THE THEØRY ØF HØPE

STORY OF A QUANTUM TRAVELLER

FARABI SHAYOR
Chartered Scientist

The Theory of Hope: Story of a Quantum Traveller
Book 1 in the Series: ***The Sentience Codex***

First published in Great Britain in 2026.
Hardcover Edition | 354 Pages

This edition was first published in 2026 by NarrativX, an imprint of ChapterOne Press Ltd.

Correspondence Email: author@thetheoryofhope.com

Publisher: NarrativX
Location: London, United Kingdom

A CIP catalogue record of this book
is available from the British Library.

ISBN: 978-1-7393498-6-8.

thetheoryofhope.com

Developmental Editor

P. J. Hoover
4X award-winning author and editor

Story Editor

Payton Ressen

Written in **early 2022**,
edited by *PJ Hoover* in late 2023.

The Theory of Hope: *Story of a Quantum Traveller* is the first book of a six-part series, **The Sentience Codex**.

Limitations of Liability: All the characters and companies/start-ups in this book, other than the ones in the public domain, are fictitious; therefore, **any resemblance with a real person or company is purely coincidental**. A combination of real-life photos, 3D rendering software and generative pre-trained transformer models have been used to depict and generate the images of characters.

AI Disclaimer: The author and the publisher declare that artificial intelligence **played no role** in the composition or narrative development of any sections within this story or manuscript.

Category: Science Fiction.

This book is dedicated to all those who helped make this dream a reality.

Visit the website and see the characters in action.
https://thetheoryofhope.com

Contents

This page has been left blank intentionally.

Chapter 1: Ashaar

October, 2020

The monotonous droning of the alarm wound itself into Ashaar's dream of discombobulated nothingness. Out of part reflex and part desperation, he slapped around the side of his bed blindly for his phone, shutting the belligerent sound off as soon as he found it.

He groaned into the mattress. With one eye screwed shut against the light filtering through the blinds, he looked at the time on the screen.

06:32 a.m.

Two minutes into his day and Ashaar was already dreading it. He had hardly slept, having gone to bed only four or five hours ago. Somehow his evenings got away from him, not that he had done anything of note. A half-hearted attempt at dinner and what felt like a few minutes of scrolling through his phone and suddenly it had been one in the morning. Now here he was, back at it again. He flipped through the news, his email, the lack of texts, trying to encourage his brain to wake up, to find some excitement in the day.

It wasn't until the time read 06:54 am that he ripped the blanket back and stumbled out of bed in search of trousers. His mood wasn't because he disliked today any more than the rest, it was because he disliked most of his days. He had a job and a flat and a few close friends but somehow none of it was right.

And he didn't know why.

He shuffled to the pile of clean clothes that was suspiciously close to the pile of dirty ones and yanked on a shirt before moving through the flat to find his shoes. The small one-bedroom unit was bereft of any hominess, looking more like a half-forgotten storage unit for lost cables, spare keyboards, a frayed couch and his laptop, which he snagged and stuffed into his bag. Giving up the search for his shoes, he headed for the bathroom.

As he scrubbed viciously at his teeth, he thought of all the work he had to do today.

His phone beeped in the other room, reminding him he was going to be late for work. He tossed the toothbrush onto the counter and went back into the living room. There, next to the books scattered over the floor were his shoes. He sighed, tugging them on. He didn't bother looking in the kitchen for food. There wouldn't be any. Swinging his bag over his shoulder, he headed out the door.

Summer still gripped London firmly in August as he hurried down the pavement to his car. Just as he got in, his phone beeped again. It was his mother. Ashaar let out his second sigh of the day as he opened her text.

Mum: When are you coming to see your father?

Ashaar tossed the phone onto the passenger seat and started the drive into London traffic.

He gripped the steering wheel as he drove towards London, his mother's voice coming through the car's speakers.

"Why aren't you picking up my calls?" she asked, her tone laced with concern.

"I'm swamped with work, Mum. Can't make the trip back home right now," Ashaar responded, his eyes fixed on the road.

"You and your job," she sighed over the phone, with a tinge of disappointment in her voice. "Family is important, Ashaar."

Guilt pricked him, combined with the usual frustration. "I know, Mum. It's just ... it's not that simple. We are about to release a new version of our AI software and I need to be here to make sure everything goes in the right direction."

There was a pause, filled with unspoken words and years of similar conversations. "Your father misses you," she finally said, softer now.

"I miss him too," Ashaar admitted, the London skyline coming into view as he drove down the M11 motorway. His mother's love, always entwined with expectations, weighed on him even as the morning sun pierced through the heavy cloud.

"We should go together to visit my sister. She isn't feeling well. You barely speak with her these days," his mum replied. They had variations of this conversation over and over again. His parents loved him, but their love was a harsh thing.

They had always doubted his choices and he didn't need his mother to tell him about how he talked with his aunts and uncles.

She would tell him anyway. In her mind, salt in the wound was the best encouragement.

The London traffic did little to ease the knots in his stomach and he picked at the steering wheel the rest of the way. He didn't fully understand it himself, but he *had* to continue down this line of choices he made.

In the background, the familial sound of another warning alarm from his car echoed. "Not again," Ashaar muttered under his breath, his frustration mounting. He found himself counting down the days to the next three weeks—the expected arrival of his new SUV. The thought of finally getting rid of this lemon of a vehicle and stepping into a new, problem-free one brought a sense of impatient excitement. *Can't come soon enough,* he thought.

He parked his car in a car park next to his office, a massive structure, and made his way to the door where a few others were heading in as well. Ashaar gave them tight-lipped smiles as they sardined their way into the building.

On the way to his desk, Ashaar made a beeline for the coffee station, trying to be quick and efficient. He didn't want to get wrapped up in a conversation with—

"Morning, Ashaar!"

Ashaar clenched his jaw but forced himself to relax. "Hi, Natalie," he said, turning to look at the physical embodiment of the sun. Who smiled that much before eight in the morning? It was nauseating, but he tried to be polite. Ashaar moved aside as the other guy reached for the coffee, itching to escape.

"So what happened with Oscar last night?" Natalie asked, adjusting the badge on her lapel, ensuring it sat just right. The gleam of the polished badge caught the light, drawing his attention. He noticed the bold print—*Natalie, Project Manager, Cognition*—emblazoned across it.

Ashaar really didn't want any small talk this morning, but his day was already shot. "CognitionGPT started talking in an alien language after my team activated its voice feature. Oscar asked me to shut it down." He tapped his feet, gripping his mug. "We've got only one complaint filed so far."

"That so?" Natalie said, looking up as she poured an unholy amount of milk into her coffee. Her eyes lit up. "Hey, did you hear that Hyperion's engineering team is moving into the building today?"

"Is it related to the merger of our research projects?"

"Yeah. They are a start-up...."

He tuned her out, feeling a lot like when he woke in the dead of night to the TV still on but muted. The ecstatic faces of the infomercial host trying to sell its audience some revolutionary orange goop that would change how one cleaned their house, but only if they called right away and put their credit card down. Natalie's face was an exact replica of the infomercial host Ashaar was picturing, eyebrows glued up and a too-wide smile. And Ashaar, being the sucker he was, smiled and nodded, not wanting to disappoint such eagerness. It was a miracle he didn't reach for his wallet.

Behind Natalie was a huge hallway with offices on the other side and employees just getting in for the day. Hundreds of companies worked in the building. Ashaar knew a few of them, but not nearly enough that he could pretend he saw another co-worker and make his escape.

He should have called in sick.

It was nearing the three-minute mark of Natalie's jabbering when some divine force of gravity commanded Ashaar's eyes over Natalie's left shoulder, across the massive hallway. On the other side was a group of people shaking hands, but Ashaar's eyes fell on the woman in the middle. His vision narrowed to a pinprick.

Dark-blonde hair grazed her jaw as she reached forward to shake the hand of the man across from her. Ashaar couldn't pull his eyes away as he watched the woman smile wide and endearing at the man, nodding along with something he said. Other introductions seemed to be made in the group but something about the woman made Ashaar's brain wide awake, like he was looking at something of extraordinary importance. She was young, probably in her mid-twenties, but held herself with authority, like she had earned it.

"I think it really gives me a good edge and you know how everyone always likes—"

"Who is that?" Ashaar interrupted Natalie who turned to look where Ashaar was gazing.

"Oh, that's them. I just told you their engineering team was moving into the building today. They'll continue building a working prototype of the Martian habitat. Were you even—"

"But who is she?" Ashaar asked.

"Which one?" Natalie asked.

Ashaar had hardly realised there were any other women in the group. “The one in the middle, in the white shirt.”

“That’s Emma Herrmann, the new project lead for Hyperion. She’s a quantum physicist. Aren’t you going to be working with them soon?” Natalie asked, turning back to him. “I thought *you* were leading the joint project.”

“Yeah, I am leading it.” *Emma, the quantum physicist.* He had to talk to her. He needed to speak with her directly, wanting to avoid the discomfort of an awkward, impromptu introduction by his boss, Oscar Williams. His best bet was to play it cool. If she was the project manager from Hyperion, then Natalie was right.

“Oscar wants both companies to work closely together.” She added, “Once our AI is integrated into their habitats, Hyperion can build self-sustaining Martian....”

Natalie kept talking, but Ashaar was already deep down a rabbit hole of the possible ways he could introduce himself without looking like an absolute fool.

With more willpower than he realised he had, Ashaar turned his gaze away from Emma and headed down the hall in the direction of his desk, leaving Natalie shouting an “I’ll finish telling you later” at his back.

Ashaar wasn’t listening. He was starting to realise the day might not have been a total waste.

***

“Yeah, only a few more days and I can have the AI dev team send a full diagnostics report,” Ashaar said, tucking his laptop under his arm. He stood with Oscar, his boss, to the side of Oscar’s desk, watching the people pass by in the hall. Oscar was Cognition’s CEO but he also held stakes in Hyperion.

It had been a few days since he had seen Emma in the hallway, and he had been spending quite a lot of time thinking about her. It wasn’t lost on him how absurd it was to have one’s thoughts revolve entirely around a person he knew nothing about. Yet here he was, wondering where Emma was in the building today. He had discovered where her desk was, not far from his own, but she was frequently not there. Not that he planned on talking to her.

"Good, that's really good. We can't be receiving complaints anymore," Oscar said. "Once we've got that squared away, I think we can have you start on the project with Hyperion. They'll need several more weeks at least to get caught up and settled in, but it wouldn't be a bad idea to have you get started in the meantime. What do you have left to do?"

Ashaar was nodding in agreement. "Just a few more—"

"Oh, hey Emma!" Oscar said, looking over Ashaar's shoulder. Ashaar turned to find *her*. "Emma, this is Ashaar. You two will be working quite closely in the coming weeks. Ashaar," he said turning to him, "this is Emma Herrmann, our project lead from Hyperion and a physicist by trade."

She wore a pale blue shirt that brought out the colour of her eyes as they pierced into Ashaar's. He couldn't help but feel the quickening of his heart rate.

"Nice to meet you," she said, her smile bright as she held out her hand.

Ashaar took it and he swore an electrical charge singed his skin everywhere they touched. "You as well," he said with a tight smile. The effort to keep her from picking up on his discomfort was monumental. He turned back to Oscar hoping she wouldn't notice.

"Well," she said, checking her phone for the time, "I have another meeting but I'm sure you and I will have time to chat. Let's catch up over coffee next week."

Ashaar nodded as she left and picked up his conversation with Oscar where they had left off, as if nothing had happened.

It wasn't until a few days later that Ashaar could really put a label on the increasing entropy that was his thoughts surrounding Emma.

He took every distraction he could, including calling his aunt back which he should have won a Nobel prize for. He spent fifteen minutes barely noticing the underhanded comments about his life choices peppered with a few pleas to visit his extended family members in London. He promised her he would when he could. Thankfully Ashaar's niece Tiffany was calling him on the other line, and he silently thanked his sister for the child's existence.

It was Friday of the following week when Ashaar sat in a cluster of chairs near his co-working space. The office was a little quieter today, but he was wrapped tight in his work despite the sunny weather that enticed him from the window nearby. Since the space was a shared one, a few other employees dropped in and out of the surrounding chairs, keeping their conversations low. A guy he didn't know very well suddenly sank into the chair next to him. Was his name Ned? Niall?

"How are things?" the guy asked, turning to Ashaar as he opened his laptop.

"Great. You?" Ashaar said with a nod as he finished typing.

"I'd rather not be working but it could be worse," the guy said, chuckling.

They sat in silence as Ashaar continued down his wormhole of a project, oblivious to the people walking by. It had started to get a bit louder. A meeting had let out in one of the nearby rooms, but he tuned it out.

"Ashaar, you think she's single?"

Ashaar stopped typing abruptly. Ned—or Niall, whatever—had his chin propped on a fist but he was looking across the way and two people talking outside one of the meeting rooms. Something prickled along Ashaar's spine when he saw Emma standing there with one of Hyperion's other employees.

"Who? Emma?"

"You know her?" Niall asked, looking at him, eyes widening.

"Not well. We're on a joint project but I spoke to her a few times," Ashaar said, looking back down at his keyboard. A cloud had passed over the sun, darkening the windows.

"Could you find out for me?" The eager look on Niall's face made Ashaar want to throw up, to smash his keyboard, to storm off, to scream.

“Sure.” The word tasted like acid in his mouth. Why did he say that? Why couldn’t he have just said that he was interested in her?

Ah. There it was.

He was *interested* in Emma. And judging by the state of his mind the last few days, he was *very* interested. Suddenly a million possible outcomes unrolled before him. It made him a bit giddy to think of her as his girlfriend, but he was getting ahead of himself.

“Thanks,” Niall said with a nod. Remembering him dampened Ashaar’s sudden mood change, and he decided he would not be finding out anything for Niall.

Across the way, Emma laughed out loud at something the other person had said. Ashaar had to tell her. Even if she rejected him, he had to tell her.

He opened their company’s CognitionGPT app, pressed the voice button, and muttered, “Hey, I think I have a crush on a co-worker. Should I ask her out?”

He smirked at himself. *Asking an AI for dating advice—how pathetic.* Of course, it would spit out something cheerful and predictable.

Then, his brows shot up.

“Sorry, what did you just say?” he asked the AI, frowning.

The AI’s voice warped into static, spilling out garbled sounds. It didn’t stop. It kept speaking and twisting into something that didn’t sound human.

Ashaar’s heart pounded. He tapped frantically at the glitching screen, then slammed the side button to force a shutdown. The phone went dark. He stood still, his breath caught in his throat.

He thought, *fuck. I need to investigate the code.*

Something was wrong.

Chapter 2: Emma

A few hours earlier, the same day Emma and Ashaar had their first meeting

Emma had been on turbo-drive since five in the morning. Texts from someone on the marketing team and one engineer had her calming a dispute between what the marketing team was promising and what the back end was actually going to deliver before she'd even had her coffee. That was assuming their habitats were functional anytime soon.

She had thrown on an outfit and was headed to the office in her rental car earlier than normal. Oscar had thrown a meeting on her calendar for 7 a.m. this morning and Emma knew what it was going to be about. Hyperion needed to secure funding as soon as possible if they didn't want to tank within the next two years. Her phone rang through the Bluetooth in her car, and she smacked the button to answer the call.

"So was that a 'yes' or a 'no'?" the marketing coordinator, Tia, asked.

Emma sighed. "No, we can't add any official release dates for the Habs if we don't even have them working yet. We need to host a PR event. Like a proper launch event."

"Okay, but if we don't put something down, investors are going to think it's hypothetical and that we can't actually produce anything," Tia said. "We need to give them a carrot."

"It is hypothetical, technically," Emma muttered. "Just hold off on that for now and we can chat about it later. I should have time this afternoon."

She could hear Tia clicking on her computer. "No ... you're booked the rest of the day. Jeez, Emma. Do you even have time to eat?"

Emma's clutch on the steering wheel intensified. She had forgotten she had a meeting with one of the guys from Cognition today—Ashaar. There hadn't been time for them to really talk yet even though they had been working together for weeks. Plus another meeting with another one of Hyperion's engineers in the afternoon that she was dreading. Trying to connect with them was like pulling teeth. Everything was one-word answers—yes, no, bye.

"I can give you a call in between a few meetings later."

"But we really need to—"

Emma hit the call button again, disconnecting the line. She drove the rest of the way to the office in silence. She spent the entire day speed-walking back and forth from her office to the coffee machine. She had sent Oscar an update just yesterday on their funding status and she triple-checked the numbers and pulled a few other things together in case he asked.

Hyperion's habitat was one of the most sophisticated designs ever created, receiving grants and awards from NASA and every other space agency in the world. Now, they were days away from integrating Cognition's AI within their systems. She had to make sure that everything worked out.

***

When Emma opened the door for Ashaar, she wasn't prepared. Her face looked pale and her desk was covered in papers. "Hi," Emma replied, her lips curving into a smile, "Come in." She rushed back to her desk, organised the papers and craned her neck awkwardly. "Sorry, just one of those days."

Ashaar's brows shot up towards his hairline, replying, "It's okay. Take your time. I'll wait outside."

"Give me a couple of minutes. I'll meet you at the park."

A long few minutes later, she met Ashaar at their indoor park, lined with long tables and bar-stool-like chairs. "Sorry, it's been a long day for me."

Ashaar nodded and pulled another chair next to him.

"How's everything on your side?" Emma asked. Her lips turned up in a strained smile, her eyes flickering as she struggled to keep her composure. Her shoulders hunched up slightly, and she fidgeted with her hands.

"Things are great! Cognition's app just hit 100 million users, and 10 million in the UK."

Her phone chimed a mellow ping. "Sorry," she said, chuckling nervously and yanking her phone from her pocket. Her brows wrinkled slightly as she glowered at her phone and then typed a response. She pressed the power button on the side and turned it off.

"How about you?" Ashaar asked.

With a faint smile, she explained her sense of disillusionment. "I came here with dreams of making a real difference, but instead, I've found myself spending the last couple of months screaming internally." She paused, her expression reflecting a deep-seated frustration. "There's more. Let's walk and talk."

They jumped off their seats and walked back towards her office. Ashaar and Emma's offices were opposite each other, separated by a giant hallway, a coffee station and a few haphazardly spread-out tables. Most people who walked past the building from the outside could see through the floor-to-ceiling glass walls.

This time her phone chimed four times in a row. She glowered at the screen. "Can you lot just figure this out? C'mon people, you can't lose a screw and panic about it." She shook her head, breathing heavily.

Ashaar pursed his lips. "Emma, you should go ..."

"I'm sorry, it's my team," she said.

"You have a lot on your plate," Ashaar said as he leaned closer. She could feel Ashaar's minty breath brushing her cheeks. He arched one brow slightly, his eyes narrowing in suspicion as he studied her. "We can talk later if you want, maybe over coffee?" He pursed his lips, shooting a wide grin.

Emma swiftly dismissed Ashaar's offer for coffee with a click of her phone, which she then tucked away in her pocket. She resumed her conversation, pouring out her emotions.

They'd been talking to each other for almost half an hour now. She could have done so much work, but this was important. She needed to trust Ashaar. "Please keep these matters between us, okay?" She nodded and looked away, exhaling through her teeth.

"Of course," Ashaar replied. Emma's phone chimed its tenth ping. Emma arched her brows and pursed her lips. "Fuck. My boss is here with the entire board." Emma cocked an eyebrow. "He didn't tell me anything about this meeting. Fuck."

"Woah. The entire board? Must be something urgent."

Despite her attempts to hide it, her annoyance was clearly visible. She darted around for a couple of seconds before continuing, "It's about money. My only goal is to raise funding. This start-up is not going to survive if we don't find money in the next 24 months. I have to make this happen." Her eyes narrowed and jaw clenched as she glared at Oscar approaching from the distance. "I need to go."

***

The meeting with Ashaar had unfolded better than expected. He had even offered to give her a ride home. This gesture opened an opportunity for Emma to discuss matters more candidly, away from the hustle and bustle.

She hardly noticed the people trickling into the building and how busy it had got. Five minutes before her next meeting she checked what room it was in.

"Shit!" Grabbing her laptop, phone and coffee, she practically ran across the building to make it on time. She turned a corner and saw a group of people entering the room she was headed towards, and she started to sweat.

The fucking board was there. Oscar had called a board meeting with Emma and hadn't told her. Thankfully she had checked all her numbers and had extra material ready, so she clenched her jaw and walked into the room.

"Afternoon, Emma." Oscar sat at the other end of the table. A few of the board members gave her a brisk greeting and she returned a clenched smile. "Sorry for springing this on you, but I thought we needed to obtain a deeper understanding of Hyperion's financial situation."

For the next forty-five minutes, she was grilled over the lack of funding Hyperion had received so far and was reminded how it was her job to secure it. When Emma had first met Oscar, he had so much faith in her and said he knew she was going to succeed. The fatherly pride was unusual to her but she found she craved that same validation she had when they first met. Now he was staring at her with cold eyes and allowing the board to eviscerate every decision she had made so far with Hyperion.

"And what about Xplorer?" one of the members asked. By this time, Emma's stress levels were through the roof and she dug her nails painfully into the palm of her hand. She should try to relax her shoulders. "Surely you've tried to obtain a partnership with them?" the board member asked.

"Yes, but they've been hesitant to join with a smaller start-up like ours. They wanted to see the Habs but I have a feeling they might try to set a sell offer on the table instead."

The board members scoffed, some rolling their eyes and a few others shaking their heads.

"When ... is your next meeting with them?" Oscar asked tersely.

Emma started frantically looking through her calendar. It sounded like Oscar and the board were looking for a fight and she saw the impending wave coming right at her. "I don't have—"

"What?" Oscar barked, leaning forward. "You have nothing with them? Emma, it is your job to be on them to secure this! Do you not understand if we don't get funding for the next round—"

"Of course, I do! I know we won't survive another 24 months without it." She could barely get the words in. "Xplorer has hundreds of others vying for the same partnerships. We aren't the only ones out here."

"Make this shit work!" Oscar's teeth were on edge as he sat back, shaking his head.

Emma found no sympathy in the eyes of the other board members. At best, some of them looked down at their clasped hands. Her jaw ached with how hard she was clenching but she lowered her brows and nodded. "I'll set up a meeting with them." She had no clue how to do it.

Oscar's scepticism cut through her.

She had to make it work. Inhaling, she forced a smile on her face and assured them that she would have updates by their next planned meeting. They filed out in a blur and Oscar picked up a call as he left, leaving Emma to drop her head in her hands as the door clicked shut. She had always known this job was stressful, but things had been piling on lately.

Taking a few deep breaths didn't help, so she left and headed back to her office to figure out how to beat Xplorer into submission.

Chapter 3: Ashaar

A week later

Friday evening was descending as Ashaar dropped Emma off, the sounds of laughter from the work event still ringing in his ears.

"No Natalie," Emma yelled over the phone. "If you say extraterrestrial habitat on the press release, people will think our Habs are a fucking straw hut made for aliens." She killed the connection and exhaled a long sigh.

With her arms resting on the side panel, Emma rolled the windows down to feel the cool breeze of London's winter. "We are devoting a lot of time and money trying to find these American and European investors. I hope I'm doing the right thing."

Ashaar pressed his indicator and shifted to the left lane. "It's a risk. But you are doing well under pressure." His face was lit by the yellow decorations hung across the empty streets. "By the way, I'm glad to be able to drop you off."

Emma smiled and eyed him. "Thanks, very kind of you." Her chest rose and fell with the rhythm of her breathing. "You know I work so hard, but then I feel like my boss is constantly undervaluing me."

He noticed a subtle change in her attitude. Her movements became more graceful, as if the champagne was starting to weave its magic in her mind.

"It's okay. You'll be able to manage Oscar," Ashaar cleared his throat, glaring at her puffy red sweater she'd been holding. The white polka-dotted black dress suited her well.

"My start-up works on space technology. It's hard to find investors for a start-up like ours. You, on the contrary, are working on AI. It's literally the most hyped technology right now," Emma said.

"But it wasn't easy to build Cognition, Emma."

"I get it. You've built your company's reputation over time. That's why he's merging our projects, trying to use the words 'artificial intelligence' to find more funding to build Martian habitats."

As she tried to speak more, her voice came out hoarse and raspy, barely audible above the hum of the background music. Ashaar reached into the door pocket and retrieved a bottle of water, unscrewing the cap with a soft hiss. "Whatever happens from this point onwards, I'll have your back."

Emma took the bottle and raised it to her lips. "Thanks."

As Emma handed him the bottle back, their fingers brushed against each other. In a half-hearted attempt to shift the topic, she asked, "How's your investigation going? Did you find out why your AI is malfunctioning?"

"Not yet, Em. We've looked through thousands of lines of code, but couldn't find anything."

Emma swallowed hard, then glanced at Ashaar. She asked, "Did you ask Oscar?"

"He doesn't seem to know anything. It looks like I have to be the one to figure this out."

"I'm sure you'll fix everything," she said, her voice soft as she placed her hand on Ashaar's. He had a surge of energy when Emma's hand met his, his heart racing as he turned to see into her eyes. He continued, "I feel like money may be a reason for this project merger. Oscar has a reason behind everything. Only time will tell."

Ashaar's gaze momentarily drifted to his phone, catching sight of the "Microphone" and "Location" indicators flickering on the screen. He wasn't on a call or using his satnav. It was like someone was tapping into it, except that was paranoid, so he brushed off the thought. Probably just one of his apps trying to access the microphone. Just as quickly as they had appeared, the symbols vanished.

"You're right. Oscar calculates his every move." Emma browsed her Spotify playlist on the infotainment system.

"Hey, I wanted to ask you something," Ashaar said, licking his lips and ignoring his inner thoughts. "If you don't mind."

"Sure." Her fingers twisted together in her lap, and she avoided looking at him directly.

Ashaar noticed Emma's attempt to avoid eye contact, watching a group of pedestrians in the distance. He forced a tight-lipped grin, his jaw clenching as he tried to hide his apprehension. "Since I finally have the chance to talk to you outside the office, I wanted to ask...."

"What?"

"Are you dating someone?"

"No." She was lost in thought, staring at the distant lights with a wandering mind.

"Do you want to go out with me for a drink?" He flared a lopsided smile. This was quite a risk he'd taken.

Emma held a blank stare momentarily.

Shit, I've fucked up. Ashaar avoided gazing at her. "Sorry, it's okay if you don't."

The moment paused, his car's headlights casting a white glow on the rain-slicked pavement. A constant stream of vehicles flowed in from all directions, merging in a chaotic dance of metal and rubber. Brake lights flashed red as drivers slammed on their brakes, narrowly avoiding collisions with the other cars jostling for position.

Emma craned her neck, smiled and gazed at Ashaar. In the next second, her face hardened. "Shall we go for drinks as friends?"

Ashaar gave her a half-smile. "Of course." He offered a prayer and swallowed, *oh God, please don't make this anymore awkward than it already is.*

Emma turned around, smiled and shifted the topic. Ashaar assumed she wasn't interested in anything more than a friendship.

Not at that moment.

It was an expedition set alight by the lively decorations on the streets of London, the pleasing sound of the city's never-ending traffic, and the lights shining from the distant, tall and wide office buildings.

His shoulders slumped as he continued driving.

The gentle, romantic music in the background wasn't helpful at all. "I'm sorry for making things awkward, Ashaar. I shouldn't have done that."

Ashaar turned his steering wheel to enter the narrow road where Emma lived. He checked the satnav—they were a minute away. "Don't worry. It's okay."

Ashaar's car came to a gentle halt. Silence stretched the distance between them. His heart pounded. Ashaar waited for Emma to say something.

Emma opened the passenger-side door a few seconds later. She shifted her sight to him and said, "I'm sorry, Ash, I know it wasn't the answer you were expecting."

"I'm happy to be here with you," Ashaar said.

After she got out, Ashaar locked his car and drove away as fast as possible. *Shit. It's fine, everything's fine.* Ashaar drove out of London and joined the motorway.

As he drove back home, the probability of a future with her was long gone before his stunned brain could come up with a plan.

The red light at the junction held him up for too long. Anger raced up his spine, attacking the back of his head.

The silence was broken when the speakers in his car, connected to his phone, began making glitching noises. His face contorted from the brash noise firing from all speakers. He spun the volume knob down, stifling the noise and disconnected the phone. "This isn't working at all." The white, glitching noise was growing into a deafening roar with each passing second.

A brief pause followed. Next, the glitching voice of a man crackled through the speakers, barely audible. "Quantum Traveller Alpha November, this is a one-way channel. From the junction, turn right and then continue on route Alpha 4-0-6 before heading home via Alpha-1-2."

"What in the world just happened?" The cars behind him honked a few seconds later, right as the light changed. The engine roared to life as he hit the gas pedal, the car leaping forward with a burst of speed. "Fuck this," he screamed. "I'll find out what's going on once I'm home."

Ashaar's attention was abruptly drawn to his left by a rapidly approaching light. His heart raced as he realised the imminent danger, but there wasn't enough time to react.

In an instant, the oncoming car collided with a deafening crash into the passenger-side door of his new SUV. The force of the impact was monstrous, wrenching his vehicle sideways with a violent jolt.

The sound of shattering glass filled the air as his SUV flipped. Ashaar was tossed around like a ragdoll inside the cabin. The screech of metal grinding against concrete was ear-piercing as the SUV rolled over.

His body jerked violently with each tumultuous roll. The airbags deployed with a whoosh, rapidly filling the surrounding space, cushioning the relentless battering his body was enduring. The taste of fear was bitter in Ashaar's mouth, as the smell of burning rubber and his own thundering heartbeat overwhelmed his senses.

As the SUV came to a jarring stop, lying on its side, a cloud of smoke billowed from the engine. Shattered glass glittered on the concrete around the wreckage.

Ashaar, dazed and disoriented, tried to gather his senses. His mind was struggling to process the catastrophic event that had just unfolded. The world outside, the shattered windows of his SUV seemed distant, surreal, as if he had been thrust into a nightmare.

***

Ashaar's head ached.

Migraine was a criminally underrated chronic illness.

Migraines, unlike headaches, could last up to 18 hours. This was just the beginning. Resting his head on the pillow, he glowered at his phone and then closed his eyes.

He couldn't figure out whether it was a dream. It appeared he was slumbering in the luxury of his bed. Seconds later, a deserted hallway appeared, the ceiling lined with neatly spaced-out LED strips arching above, giving off a spacecraft feel. He tried to remember how he'd ended up in an empty hallway. He placed his hand inside his left pocket and pulled out a card. Off to his left was a door, on which handwritten words said:

Built using Hyperion's Technology

Ashaar tapped his card to open the door to a quarter. The bottom of the sliding door made a hissing noise. As the door slid open, the sound of whirring mechanics filled the air and an animation flickered to life on the display terminal to the left.

Ashaar realised his mind travelled across millions of miles to a new planet. *The gravity feels different. This can't be Earth.* His feet pounded against the stairs with wooden steps and found a bedroom on the gantry. He sat on the bed, and the hissing sound faded as his body distorted the curve of the mattress. He cocked his head from side to side and looked upwards. A few pictures were hung on the wall, and he stared at them. Some of them were recognisable, while others were new. A frame with a Lindt box was strapped inside an acrylic frame. He studied the crimson box intently, wondering who had given it to him.

Eyes narrowing, he looked out through the circular, thick window. Outside, the windows were gritty with Martian sand, and beyond, a series of cranes were visible. The vast construction ground was deserted. Hanging threads from the cranes were dangling from left to right like a pendulum. His eyes darted to the reddish ground—tens of dead bodies lay dispersed. They had their EVA suits on and were face down on the dirt-ridden terrain, looking dead. Among them were civilians and military officers with their weapons. Looked like they had collapsed abruptly. A fast-moving sandstorm was advancing from a distance, making it harder to see anything beyond 200 metres.

It was Mars.

Shivers shot up his spine, erupting through his nerves. The cold was getting under his skin. He had clothes on. But the temperature was dropping fast. Someone had turned off the internal heating, or it was damaged.

He clenched his jaws, teeth clattering. Eyes darting across the habitat, he looked for an EVA suit or a jacket.

Ashaar hurried down the stairs, convincing his eyes to believe it wasn't Earth. His brain couldn't conceive that Hyperion had built these Martian habitats. His head swirled from his left to the top of the ceiling and then to his right.

He wasn't supposed to be in Hyperion's living quarters because they didn't exist. Emma's start-up was still in its infancy.

A vibration from underneath the floor intensified.

He was trying hard to battle the gravitational anomaly.

Ashaar gasped out loud, choking on his breath. He coughed as hard as he could and cleared his throat, slamming his back on his bed.

***

From the distance, with his blurry vision, he observed a nurse running towards him.

Ashaar's eyes fluttered open, the blur of his dream fading as the stark, white walls of a hospital room came into focus. He tried to sit up. His movements were sluggish and his mind was still groggy. A nurse approached his bedside with a sympathetic smile. "Mr. Naveed, you ... you're awake. We've informed your parents. They're flying to London today," she said, her voice gentle.

Ashaar's brow furrowed in confusion, his memory hazy. "My parents?" he murmured. In his mind, he was trying to piece together the events that had landed him here.

"Yes, and we've also contacted your office. It was the only other contact we found in your medical file," the nurse continued. "Oh, and there's someone here to see you."

"Who?" Ashaar asked, curiosity piquing through his disorientation. *Right, I had an accident.*

"Someone named Emma from your work," the nurse replied. She stepped aside, just as the knob on the door unlatched. Emma walked into the room with a smile.

As Emma walked in, Ashaar's eyes softened, a smile tugging at the corners of his mouth. His gaze lingered on her, eyebrows slightly raised. She took a seat next to his bed. "Hi."

"Hey, you didn't have to come here."

"No, I absolutely did. What happened?" Emma asked, her eyes searching his for answers.

He shook his head slightly, struggling to recall. "I ... I'm not sure. It's all a bit blurry. After I dropped you off, everything seemed fine. Then, I was at a junction, when a car came out of nowhere and hit me from the side. But I don't think it was just an accident."

Emma leaned in closer. "You think it's connected to the anomaly you've been investigating?"

"Maybe." Ashaar nodded slowly. "I need to look into the code. There's something not right, like ... someone's trying to silence me."

There was a moment of quiet, plagued only by the beeping sound of medical devices.

"Maybe this was just a coincidence because you were distracted after what I did," Emma replied, exhaling a sigh.

Ashaar said, "Anyway, how are things with you?"

Emma sighed, her frustration being evident. "Nothing much. Last night I had an idea. Maybe I can strike some partnerships that will give us some leverage."

From his hospital bed, Ashaar found an unexpected comfort in Emma's visit. Despite the accident and the sterile hospital surroundings, their conversation settled into an oasis of normalcy.

Emma spoke about her work and the mandate from Oscar to build partnerships with major corporations. Ashaar couldn't help but grin, even though it strained his injuries.

As he narrated recent events at Cognition, including the anomalies that had arisen, Emma's laughter echoed through the room. He embellished his stories with light-hearted commentary, drawing more chuckles from Emma.

Ashaar's eyes hardened with resolve. "Speaking of partnerships...." he cleared his throat. "I might have a lead. Stephanie Maddox, from Xplorer's space division. They're based in California but Stephanie manages the London team. I could introduce you."

Emma's interest was piqued. She said, "That'd be amazing. But what are we going to show?"

Ashaar nodded. He said, "Talk to her. They have a facility in Turin, Italy that they manage alongside European Space Agency. Maybe you can use their facility. With their technology and Hyperion's expertise, you could push the boundaries further than ever before."

Emma sat back, and contemplated the potential of this new partnership. She looked through the window as her mind drifted away for a few seconds. Then, shifting her eyes to Ashaar, she said, "This could be the break we need, Ashaar. Thank you!"

"No problem." He smiled, watching Emma gently grip his hand.

"And if you need anything, let me know," she said. "My quantum physics degree could come in handy after all."

"Sure." Ashaar's determination grew stronger. Despite his current state, he knew that this was just the beginning of a new chapter.

The hospital room fell quiet once Emma left, but the air was charged with a new sense of hope.

His phone chimed an alert.

He grabbed his phone from his bedside table, swiped up and unlocked it. When the words became legible after he strained his eyes to read them, a cold shiver went down his spine.

> Anonymous: The code you are searching for in Cognition's backend systems was not written by a human.

The only way to know the truth was to discover it firsthand. It was time.

Chapter 4: Emma

Two months after Ashaar's accident

The announcement of a train delay chimed, making her growl. *Fuck this shit.*

When she watched the announcement board say one minute, it gave her hope of reaching the destination on time. Today, of all days, was important. She was meeting with Stephanie from Xplorer, the operations lead for the largest space company in the world. Emma couldn't afford to be late in the middle of chasing a partnership.

Ashaar's friend, Stephanie, had helped Emma build the bridge between her start-up and the largest private space agency, Xplorer. She had set up a meeting with them to use their lab for Hyperion's research, marking the expansion of their start-up to Italy.

Emma was desperate to strike a relationship with Xplorer since it would encourage investors to contribute to their next round of funding.

Her mum said Emma lacked confidence. But she didn't. She used to be a part of theatre drama since she was little when her mum used to be around to support her. This time, she had to handle her job by herself.

Ashaar was supposed to meet with her at Stephanie's residence.

"I think Ashaar is brilliant," Natalie said, standing next to her on the platform.

Emma's nostrils flared as she inhaled sharply. "Yep, thanks to him, we are here."

Natalie glanced at a young kid looking down at the tracks. Her guardian, probably mother, pulled her back behind the yellow line. "Emma, would you mind if I share something about Ashaar?"

Emma raised her brows, "Sure, why not." She pressed her lips together, a faint exhale escaping almost involuntarily. Her eyes narrowed slightly, focusing on what had stirred her irritation, yet her expression remained relatively composed.

"I know Ashaar is struggling with work after his recovery, and that's translating him being aloof. He'll come around."

Emma turned her neck, staring at Natalie. "And what made you think that he's avoiding me?"

Natalie clicked her tongue, "I'm saying if he acts weird, it's because he has a lot on his plate."

"Sure."

The station sprang to life when the lifeless track was covered with a futuristic-looking train made by a company called Bombardier. She waited for the doors to open, watching the yellow lights around the button flash. Two men armed with tasers on their belts and bulletproof vests with their bikes jumped out, making her recoil.

One of them had a slow staring contest with Emma before he darted towards the lift.

She leapt out of her skin as another train's siren honked.

Natalie tugged her by her arm. Emma stepped in, took a seat and placed her bag on her lap. At least the tube didn't smell like armpit sweat and wet socks during this time of the day.

After a forty-minute train ride and fifteen minutes on foot, she'd reached her destination on time.

The garden felt far too big for a single home. It was an expanse of trimmed grass and carefully placed flowerbeds stretching all the way to a small lake. It should have been peaceful. Instead, the air carried a faint charge, the kind that prickled at the edges of her skin.

In the far corner, a detached structure stood apart from the main house. Its walls were plain enough, but the tangle of cables and oddly positioned security cameras gave it away.

She glanced back, half-expecting someone to stop her. Ashaar was still deep in conversation with Natalie, both of them looking like they were plotting the fate of the world. Her path was clear.

The nearest CCTV camera shifted. Deliberately. She froze. Its lens angled down until it was staring right at her, the black glass swallowing her reflection. For a moment, she felt pinned under its gaze, like something inside was studying her. Then the red light blinked out.

No mechanical hum, no stutter.

The air seemed to lean in, and the silence itself had weight. A pulse of something unseen brushed the edge of her mind. It wasn't a sound, but she understood it.

The separate building suddenly resembled a less structural and more open doorway. Her steps were quiet as a cat and her eyes flicked to the other cameras around the garden. Whatever had been looking at her ... wanted her to follow.

And she couldn't tell if she was walking towards trouble, or if trouble always had a way to find her.

She gently placed her hand on the door of that detached house, and wham, it slid open. *What the fuck*, she whispered. The inside of the house looked nothing like it. Inhalable smoke emitted from the sides, mixed with some form of disinfectant. In front of her, she found an antechamber that led to another chamber. She made a U-turn and waved at Ashaar, but he was too busy chatting with Natalie. Well, she wasn't waiting for him. She walked inside.

It was like entering the antechamber of a spaceship since the corridor was hexagonal in design. Big, fat pipes were pushing high-speed fibre-optic cables into the wall, some form of data transmission pipeline. Bright LEDs in the centre of the wall could have easily been misconstrued as sunlight streaming in through a window. Ceiling-mounted LEDs illuminated the corridor's ceiling, and a metal off-white door stood at the end. The door's thickness was identical to that of a bank vault.

She stepped in, and simultaneously, the cameras' red lights ceased their rhythmic blinking.

One after another.

This place has a dense radiation insulator and a heat signature that can't be read outside. Once she got to the far side of the antechamber, she found a lock—not a titanium-sealed lock with a passcode. Instead, Emma discovered a hologram that emitted a number pad she could interact with. *What the actual fuck?* Her brain cells were flooded with endorphins. She accidentally touched the surface of the sliding door that looked like a chamber taken out of a spaceship. Inside, a room full of fluids in IV bags, hanging from metal rods. Hundreds of them. The resemblance to a spaceship was uncanny, down to the structure of the med bay that sat right in the middle. The cold air had turned warm, as the lights lit up once she stepped foot on the metal welcome mat. *This must be a sensor*, she looked down at her feet, looked around and found laser arrays intended to frighten everyone. All three walls had light blue coloured IV bags. She stepped closer, brushing her hand over one of the bags. On the sticker, it said, "DNA data, September 2015-November 2018."

This is a DNA data archive. How is this even possible? How the fuck—

Shit. Emma heard Steph's voice approaching from the distance and stepped out before the woman found her inside the vault.

As the door behind slid close with a hiss, a sudden, overwhelming wave of disorientation swept over Emma. It was as if she had collided head-on with a vision, a cascade of memories flashing before her eyes, disjointed and surreal. She couldn't place these memories, yet deep down, she sensed they were intrinsically hers. Maybe they weren't. She couldn't figure. Shaking her head in an attempt to dispel the confusion, she steadied herself against a nearby wall.

With a deep breath, she gathered her composure and hastened towards Stephanie's primary residence.

Stephanie greeted her at the door, her expression shifting from cordiality to concern in an instant. "You okay, Emma?"

Emma knew Stephanie's inspecting stare was on her, it cut through her effort to seem calm.

Emma, putting on a brave front, waved away the concern with a forced smile. "Oh, it's nothing. Just a bit of fatigue. I'm completely fine," she assured, though her voice lacked its usual conviction.

They moved into Stephanie's home office, where the air was filled with the anticipation of important discussions. Emma couldn't shake off a nagging feeling about Stephanie's attitude. There was something unsettlingly evasive about her, a hint of something cloaked just beneath the surface. She had to know why Stephanie had built a DNA data archive. More than that, she had to learn why she'd been struck with a vision. That had never happened before. Despite this, Emma recognised the critical need for the partnership with Xplorer. The future of her company, teetering on the brink of financial challenges, depended on this alliance.

As they settled around her office table, the conversation shifted to the promising prospects of their research collaboration. They spoke of establishing a state-of-the-art research facility within Xplorer's lab in Turin, Italy, a venture that promised to push the boundaries of their current capabilities of Habs.

Ashaar leaned forward. “Stephanie, I need to be frank with you, as a friend. Emma’s company is facing a bit of a financial crunch. They could really use your support. It’s important for them to find partners to increase VC confidence. We both know that having an advanced AI is a great asset, but it’s not everything.”

“Uh ... I don’t know man ...” Stephanie clicked her tongue, a long exhale escaping her lips. “I need our CEO, Nolan’s permission to make it work.”

Emma, though doing her best to focus on the conversation, found her thoughts repeatedly drifting to the enigmatic word from her vision “Sentinel.”

She couldn’t fully grasp the word’s significance, which felt like a puzzle piece she couldn’t locate. The significance of ‘Sentinel’ in the grand scheme of their work was unclear.

As the meeting progressed, her internal debate intensified, weighing the potential risks and benefits of disclosing this mysterious piece of the puzzle.

***

It had been a week since her meeting with Stephanie.

Emma consolidated all her thoughts. Her heart wanted to speak to Ashaar and tell him everything. She had to explain what she’d experienced after walking out of that archive.

Her feet pounded against the floor as she walked purposefully down the main hallway of her office building. Her arm swung back and forth at her side, and her breaths came in short, rapid bursts.

She watched Ashaar speak to another woman at the office reception. From a distance, it seemed that they were having a serious conversation.

Who the fuck cared? She needed to speak with him right now.

"Hey, can I talk to you for a second? It's important." She cut in, her words sharp and urgent. She leaned forward, cutting off the receptionist's words before she could finish. Emma stood next to Ashaar, gripping and pulling his arm.

The receptionist glared at her. Emma watched her shift her eyes and smile at Ashaar.

"What's up?" he asked.

"I need to talk. Shall we go somewhere I can sit down and talk in private?"

His left hand reached around to touch her back, drawing her closer. "Let's go there," he said, pointing at a corner.

Ashaar shot Emma a blank stare as he sat down. "What's going on?"

Her eyes dropped to her feet. "Ashaar," she swallowed as her expression altered. "This is going to sound crazy but you need to trust me."

"You're making me nervous, Emma."

Emma pinched her lips, moving closer to him, "There's something ..." Emma held Ashaar's forearm and pulled him closer. She remained silent for a heartbeat.

"Ash, have you ever heard anything about Sentinel?" Emma asked. "I've had this vision about it. I can't really explain." She considered if it was sensible to speak about her visions, pressing her lips together.

"What did you see?" he asked.

"Like I'm experiencing a memory from a different past." She shifted further towards him, her arms crossed tightly over her chest, hair rising above her neck. *First, the data archive and now the visions. They might not be coincidences. I don't know.*

It was as if her emotions were radiating off her in waves.

Ashaar's brows furrowed slightly. "It's got to be a hallucination."

"I don't think so." Emma's pupils dilated. "You may have some info on this through your AI. It's literally a search engine. See if there's anything about it."

She watched a group of people from their co-working space approach them from the distance.

Ashaar's eyes widened. He lowered his voice and replied, "I'll look into it and come back to you tomorrow," Ashaar spoke in a reassuring voice. "How long are you here for?"

"I'll be here until late, don't worry. We can talk then," she replied. "Thank you," Emma smiled and exhaled a sigh of relief.

***

The following day

Emma twisted her wrist to check the time—it was almost 9 p.m. Another late-night-er she was getting used to. Her phone buzzed a mellow chime.

Ashaar: I'm coming over now.

Moments later, she watched Ashaar approaching her desk, keeping her eyes glued to the laptop.

Her fingers moved and shifted across the keyboard with precision.

"Everything okay?" Ashaar asked. He placed a cup of tea next to her keyboard, grabbed a chair and sat beside her.

Emma gave a strong nod. "Decaf?"

"Yes, Emma. Sorry I didn't have enough time yesterday to do your research. I need more time."

"It's okay. I found something the other day." Heat gathered in her chest. *Think about what you want to say. Think fast.*

She was at a loss for words, so he drew her in close and held her hands, his fingertips running over her flushed skin.

Dressed in her fitted white top and black skirt, Emma had a rush of nervousness despite the outfit hugging her curves just right. The tumbling neckline, now made her self-consciously tug at the fabric, second-guessing her choice. Her strappy black boots, usually a source of confidence, seemed to echo her unease.

She could feel Ashaar's eyes on her, intensifying her sense of vulnerability. She shifted, took a deep breath and rubbed her hands over the discontinuities on her skirt. "I found something in Steph's backyard."

"What do you mean?" His eyes widened.

"Before I went inside, I snuck into that detached house in her backyard."

"You sneaked in? What did you find?" Ashaar clutched Emma's chair by its armrest and pulled it closer.

Her eyes shifted from his face to the palm of his hand, then back to his eyes. She cleared her throat and said, "Really futuristic stuff. Inside, an antechamber and then the main chamber." Emma pursed her lips. "It was a container full of IV bags. Fluids. Like a data archive." Her shoulders hunched up slightly while she continued fidgeting with a pen.

"She must be doing some form of research." Ashaar gently gripped her shoulder. "I can look into it."

Was that it? Emma stared into Ashaar's glassy brown eyes and thought, *why isn't he reacting?* She tried to discover a million reasons why Ashaar's jaw wouldn't hit the floor. It almost felt like Ashaar had prior knowledge of Stephanie's research. Whatever it was, she didn't regret a word.

"Honestly, I kind of feel relieved to share this with you." Emma crossed her legs and turned around to face him.

"Ashaar ..."

"Yeah?"

She leaned in further and said, "I know you asked me out, but back then, I didn't trust you." Her eyes widened. She realised Ashaar had already noticed her awkward behaviour, and her posture didn't make things any better. She brought the mug to her lips and took a sip, trying to act normal.

"It doesn't matter," he said, "You're the best thing that has happened to me."

She replied silently with a smile. She felt the words energising the nanoparticles that went through her body like electric charges, exploding into her heart. Her eyes were glued to her nails.

"Emma," Ashaar exhaled a smile, his voice dropping to a new low. "I'm happy whichever way you want to take this, and however slow it might be. I just want you to know that I like you. A lot."

Emma couldn't stop smiling.

Emma sensed something scorching entering her heart, and she had emotions that her brain prevented her from stating.

He turned his face to stare at the unfamiliar figures outside the lab, then put his hand around hers, his cheeks against the bare skin on her arm.

Emma took a few seconds, and tried to stop the time from rushing away. A long few minutes later, he pulled back. She watched him observe her from a close distance.

It was about twenty degrees outside, and the enormous glass windows of her office let in most of that heat. Even inside, the temperature was rising, and the air conditioner had difficulty keeping up with the external heat. It was late, but she seemed perfectly awake.

Emma, who felt as if the air had shifted at the time, realised that Ashaar's hands were brushing against her left shoulder blade and bra straps, as if he wanted to make her bend towards him.

"I think you should call it a day." Ashaar stroked his fingers on her cheek, pulled a few strands of hair away and dragged them behind her ears. It took a few moments to adjust, as Ashaar inhaled deeply and inclined his face towards her.

At first, the fingers touching her face startled her. A rapid puff of air blew on Emma's neck. She could see his face from her peripheral vision as she turned towards him in that agonisingly slow moment. Afterwards, she sensed his hand had been pulled back. Ashaar wasn't smiling, yet she perceived how differently Ashaar looked at her—it gave her the impression of being the absolute centre of his world. In the abrupt and profound silence, she saw a face, a pleasant, comforting and warm human being. A strange, wireless transmission of a type of energy occurred. It was different. Few people had made her feel that way, pleasant and fuzzy and jubilant and exasperated and demented, all simultaneously. His hand travelled from the dark golden hair to her jaw as his fingers brushed against her cheek. She did not want to and had no plans to enjoy that, but her brain was split into two different opinions. It was in a state of superposition, yes and no simultaneously. The second he pulled away, she grabbed his hands, wrapped her fingers around his palm and squeezed them tight for one second. Then she let him go.

He will not kiss me in my office. Why isn't he moving? Go away. Leave this office.

Ashaar leaned in, rolling his chair an inch forward.

She felt the soft and warm touch of his hands.

The sudden chime of her phone shattered the silence like a gunshot. Her body jolted with the surprise. She reached for her phone, turned it around just as she saw the name David.

> David: I'm glad you came to that singles event. Maybe we could catch up soon?

Ashaar's frustration was visible on his face, etched onto his forehead in lines of tension and stress.

Shit. Oh my God. He saw the text, didn't he?

"Let's go. You have a long day tomorrow," Ashaar said and stood up. He pushed the chair under the table, turned the other way and grabbed his coat.

She let out a long exhale she didn't realise she was holding. The tension in her shoulders began to ease.

Ashaar walked out of the office.

In the deep trenches of her consciousness, she knew that her logical side could easily blunder the feeling of this relief as a sign of avoiding danger.

The soft buzz of her phone broke her chain of thoughts. As she looked at her phone, her pulse raised again. She quickly picked up her bag, locked her office and left.

She tapped the notification while dashing towards the exit. The AI on her phone read the message out loud.

> +17: Quantum Traveller Echo Mike, this is a one-way quantum communication channel. Do not resist Ashaar Naveed's departure from Cognition or share intel on the data archive. If you do, it will lead to catastrophic consequences.

Just as she stepped out of the building entrance, the phone slipped and dropped onto the concrete.

The screen was shattered. Glaring at the concrete pavement, she growled for a couple of seconds. She picked it up and stared at the broken phone for a while, before heading off to the bike rack.

It was the first time she'd received this text. Where the hell was this text coming from? Now, someone knew she had been trespassing on Stephanie's property.

This is freaking me out.

She needed an answer, and soon, before irritation boiled over into something volatile. She had to find out about the source.

Chapter 5: Ashaar

A week before Emma broke her phone

In the dimly lit privacy of his office, Ashaar sat motionless, staring at the terminal that illuminated his face with an eerie glow. Over the past couple of months, several new users had reported unusual behaviour in Cognition's AI—it was speaking in unnatural "human" ways. Meanwhile, others found it making up its own alien language. The possibilities were narrow: either someone inserted an unknown code, or the AI was rewriting itself, the latter of which Ashaar knew was impossible.

CognitionGPT, the AI they were building, was a different beast altogether. It was more advanced, more powerful than any other AI software in the world. But it wasn't smart enough to re-write its own code or make up its own language. Watching a video embedded in the report, he observed how their AI reacted with almost sentient-like articulation. It was speaking, and then suddenly, making up an alien language. He knew it wasn't truly sentient, just an illusion of consciousness, a trick of programming and data. But as the AI spoke in the video, Ashaar couldn't help but feel a flicker of doubt.

Hours turned into days as Ashaar delved into the AI's intricate web of code, his eyes flickering across the screen, dissecting lines of programming in search of anomalies. The night was quiet, save for the occasional hum of the computer and Ashaar's focused breathing. The more he investigated, the more baffling the situation became.

Code segments began appearing that were clearly not the work of any known employee—at least not anyone in his team. Ashaar spent his time writing a custom script to sift through large datasets generated by the AI, looking for hidden patterns or anomalies.

A week later, after nearly four hours one evening, Ashaar found the root of the problem. A piece of code, so sophisticated and foreign, it seemed impossible that it was human written. It was as if invisible hands belonging to people who had never set foot in the company were writing these codes.

The discovery consumed him. The following night, Ashaar tirelessly traced the code's origins. The code seemed to pulse with a life of its own, and led him to a startling revelation. The first piece of anomalous code he found was installed by an insider.

The clock struck 10 p.m. as Ashaar accessed the terminal's logs, the only sound in the room being his steady keystrokes on his laptop. His heart pounded as he found the entry he was looking for.

The person who added the first code was none other than Oscar. And he'd done that almost a year ago.

A chill ran down Ashaar's spine as he pieced the information together. After Oscar's initial interference, the AI had evolved autonomously, code segments sporadically appearing as if the AI was in communication with an unseen entity, possibly another AI. With his mind racing, Ashaar reached for the phone and called Emma.

"Hey, everything okay Ashaar?"

"Emma, Oscar's tampering with Cognition AI. I knew it! I fucking knew it! And it's been self-evolving, as if it's merging code from somewhere else."

"What exactly do you mean by somewhere else?"

"Em, after Oscar hid a piece of code, the AI has been literally generating code by itself. But it would have made sense if GPT could re-write its own code."

"But it can't," Emma replied. "It wasn't designed to access its own code, right?"

"Correct. So this is it. I don't know what to do now." Ashaar slammed his laptop close and chugged the rest of his leftover tea.

"Ash, this might sound crazy, but can I share something as a physicist?" Emma's response was filled with intrigue and a hint of apprehension. "Only a quantum superintelligence can do that kind of stuff."

"What kind of stuff?"

"Do you reckon it's speaking to an upgraded version of itself?" Emma replied, and added, "Theoretically of course."

"I ..." Ashaar clicked his tongue. *Nothing had happened that would make her think this. Does she know something?*

Emma continued, "What if ... he's testing a new algorithm on Cognition, and then use it to build a more powerful quantum AI? I know this sounds downright crazy, but—"

"It's the only theoretical explanation that makes sense," Ashaar replied. "I also think he's trying out a new algorithm using Cognition's backend terminal. Wait, Emma, do you know something that I don't?"

"I don't think so," Emma replied. She paused for a second, and replied, "I thought we trusted each other?"

He swallowed a lump. "Yes, of course I trust you, Emma," he replied, exhaling a sigh. Deep inside, he felt Emma wanted to share something more. Something that she was trying to hide. He cleared her throat and said, "There must be something in his office that will prove all these."

“Why is he keeping this a secret then? That’s a scientific breakthrough.” Emma said.

“Probably because no one will believe him.”

Their conversation deepened into theories of quantum computers and multidimensional access. Emma shared her insights, and her was voice tinged with excitement and concern. “This could explain so much, Ash.”

“Oscar’s actions, the AI’s behaviour, your visions, the archives ... they’re all part of a larger puzzle.”

An hour passed as they pieced together the fragments of information. After the call, he paced across the room from one side to the other while his office room was shrouded in darkness, save for the faint light from his monitors.

The clock continued its steady tick.

***

April 2021, a couple of weeks later

Last week, Emma’s team member Kjell Abbott stole confidential research documents on Hyperion and left the company. Kjell was under her direct supervision, and that made her responsible for this mishap.

Now, Oscar wanted Emma to suffer.

Ashaar knew Emma was overstressed. She broke her phone, and then took a few days off to let go of her steam. One week away from work was enough to cause a meltdown.

Ashaar drained his coffee from his stainless-steel mug and looked at Emma from a distance as she walked away. After several closed-door conversations, Ashaar and Emma had come up with a plan earlier today.

It was time for Ashaar to be her shining knight and save Oscar from ending her career. Risking his job and going against his own boss was something Ashaar wouldn’t typically do.

Oscar had just returned from his trip to Monaco, and it was the right time to have a serious conversation like that. With the intent to set up a meeting, Ashaar walked into his room. He needed to take that risk. Without Emma, the whole deal with Xplorer would slip through the gaps.

A while later, as he waited on the sofa in Oscar's room, Ashaar received a text from him: I'll be late. Send me a Teams invite, and we can have a chat. He shook off his breath and walked towards the door. On his way out, a peculiar binder caught Ashaar's eye as he tapped a digital scanner to open the door. He closed the door behind him and walked carefully back to Oscar's desk. Then, he quickly scanned the area to make sure he was alone.

Oscar's office, notably devoid of any surveillance cameras, reflected his fondness for privacy. As the CEO, he had the liberty to choose where CCTV surveillance was implemented. He approached the desk, carefully pulled the binder towards him, and slowly opened it to uncover its contents. A lime green marker was used to emphasise several sentences on the first page. Turning to the second page, his eyes nearly popped out of their sockets. The words "Sentinel—A new era of AI" was printed in large, bold font. "Strictly private and confidential" and "SECRET" watermarks were printed across the page.

He slammed the binder closed.

A wave of vertigo washed over Ashaar. It felt like the floor was trembling beneath him. This sensation struck just as Emma had shared her vision of "Sentinel," experienced right after she walked out of the data archive. The other night, Emma casually linked the unknown codes Ashaar had found in Cognition's backend to a hypothetical quantum superintelligence. The way she said it made him feel like she was holding something back. Now, in a moment that seemed far from coincidental, Ashaar stumbled upon a binder on Oscar's desk, eerily labelled "Sentinel."

But what sent a jolt of shock through him was the revelation tucked within its pages: Sentinel, contrary to everything Emma and Ashaar believed, did not actually exist.

He yanked his phone out and took a photo of that page after opening the binder.

The fire alarm blasted in the office, pulling him out of his thoughts.

It was loud and ear-piercing. He craned his neck, and watched everyone in the office stand up. Ashaar shut the binder, and sprinted out of the room and towards the exit—red lights flashed all over the building and the space was drowned with the stomping of boots. He pushed the emergency fire exit, opened the glass barriers and exited the building.

He heard hurried footsteps—the sound of Marshalls in their high-viz walking towards the building. Ashaar dashed and ran towards the car park.

***

After stepping inside his flat, Ashaar sat in his kitchen behind his laptop, and waited for the clock to hit 8.30 p.m. He shook his legs, and repeatedly checked his clock.

Oscar rang on Teams.

Ashaar received a text, his phone humming with a mellow ping.

> Emma: Good luck tonight. Let me know what happens.

Ashaar poured a cold drink and opened his laptop. He clicked a button and turned on the video feed labelled Oscar Williams. He felt his pulse pounding in his head like a hammer on a metal plate.

Oscar and Ashaar continued the conversation for an hour.

Once the conversation was over, Ashaar finally had the guts to say what he wanted. He asked Oscar to keep Emma in the team. Otherwise, Ashaar said he'd reveal Oscar's plans—how Oscar had used his profits to build his secret project "Sentinel."

Oscar took the plea like it was no big deal. "What I do with my personal wealth isn't your business, Ash."

"It is *my* business if *I* start finding anomalies in Cognition's code, Oscar."

"And how exactly does that relate to my project, Ashaar?"

Ashaar swallowed a lump before replying, "I've investigated. There are codes within Cognition's AI that aren't written by anyone in our team."

"The anomalies have nothing to do with Sentinel," Oscar replied, his voice deepening. "Sentinel is a quantum AI that I want to build in the future. It's for the benefit of my companies."

"But it's a lot of money. You can use that money to fund Hyperion and keep it afloat for a few years."

Oscar exhaled a sigh. "Hyperion needs to stay afloat on its own. We need to find investors who are willing to fund the research!"

"If Emma signs this partnership with Xplorer, VCs will throw their money at you," Ashaar said.

Oscar leaned in, "When I left that folder in my office earlier today, I knew someone dug into it. Some part of my sixth sense told me it was you. Now you are using it as a bargaining chip for Emma."

"You wouldn't have kept Sentinel a secret if it was for a good purpose." Ashaar took a few seconds to gather his thoughts, and stared at him, brows furrowing. "Emma stays here with me. Otherwise, I'm out."

"I get that you have moral conundrums."

"About your companies?" Ashaar said. "Hell yes! And now I find out that you're building a fucking artificial superintelligence?" Ashaar could hear his heart punching out of his chest.

There was silence on Oscar's side. "How the fuck do you know that Sentinel is a superintelligence?"

Ashaar lowered his eyes and shook his head. "I didn't." He chuckled, "You just confirmed it. I have journalist friends who'll dig for a story like this."

A strained and jittery laugh escaped Oscar's lips, betraying his anxious state. "You're blackmailing me."

Ashaar shrugged and said, "Oscar, all you need is one incident and that'll trigger the sentience to go rogue. This is by far the biggest technological revolution the world has seen, yet we have barely any virtual hard walls to protect the users!"

"We'll shut it down just like Facebook did," Oscar folded his hands and leaned back.

"We both know it won't be that easy," Ashaar said.

Oscar went away for a few minutes to make a couple of calls and put the video call on mute.

A few minutes later, Oscar's video feed returned. He said, "I will go ahead and hope that Emma can handle her team. I could have found someone who knows how to manage their fucking team better."

Ashaar bit his lip with his mouth and waited for his agitating panic to blow over, while nodding at Oscar ranting about his work. His words were as blurry as a window on a cold winter morning.

"I'm glad we've reached an agreement." Ashaar folded his hands, head tilting to the side, "Why do you want Emma to leave so desperately?"

"Because she's meant to do great things someday."

"For what purpose?"

"I gotta go." Oscar killed the connection in the next second.

That was the weirdest thing any boss ever said. But it was Oscar, after all.

Ashaar turned off his laptop and went to sleep straight after the call.

***

> News Reader: Last week, CognitionGPT, which has already been integrated as a third-party extension to browsers and alike, was under investigation. One internet user used the AI to carry out his research, and as a part of his social experiment, he asked the AI what it would do if he hacked into the GPT. The AI, in response, threatened the user by using words such as "enemy" and "revenge" which shocked the world media.
>
> After the video went viral on the social media app TikTok, Cognition has come under heavy scrutiny. Following reports from several of Cognition's users, the start-up has

> yet to investigate its anomaly. We've reached out to the start-up, however, the company declined to comment.

After listening to the newsreader, Ashaar closed the laptop lid. His email was bombarded with questions from all over the news media, left and right. The inaudible hum of his colleagues talking to each other in the office was making him feel anxious.

If Oscar were to be summoned to testify before the US congress, the situation would likely worsen. Ashaar's company, Cognition, was building the most technologically sophisticated AI, but someday, that'd be trumped by the computational power of quantum physics. Considering the sizable risks AI posed to humanity's future, the government's interest in overseeing its progress was comprehensible.

Their AI was already showing signs of sentience.

I'm not going to lie, I'm nervous about what will happen from this moment forward.

He shifted his eyes to Emma to use her as a distraction.

The innocent-looking woman in blue jeans and a white top captured his attention as she pitched her project.

I need to have coffee right now.

He glanced at the large digital clock on the towering screen at the reception. It was 11 a.m. on a hot, sticky May afternoon. The heat was unbearable.

Half an hour later, Ashaar returned to his office carrying two coffee cups in one hand and a stack of papers in the other. He stared at the woman in his office, reading a magazine, wearing her black top, grey chequered trousers and white trainers. Her judgemental look spoke volumes.

With a twirl of his chair, Ashaar sat down, facing Stephanie on the other side of his desk. He passed the coffee and smiled, "You've got half an hour. Talk."

"Wow, a whole half-hour, huh? That's quite the generous trade-off for helping Emma and her start-up in building an entire fucking Habitat lab in Italy." Stephanie raised her brows, bringing her cup to her lips.

Ashaar shrugged. "I'm kidding."

"I think it's time for you to think big," Steph replied.

His phone chimed with an alert:

> Emma: I'm having those visions again. This is too much to handle. I'm going home.
>
> Ashaar: Sorry! Maybe you should ask Oscar to give you a week off.

"What's wrong?" Stephanie asked, taking a sip of her coffee. "This coffee is great, by the way."

"Emma needs to go home, I think she's ill," he replied.

"I'm sorry to hear that. I hope she feels better." Stephanie's eyes shifted at the blueprint resting on the side of Ashaar's desk. "What are your thoughts on joining Xplorer?"

"Your team in London?"

"No," Stephanie replied. "Their HQ is in California."

Ashaar said, "Someday Oscar will sell his soul to build an artificial superintelligence, and I'll have moral obligations to leave his company. After the news about the AI's anomaly broke, I was researching on twitter, and here's what I fucking found." He unlocked his phone with a swipe of his thumb and scrolled through twitter's home feed.

Stephanie leaned in and stared at Ashaar's phone, squeezing her brows. "Interesting," she said, after reading through some negative comments. "Ash, this is more the reason you should work for Xplorer's space division instead. Then you wouldn't have to deal with all this bullshit."

"Thanks, Stephanie, I need a solution to stop this, not a job offer!" Ashaar took another sip, and made a clicking noise with his mouth. Tapping on the side of his phone, he switched it off. "Come with me. Outside, now." He stood up.

Stephanie walked along Ashaar. She stood next to a steel beam painted bright pink and whispered, "Is everything okay?" She crossed her hands.

"There's something I wanna ask." Ashaar leaned closer. "Remember our first meeting with Emma? She experienced a vision after accidentally discovering your lab."

"What?" The skin on her forehead furrowed.

"Look, I know about your and Bryan's DNA drive research." Ashaar turned and eyed a security guard watching them from a distance. "Bryan's one of my good friends. And I know it's all experimental stuff that Xplorer is secretly buying from his start-up. But I didn't know you had an entire archive of IV bags stashed away in your fucking backyard."

She exhaled in disbelief. "Emma had a vision about what? But ..." Her words stumbled and faltered, coming out in hesitant, broken fragments. "Ash, I know she was trespassing in my backyard." Her face was etched with worry, the creases around her eyes and furrowed brow clearly conveying her deep-seated concerns. "It doesn't matter. What did she see in her vision?"

"Memories that didn't make sense. Emma told me that she heard the name Sentinel," Ashaar said.

The electric engines in the back hummed to life. A group of engineers from a different company were testing their prototype vehicle.

"And what else?" Stephanie's eyes grazed over Ashaar's face.

"It can't be a coincidence that the *second* she walked out of your lab, she had a vision about Sentinel. Weeks later, I find Sentinel's file on Oscar's table. Meanwhile, I'm investigating anomalies at my company. There are codes that literally *none* of us recognise. It's almost as if someone, or 'something' has connections to it. Those codes were not written by a person. And now the visions are starting to affect her life."

Stephanie pursed her lips. "Ash, there are things that I can't tell you right now."

"So—" Ashaar exhaled a chuckle. "I am breaking my non-disclosure, but you can't?" Ashaar sunk his teeth into his lips, "Look, Emma is a quantum physicist. I'm worried that her theory might be true. Cognition's AI is learning to access higher dimensions. Oscar will take that algorithm and build a more powerful quantum AI. And even if Emma knows something, she won't share anything to protect herself. Do you see where I'm going with this?"

“It’s just a theory.” Stephanie’s phone chimed with a buzz. She yanked it out of her pocket and stared at it for a short while. “Look, Ash, I promise you that I know *nothing* about Oscar’s motives. And there’s only one way I could tell you about the DNA data archive—if you join Xplorer.”

Closing his eyes, Ashaar exhaled a sigh, his nostrils flaring. “Thanks for the job offer anyway,” he drank the rest of the coffee and threw the plastic cup in the recycling bin. “I need to think about it.”

“How about by the end of this week?”

“No.” Ashaar shook his head. “I need a couple of weeks.”

“Fine. Just make sure Emma keeps her mouth zipped.”

Chapter 6: Ashaar

May 2021, three days later

Ashaar turned his eyes towards the driver-side window, waiting for Emma to reply.

Emma and her flatmate Aggie lived on a little street in Hackney, East London. Everything about the place was ridiculously pricey. Rent increases made it nearly impossible for city dwellers to find affordable housing.

The neighbourhood was filled with clusters of similar three- or four-bedroom homes with red roofs, white siding and enlarged windows. A thin, easily breakable divider split each dwelling, even though house prices were far over one million.

Ashaar shifted his eyes to his phone, scrolling through the texts he'd sent earlier:

> Ashaar: I'm here at Ikea. I found a Monstera. It's the last one. Sending you a photo.
>
> Emma: I'll take it, it's beautiful!

Just as Emma walked out of her house with a grin on her face, Ashaar jumped out of his car, grabbed a blue Ikea bag and dropped it on her driveway.

They stood a foot apart from each other.

Emma peeked through the bag, "Wow, it's so pretty. I'm so excited."

"I'm glad," Ashaar replied with a smile.

"Thanks for going all the way to Ikea to buy a plant."

Ashaar cleared his throat and said, "There's something I need to tell you."

"What?"

"I had a chat with Stephanie."

"Ash, please don't tell me ..."

"Yeah." He rubbed his palms together repeatedly, the friction causing a soft rustling sound as his skin grew slick with sweat. Raising his brows, he added, "I asked her."

Emma dropped the bag, and covered her mouth with both hands, "I cannot believe this. I think I'm gonna throw up."

"Emma, she needs to know. It's okay, she's not done anything." Ashaar replied, cradling her arm.

"She's never gonna help me with my funding deal," Emma replied. A flush of red spread across her face.

"Look." Ashaar unlocked his phone to show Stephanie's latest text. Emma leaned in as Ashaar stood next to her.

> Stephanie: Let's pretend nothing ever happened. Just make sure that Emma doesn't share with anyone else.

"Why is she letting this go?" Emma's brow furrowed, her eyes reflecting a storm of concern.

"I don't know, she's nice," Ashaar replied with a shrug.

"This can't be. There's more to this than you think, Ash."

"Em, do you want her to prosecute you? Just let go of this matter already."

Emma exhaled through her teeth, clenching her jaws. "Fine."

"She's gonna help us figure out the visions. But there's a condition." Ashaar clicked his phone off, standing up to face

Emma. A lump formed in his throat, which he swallowed with effort.

"What?"

"I have to join her team. Steph offered me a job at Xplorer."

Emma returned a blank stare. She subtly cleared her throat, steadying her voice, and reached out to tenderly grasp his forearm. "Ashaar, what? No, you don't have to leave your job to help me out. It could just be a neurological problem."

He said, "Here's the thing—I can have some real intel on what's going on. Stephanie's under strict NDA, so she can't risk discussing their internal things. Xplorer must be working on a secret quantum AI project she doesn't want anyone to know about."

"What makes you think that?" Emma asked, swallowing a lump forming in her throat.

Ashaar unlocked his phone and held it in front of her face. "I found out that Xplorer has a secret project called 'Quantitative.' If that has something to do with the DNA archive, and that triggered your visions, then they must be related. I need to figure this out."

"Ash, if you want the job, just take it."

"Emma, this whole situation is making you ill. You've had over ten visions, and now your health is deteriorating. You need to rest."

"I will." Emma replied with a soft nod of her head. "Once you're done talking about this, we can go back to discussing Hyperion's upcoming PR event."

Ashaar stepped back, blew a kiss from a distance and left. He observed her walk into her house.

She clearly didn't react to the intel about Quantitative, he thought. *There's a 99% chance that she's hiding something.*

He sped away from Hackney and onto the highway, scowling at the streetlamps and replaying what had happened. Ashaar wanted Emma to give this relationship a chance.

As he drove, lost in reflections about their intertwined lives, his phone buzzed with an unexpected message that made his heart skip a beat. The screen displayed text he never expected to see.

It was Xplorer's CEO, Nolan. *What the actual fuck is even happening!*

Hey Ashaar, I was hoping we could talk. N.

He gripped the wheel tighter and hard pressed the gas pedal. In his mind, Ashaar had already sketched out his next moves before even thinking about saying yes.

But first, he needed Bryan to help find an antidote for Emma. Second, he had to dig up dirt on Xplorer's secretive project. Ashaar had to be sure of exactly what he was walking into before signing any contracts.

***

Ashaar's visit to Bryan's lab in Dagenham took him to an area shrouded in secrecy and high-end security. The lab, located in an isolated area within an industrial complex, was a fortress of modern technology. As he passed through the multiple security checkpoints and 15-foot-tall gates, he couldn't help but admire the precision and difficulty that safeguarded the facility.

Inside, the lab was a hive of activity. Scientists and engineers wearing white aprons and goggles moved with purpose among the sleek, high-tech equipment. The air was filled with a subtle hum of 3D printers. Bryan, the lead scientist, greeted Ashaar in a room that was more of a technological sanctuary than a mere office.

Ashaar's eyes drifted over the soft glow of the white LED strips lining the room. His mind flicked back to the conversation with Bryan the night before. Bryan had agreed to help but only on one condition: that Ashaar would seriously consider the job offer from Stephanie.

After exchanging pleasantries, Ashaar sat next to Bryan and delved into the reason for his visit. He shared with Bryan that Emma had experienced visions since her visit to the DNA data archive. Bryan listened intently as his face masked concentration.

"Emma is stubborn. She won't tell anyone, and her symptoms are getting worse."

"Ash, I'm glad you're here. I have something that could help," Bryan said, leading Ashaar to a secure section of the room behind another set of doors. Tapping his ID, he opened the door, and Ashaar followed him into a vault.

"I'll give a dose of nanobots." Bryan opened a safe deposit box, one of hundreds inside that room. The looks mimicked the vault of a bank. He presented Ashaar with a batch of experimental nanobots inside an EpiPen, "These are still in the testing phase, but they should prevent Emma's visions."

Ashaar examined the nanobots. *There is no way I'm putting nanobots inside Emma.* Despite Bryan's reassurances, he couldn't shake the feeling that Bryan and Stephanie were holding back crucial information about these nanobots. Ashaar looked up and stared at Bryan for a few seconds before saying, "Bryan, I hope you and Stephanie aren't playing God."

Bryan chuckled. "My nanobots will be the only way to store data inside DNA. This is the future, Ash."

"Bryan—"

"You trust me, right?" Bryan gripped Ashaar's shoulder.

Ashaar nodded and took the EpiPen from Bryan's hand.

He'd been friends with Bryan and Stephanie for a long time, but their work on DNA drives and nanobots were wrapped in mystery and secrecy. Ashaar contemplated this as he tucked the nanobots into his pocket.

Later that night, Ashaar met with Emma outside her house. The street was quiet and bathed in the soft glow of the streetlights. Emma, surprised by his sudden visit, sprinted out of her house and jumped into his car. In a fluid motion, she tied up her robe over her grey tank top and shorts.

"I have something that might stop your visions," Ashaar said, his voice hesitant. He showed her the EpiPen, which contained a thick, black ferromagnetic liquid. The nanobots shimmered slightly under the car's dim purple light.

Ashaar extended his hand, holding out the EpiPen loaded with nanobots. He watched as Emma took it, turning it over carefully in her fingers. "I got this from Bryan's lab," Ashaar said quietly. "He's the one who came up with all of this—storing data inside DNA drives using nanobots. He even helped Stephanie set up the data archive in her backyard." Ashaar shook his head slightly. "But I have no idea what kind of data they're storing."

Emma swallowed a lump. "And you didn't bother telling me about it?"

"Emma, I'm trying to find out the connection between the data archive, your visions and Sentinel. But I trust Bryan with my life. I know if he's into something, he'll do it for the right reasons."

Emma pushed Ashaar's hand away. "I can't use this, Ashaar. It's untested, and we don't fully understand it."

"Emma," Ashaar exhaled sharply, touching the cold skin on her arm, "these visions will fry your brain if you don't do something. Remember, we have to attend your launch event in a few days."

Emma gently placed her hand on Ashaar's. "Ash, I don't even take paracetamol when I get migraines. You're asking me to inject my blood with medical nanobots that have yet to receive approval. Not gonna happen."

Her refusal hung in the air between them.

"Keep it." Ashaar watched her swallow twice, shifting her eyes between the device and his face. Without another word, she opened the car door and stepped out, slamming the door shut behind her. He watched her walk away until slowly her figure retreated into the haze.

***

A few days later

Ashaar's stomach churned as he stared at his buzzing phone, the unknown number flashing like a threat. He ambled over from his kitchen to his sofa and sat down. With a response that was a mixture of both curiosity and caution, he was answered by a voice that was hidden in secrecy.

"This is the London Relay UK service. Am I speaking to Ashaar Naveed?"

"Yes," Ashaar said.

"Have you used a relay service before, sir?"

"I have, yes, please connect me to the user," Ashaar replied, swallowing a lump.

"Excellent. Your identity and data remains safe with us. Our client will type a response, and we will relay it back to you, is that okay?" the operator said. "Once you finish speaking, you will then need to say, go ahead."

"That's fine," Ashaar replied.

"Is this user4351?" the relay operator asked.

Ashaar froze for a second, his phone pressed to his ear.

"Yes, speaking," he answered cautiously. The man on the other end knew his DeepChat handle. This had to be about the post he had made two nights ago, the one asking for anonymous leads on Xplorer's internal project.

"Sorry," Ashaar continued, his voice tight, "who's this? Go ahead."

His pulse quickened. He had expected no one to actually call. The operator replied, "I'm DeepChat user 45boogieman. I saw your post about finding info on Xplorer's quantum research."

"Right," Ashaar cleared his throat, "How do I know it's really you? Go ahead."

"I've learned that you had a conversation with Miss Stephanie Maddox about your job," the operator replied.

"Erm ... how do you ... never mind. What intel do you have? Go ahead." Ashaar replied, swallowing a lump.

"I have some information you need to know about their Quantitative lab," the operator said.

Ashaar's interest was immediately piqued. "I'm listening, go ahead," he urged, his mind racing with the implications of this unsolicited contact. He placed his drink on the side table and picked up his notebook.

"The research they're doing on quantum AI ... it's beyond anyone's comprehension, even Xplorer's. Nolan, Xplorer's CEO is funding this research out of his pocket."

"How do you know all this? Go ahead." Ashaar asked.

"I used to be one of the lab's construction workers for years. Now I've been diagnosed with an unknown neurological condition. It made me sick. Take the fucking job Ashaar. Nolan wants you to take it. Then, stop them. If you don't, their quantum device will annihilate the world."

"I don't understand. Go ahead." Ashaar's brows creased.

"Meet me at Caffe Concerto next to Trafalgar Square tomorrow. I'll hand over to you some files ... our client has hung up, sir. Thank you for using—" Ashaar ended the call.

The following evening, in the café, Ashaar sat at a corner table, his vision scanning the bustling crowd. Across the room, the whistleblower, a figure swathed in anonymity sat at a separate table. Their eyes met briefly.

Ashaar watched as the whistleblower, with a calculated nonchalance, stood up and casually strolled past his table.

As they passed, the person subtly dropped a file next to where Ashaar was seated, and offered him a fleeting smile before exiting the café. The exchange was seamless.

Ashaar waited a beat to make sure not to draw attention. He then casually leaned over, his hand sweeping the file off the floor and onto his lap. He quickly scanned the room, his heart pounding with adrenaline.

With the file now in his possession, Ashaar stood up and rushed to the exit. His heart was beating out of his chest, and mind was already racing with the possibilities of what the file might contain.

Once outside, he made his way to his car. After settling into the driver's seat, he placed the file on the passenger seat. The file, unassuming in appearance, held secrets that might alter the course of his life and perhaps much more. It could affect Emma's life and he wouldn't allow it to happen. The folder was brimming with evidence. There were internal reports, confidential emails and documents detailing Xplorer's quantum research.

Ashaar combed through the documents as his expression shifted from disbelief to concern. "This is ... it's unbelievable. What the fuck am I supposed to do with this?"

He gazed out of the window. He didn't know what he wanted to do, but he needed to decide fast.

Chapter 7: Emma

8 June 2021

“Eighty-one years ago, when the war among the nations ended, the world began to see more progress than ever before, exploding on the verge of exponential technological success. Then Italian American scientist Enrico Fermi had built a self-sustaining nuclear reaction, propelling humanity into another dimension. Then, NASA sent astronauts to the moon, and Xplorer built the self-guiding rockets that left Earth on its own and flew back at the speed of sound.”

Emma shut her eyes as she listened to the narrator.

“Fortunately, the political fight did not stop the innovators from continuing to build their world. And now, companies like Hyperion are building Martian habitats, and designing nuclear-powered rocket engines. Dr Fermi would have been proud to see his work being used to propel humanity to the outer terrestrial colonies.”

Emma heard the narrator's voice rise above the background noise, cutting through the chatter. She sat outside a conference hall on a wooden bench, and grazed over the blueprint of Xplorer's plans for building a new military-class spaceship. Everything at this point was theoretical. Oscar's Hyperion Drive project didn't work, not yet. The idea, though, was one of a kind and extremely valuable. Their habitats were hardly functional, and without funding, the start-up would go bust in less than 18 months.

"Gliding through the darkness of hard vacuum, Earth has been carrying the burden of humanity for too long." She heard the announcement blasting from the speakers.

"Xplorer's spaceship pointed its mighty cone towards the red, dimmed star, two hundred million miles away. Roughly two-hundred feet long and thirty feet wide—shaped like an aircraft fuselage but without wings. And prepared itself for transporting Hyperion's habitat to the red rock. Six months later, the spaceship reached its ultimate destination."

The crowd gathered in the middle of the hall, watching the awe-spectacle documentary on how Xplorer and Oscar's start-up would build the capital city on Mars.

Hyperion's PR stunt was about to kick off. Emma realised Ashaar had cloaked himself around the project, which made her feel secure.

Standing in the greenroom, Emma looked around. The hall was filled with food, people, music and a live demonstration of the 3D-printed parts. Their habitat was placed right in the centre. There were iPad terminals connected all around where people learned about the technology and watched how the temperature-controlled system worked. Since it was impossible to mimic the Martian temperature in real-time, part of the warehouse was insulated to mimic a colder environment. Within that cold patch, guarded by acrylic walls, people hung around in their jackets.

Emma adjusted her crimson leather top and glanced at her reflection again. The matching trousers looked sharp under the lights, but something felt off. The outfit fit well and looked good, but her mind kept drifting to the fact that they needed this event to be successful. Her company's name was about to go public after this party. And she wasn't sure if she was ready for that kind of attention.

When Emma walked into the hall, she felt eyes on her. She looked around and it was perfect. The room was filled with displays, and lights—pink, purple and blue. The journalists and influencers were the ones most excited. It was almost like a swarm of people walking around with selfie sticks and vlogging cameras. She ambled towards the centre where the habitats were being displayed. As she walked along with the lights, people turned around and looked at her. She never wore high heels at work, but today, she made an exception. She spotted Ashaar in one corner, at a distance. She got closer and waved at him.

He smiled back.

A second later, Emma received a terminal from one of her colleagues, which she could use to control various aspects of the habitat. She placed her thumb on the under-screen fingerprint and unlocked the screen.

"The stage is yours, Emma." Her colleague left the area and walked towards a group of people who stood around the corner. Emma took the microphone.

"Thank you," Emma began, her voice resonating with a mix of pride and anticipation as she addressed the gathered crowd. "Today marks a monumental step for our company and for humanity. With the launch of our first-ever Martian Habitat, *Habs,* we're not just unveiling a prototype; we're opening the door to a new era of space exploration and habitation. This habitat represents the culmination of years of dedicated research, innovation and an unwavering belief in our mission to extend human presence beyond Earth. Together, we're stepping into a future filled with boundless possibilities." She paused, letting her words sink in, her eyes sweeping across the audience, each member hanging onto her every word.

Her five-minute speech ended with thunderous applause.

A journalist stood next to the habitat and spoke to Emma, "We learned that your board would bring funding from Roscosmos. Do you think you'll be able to raise enough funding to survive?" The woman with a blue badge asked. The journalist lady continued asking questions while Emma confidently tackled her.

When it was over, Emma walked towards Oscar and Ashaar. She wasn't happy about Oscar being ready to sell his companies to Russian investors for money. He just didn't have the patience.

"Ashaar, I'm so glad we did this." Oscar tapped his glass against Ashaar's.

"Oscar, why did you make the announcement to bring foreign funding? You should have told me first. Now I look like an absolute fool!" Emma said.

The bottom row of Oscar's teeth was uncorrected and shaded because of smoking. "If I have offers from Russia or China, the West will jump up and down to fund the company. We need to create a 'fear of missing out' idea for the investors. FOMO."

F.O.M.O., pfff, she thought, mocking Oscar. "It's pronounced *fomo.*" They stood right next to the drinks counter. The purple light reflected off Ashaar's face while he drank his cola.

Emma stood next to Ashaar, "People are asking me questions I can't answer. Hyperion can't sell their products to Chinese and Russian investors before we commercialise."

"You mean ... what? Starve to death as the company runs out of funding?" Oscar disregarded Emma's idea, chucked his cocktail and grabbed another one.

"Selling the start-up to Xplorer is always an option," Ashaar replied.

"I'm asking Emma to chase up a partnership with them, not sell my company to them. It's not the right time."

Emma clenched her jaws. "Well, you're wrong, Oscar."

Ashaar gave her a sharp look, his eyes narrowing as he leaned in close, as if he said, *stop fighting with your boss.*

Emma blinked hard and looked away.

"Russian and Chinese space agencies have an actual plan. Their investors have funding ready to be sent. If we say yes, we don't have to worry about money for at least a decade," Oscar added with a hefty voice. His vocal cords got deeper when he drank alcohol.

The music was getting louder. Emma turned around, stared at the DJ for a few seconds, turned her eyes back at Oscar and spoke loudly. "Oscar, between your two start-ups, you have IPs for a quantum AI, a Martian habitat and the blueprint for the Hyperion nuclear fusion drive that *no one* has ever built. If we put these technologies in their hands, then those countries will win the space race, and we lose the credibility. The West will literally start a war over the lands on the Moon and Mars. You own shares in both companies, and you have the power to change things," Emma replied.

One journalist from a tech magazine walked past her.

Fuck this, she must have overheard our conversation. Shit.

"We can talk about this later," Emma shot a fake smile, her face twitching.

"Oscar, I'm sure sparing a few million won't make a dent in your bank—" Ashaar was interrupted again.

"Well, the board told me that Emma is going to be named 30 under 30 in the SpaceTech world, so I'd better listen. Meanwhile, I don't get nearly enough credit." Oscar forced a smile, slammed his empty glass on the bar, and walked towards the restroom.

Emma stared at Oscar and tightened her jaw again. His constant condescending behaviour wasn't easy for her to handle. As her boss, he should be proud. But she was now mocked for having been nominated for an award.

Emma gave Ashaar a big smile, "I need to go." Emma held her clutch, turned around and walked in the opposite direction. *That's it, I'm fucking done,* she told herself. The back end of the warehouse had a fire exit. She walked through the entrance lit with a green sign at the top and slammed the door from behind.

She noticed a dark-skinned woman wearing a saree staring at her as she left.

***

Emma tapped the delivery lift repetitively. Her face turned red, her jaw clenching as she gritted her teeth. She slammed her fist on the switch and mimicked Oscar.

She paced back and forth. Her face was contorted with rage. "You don't get a bloody credit because I'm the fucking lapdog that's doing all the motherfucking work for *you*!"

The corner of her eye caught a CCTV camera in the corridor twitch, its red light flickering. Emma paused. The lens seemed to tilt ever so slightly towards her before the blinking stopped altogether. The hallway fell silent. She waited for something ... anything ... to happen. Then, she decided it wasn't worth her curiosity.

She tied her hair with a band, observed Ashaar walk closer and stand beside her. Her face twisted in a scowl. "You just stood there and did nothing," she said.

"Emma—"

"What? I didn't want to slap my fucking face all over the internet. Now that I have, he's bringing investors and clients from Russia and China. How dare he flaunt his arrogance?"

Ashaar sighed in response.

Emma blinked hard and looked up as the lift pinged. "How did it look when my project partner stood there and let my boss humiliate me in front of the *fucking* world?"

"I'm sorry. I'll remember that next time," Ashaar replied in a mellow voice, gently approaching.

"Don't *you dare come any fucking closer*! This is over." Emma's voice echoed in the hall as she walked into the lift and pressed the button inside until it shut in Ashaar's face.

Chapter 8: Emma

The following week

Emma scrubbed her bottle and poured a drink in the kitchen. The smell of eggs and brewing coffee filled the small room. Unprepared for what would happen next, she turned around and watched Ashaar walk into the kitchen.

She shunned him for a week, like a complete U-turn. She thought he must be feeling terrible. But she didn't care.

Yes, it had been that sort of work week. Emma didn't have the mental capacity to deal with Ashaar's annoyance. Or him trying to ask her a hundred times if she was okay. The water from the tap was cold, but vital for her skin.

The event last week proved to be largely successful. But the past few days far from useful.

She thought about last night, when she became a tad too desperate to find another job. Emma was in her dimly lit bedroom, which was silent except for the sound of fingers tapping on the laptop keyboard. She sat hunched over the screen, her brow furrowed with concentration and anxiety. An occasional sigh or groan escaped her lips. The only source of light was the soft glow of the laptop screen, casting an eerie pastiness over her face.

Emma felt a slight pinching ache in her head when she realised her visions were coming back. In a flash, she saw a shape, a prism. Next, the name Sentinel sprang up in the middle. She heard an old man speaking in the background, but it was unintelligible. The vision disappeared in seconds.

Then she received a notification.

+17: New Message.

The number was familiar. The text, also familiar. She glanced at the notification and deleted it.

Echoing footsteps brought her back to reality.

Back in her office kitchen, Emma continued to disregard Ashaar's presence and stood right next to him, brushing her arm against his.

"Can we talk, please, Emma?" Ashaar said quietly.

"What's on your mind, Ashaar?" Emma scrubbed harder, avoiding eye contact.

"The elephant in the room," Ashaar replied and drifted away. He opened the fridge and looked inside, "Can we talk now?"

"We don't have to. Since, you know, I'm not your friend." Emma, out of the corner of her eye could see Ashaar looking at her, while she focused her eyes on the yellow scrub forming bubbles. Her breathing became shallow and her nostrils flared.

"Why are you so angry at me? Why do you *always* have to say something provocative at the beginning of a conversation?" He slammed the fridge door and walked towards her.

"I don't know, I'm not in a good mood. What do you want?" Emma turned the tap off, shook her hands and sprayed water all over Ashaar's jumper. "Sorry." Emma frowned, wiping her white top and black tights with water droplets all over.

"I want you to move on from this." Ashaar wiped some droplets off.

"I have put a lot of work and effort into this job, and it seemed like we were both in different boats." Emma spun around, trying hard not to look into Ashaar's eyes.

"We are not." Ashaar stood closer to her.

Emma was silent for a heartbeat. She sensed her pulse increasing. She swallowed a lump. "Yes, we fucking *are*! Hyperion is a fucking laundromat for his profit!" Her vocal cords felt strained, "He can easily re-invest that money. Instead, he's funding his own secret AI and *lying* about it. Now, I'm being talked down because I have the guts to resist the Russian and Chinese money."

"What's the worst thing that could happen?" Ashaar asked, folding his hands over his chest.

"Selling British IP to them will start a fucking war between the East and the West! How can you not see that?"

"Yes, I get it. Is that why you're mad at me?"

"No," her lips pressed into a thin line as she let out a long sigh. Emma struggled to push her bottle down the side pocket of her bag and attempted to walk away from the conversation. "I don't fucking care. I don't want my *fucking face* associated with Hyperion anymore. And I'm done with you, Ashaar." Her hands shook slightly, and she had to take several deep breaths to calm herself down.

"You're done with *me*?"

"I'm leaving now."

"Wait." Ashaar held her arm, clenching his jaw firmly. "At least listen to my plan and see what I've come up with."

Emma stared at his hand. She swallowed hard, looked up and stared right into Ashaar's eyes. "What do you want to explain, Ashaar?" Her voice sounded mellow. She took a deep breath, but her heart had been pumping adrenaline. "I understand that you are trying to make me feel better." Emma freed herself and darted to the exit.

Emma marched away, assuming she would not fix everything at that moment. Her fingers trembled as she typed out a message on her phone, her mind racing with doubts and fears. She took a deep breath, steeling herself for what was to come, and hit the call button. As she waited for the man to pick up, her heart pounded in her chest like a drum. "David?"

"Hey, Emma? Everything okay?"

When she heard him on the other end, she spoke with a shaky voice, her nerves barely under control. "You wanted to spend some time, remember? How about this week?"

"I'm going to Soho for a launch event. Join me?"

"Yeah, sure. Will see you on Thursday." She killed the call and raced to the bike rack.

***

Emma was cycling along the canal side in Hackney, her legs pumping rhythmically as she wove through the evening crowd. The afternoon breeze against her face was a welcome relief from the day's stress. As she reached home, her phone rang, the caller ID flashing Stephanie's name.

"Hi Stephanie, what's going on?"

"Emma, we need to meet tonight. In Stratford village. There's a secluded spot in the park there." Stephanie's voice sounded urgent yet hushed over the phone.

Despite the odd request, Emma agreed. The vast park in the residential area promised a discreet meeting place, away from prying eyes and ears.

Under the cloak of night, Emma found Stephanie waiting for her around 10 p.m. There was a palpable tension in Stephanie's demeanour, her usual composure replaced by something edgier.

"Stephanie, what's this about?" Emma asked as she approached.

Stephanie took a deep breath before speaking. "Emma, I'm gonna tell you this once. There's only one way you can save your job and Hyperion. I will make sure you secure that funding deal with Xplorer and set up the lab in Turin. But I have two conditions." Stephanie's voice was firm.

Emma's heart raced. "What conditions?"

Stephanie paused, her sight fixed on Emma. "First, Ashaar. He needs to leave Hyperion and join Xplorer."

Emma's eyes widened in shock. "Why? Do you know about Sentinel and the messages I've been getting? Does it have something to do with that?"

"It might come as a shock to you, but Xplorer's CEO, Nolan Harvey reached out to Ashaar."

"Is that the answer to my question about Sentinel?" Raising her brows, Emma said, "Ashaar didn't tell me anything."

"Nolan gave him until the end of the year to decide. But I need him to move ASAP."

"What about Sentinel? What do you know about it? Why are you storing data on DNA drives? Is it for Sentinel?"

Stephanie glanced around, her eyes settling on a distant dog walker. "I can't discuss this with you, Emma. Just know that Ashaar's life might be at risk. But you ..." Stephanie paused for a second before speaking, lowering her tone. "If you ignore those messages, you're jeopardising more than just your career."

"You're blackmailing me, Jesus."

"I'm trying to protect both of you."

Emma's mind reeled with the implications. "It's my decision whether I choose to be a part of whatever you are doing, Stephanie."

"If you want to save your career and Ashaar's life, you might want to reconsider," Stephanie replied with a note of finality in her voice.

"What's the second condition?"

"You cannot tell *anyone* about Sentinel."

"Steph—"

"I'm sorry, Emma. That's it for now." Stephanie turned and walked away, her silhouette gradually disappearing into the darkness, the dim lights of the park casting long shadows along her path.

Now that she knew she had to let him go, Emma, in the corner of her head, needed him to stay.

***

On Friday morning, Emma stumbled into her office, nursing a hangover. The bright office lights seemed to pierce straight through her, each ray like a needle against her strained eyes as she slumped into her desk chair.

Her drink with David the previous night had been less than ideal. Yet, she wasn't ready to write him off completely—not just yet. Truth be told, David barely registered in her mind, particularly when thoughts of someone else overwhelmed her every waking moment.

And suddenly, she found herself listening to the clanking and cluttering of Ashaar's heavy keychain. *Good,* she thought, *now I can ask him about his so-called plan.*

As Ashaar asked to speak with her alone, she stood up and walked towards a quiet corner of the building. "What happened?" Emma asked.

He looked up and stared at the blinking lights from the network routers strategically hung all over the campus. "I think I might take up on that job offer from Xplorer."

Emma stood right in front of Ashaar, pulling and brushing her golden necklace with her index finger. "No, don't."

"Why?" He gripped his laptop. His eyes were drawn to her bright blue top and white trousers.

"I have—" She let out a nervous laugh and ran her fingers through her hair. The weight that had been crushing her chest began to lift, and she felt like she could breathe again. Emma looked into Ashaar's eyes without blinking once. "I may have overreacted."

Ashaar continued, watching her ears flushing, "Emma, I grew up in a strict South-Asian household. I was taught to suppress my anger and I've learned to bottle it up until it explodes."

She exhaled a long sigh. "Your reaction was justified."

"Why do you need Oscar's constant approval?" Ashaar asked.

She fidgeted with her necklace, her fingers twisting and pulling at the chain as she glanced at him. "Because we work in a network-dominant world and good things happen when you know how to maintain them."

"Maybe he doesn't like you because you know he's building a secret quantum AI. You want the research money to go in the right direction. And he won't win against you because your plan will be thorough, and his one will be downright crazy." Ashaar's eyes trailed a path from her lips to her eyes.

"Is that the plan you wanted to talk to me about?"

"Yes. Two important things, Emma. One, your face now represents Hyperion. Two, the board will be in your favour if use the 'don't bring the Russians' card. Your intel against Oscar gives you leverage. Use them."

"And how do you suggest I 'use it'?"

He lowered his eyes again and stared at the yellow laces of her boots. "Time for you to break people."

She noticed his stare, but the words being launched from his mouth hit her at the speed of bullets. Stephanie told her this week that she wasn't allowed to throw Oscar under the bus, because that would stop Sentinel from being funded. Emma folded her hands in a defensive posture and moved one step forward towards him, "I don't—"

"What, Emma? You're gonna say that you can't break Oscar?"

"What happens then?" Emma asked.

"They'll investigate Oscar's assets and hit a pause to his profits," Ashaar said.

"Ash, he will lose his fucking job!" She spoke in a booming voice that echoed through the corridor.

"Lower your voice," Ashaar whispered.

Emma's exhale was loud, "So ... now that I'm cornered, you want me to feed him to the dogs as a whistleblower? They'll ask a thousand questions I can't answer."

"Emma, Oscar's using you as a shield between him and his personal agenda. It's literally driving a wedge between the two of us. If he's really interested in selling Hyperion to the East, you'll have to face the public. Don't fall for that fucking trap. I'm trying to protect your ass here."

"I need to think about it. If Oscar hates me—"

"Well, Emma, I'm fairly sure you hate me. Yet you've missed the first ten minutes of your meeting because of this conversation. I must be important," Ashaar said.

She chuckled at his response, lowering her eyes. She walked back to her office with him. Her walls clamped, and she felt like grabbing and holding him inside her arms. Emma beamed and stirred back a little. She smiled and didn't smile simultaneously.

"We have two options," Ashaar said, opening the door for her. "Sign a deal with Xplorer that's guaranteed to bring VC funding. And if it doesn't work, you know what to do."

"I'm ... uh ... gonna join my meeting, Ash."

Ashaar smiled, turned around and left.

She stood there, gawked at Ashaar and watched him walk away.

***

The following week, Emma had a lot on her plate. She needed Ashaar close. That's why she scheduled time with him, using it as an excuse to keep him nearby for moral support. It was her quiet, unspoken way of trying to make things right with him.

She watched Ashaar lift his eyes and lock with hers.

"Are you busy this afternoon?" Ashaar said, sitting at his desk, gazing at Emma. The low rumble of other offices in the background, the keys clicking inside his mechanical keyboard and intermittent pings from the computer added depth to the atmosphere.

"No, actually, I'm free." She tried to tie her hair.

"You look like you want to go out." Ashaar said. She watched him gaze over her outfit—the billowy oversized shirtdress with a leather belt that revealed her legs. Her chunky platform sandals added height to her frame.

"I want to stay here with you and get our project plan done by the end of this day," she replied.

That evening, the entire campus was bustling with a chattering crowd. There were lots of people passing by his office. But none of that mattered because she was sitting there with Ashaar beside her.

Emma tucked her feet under Ashaar's desk. Leaning in, she asked, "Wait, why is everyone still here? It's seven o'clock. People should have left." She placed her arm on Ashaar's armrest.

Ashaar chuckled and gently smacked his head on her right arm. He brushed his forehead against her skin and said, "Did you just say it aloud in front of *everyone*?"

Emma glanced around with a grin on her face, realising how loud she had spoken, "Oh shit." But they both laughed.

A couple of hours had passed, and Ashaar's cognisance felt a little different. Emma loved how he touched and handled her every single time with utter delicacy. Like handling a frail piece of cake. A fragile artefact. Or perhaps treated her the way he was. Those moments made a lot of difference. Made things easier to deal with, given all the pressure they both had to face daily.

The entire campus had emptied by then.

I cannot believe he said I'm the centre of his universe, she thought, eyeing him. Her heart fluttered.

A rare feeling sent a spasm of serenity down the spine. He might break her open and crack her guards with a simple wrong move.

Emma felt a sense of relief. After what seemed like an eternity, things were healing. Every day of the week was spent working together to get things done. Her words were full of humour, and her assertions rang with the ring of happiness. Intrigued, she allowed her thoughts to drift to whether she should pull Ashaar closer. She'd been having a pleasant time. In a way, it was refreshing.

"What?" Emma asked when she noticed him staring at her. She uncrossed and crossed her legs.

"Nothing," Ashaar turned his gaze at the monitor.

She could feel him closer. But it didn't feel forced. She leaned in. Her lungs caught warmth when his legs brushed her skin. His eyes met the inner curves of her breasts.

Emma leaned in closer, her breath mingling with Ashaar's. Their eyes locked, a silent understanding passing between them before their lips met in a hesitant yet electrifying kiss.

It was a gentle melding at first, cautious, but soon deepened with a passion that had been simmering just beneath the surface. Emma's heart raced, her smile growing as she pulled back slightly, her eyes sparkling with a mix of excitement and contentment.

They both paused, savouring the moment. "This doesn't mean anything, okay?"

He hesitated, just for a second, eyes searching hers. "Ha! Okay!" Ashaar replied with a smile. Ashaar looked, and put his left hand on her forearm as Emma kept sharing her ideas.

An hour later, Emma squinted at her Apple watch. It was already 9.30 p.m. She looked outside, watching the clouds gather.

"Don't worry about the rest. I'll finish up." Ashaar gently held her arm.

"Okay," Emma smiled, picked up her jacket and left.

She ran down the stairs, reached the ground floor and ran for the exit sign, watching a stranger hold the large glass doors. "Thank you," she said. Her eyes were glued to her feet as she marched towards the basement. With arms, she pushed two sets of doors open and ran towards the cycle rack downstairs. When her phone chimed an alert, she yanked it out, and read the text she'd received over twenty times.

She hard-pressed the power button repeatedly to turn the phone off, but she struggled as her phone's AI read the text out loud.

> Quantum Traveller Echo Mike, this is a one-way quantum communication channel. Do not resist Ashaar Naveed's departure from Cognition or share intel on the data archive. Refrain from causing intrusion in the coming

months, otherwise it will cause catastrophic consequences.

It was time to tell Ashaar about her conversation with Stephanie. But she couldn't.

***

September 2021

Emma leaned back in the passenger seat, watching the city lights blur past as Ashaar drove. She could still feel the rush of the afternoon—weaving through Ikea, tugging him by the arm, laughing as they fast-tracked to the checkout. She had planned nothing fancy for his birthday, just this brief shopping trip, but somehow it had felt ... right.

She smiled to herself, remembering the way he grinned when she slapped the silly "Good Boy" dog sticker on his shirt. It was stupid, playful and so perfectly her.

Now they were headed back, and soon he'd drop her off. She glanced at him, her heart warm as she saw the radiant look on his face. Her mind drifted back to the moment they had shared their first kiss. He tasted of trouble and something safe. She hadn't felt this calm, this content, in a long time. Not since after the Hyperion event. Maybe she hadn't planned the perfect day, but somehow, it ended up being exactly what they both needed.

She felt a strange sensation, as if an unknown vortex was drawing her in. The prism shape was the first thing she saw, and a sense of familiarity washed over her.

Wait a second, she thought, *not this again.* She watched herself lying on a flat surgical bed strapped with cardiac and neuro-monitoring devices. Then, a flurry of recollections that she couldn't make sense of. *These aren't my memories, so what am I doing?* She felt as if she were in a different universe.

Emma heard a woman talking in the background. "Sentinel calculates the probability of a dystopian future," the voice started fading away.

She was meta-consciously aware that she was trapped. But she was at ease. A burst of memories from her time at Hyperion flickered before her eyes.

She experienced a moment that made her blood run cold.

She was sitting in a car next to Ashaar, discussing future lives. She thought, "Why am I experiencing the exact moment that happened ten minutes ago?" Emma, as a physicist, couldn't tell whether she was in her own world or a dream. It felt like a hallucination. The head flooded within her once more, knocked the air out of her lungs, left her open-mouthed, bright colour bursting behind her blue eyes.

Emma slowly opened her eyes, her chest heaving with fatigue.

"Are you okay?" Ashaar gently placed his palm on her knee.

"I don't know. I feel kind of lightheaded. I feel like something is inside my head."

"What do you mean?"

"I felt like I was having a déjà vu moment." Emma couldn't figure out why it had happened.

"What exactly, Emma? You know déjà vu—"

"It wasn't my pre-frontal region adjusting a memory. I felt like experiencing a fall for a second, some form of quantum cryptographic flash appeared in front of me. I saw a shape. It was a prism. As you see in films, I was vacuumed into a quantum realm and thrown out almost instantly. Memories—I experienced them, but," Emma paused for a second, frowning. "Uh, possibly ... don't know what prism means. I don't know why that would happen. I felt as if I was strapped to a flat surgical bed."

"Emma, it's your visions. I think it might be a message."

"I can't see anything else other than that prism and Sentinel."

"We are going home for now." Ashaar floored the gas pedal, the sound of the engine rumbling in the background.

"Anyway, look, that pub is actually great." Emma pointed to a pub near her home, trying to distract herself. Her breathing slowed down. Emma continued to show the places around to

Ashaar as he drove. They kept talking about how great it would be to buy a nice townhouse next to their workplace.

Ashaar listened as Emma began speaking about her long-term plans and what life would be like in a few years. She felt grateful and wondered whether it'd be the same the following year.

It wasn't until a week after his birthday when things started to crack at work.

Chapter 9: Ashaar

A day after Ashaar's birthday

Ashaar ambled down the Hackney Canalside in silence to buy his morning coffee. The dim wind, and the background hum of people sitting in cafes and on park benches filled the void between them. East London was a beehive of activity throughout the summer months, with visitors from all over the UK flocking to the neighbourhood.

"I read that book you suggested, Ashaar," Emma shot a grin and stood beside Ashaar.

"Did you? That's amazing. I love that book. Wait. Which book again?" Ashaar continued to walk.

"Midnight Library. Shall we get some takeaways?" Her head tilted, eyes grazing over the crusty croissants and pain-au-chocolat on display inside a glass box.

"Sure. Yea, love that book. The science behind it is subtle, but it's nice."

"I feel like I should have more time to experience life." The gentle wind scraped her shoulder-length glistening hair.

"You want to leave Hyperion? I'm confused." Ashaar found a separate window for takeaway customers next to their entrance.

"No ... I'm wondering. I don't know what you are going to do." Emma looked down while opening the menu. "Anyway, what's up?" Emma asked.

"Emma, after months of digging, I finally found some evidence." He paused for a moment and said, "Let's grab the food first."

"Fine," Emma said while flicking through the menu. She grabbed the phone from her pocket, "Hi, can I get a sausage roll, please? And what do you want, Ashaar? Try the brownie maybe?"

"Sure."

"I'm going to have the brownie, please! Thank you." Emma hovered her Apple Pay over the payment terminal. Emma shifted her gaze back to Ashaar. "Is Oscar building his quantum AI with Xplorer's help?"

"No." Ashaar's voice went low, stepping closer to Emma. "I believe Xplorer is building a portal to another world."

"What? How do you know this?" Emma's face registered the shock, her mouth dropping open in a silent gasp.

"I have evidence," Ashaar replied, almost whispering into Emma's ears. "I won't know unless I join their company."

"Is Oscar building that quantum AI for Xplorer? That's the only explanation for it." She crossed her arms protectively over her chest.

"Emma, you're a scientist, right?" Ashaar asked, squeezing his brows. "Do you really think we have the technology to build that shit?"

"I don't know," Emma stared at the distance boats floating on the canal. Meanwhile, her hand absentmindedly fidgeted with a small device. "On one hand, I wanna see what Oscar and Xplorer are building. However, I don't want all of humanity to be in jeopardy."

Their conversation was interrupted by the loud announcement from the man behind the counter. "Order number 67," his voice cut through the air.

"If a fucking GPT can be this good, imagine what a quantum AI can do. It'll be great if used in the right way," Ashaar added, then grabbed the two brown bags. They headed back to their office.

"And what does 'using the right way' mean?" She raised a brow. "From your point of view."

"It's about ethics and morality, Emma. Quantum AIs would be the true superintelligence. But for them to make moral and ethical decisions, they need to be trained using the correct dataset. Humanity could be wiped out if it makes a wrong decision." Ashaar grabbed his brownie and returned to the office with her.

"The stories from the book Humankind. Remember the book I suggested to you last year?" Emma asked.

"Of course, it's harrowing."

"If an AI is built and given the power to make tactical military decisions, they need to be ethically strong enough and capable of never choosing to end a person's life without a valid reason," Emma tapped her card on a reader to open a security barrier.

"Imagine the antagonists working under the shadow, filtering old data and only focusing on storing selective information they need. Eventually," she said and moved in closer to him, their arms touching. "The AI will learn to think about destroying countries and then the planet."

As they walked inside the basement, they came to a halt.

Ashaar stood in the empty L-shaped corridor barricaded by two security doors on both ends—the perfect place to have private conversations away from their colleagues.

The warmth of her presence enveloped him, and he felt the steady beat of her heart against his own. As he looked into her eyes, the depth of Emma's emotions reflected back.

"AIs can replace us to take their place in the society." Ashaar took a bite of the brownie. "You want a bite?"

Emma watched as Ashaar passed it to her. She grabbed his hand, pulled it closer and took a bite straight out of the packet, "Why do you always have to think about the worst? I was giving you a realistic scenario."

"I like sci-fi dramas." Ashaar bit a nut.

"Of course, you do, savage," she gazed at Ashaar, put her right thumb on his lower lip and wiped off some chocolate.

"You think I want an AI to destroy the world?" Ashaar continued to shove a heap of the brownie into his mouth. "You know, after we achieve post-quantum cryptography, things are going to escalate pretty quickly." The brownie was as good as Emma had promised him.

"Yes, probably. But sometimes, you may want to be a little more optimistic."

"I might reconsider joining Xplorer," Ashaar said. Her faint fragrance caught up with him. He grazed his eyes over her lips. "It's the only way to find the connection between Sentinel and Xplorer's research and keep you safe."

Ashaar's mind was a whirlwind of thoughts. He was grappling with the decision of whether to share with Emma the unexpected text from Nolan Harvey, the renowned multi-billionaire behind Xplorer. Nolan had extended an invitation for Ashaar to join his team, a once-in-a-lifetime opportunity. Ashaar knew he had a limited time to make his decision, but he found himself hesitating.

In the stillness of the basement, Emma took a step closer to Ashaar, her gaze involuntarily drifting to his lips. "You don't have to worry about me all the time, Ash."

"I do," Ashaar replied with a smile.

Emma's eyes met his, sending a flurry of signals that Ashaar found hard to interpret. Emboldened yet uncertain, he leaned in, driven by a moment's impulse.

But just as her lips met his, Emma stepped back.

A palpable wave of awkwardness surged through the space between them, and the charged moment dissolved into a painful sting of rejection and confusion.

"I'm gonna go," Emma said.

Her words hung heavy in the air.

Ashaar, taken aback, could only purse his lips in response. He stood rooted to the spot, watching as Emma turned and walked away. With every step she took widened the gap that had just opened between them.

***

Ashaar couldn't recall arriving at work, but he made it safely, thanks to the autopilot called "brain." He was waiting for the red and white barrier to open, his hands gripping the stitched leather on both sides of the steering wheel. As the metal ramp bumped against the stiffness of the shock absorbers in his car, Ashaar thought about the past week's events.

His circumstances with Emma took a sharp downturn this week. Meanwhile, work pressure mounted on Ashaar and he made a mistake. Under intense pressure from the press, Ashaar couldn't give a straight answer to the journalists when they asked about Hyperion. The cautiousness in his words were twisted by one of the American VCs who was interested in investing.

A day later, the VC pulled their offer.

This time, Emma's anger tripled.

The memory of their awkward moment in the basement was still alive, as if he was living that moment.

Ashaar pushed his gear into "P" and jumped out. He locked the car with a tap of his car key.

Ashaar swallowed, trying to reduce the itchiness in his mouth. This was absolutely outrageous. He hadn't even known this woman last year, and now, her aloofness caused him sleepless nights.

From across the hall, through the transparent walls, Ashaar noticed an unknown person—a tall, striking blonde man—approaching Emma's desk. His body language was confident, his eyes locked onto Emma's as she spoke.

Ashaar couldn't help but sense a tension, a subtle energy in the room. They both seemed excited. The man leaned close, as he whispered something in her ear. She turned to face him, and her expression was a mix of surprise and pleasure. The man reached out for a bunch of folders without warning and brushed his arm against Emma's.

A few moments later, he left.

Ashaar slowly opened Emma's office door.

His jaws clenched as he watched her type and laugh at her laptop. His heart was twisting with a feeling he couldn't quite place. He tried to keep his expression neutral, not wanting to give away the jealousy that was simmering just beneath the surface. In his heart, Ashaar knew he didn't have the full picture, didn't know what their relationship really was, but that didn't stop the feelings of possessiveness that were bubbling up inside him. He took a deep breath and reminded himself to stay calm, to trust her until he had a reason not to.

"Emma."

"I don't want to talk."

"You are avoiding me," he clarified. His voice rumbled through the cold air in her office. "Is it because of that kiss?"

"Why would it matter to you? We are colleagues, right? I shouldn't have done that."

"Emma, I have always prioritised you over anything and everything. Do not question my judgement." Ashaar made a fist with his hand. "The fact is that Hyperion is struggling with funding. I had to tell the truth. That didn't mean you had to scream at me in public." He reached out, as if to touch her arm.

"Ashaar, stop!" Emma's words were loud and sharp.

Ashaar took a step back. "Why don't you talk about this?" he asked.

Emma, swallowing hard, closed her eyes and exhaled a sigh. "I don't want to. I have so much work to do, honestly," she shook her head, avoiding eye contact.

"You are going to say that for the rest of your life. The only time you open up is when you *shout* at someone. I'm like a fucking *bin* to you. When you are stressed out, you need to throw your anger at someone. I'm that someone." His voice was rattling.

Ashaar was breathing rapidly, as short, shallow breaths were escaping his lips.

He could let out his pain at the top of his lungs, and that wouldn't be enough to calm him down. He clenched his jaws and stood with his hands folded.

She rolled her chair back slightly and turned, toes pointing at him, "Look, I didn't mean to. I want to tell you that we are colleagues, and I don't want to have anything more between us."

"That's fine. If you want, I can walk away from this." Tears stung in his eyes.

Emma shifted, uncrossing her arms and sitting upright. She dropped her mouse from her hand and looked into Ashaar's eyes. She asked, "What do you mean by walking away?"

"Life goes on, Emma. I've done this twice. I have been heartbroken twice. I recovered and walked away unscathed."

Ashaar paused for a second, struggling to swallow the lump that had formed in his throat. Emma returned a blank stare.

"Look, Emma," Ashaar said, "I wanted you to give our relationship a chance. If you don't want to, that's fair. There's no reason for me to stay here anymore. I still have an offer on the table, so I can jump ship anytime."

"Ash, I may have acted differently but it wasn't because of you."

"Are you serious, Emma?" His vision became blurry as tears welled up. "You are *too* afraid to face your own feelings! So instead, you push me away and now, you can't even decide whether you want to let go of me." Ashaar exhaled a chuckle. "This is insane."

Her face crumpled with rising pain. "You are complicating this."

"You think I am complicating this?" His mouth hung open, his eyebrows furrowed, and his eyes widened as he stared at her. "That's all. Thanks for everything."

"Ash, please wait—" Emma said as Ashaar turned to leave. He slammed Emma's door and stood outside in the corridor for a second. The glass wall shuddered for two seconds before the vibration came to a halt. Ashaar took a breath. But he ran out of oxygen.

Half an hour later, he was stuck on the A12, slowly moving towards the motorway.

"Boss, I think I need a break." Ashaar was speaking to Oscar on the phone.

"We all need a break. Is there anything you want to share with me now?" Oscar replied.

"I think I might need you to consider the possibility of me moving somewhere else," Ashaar replied.

"Where?"

"Move from the UK. I had a few offers from companies in America."

"You didn't tell me you had offers on the table," Oscar said. "Shall we talk about this later next week?"

"Sure, but for now, I need you to give me some time away. I need to think straight." His voice appeared furious, but he schooled himself back into reality.

"It's up to you what you decide. I can say a thousand things to you right now that wouldn't make a difference. Take a break, refresh your memory and come back."

"Thanks. I will send an official request."

Instead, when he went home, Ashaar resigned.

Chapter 10: Ashaar

24 September 2021

Ashaar sat on the flight back to London, staring out the window at the fading light.

The day in Turin had been nothing but tense—setting up Hyperion's lab, Emma snapping after Oscar's usual outburst and Ashaar keeping quiet ever since. This trial was a do-or-die situation for Hyperion. They had to produce some solid results in under a week to bring Xplorer onboard.

Now, in the stillness of the plane, he recapped the entire trip, wondering if all of this was worth fighting for. He knew part of her edge wasn't just the stress. She wasn't happy about him resigning, signing up for a job not in London, not even in the UK—but in California. Emma could have been on another planet, for all she knew.

Her behaviour towards him had shifted, and Ashaar knew that was the reason.

Turbulence shifted the aircraft.

Ashaar was drifting off to sleep, but the heavy shaking broke his chain of thoughts. He said, "Woah, this—"

"Isn't just a little turbulence." Emma was smiling, despite the fear on her face. "This is rather unsettling."

The seatbelt warning sign was turned on.

Outside, the aircraft began a rapid, uncontrolled descent, plunging towards the cloud. The cabin was filled with tumultuous screams. People onboard weren't simply scared. They assumed it was the end.

Fuck it.

Emma grabbed the glass of bubbly, chugged it in one go and held Ashaar's palm, sitting on her right-hand side. "This isn't good. Oh gosh, I'm starting to feel nauseous."

The overhead lid popped, throwing their hand luggage into the cabin, and hitting one of the passenger's arms. The woman tried to deflect but bent her finger.

Her face turned crimson as she let out her cry. Seconds later, her voice was drowned by all the screaming passengers.

"Everyone, can you please calm down," one of the air hostesses shouted from the front of the aircraft. The screens in the cabin flickered erratically, signalling trouble.

Ashaar thought this probably wouldn't be the end, but it would be a trip to remember. He gathered his strength because Emma was there along with his other colleagues.

Natalie grabbed a brown bag and retched into it. She coughed vigorously, trying to clear her throat and regain her composure. A woman right behind their aisle held the side of her head and screamed. Then a second. Then a child. After that, a man. A grown man rolled over from his seat, clenched his jaw and let out his pain.

"What the actual fuck?" Emma released her bundled-up fear and tossed it right onto Ashaar's face. "I don't know what's happening."

Ashaar looked at his other colleague sitting on the other side of the aircraft. He passed out. Natalie was throwing up again.

Emma clenched her hand, grabbed Ashaar's muscle and squeezed it.

Ashaar, in a moment of panic, prayed. He strongly believed in the power of God, especially during these moments.

The aircraft pulled up and stabilised. It felt like a miracle.

"Oh my God, I'm not gonna lie, I thought that was it." Emma stared at Ashaar's arm. She pressed her nails so hard that he had blood squeezed out of his skin. She gasped breathlessly in shock, not at Ashaar, but at the wound she had caused.

"It's okay, don't worry. We're safe," Ashaar replied.

His only stronger emotion was anger, but this time, the overpowering turbulence had trumped everything else. He locked his phone, put it away for charging and put on his gleaming headphones, anxiously waiting for aircraft to start falling out of the sky again.

He couldn't wait to get back home.

***

The aftermath of Ashaar's harrowing flight to London had ignited an immediate investigation by the Air Accidents Investigation Branch. Media outlets were abuzz with reports of the flight's near-disastrous descent, speculating on the cause. As news anchors discussed the preliminary findings, which pointed to no mechanical failures or fault of the pilots, Ashaar's mind raced with suspicions.

He reached for the laptop and muted the sound while his sight fixed on the now-silent screen. The possibility that someone had sabotaged their flight to target Emma loomed in his thoughts. Sitting alone in the dimly lit confines of his desk, Ashaar thought of various scenarios. He weighed each possibility, seeking to understand the puzzle and the connection to the DNA data archive, Cognition and Sentinel. His six-month armed response training at the Police Academy might come in handy after all.

Amidst these unspoken feelings, Ashaar had to focus on the task at hand—a party hosted by Xplorer in Soho, and Emma needed to be there with him. It was an important event, possibly her last opportunity to sway the inebriated rich crowd in favour of her ambitious plan of a tech start-up building houses for future Martians.

Once at the party, the night stretched on, unusually long and demanding. Both Ashaar and Emma were visibly worn out. His return flight from Italy had been anything but smooth, and the relentless pace of the past four days had offered them no respite. The weight of exhaustion hung heavily on his shoulders as he navigated the evening's challenges.

After the party, Ashaar dropped by Tesco's because Emma wanted some ice cream.

He observed her walk along the frozen aisle section, step by step. She opened the transparent freezer door and grabbed a couple of ice cream tubs from the top shelf. The cold wind from the freezer kept hitting his face, so he stepped back a few inches and stared at her. The aisle smelled of disinfectant. She looked confused. He watched her raise her ankle to try to reach the topmost shelf. Her party attire, which was a combination of a black short skirt, black boots and a black jumper made her look much younger. He offered to help, but she declined. He stood there while she suffered from indecisiveness.

After she'd picked out her ice cream, Ashaar was driving through the narrow roads of southeast London. Cloudy sky, 11 p.m. near Greenwich.

"Everything okay, Emma?" Ashaar asked.

"That car has been following us for a while," Emma kept looking in the side mirror.

Ashaar made a couple of turns, going in circles. The SUV continued trailing him. "I see."

Before dropping Emma off, he needed to make sure they weren't after her. *They might be trying to find where she lives or might be after me. Who knows?* He held the steering wheel with a death grip, his knuckles turning white as he rushed down the deserted road.

Emma's eyes darted nervously between the road and her mirrors, and she winced every time a car passed her by.

Ashaar was driving fast enough to leave them behind at a red light.

"Why are you driving so fast?" Emma asked.

"Wait." Ashaar steered his car into an empty parking lot adjacent to the O2 Arena. It was a quiet Thursday night, and the venue was shuttered, bathed in the stillness of the off-hours. He started carefully manoeuvring his vehicle, parking it out of plain sight behind a large, abandoned shipping container that loomed in the corner of the lot. With a swift, almost urgent motion, Emma opened the passenger door and jumped out, and her eyes quickly scanned the deserted surroundings.

Earlier that week, the O2 Arena and its nearby vicinity were forced to evacuate owing to a potential fire risk. The entire stadium was deserted. It was dark and unnervingly quiet. There was no one in the nearby venue parking lot either.

"Ash?" Emma squealed from a foot distance.

"Give me one second," Ashaar reached under his seat to grab a handgun, slammed the doors and activated an emergency alarm that'd be sent to police if they broke in.

They walked towards a white container with a door slightly open, hoping he would find some space inside. Hide. He held her forearm and dragged her in.

"Are you sure this is a good idea?" Emma asked.

"First, we both have visions. Then an entire fucking aircraft falls out of the sky. And now, these people are following us. Don't tell me I'm overthinking." Stepping into the vacant room, Ashaar surveyed the surroundings. They were inside a compact office space, set up within a small shipping container. A window punctuated the wall, offering a limited view of the outside. The interior was cramped; a single table, chair and computer were squeezed in, surrounded by an array of boxes. The confined space was just enough for the two of them, though it offered little room to stand or manoeuvre comfortably.

The container, one of many in the sprawling car park, served as their temporary refuge.

"Wait, look, they did follow us." Emma was rubbing her arm against Ashaar's. They stood really close.

"Three men, armed," Ashaar whispered, watching two of them jump out and wave their torches at his car. They found nothing.

"Oh my God, they will come and look for us here and—" Emma kept rocking her leg.

Ashaar placed his palm over her mouth. "Shh," he whispered.

Emma bent down and peeked. Ashaar heard her heart beating fast but she remained silent, cheeks flushed and breathing hard.

One of the armed men turned and waved their torch at them. Ashaar knelt before her, holding Emma with both arms, pushed her shoulder blades down and pulled her towards him. She turned, placed her head on Ashaar's shoulder and pressed her nose against his cheek.

"I'm scared," Emma said, whispering, her lips gently scrubbing his beard.

"It'll be okay," Ashaar reassured. Just as her hand reached his back, he gently shifted her hand to the front.

"I hope so, otherwise we're fucking dead," she whispered.

A red laser light zoomed past Ashaar's face.

The only sound was their hushed breaths, blending with the distant murmur of the cars driving past on the highway.

Outside, the rhythmic thuds of heavy boots echoed as armed men conducted a methodical search. They peered into each container methodically. Ashaar, his eyes fixed on the approaching figures, signalled to Emma, and they quickly knelt, sliding underneath a sturdy desk that occupied the cramped space.

The door creaked open, casting a sliver of light into the darkened interior. Flashlights flickered on, beams of light dancing across the walls as the men searched for any signs of occupants. Ashaar felt the tremors of their steps from where he was.

Their hiding spot, fortuitously shielded by a wooden cover in front of the desk, kept them hidden from view. The cover's plain appearance belied its significance and rendered them invisible in the shadowed recess. Ashaar placed one hand on the back, trying to reach a handgun tucked in his trousers. Gently shifting, he placed his hand on the trigger.

A sudden, sharp sound shattered the silence as one man kicked the opposite side of the desk. Emma's lips parted slightly in a silent gasp, but nobody saw. The tension in the air was palpable, a long, agonising moment stretching out as the men lingered, scanning the space.

The men eventually departed, and their footsteps faded away. Ashaar let out a slow breath, feeling both relief and confusion at once. Their conversation was an unintelligible puzzle to him. Moments later, Ashaar could hear them searching through every other container in the car park.

Emma asked, "Ashaar—"

"A few more seconds," Ashaar gently stroked her cheeks with his other hand.

Ashaar, through the corner of the window, watched them tempestuously throw a small device. He could barely see them in his peripheral vision. Keeping tabs on them was a daunting task. A holographic projection appeared. He kept his mouth shut and watched. A woman appeared, in her 40s, face covered.

His heart pounded.

The armed men gestured with their hands, communicating in swift, silent signals to a figure that appeared on a holographic display. How did they have access to such advanced technology? They appeared to have aborted their missions because they quickly hopped back into their vehicle. As the car made a sharp turn, Ashaar noticed the absence of a number plate. Through the rear window, he could see the boot was occupied by a large, metal circular copper case, its shape and design reminiscent of a quantum computer. Why would anyone transport such advanced technology in an ordinary SUV? The situation defied logic, leaving Ashaar with more questions than answers as he watched the car disappear into the distance.

Nothing made sense.

Emma had her eyes fully closed, folded legs tucked against his stomach and her nose and lips pressed on Ashaar's neck.

Ashaar's adrenaline kicked in. If he had to use the gun, he'd use it. He lingered for a few more minutes and softly pushed her back. "They are gone."

"What are we going to do?" She gasped and freed herself. Her pulse pounded inside her ribcage.

"Nothing. You need to calm down, Emma." Ashaar held her cheeks with his palms. "We wait here a little more, then take a different route."

"What were they looking for?" Emma's eyes darted between Ashaar's lips and eyes. "I don't like this."

As they emerged from their hiding spot, the reality of their narrow escape set in. The night, once an oppressive shroud, now felt like a protective cloak as Ashaar and Emma cautiously stepped out of the container.

"Thankfully, I'll be out of this fucking country for a month as soon as Xplorer signs the partnership." Emma stood up, tensely walked towards the SUV while grabbing Ashaar's white shirt. They jumped in and drove back to Hackney, where Emma lived. They took a different route. When she saw Ashaar turn onto the street she lived on, Emma grabbed his left arm and pressed it with her nails, letting her fingers loop around his muscle.

"Don't worry, I will see what I can do, Em."

"Thanks, Ashaar, don't park. I will jump off right here."

"Okay."

Emma leaned in.

Ashaar grabbed her by the neck, pulled her close and locked his lips on the side of her head.

Emma thanked him again and left.

Ashaar drove back. On the way, he tapped on his infotainment tab, and found the name, "Joseph Cabrera Navy."

He pressed that name and rang the person. They planned to meet up in London in the next few days.

Everything had to be intertwined. Ashaar discovered an unknown piece of code in Cognition's AI. Emma accidentally walked into a so-called archive full of DNA drives. She experienced visions multiple times, repetitively observing the word "Sentinel." Ashaar then found a folder with the same title on Oscar's table. He received the same job offer from Xplorer *twice.* A whistleblower from Xplorer reached out, asking him to stop their secret quantum research. Then their plane plummeted 15,000 feet in the air. Now they were being followed by an armed militia.

God knows if Emma was hiding anything.

Lights from the motorway intermittently hit Ashaar's face while he drove home.

What if all these events were linked together?

Chapter 11: Emma

One month later

Emma, sat before Ashaar in a closed-door meeting room, trying to push the feeling aside, knowing that it was too soon to let her guard down.

"I want to give you some news," Ashaar said, sitting across the table. It had been a month, Emma had been on holiday, and things were uncomfortable.

"Thank you. What's the news?" she asked hesitantly.

"One of the companies on our campus is interested in hiring you. They were impressed by the way you signed the deal with Xplorer and brought two more investors."

"That's great! You don't know how difficult it has been since I came back. I don't feel safe in London. I can't stop thinking about that night at the O2," Emma looked away, blinking hard.

"Yeah," Ashaar cleared his throat, "I haven't slept in weeks. I don't even know if they are still following us."

There were things Emma wanted to be competent at—riding a bike like a pro, being skilled at managing projects and dealing with her post-traumatic stress. She wanted to play netball with her friends. She wanted to be free of any shackles.

She wanted her mother to be proud and to recognise that her pipedream had turned into a reality. Understand how her physics degree was a key reason behind raising fifteen *million* dollars for her start-up.

Emma's heart leapt out of her chest. She felt the subatomic particles vibrating through the air, sending the message to project how important she was in Ashaar's life. Her eyes locked with his as butterflies beat their wings, sweeping across the serendipity of their professional relationship, overshadowed by the friendship that had broken the rules long ago. "Wow," Emma said. "I can't believe you are moving so far away."

Ashaar turned his eyes and stared at the laptop.

This man just kept surprising her. She'd maintain a curtain and be a professional with everyone else in the world. She didn't need to do all that when she was with him. Because this one person in the entire world would never judge her for anything.

With a sigh, Ashaar took a black device from his pocket and handed it over to her, "Here."

"What's this?" Emma reached out, and their fingers touched.

"You'll need this. It's a covert communications device."

"What do I do with this?" Her face twisted, expressing the inner fear she had been hiding since the night they'd been followed.

"It's like a transponder. Page this when something like that happens. When someone is following you." Ashaar added, "I have a friend who works for the UN Navy. He'll help you. Please stay safe."

"Wow, okay." She took the device from his hand. "I'm not gonna lie, I've had so many nightmares. While I was on holiday, I kept thinking that people were following me," Emma said, spinning the device with her hand.

"Just use the device," Ashaar insisted, gesturing towards the pager. "Right now, we're in the dark about their motives and how this all ties into your visions."

He paused for a moment, his expression softening as he shifted the topic. "Look, my part here is over, Emma."

He might be thinking that she was a spoilt, blonde woman who'd been floating in a sea of wealth. Only if he knew what she'd been through to get to that place. It had been so long since she'd been treated like this. It'd been so long since she had found someone who'd catch her if she fell backwards with her eyes closed.

At that moment, as Ashaar sat right in front, she could feel the pulsating nerves in him. It was a bag of mixed emotions, as Emma's German mother would say, *Kabelsalat.*

The second he left the room, she exhaled through her teeth. She closed her eyes, waiting for her next meeting. A million things ran through her head. Should she walk over and offer him a hug? The future was a mystery to her.

Life had been incredibly difficult, and she had trouble handling her responsibilities. She had wanted to quit her job so many times. She wanted to throw her laptop and notepad at Ashaar whenever he came to her, trying to pull feelings out of her burial ground.

But moments like today reminded her that those trivial things turned everything upside down and made her day. And now, in three weeks' time, Ashaar would be gone forever. Just after she'd managed the funding for Hyperion, the subplot in her story would collapse.

She had to stop Ashaar from leaving. Emma jumped out of her chair and left the meeting room.

Her long strides ate up the distance as she covered ground with an urgent gait. She appeared determined, her gaze unwavering.

The phone chimed and AI started speaking out loud again.

+17: Quantum traveller Echo Mike, refrain from causing intrusion to Ashaar's plan, otherwise it would cause catastrophic consequences.

Her whole body shook with fury and her face twisted into a scowl. Her voice grew low and menacing as she murmured, "Fuck my life!"

With tears gathering, she quickly typed a message, eyes struggling to see the screen clearly.

Emma: I can't do this anymore, Steph. I just can't. Tell me everything I need to know otherwise I am out!

Within seconds, her phone chimed.

Stephanie: Let's meet this evening. I'm free.

Chapter 12: Ashaar

April 2022, Iceland

The hike was precipitous, and heat sweltered underneath three layers of trekking gear. But when Ashaar saw the glacier from the crest, he absorbed the extraordinary splendour of nature. A meandering, curvy path cut through large chucks of white ice, floating on the chilliness of the ocean, to a small mountain painted in white. Its edge slowly disintegrated, melting ice hurried and spattered onto the sea.

Splash down.

An archaic mountain was being speedily fragmented by the melting heat from global warming. *Climate change is real.* The only nuance evident on the fringes was a group of birds flying across the clear blue sky. On the ice shelf, a wild Arctic fox stood among the stranded seabirds, the wind carrying the sounds of their calls, all bound by the same quiet desperation.

The visual experience was nothing like an average Netflix documentary.

It was more than flawless.

Ashaar was taken aback when he realised how far he'd come in such a fleeting time. He and his coworkers would go hiking every other month, but he didn't like it. This trip was to the highlands of Iceland, far away from where he moved to—far away from his new home and old home. Inexplicably, these trips made a difference. The surface temperature was not tolerable, and they could barely see the sky.

Ashaar felt captivated by being among young hikers and scientists who were there to achieve something. They were on a trip to save the Earth, observed the glacial change and fed it back to their headquarters for research. He had a brief conversation with a woman in the same group but did not exchange any contact information.

That new life became intense but enjoyable, although, it was all a little blurry. Every day, Ashaar had to battle with flashes of memories. Slowly, the sporadic aide-mémoire of Emma's reminiscences was evaporating, just like the glaciers disappeared into the void. Emma Herrmann—the name of the woman he was hopelessly in love with before he moved to the US.

This was the beginning of a new journey.

The following evening, the pub was busy and the humming noise in the background felt slightly uncomfortable. But it helped keep him distracted from his inner thoughts. From a distance, Ashaar watched as one of his colleagues from his hiking group sat alone at the bar and fiddled with a beer mat.

Ashaar's expression turned into a scowl as he stared at his phone. He quickly typed out a message to Stephanie.

> Who am I meeting?

Stephanie's response came promptly.

> Look for a brunette with long hair, wearing a t-shirt. Introduce yourself and try to learn more about her. She's your key.

The walls and floors were all created from wood, uneven and the ceiling had lots of chandeliers. Photos of different celebrities hung on one side, and the other was covered in a series of barren alcohol bottles—wines, beers, spirits and champagnes.

"Do I know you?" Taya grinned, trying to tie her thick, dark hair. "Haven't we met during our glacial trip? I like your jacket."

"Hi, yes we did." Ashaar extended his hand. "I must say, you have a beautiful smile."

"Thank you," she chuckled, "I heard you work for the space division, right?" Taya shook his hand with a firm grip.

"In fact, I do. How do you know?" Ashaar spoke loudly over the music.

"Your colleague, Tom, he's my friend too." Taya's eyes glowed from the bright pink and purple lights, "he told me about you. And I may have read your paper, too."

"Nice." Ashaar awkwardly continued their conversation, looking into her eyes. "Glad to meet a fan of my work!"

She shrugged, smiling sheepishly.

"What division are you working for?" He turned his neck to check out her outfit, a black AC/DC t-shirt tucked into her denim jeans, adding edginess to her charm.

"I'm working for the quantum research division at Xplorer. It is a separate division." She took a large sip. "I moved there because the pay is much better."

"So, what is your focus area?"

"Quantum entanglement." Taya leaned in and spoke, "I'm an engineer, working on unlocking the mysteries of the universe."

Ashaar raised his brows, smiling. "Wow, mysteries of the universe!"

"I still don't know how you ended up here, in the United States." Taya's exhale was a response filled with confusion. "Why did you move here?"

Ashaar shifted his eyes, raising his hand to get the bartender's attention. "Just starting a new life."

"Intriguing." Taya bobbed her head.

"What is your name again? Sorry, I forgot to ask your name...." Ashaar smiled at her and expressed his guilt.

"I'm Taya Leah-Jones. You can call me Taya!"

"Shall we grab dinner, Taya? As friends, of course."

"I'm game!"

***

May 2022, California

Almost ten-million-square feet, roughly the length of one hundred football fields and mostly vacant, Xplorer's California facility was painted in a calming shade of blue, and there were potted plants and elegant light fixtures scattered throughout the space. The desks were made of sleek glass and chrome, while the shelves were lined with books and mementos that hinted at the designer's impeccable taste.

The campus was divided into separate buildings, one of which was dedicated to the Quantum Consciousness Transfer Initiative. It was packed with supplies, machines, people and most importantly, faith. The faith among a group of scientists was that one day they would crack the code of consciousness transfer and access the higher dimension. Xplorer had nearly one hundred employees working in that division, led by a scientist named Dr Ben Weiss and his co-lead, Taya Leah-Jones. Stephanie used to be one of the lead scientists too, but she was transferred to London to spearhead their British space engineering team.

Underneath the building, they'd built a looped tunnel that mimicked the large hadron collider. Taya's team had made it much smaller, yet ten times more powerful. It was a giant doughnut-shaped metal object, twelve feet tall and fifteen feet wide. Ashaar stood outside the chamber, protected by a series of radiation shields made of fibreglass.

Ashaar looked back at Ben working in the control room, towering over the primary lab. He walked up the stairs to reach the control room separated by another layer of radiation-proof glass barriers. Taya sat behind Ben, sporting her goggles, white apron, blue gloves and hair tied like a ponytail. Their staff ran around the lab wearing aprons and carrying more items to the vault. The room behind the lab had computing servers that ran a series of cables through the false overhead ceiling and met the quantum tunnel. He grazed his eyes over the cables hanging from the top.

Friday morning and Taya's team was ready to fire up their tunnel. Taya bobbed her head at Ashaar and shifted her vision back to her terminal.

For the past few days, they'd been running the quantum tunnel without hesitation. Unlike early-stage rockets, this device had little to no chance of hurting anyone—unless they deliberately created an implosion bomb with it.

Ashaar stood with his hands folded, watching Ben approach him. He asked, "What happens to the consciousness of those people in another universe? Not killing anyone, are we?"

"No, if we send a consciousness to the other Earth, it's temporarily overwritten as long as the quantum entanglement works with precision. A slight diversion could cause a massive ripple in space-time." Ben kept crossing, checking all the data before moving forward.

The cacophony from the quantum tunnel had begun to fill the room. It forced everyone to cover their ears with protective headphones. The sound wave from the noise made the glass walls vibrate, and the floors beneath wobble. As the smoke billowed out of the tube, Ashaar saw the lights begin to illuminate one after the other.

The flickering became more and more pronounced.

"Three, two, one—" the announcement filled the room.

Ben rapidly powered the device by pulling up a slider on his terminal.

Ashaar watched the trial intently, dreaming of the day he could explore the distant galaxies. His eyes flickered over the screen, absorbing the data displayed on the digital gauges and charts. They planned to keep the tunnel running until it successfully generated sufficient data to show them how to generate a wormhole.

That night, Ashaar remained at the lab, and sat on a sofa, giving himself gentle hope while scrambling to understand as much as he could before their trial next week. The lights inside the lab were turned off. Only one LED was hovering over his head, shining a light on his desk. The rest was plunged into the darkness, the reactors and the servers powered down.

After delving deep into the secrets of the Quantitative lab, Ashaar realised it bore no connection to Oscar or his Sentinel AI project. Instead, the lab was venturing into uncharted scientific territory, daring to test a theory too crazy for most research companies, funding and audacity notwithstanding.

This was a realm where even the CERN supercollider hadn't yet stomped their feet. Creating a wormhole required more than high-velocity collisions. Ben and Taya's team had somehow unravelled this complex puzzle.

Nolan, recognising the groundbreaking implications of their work, had chosen to keep it shrouded in secrecy. Though the portal was a gateway to understanding more about Emma's visions and their link to the data archive, with it came substantial risk. The creation of a portal carried the alarming possibility of imploding and annihilating the planet.

Ashaar found himself poring over a dataset, his mind racing to comprehend how they had managed to achieve something so monumental and fraught with danger.

Suddenly, he heard a muffled noise coming from the dark. Then, the hanging terminal above chimed a mellow ping. A flashing message materialised written in white, bold font inside a red rectangle.

Portal Generation Successful.

Did the tunnel just generate a wormhole?

He stood up, and gently took three steps towards the lab.

There was no one inside the primary lab. The door to it was locked, and one could not have entered the lab without passing his desk.

The loneliness of working on Friday night was finally catching up with him. He marched towards the command centre and brought the terminal to life, then tapped a few buttons to see the findings.

Nothing. None of the charts indicated that their device created a wormhole. He yanked his phone and checked the network bar—something was blocking his reception.

With the press of a button, he locked the phone and placed it in his back pocket.

With a silent curse, he held the door handle to the primary lab and tapped his ID to unlock it. The metal cranking from the magnetic lock filled the silence.

In the darkness of the lab, he took one step at a time and walked down the stairs.

"Hello?" He could only hear his own echo.

Leave it, don't go, he thought. Young Ashaar would be terrified of ghosts and thieves. He'd struggle to go back to sleep if a noise woke him up in the middle of the night.

When he was a child, thieves breaking in was a common occurrence. Once, armed robbers infiltrated his parent's house when he was 9 years old. He'd never stopped being that scared little boy.

Part of his brain thought that people from a different timeline might have walked through a gigantic wormhole, like the ones he saw in Avengers.

With his shoes squeaking on the tiled floor, he walked over to the tunnel. The repeated hum became more and more pronounced as he approached the quantum tunnel.

Ashaar should notify Ben or Taya. But it was almost 10 p.m. He knew both of them would be asleep. Taya had been busy attending a conference all afternoon and Ben was an old man.

He glanced to the side and flinched at something in the dark. It was just a shadow.

When he tapped his card again on the lock, opened a steel door and pulled a metal lever, his nostrils weren't ready to be invaded by the unusual smell dissipating from inside. He needed to enter the tunnel and circle around to find where it was coming from.

His stomach was empty, and his brain was filled with adrenaline.

Nothing compared to walking inside a tunnel and having a eureka moment. The tunnel was deemed extremely safe when it was powered down, and anyone working at the lab could walk in and out with no protective clothing. Ashaar checked the terminal again.

Power level: 0%

A thud sounded, like someone had been beating a metal beam with a hammer.

He craned his neck up and glowered at the ceiling. Two large electric metal blades were pointing at him. That must be a way to trigger electrical charges inside the station. If someone had turned on the device, his organs would have been deep-fried from radiation instantly.

The tunnel was built to create a wormhole the size of an atom, and through that, they had planned to transfer human consciousness across time.

The possibilities were endless. They could travel through time, or if luck persisted, they might reach another universe. Their team needed to run enough tests to figure out if TAC worked—Time, Amplitude and Coordinates—a set of rules that defined where and how they'd transfer the consciousness. He could also figure out how Emma was having visions from a different past. If Emma's theories were true, the tunnel would be his gateway to solving every mystery that had plagued his brain since meeting her.

He was desperate to get closer to the source, despite knowing that one slight mistake would end his life.

Ashaar stepped on a loose metal beam, which activated a cranking noise. The resounding echo sent a shiver up his spine. He huffed a breath. He'd rather risk his own life than anyone else.

Maybe a part of him wanted to discover something bizarre. Something he didn't want anyone else to know. Given his team's all-time presence, he almost never found the lab to be empty.

"Be careful, Ash. You are literally sitting on a rocket that has never flown." He said to himself, and walked to the centre of the tunnel after two long minutes.

A layer of thin, blurry material blocked his view to the other side.

He wasn't sure what it was.

Ashaar wanted to run back to the command centre and call everyone. But he also wanted to run towards the anomaly and see what it was.

Ashaar swallowed the lump forming in his throat. This was the moment they had waited for. A shudder rose up his spine, sending goosebumps all over his body.

Years of research might had come to fruition.

He'd be part of a team that created time travel.

Or he'd end up creating a black hole.

His thoughts were interrupted by an unexpected warning light overhead that flashed for one second.

Ashaar took five more steps, getting closer. If he didn't find out what it was, an accidental black hole could consume everything or everyone in its way. Shrink hundreds of people into dust.

If he did, and it was an anomaly, it could end his life.

The feeling was unlike anything else. It felt like he was in a bed, desperately trying to get out but struggling because the atoms and molecules bonded with his body and pulled him back into the bed frame like a magnet.

He moved forward, lured by the anomaly. The silence broke when the floor vibrated.

Ashaar let out a guttural scream. He curled in a ball on the floor and held both sides of his head. His entire body began to shake, eyes bulging, blood draining from his nose.

***

Ben jolted awake at the sound of his alarm. He threw on his coat, grabbed his bag and bolted out the door, heading straight for the lab.

"What's the matter? Ashaar? Are you here?" Ben sprinted to the lab and switched on the lights. His mouth fell open when he saw that the metal door to the quantum tunnel was ajar.

"He's inside the tunnel. Fuck!" Why had Ashaar entered the tunnel by himself without notifying him?

Ashaar's screech became louder and louder by the second.

"Ash?" Ben rapidly climbed down the stairs to the primary lab. Slowly, he opened the door to the tunnel, a screeching noise filling up the silence.

A boom sounded.

The reactor exploded, hurling Ben off the stairs and onto the lab's ground level.

Ben lay on the floor, face down, as smoke began to fill the entire area.

In the distance, Ashaar's unconscious body rested on a pool of thick blood, his white apron vest soaked in the ocean of grim red.

Chapter 13: Taya

May 2022, California

Taya, apprehensive and anxious, described the event to Nolan over the phone. “There’s been an explosion at the quantum lab.”

Taya, struck with a disconcerting reality, suffered a stinging feeling all over her neck. At that moment, she acknowledged that their research project had made a razor-sharp hairpin turn into the acrimonious wild west of quantum mechanics.

At the expense of a life.

The celebratory mood among employees at Xplorer for their 400th launch had raised expectations to where nobody ever predicted such a tragedy.

It wasn’t until 10.35 p.m. when Taya heard the announcement from the Fire Brigade. The quantum lab had been completely destroyed, as the smell of petrol and burnt copper wire had overflown. The adjacent hallways had been evacuated. The false ceiling collapsed—a dark, grey smoke had soaked the room. Some LEDs were still blinking, but the smoke from the explosion made it impossible to see them through. The fire alarm was throbbing throughout the building.

Taya, strapped with a gas mask and hazmat suit, followed a group of firefighters with their beige-coloured fireproof clothing, gas masks and red oxygen tanks on their shoulders smashed the partition and shouted, "Can anybody hear us? Firefighters! If anyone can hear us, please speak now!"

Two firemen valiantly walked towards the end of the chamber amid the brutality of destruction. Inside, the smoke was thick enough to congeal the lungs in seconds. Next to the tunnel built with metal sheets was a device resembling a giant doughnut-shaped paddock.

On the floor, they found Ashaar in a shredded lab coat, sporting a black shirt, and grey jeans, resting flat with his eyes closed. His body was surrounded by a thick pool of blood.

The firefighters tapped their hands on him and held their fingers on his neck.

There was a faint pulse. Taya stood two steps away and watched in agony.

The fireman on the right pressed the radio and advised his colleagues. Taya nodded at them, signalling Ashaar's identity.

They dragged Ashaar outside the tunnel, placed him on a stretcher and dragged him to the small car park, where a medical helicopter waited.

Paramedics hurtled towards the aircraft, cutting its rotating blade through the smoke released from the building, blasting the wind and pushing people away in its adjacent vicinity. Taya shouted over the rotating blades, "You need to let me know ASAP about his status."

They replied, "Copy that, ma'am."

The pilots pulled and slammed the door from both sides and were airborne within the next two minutes.

They recovered a little square Polaroid-style photograph of Ashaar and another dark-blonde, short-haired lady smiling for the camera. Taya glowered at the photograph. Underneath the photo was a handwritten message that said,

"For Ash, from Emma Xx."

Half an hour later, flashing red and blue lights from ambulances and fire engines warped the entire campus. Taya stood outside—the light from the hand terminal shone on her eyes and face. She said to Ben, "Looks like our device couldn't handle the electrical surge. A massive spike in Hawking radiation caused the explosion."

She felt her blood about to start boiling, watching Ben being treated inside an ambulance for minor injuries. He escaped unscathed.

Two guards and a group of other individuals paraded into the cordoned zone, strapped with yellow warning tapes. The sound of boots stomping stopped. One of them shot a worrying gaze at Taya and said, "Ma'am, Ashaar Naveed is in a coma."

Taya gulped with a sense of downright fear of losing her friend. She could hear her heart beating out of her ribcage. "Is he going to be okay?" Blood rushed in her veins, preparing her for the worst-case scenario.

The guard, strapped with body armour that appeared to be some type of carbon fibre, moved his rifle and freed up his hands. He opened his tablet and said, "His pulse is active. But initial assessment suggests reduced brain activity." He tapped, flicked his fingers and sent the data straight to Taya's terminal.

Nolan raised his badge and paraded in with a couple of employees. His turtleneck jumper and blue jeans made him look like Steve Jobs.

The space was filled with people and their anxiety.

Nolan's presence made it worse.

He gripped his waist, "What the *fuck* were you thinking, Ben? That Star Wars-loving dork was literally one of the best resources I had. Do you know how long it took Stephanie to convince him? *Five months*! I only let him work with you because I thought you weren't dumb enough to put him in trouble." He closed his eyes and exhaled.

"'Glad to see you alive' would've been nicer, Nolan."

"Well, you're alive and he's probably in a coma." Nolan exhaled a sigh. "What the fuck happened?"

"I think Ashaar might have helped us—" Ben paused.

"Helped us with *what*?" Nolan clenched his fist.

"Saving everyone," he held his terminal before Nolan.

He pointed his finger at it and said, "Jesus, Ben, your experiment could have shrunk the entire campus to the size of a fucking atom!"

"Nolan, I can explain." Ben gulped as sweat trickled down his forehead. "The spike in Hawking radiation means that the device generated a micro black hole. It was more of a portal that sucked everything into it. The data implies that Ashaar's consciousness may be stuck in a quantum matrix. That disabled the implosion. He saved us."

This was it. That was the only way the data could be explained. Taya knew deep in her heart that Ben was right. She shook her head and brushed her hands over her sweat-dampened hair.

Taya stood next to Nolan, and her eyes glued on the screen. Hundreds of lines of code appear on a black screen as the AI ran its algorithm to produce a wireframe. The pain in her head and back got worse when the software generated an image of what seemed to be a distortion in the space-time continuum. It was a 3D image of a flat rectangle with a tiny hole in the middle.

The pain of losing a friend, and guilt, combined with anger, turned into a hurricane. It had been growing for the past hour, and now she was about to burst out.

Her ears were ringing, palms sweating with the fear of losing everything she worked for. Her anxiety was going to destroy her before Nolan did.

"We may have created a gateway through a quantum matrix. The only—" Ben swallowed a lump, "—believe me, the only explanation would be that a civilisation from the future has built a quantum AI powerful enough to control these matrices. Or maybe the AI itself caught Ashaar's consciousness."

"I need time to think about this," Nolan replied, scratching the back of his head. "It could be our biggest PR nightmare. *Fuck!*"

"I'm sorry—" Ben exhaled a sigh.

"I wanted you to achieve this consciousness transfer programme or whatever the hell you wanted to build. It was supposed to be an R&D project, not a catastrophic failure! *Do you understand?*" Nolan turned, raised the yellow tape and walked out with his guards.

Taya followed. She caught up with Nolan and eyed him.

"Taya, I am sorry about Ashaar." Nolan's sigh was an apology and a hundred more words packed into a burst of air.

"He's not dead yet. He's in a medically induced coma." Taya frowned at her hand terminal and added, "What happens next is your decision, Nolan."

"I will do everything I can to keep him alive. And this wasn't your fault," Nolan gave Taya's shoulder a squeeze and walked away.

Ashaar was intubated and perhaps medically dead.

Chapter 14: Ashaar

The rapidly increasing acceleration pressed his chest against the chair like a huge concrete brick. His hands were strapped to the armrests, and his body strapped with a belt pressing on his skin. Cheeks flapped like paper held inside a wind tunnel. Ashaar was stuck in a capsule that hurtled through space. Or something that appeared to be space. The capsule was zooming through an archway built of LED lights. One after another, the light from the arches reflected off his eyes.

The only reasonable explanation was that the capsule was his brain trying to form a fabricated experience to keep his consciousness from collapsing, while he journeyed somewhere.

When "evaluating probabilities" becomes a daily part of your life, people become excellent at predicting everything, Ashaar thought. Overthinking was a vital part of a scientist's brain. They'd think about a scenario and figure out every single viable strategy of where they were headed.

When he was a child, Ashaar thought about becoming a world-renowned scientist. Live happily ever-after with the love of his life.

His career was a result of two working-class parents who'd given him a complicated childhood. He'd been through all of it—tolerating his parent's attitude, breaking his heart three times, breaking his bones because he wasn't good at sports and eventually, moving to an entirely new city at the age of 17.

Ashaar failed to make Emma realise how badly he wanted her. Or he failed to get her to reciprocate. He was desperately, madly and hopelessly in love with her.

But none of the calculations led to this reality.

He stared at the vast, curved windscreen at the front. There was no sense of time in this realm. He wasn't moving through time laterally. From his viewpoint, he could be stuck for an hour, a day or a lifetime. Not the type of quantum entanglement project he wanted to be involved with.

Just as his mind continued the analysis, his heart began pumping blood faster, tossing his consciousness into a panic attack.

Ashaar's consciousness was of speeding through a quantum hyperspace. Everything might just be a product of his eyes, creating an illusion to keep him safe. A technology developed in the future.

He was having a panic attack inside a quantum matrix.

Well, that's not great.

It was like a capsule spaceship humans built to send people to space. The interior wasn't beautiful but was soothing to his eyes. It was made of pure metal and some sort of sound-dampening compound attached all over the inner walls.

And now, he was starting to forget his memories. He felt an alarm pop up, more like a faint sound in the background.

His guess was correct. The acceleration increased. On Earth, his weight was 70 kilogrammes. At 5g or 6g, it would be about 350 kilogrammes or more. This was more than 10g. He tried pushing his arm up and reaching his belt. The skin on his forearm trembled, fingers bending at the increasing pressure of gravitational force. He breathed in and out five times and tried again.

Ashaar failed to move either arm an inch.

He clenched his teeth and thought about his decisions.

He couldn't stop himself from having another panic attack. Eyes pushed against the stress of gravity, he prayed. Prayed that God, and whoever controlled the quantum matrix would save him. It was harsher than his worst nightmare. He either needed to end his life or just end this insufferable journey.

He wheezed in pain.

His voice cracked as he bellowed, the veins in his neck pulsating.

Tears of agony rolled down his cheeks. He could have been anywhere on Earth—on a date with a woman, married and with his daughter, or be with his friends on a world tour. But his curiosity as a scientist and the need to escape the pain of love led him down this road. He just wanted to get back to his life. His family, friends and the woman he was in love with.

This hazardous experiment with his career, and choosing to risk his life, had plunged him into the quantum matrix.

Ashaar had lost hope.

As his promising relationship fell apart, Ashaar used Emma's memories as a picture-perfect logic to escape his convoluted life. And now, logic was thrown out of whatever science he'd learned.

He shouldn't have left her.

Now he was being hurtled down to the land of nowhere.

Steadily, his memories began depleting. *Think, think, think. What could it be?*

When the absolute worst happened, Ashaar had been trained to stay calmer than most people around him, making him incredibly tough. Before he'd set foot in the consciousness transfer lab, he thought of the probabilities of a higher dimensional being or an AI regulating quantum matrices at a subatomic level. The idea couldn't make any sense in anyone's head. But what did? 500 years after humans discovered the solar system, humans sent the James Webb Telescope into space, learning that galaxies older than 13 billion years were still transmitting photon particles. Before dying, Stephen Hawking said that time travel was possible, but we weren't there yet. If it was twenty years ago, Ashaar wouldn't even have had the opportunity to work for a space agency that landed a booster straight from orbit. And now, he had just unlocked a new level of science.

A quantum matrix built by an intelligent being on the other side of the portal.

A sudden onslaught of migraine hit his head, spreading pain across his nervous system. He was blacking out but wasn't sure if it was the sheer force of gravity or his consciousness coming to the end of its journey.

This can't go on forever.

I need to calm down.

He could see the tunnel coming to its end. Maybe this was how it felt to die. Ashaar thought about the possibilities of this breakthrough—the fact that his colleagues Taya and Ben could build a wormhole-generating device was the biggest scientific breakthrough. The next few years would be monumental for them. They might even win a Nobel prize. But Ashaar wouldn't live to see it.

He wouldn't live to tell the story to his children.

He always wanted to have children. A daughter who'd resemble Emma's intellect, and have Ashaar's personality. He shut his eyes, drifting into the thoughts that made him feel relaxed, and hoping that someone who communicated with this realm would save him. If not, it was time to say goodbye.

Chapter 15: Ashaar

Date Unknown: Location Unknown

> Atoms bond to form molecules with their electrons interacting in shared orbitals. When it becomes unstable or goes through a chemical reaction, atoms can jump from their own orbit to another to pair with another atom. If the atom jumps into more than one orbit, it's commonly known as the quantum leap. Entangled particles may be subatomic particles or particles in three-dimensional space that follow the principles of quantum physics.

Ashaar read that out from a book and sketched a figure of atoms around a nucleus, because he was asked to explain "how atoms bind to form humans." He was also asked to read that part from a book by a little girl sitting beside him.

"Dear Lord, it means I am also made of atoms, popsy!"

"Yes, you are!" Ashaar asked, "Did you understand anything I explained?"

"No?"

"Then why did you ask me to read it?" He caressed the child's hair and watched her smile.

"Because I want to know what you were reading!"

Ashaar spoke to the five-year-old in a well-lit living room. He looked around the room, and he first noticed the calendar—*2030*. He could see a bunch of photos on the wall in the next room, but they were a little far away for his vision.

He walked into the kitchen and found someone was cooking curry. His favourite one, by the smell of it, was *beef bhuna*. She had put some reconstituted onion alongside the spices, and the smell filled the entire room. It took about three hours to follow that recipe. He looked at the bunch of bananas in the basket. They looked pretty ripe. Fruits were something Ashaar never grew fond of, but he loved bananas. Ashaar felt comfortable walking around the kitchen, but a subconscious notion came up from the implanted thoughts in his head. This was a house he had bought a few years ago. Since that preparation for the second Mars-bound flight, as he was about to go to space, things had been peculiar and rather off.

This situation could be compared to Schrodinger's cat. Until he walked up to the person cooking in the kitchen, he'd never know who that was. His harsh training in Xplorer's spacecraft simulator might have affected his ability to bring back recent memories.

Smelling like the cologne that Ashaar once gifted Emma roughly eight years ago, he approached the woman and asked, "Are you cooking beef?"

"I am, does it smell okay?" The woman in her late-30s with brown, shoulder-length hair and dark eyes turned around. Ashaar recognised her face and smiled back. She cradled his hand and looked into his eyes. Immediately, Ashaar felt two rings in her left hand. An engagement and wedding ring. Ashaar's anticipation for dinner grew as he smelled the food she was preparing.

The woman asked, "Can you bring Sophia to the table and put her tablet away for charging?"

"Okay." Everything felt to be in perfect order. Ashaar grabbed Sophia and prepared the table. This night felt like a quantum leap. They discussed work, school and everything in between at the dinner table. Ashaar could feel the warmth of happiness. Seeing two important people after a long day of work was such a relief. After having dinner, he took Sophia to her bed, upstairs, on the second floor.

"A storm is coming. Can I come to you if it gets scary, Popsy?" The air smelled of ozone, and electricity made the hair on the back of her neck stand on end.

"Of course, you can." He shot a heartfelt grin.

As a scientist, Ashaar approached life the way he approached science. Unless it was logical and clearly based, nothing mattered, and there was a reason for all things. He was convinced of the concept of God, not miracles. To him, the existence of multiple universes demanded some kind of ordering force holding everything steady. Quantum physics reinforced that view. Everything in reality carried a wavelength and once light reached the eye, that wave collapsed. The brain then stitched the incoming signals into the thing humanity called consciousness.

Ashaar walked downstairs, and right at the living room entrance lay a huge wedding photo. The engraved caption at the bottom of the frame said, "Ashaar and Stella," and a love sign right next to their wedding date, August 10th, 2025.

Struggling to recall the long-term memories, he asked Stella about the wedding album. "They are in the bottom left drawer under the TV." Ashaar, a tech fanatic, bought an 80-inch quantum dot TV three years ago. It was like the memories were starting to come back. That made him buy a huge TV cabinet with six drawers. All of them were filled with either photo albums or plush toys that Sophia played with every day.

Next to the cabinet was a bookshelf with a large cube-shaped drawer containing many of Ashaar's precious memories. He pulled out one drawer and was stunned. A framed red Lindt box, the one he received from Emma almost a decade ago. Ashaar couldn't stop smiling, because that might be one of the silliest things he had done, but the intrinsic value of that box was much higher. This time, he found a way to preserve the memory. And it was still here. No matter where he had moved, the framed box moved with him. Suddenly, he felt a rush of those memories and flashbacks of all the good times he had. It was a realisation of something that Ashaar had always wanted, something that was truly pure. He had put that need above everything else, but it didn't work out.

He turned on the TV and sat on the sofa. He couldn't find his phone on the sofa because it had slipped in between the cushions. He grabbed the phone and logged into the new social media video-sharing app that was trending.

The newsreader continued to explain the situation on Mars, "Over the next ten hours, the Martian Navy reported two riots in the station. There had been minor structural damage near the habitat zone Lambda. It was being reported that a curfew might come into force. Therefore, anyone going out after 7 p.m. would be subject to arrest."

The newsreader continued, "Outside the Martian atmosphere, things were getting worse. The deep AI research lab in the Lower Martian Orbit has been witnessing protests from two AI experts who have occupied the station for the past six months. They were tasked with training the orbital AI to broadcast the location of every Martian on the surface and, in the event of an anomaly, capture ultra-high-definition photos for a trial. The first Martian society appeals for freedom. However, the military defence arm, the Martian Naval Forces, indicates that without strict measures, the entire civilisation will spin out of control. Nolan, Xplorer's CEO, is yet to make any comments."

Minutes later, he heard a noise coming from the stairs. Sophia walked up to him and stared like she was about to burst out.

"Hi." Out of the corner of his eyes, she saw the little girl running towards him, then start jumping. Ashaar extended his arm and wrapped her arm around him.

"I can't sleep. Can you help me?" she said. He grabbed her with two hands and helped her sit on his lap. Sophia snatched him and hugged him tightly.

"Do you want me to go upstairs and sit with you a bit longer?" Ashaar asked.

She mumbled, "Okay." It took about five more minutes for her to fall asleep. Ashaar gently carried Sophia to her room and put her down. Next to that room was a second bedroom for guests. There were photos up on the wall in that room too. Some recently printed photos were lying on the corner table, with some opened-up empty frames lying on the floor. The moment Ashaar turned on the light, he almost jumped out of his skin.

In front of him was a photo of his daughter, with Emma. On that table. In the house.

Ashaar couldn't remember any recent memories of having contact with Emma. He turned around and went downstairs to grab his laptop. How was Emma still in this photo? Was he still in contact with her? He opened his laptop and tried to find some recent information. He found nothing. In the bottom right corner, he noticed the date; it was *September 2030.*

Then he looked at WhatsApp. There was a chain of texts with Stella. He realised Emma had been a friend of Susan, Stella's sister, and decided to drop by. Ashaar wasn't prepared to discover that he had simply forgotten this recent memory. He wondered if he had recently had a stroke or suffered memory loss. It was evident that despite recognising everything around him, he simply couldn't accept how gobsmacked he was to see Emma's photo with his daughter.

Ashaar heard a noise in the bedroom. It was one of those nights when Sophia struggled to sleep, causing problems for Stella. She had been busy preparing a contract that she would need for her meeting the following day. Ashaar got himself together and went upstairs to see what the deal was.

Sophia quickly hid under the duvet and made a mushy noise. "Hi, popsy," a voice murmured underneath the duvet.

"Can't you sleep?"

"No. I keep thinking about the nightmare," she said, rubbing her eyes with both hands.

"It's okay. What do you want me to do? Read you another story? Something new?" Ashaar sat next to her.

"No. I want you to stay here until I fall asleep again. Remember that story you told me about Princess Martha?"

"Oh yes, that story," Ashaar tried to juggle his memory, "I think we'll try a different story tonight."

The girl stared at him and wiped her eyes. Her eyes were wider this time. He watched Sophia looking at her dad. Ashaar understood this feeling. He had been around children from an early age. In his mid-20s, he spent a lot of time with his niece and nephews, toddlers back then. Ashaar felt the strangeness of connecting with his own child. "Popsy, why are you whispering? Aren't you supposed to read the story?"

Ashaar pulled the closest available bedtime storybook. Sophia loved it when the story was read from a book, not from a tablet or a phone. Like her father, she'd liked to hold a book and draw things in it. Ashaar read the story and made sure Sophia was asleep this time. He stayed for a few more minutes before turning off the lights.

Chapter 16: Ashaar

September 2030, California

In the morning, Ashaar sat down with the members of his team to have a detailed conversation. He had been employed by the space agency “Xplorer” for some time. With the greatest launch in history on the horizon, he led the research team and put in 10-12-hour days, Monday through Friday. His agency permanently relocated two hundred individuals to the newly habitable planet of Mars, making it the largest payload ever sent. There were three further launches planned, each carrying enough supplies to construct additional homes and materials. Iron, beryllium, platinum from Mars. Water, helium-3, REMs from the Moon. Organic elements from Earth. Vegetables grew in commercial space agencies in Earth’s orbit. An outer space warehouse had been built to store small packages for interplanetary delivery. A river of wealth and space expansion unrivalled in human history had been constructed in under a few years. There was commerce between planets and crime.

There were forces to battle that crime. There were secret military routes within Earth. The airspace was divided between civilian and military aircraft. The head of the Interplanetary Security Force, Mr Banerjee, led his military garrison, funded by the wealthiest companies in the world. Ashaar was halfway through reading through the history of space travel when one of his colleagues appeared behind him.

Ashaar's office was enormous enough to fit ten people, but the space was reserved for him. It smelled of polished leather and lemongrass. Under his desk, was a safe built with titanium and had a digital lock-screen.

The walls could be operated with a remote, and he could make it opaque or transparent with one click. A wall-hanging terminal next to his desk showed the status of the ships being built.

Something felt off. The timing wasn't right. And he couldn't figure out what it was.

This life felt like a box without an exit.

Over the past few hours, he looked at his DNA records, archives and everything in between. Every detail checked out. It was like he'd time-jumped years ahead. But the past few years of his memories were missing.

Ashaar met with Master Chief Joseph Santiago Cabrera, who worked for a covert military organisation called the United Nations Space Intelligence (UNSI). Joseph was an old friend of Ashaar's and had been employed by them for many years. The purpose of his clandestine military unit was to protect key individuals. This credible association was established with other military organisations around the world, the first ones to unite were the UK, US, Netherlands, France, Germany, Estonia, Japan, South Korea, Singapore, Dubai and Qatar. Their reach had expanded, as people from different countries applied to become space travellers and trained to be payload specialists and pilots. Joseph trained as an aeronautics technician, receiving his military licence from the US Space Force and working as a test pilot for Xplorer.

Born in Mexico and raised in Texas, Joseph appeared to have a great reputation at Xplorer. After shaking hands and exchanging pleasantries, he asked, "You wanted to visit the Fusion Propulsion Lab?"

"I did a few days ago." Ashaar furrowed his brows.

"I've come to take you there. Highly restricted facility, by the way, you'll need this pass." Joseph yanked a card and handed it to Ashaar.

After leaving his office, Joseph drove Ashaar to a facility approximately twenty minutes away from his office. Xplorer conducted highly classified research at this facility. Although it looked like a normal warehouse, it was bordered with fences and gated all throughout. The high-rising fences gave Ashaar the feeling as if he had walked onto a highly secured military site.

Two armed guards checked their IDs at the entrance and let them in. One guard nodded at Joseph, who nodded back and gave a thumbs up. The red and yellow barrier opened. They drove in and went underneath the warehouse marked as #4. Joseph parked near the entrance and swiped his card.

The corridors were particularly bright, lit well with white lights. It was almost like a set design inspired by Star Wars and The Expanse, like a hybrid spaceship. They had photos of Nolan, Xplorer's CEO, almost everywhere and a video feed of him attending a press conference on the Moon. There were terminals now and then, showing various information, such as the next launch window, weather and various products available in the building. Some of these TV-style terminals were so thin that Ashaar wondered how they had designed them.

The place was crowded with people, and most of them were dressed informally. Although some were in aprons. Evidently, they worked inside the lab. Joseph and Ashaar observed two people in hazmat suits walking by. Joseph smiled and nodded at them. Ashaar pretended to have knowledge about the subject and chose not to probe, hoping Joseph wouldn't begin to question his memory problems. At the end of the corridor, they found themselves before a high-tech door with an integrated terminal.

Joseph swiped his card and the computer pulled up his ID. He placed his finger directly on the screen. "Hyperion Systems" was written in bold white font under it. Seemed like those were portable tablets, connected to the internal security network. The QLED screens had built-in under-screen fingerprint readers. He stroked his finger and nodded at the screen. "Come on in, I'll show you something new today."

Joseph opened the door with deliberation and then handed Ashaar a mask. The two of them secured their black masks. Though it was dim, a huge item at the room's far end suddenly illuminated the space. Looking around, Ashaar saw only a few individuals, all clad in hazmat suits with LEDs, working behind a glass wall.

"Welcome to Hyperion Drive, Ashaar."

"You mean the start-up, Hyperion?" Ashaar asked.

Joseph scurried his brows. "They sold their technology to Xplorer. The company didn't have enough cash to sustain, so they sold their research and made residual income."

"Xplorer bought the idea?" Ashaar asked.

"This company will buy anything and everything that's relevant on the Martian terrain. Inside these walls, scientists are creating a source of unlimited energy," Joseph replied.

"Is this going to replace rocket fuel?"

"We already have sources to produce 1TerraJoule of energy after one mole of reactions, which is approximately 0.28GWh." A giant terminal displayed an animation of the reactor as he pressed the screen. Ashaar looked at the back of the lab. The room appeared to be divided into four sections. The massive reactor at the back of the lab, resembling a mushroom within a toroidal magnetic coil, was visible behind a military-grade glass wall. They'd installed cameras inside the reactor. Because of the heat resistance of the cameras, he could observe the energy moving within the chambers. The sight of hydrogen atoms colliding at high speed was truly fascinating.

"You are not connected to the grid, are you?" Ashaar asked.

"Not this facility. We are only running tests for producing space-grade propulsion reactors. We don't plan on delivering it to the national grid."

"But it can produce an extortionate amount of energy."

"You bet. Two minutes can serve 480,000 people."

"Crazy stuff, isn't it?" A voice appeared from the back of the room. A lab assistant walked in and greeted Ashaar. "Nice to see you in person. We all know you because of that photo on the wall."

"What photo?" Ashaar asked.

"The one with the second group of people to go on a Martian trip."

"Oh ... yes, yes ... of course." Ashaar received a massive kick of memory, almost like a tidal wave flashed in front of his eyes. It didn't help him with his migraine, and those memory flashbacks were becoming terrifying.

Turned out, he'd already been to Mars.

Yet, he couldn't remember anything. None of it.

"Once we can determine the technicalities to reduce its size and use it as a propellant for our ships, it could be 335 Mega Newton thrust, with an exhaust velocity of 1.9 million miles per hour."

"You could get to Mars in less than 5 days with a 100,000-ton spaceship," Ashaar said. Everything the lab assistant said in response blurred into noise. He only clearly heard them say they needed a powerful quantum AGI to finish designing the ship's nuclear reactor. But a quantum AGI with that capability wasn't available in the world.

"Great work!" Ashaar said as he shook the assistant's hand. Without waiting, he turned and left the chamber, slipping out before anyone could notice something was off.

After their conversation, Joseph took Ashaar around the facility and gave him a tour. They met with their colleagues. About an hour later, Joseph was about to drop Ashaar off at his office. He parked, pulled out a burner phone and typed a text.

Contact established. Confirmation of subject.

Almost instantly, he received a response.

Copy. Make sure Sentinel can track him with the chip.

Ashaar, from the corner of his eye, read what Joseph had sent. He looked up and read his face. Joseph might have done it intentionally to catch Ashaar's attention.

Sentinel. There it was.

Emma used to tell me about Sentinel.

The sensation was disorienting, as if he had been in an accident and abruptly awakened to a fragmented reality. His memories were like pieces of a puzzle, some fitting perfectly, others missing entirely.

Among the fragments, he discovered startling revelations about spaceships and a journey to Mars, concepts that seemed plucked from a futuristic world far removed from his own. They were also discussing quantum AGIs.

It was as though time had leapt forward, catapulting him into an era where the extraordinary had become ordinary. He was disoriented by this abrupt entry into a world of advanced technology, and he struggled to understand what was happening to him.

To find his lost memories, he understood that he needed additional clues and links to connect the disjointed parts of his mind. The unanswered questions were like keys that could open the doors to his past. And he needed the answers soon, because some part of his intuition told him that he was running out of time.

***

September 2030, California

After enduring a day that stretched longer than it should have, Ashaar came back home in the evening. On days like this, they had a full-time nanny who picked Sophia up from school and stayed with her until Ashaar and Stella returned. Around

7:30 p.m., he walked into his house. After saying hello to Sophia, Ashaar made a cup of tea and stood outside on the balcony to take the outside view in for a second. He had a clear view of the town because of the hilly terrain. The next minute, he felt someone holding his leg and trying to climb up.

"I want you to carry me," Sophia asked, jumping.

Ashaar held her in one hand and tried to balance the cup with the other. "I won't be scared tonight anymore," she affirmed. For one second, something felt like swelling inside his heart. It was the fact that Ashaar had a five-year-old child. Sophia stared at him in a way that no one ever did before. All Ashaar could do was simply smile at her and get along. Her eyes were identical to Stella's, and those big dark eyes dilated when she was infuriated or excited about something. This was the moment Ashaar realised he could never escape this life, even if he wanted to. He felt a sense of responsibility towards the little child, something he always wanted apart from his career. During his late 20s, he thought he might prioritise his job over his personal life because it wasn't working out. Luck wasn't much on his side. He didn't find the right woman to live his life with, until then. He didn't feel attracted to Stella, it was a sense of responsibility driven by his own potential future.

Sophia put her head on Ashaar's shoulder. He could hear Stella walking down the stairs and going into the kitchen to grab a glass of wine. Ashaar put his cup on the side table and walked into the room. Stella smiled at him and continued her journey upstairs with her large transparent tablet. Stella continued to read the story and walked away with her glass of wine, "I'm going to take a bath now."

"Sure. Let me order some pizzas tonight."

Ashaar double-checked his time. It was a branded watch, but not too expensive. Unlike others, he still wore an analogue stainless-steel watch. It was 7:54 p.m., almost the hour Sophia went to bed. Her nanny fed her dinner before her parents returned home, so she was ready to sleep.

"I don't want to go to sleep right now," Sophia said.

"Okay, you can stay with me for a little while," Ashaar replied.

"Can I ask you a question?" Sophia paused, "Who do you love the most, me or Mommy?"

"I think I love you more than your mommy, baby girl."

"She will be jealous." Sophia giggled.

"I'm sure she will be, princess."

"When do you have to leave, Popsy?"

"When do I have to leave for what?" Ashaar's brows creased.

"You know that trip you have to go on for a long time."

"I'm not going to go on any more trips. I'm staying here with my princess and my wife."

She continued her line of questioning. Ashaar realised how his daughter was, exactly like him, how he was in his childhood. Ashaar would ask a hundred questions every day about everything he came across, from politics to geography, ending in scientific questions.

"What happens if you die out there?" Sophia asked. Ashaar realised Sophia was pointing her finger at the toy spaceship on a corner shelf. He remembered being on Mars, and his contract was extended. He signed up for a trip to conduct research at the habitational outpost for three years, but that contract meant that he needed to leave Sophia and Stella behind for that time. Eventually, he turned down the second offer and handed the opportunity to his friends at work, Chloe and Holly. They were both training to move to the new planet and young enough to deal with the work pressure. Ashaar, outlandishly, remembered the names, but he couldn't recall their faces at all.

"I'm not going to die. I'll be here with you."

"That sounds better, Popsy."

"And you don't worry about me leaving for a long time. I'm working from my office and have already given that job to your aunt Holly. That way I'll be able to spend more time with you."

"Can we go hiking up north with mummy?"

"Yes, we'll go up north, into the mountains and hike."

"And camping. I love camping!" she replied, smiling.

"I know you do, baby girl." Slowly, the memories reappeared. Ashaar realised this trait had been directly absorbed from her mother. She used to go hiking all the time when she returned to Germany. Stella was half-German, and her parents still lived in Frankfurt. They were settled and happily married for over fifty years. It was always a good excuse for her to take Sophia to a different country.

"And we'll go to Germany and see Oma," she referred to her grandmother. Stella's mum moved to Germany at an early age and never turned back. She and her husband both worked in the automotive sector until retirement. Ashaar found himself able to recall these memories with clarity, while others remained frustratingly out of reach. It puzzled him, this selective amnesia, leaving him to wonder about the elusive nature of the memories he couldn't seem to access.

Happiness bloomed on Ashaar's face. "Yes, a trip to Germany sounds legendary."

"I love aeroplanes. I love flying. It makes me happy."

For one moment, this felt like the perfect life. He had a family of his own, a daughter he always wanted, and a nice moderately sized house. Life was good, filled with shared investments and pure joy. "If you ever want to see where I come from, we can go and pay a visit to Bangladesh."

"I really want to go to Bangadesh," Sophia struggled to pronounce the word.

"Let me plan something with your mum."

"Okay!" She laughed, darting forward to grab him. "I love you, popsy. I like your beard."

"Thank you. I love you too." Ashaar stared at the tiny yet highly energetic soul.

***

September 2030, California

Stella took her bottle of water, looked at Ashaar and asked, "Why are you looking at me like that?" She raised her brows.

Until now, Ashaar hadn't had a chance to speak with his "wife." Stella's hair shone in the morning light. If anything, she looked much younger than she had looked when he met her. Stella wore her running gear, her sleek black Apple watch gleamed on her wrist, the silver accents catching the light as she checked the time.

"What?! No. It's nothing. It's my resting bitch face," Ashaar said.

"Yes, but your resting bitch face is different." Stella replied, giggling. "It's when you are under a lot of pressure. What happened last night? Has Sophia been having difficulties sleeping for the past few days?"

Ashaar marvelled at why Stella left all the responsibilities on his shoulder, "Well, I think you'd know better."

"But this is your week! Remember? We take turns every week. You can either concentrate on your work or play with the little monster and fulfil dad duty."

"Oh yes, sorry, I forgot." Ashaar said.

"No worries," Stella said while tying her hair with a band. "Anyway, I'll grab Sophia on my way home. I think I can get out early. My project has been reassigned."

"Really? Who's handling it now?"

"John is going to manage the M&A. My part is done, so it's time for me to get rid of that shit." Stella brought her handbag and left it on the kitchen counter right in the middle of the room. Her ID badge hung from the bag, where Ashaar could see her name Stella Schmidt, and her designation. She worked at an investment firm as a senior vice president and looked after deals specific to start-ups.

"As soon as Cognition is acquired by Splinters, I can rest."

"Really?" Ashaar paused, "I mean, I know."

"I thought you knew about my project?"

"Yes, of course, I do," Ashaar walked towards a cupboard and grabbed a glass. As morning dawned, beams of light streamed through the kitchen window, bathing the kitchen in a warm, welcoming glow.

"What's your plan tomorrow?" she asked.

"Erm," Ashaar hesitated, "nothing?"

"If you want, I can join you tomorrow afternoon, and we could go out for dinner."

"That sounds amazing," Ashaar said.

"Cool." She took her handbag and left for her office.

That night, Ashaar sat down and had a conversation with Stella. She discussed life, work, the future and where they wanted to buy a new house. Stella showed him photos of her colleagues. The fake candles diffused the smell of lavender and the faint smell of wet grass passed through a slightly opened window. Outside, there was light rain. Stella held her Sauvignon Blanc in her right hand and sat next to Ashaar in the oversized jumper she borrowed from his closet. Her legs felt warm, encased in her tall Nike socks. With her knees resting on Ashaar's feet, she tucked her uncovered pale skin under a woollen throw. They were streaming a romantic comedy on Netflix. Stella felt like watching a film that was emotional.

One hour into the movie, she placed her wineglass on the side table and reached for her iPhone. "Do you remember the time when you asked me out?"

"Yeah ... ?" Ashaar conveyed his confusion with a creased forehead. "Why?"

"No, just asking. We really weren't in a proper relationship, until you—"

"Until I what?" Ashaar gazed at her.

Stella browsed her cloud storage to find a photo. "Wait, let me show you the photo."

It was a photo of Stella, on a farm, walking carefree. She was sporting a white tank top, a red skirt and a loosely fitted dark green shirt that brought out the richness of her complexion. "Do you remember this day?" Stella raised her suspicions through the tone in her voice.

"Yeah, it was great." Ashaar wanted to avoid extending that conversation anymore. A lump formed in his head.

Ashaar noticed the awkwardness on Stella's face. She said, "It was great? It was the day you said those three words for the first time!"

"I love you?" Ashaar felt his heart beating faster, as he observed Stella's doubt. That was it, three magic words, and the world had changed around him.

"Yeah! A year before we got married. I'll never forget that day!" Stella grabbed her glass, leaned in, brushed her head on his shoulder and rubbed her head against his face.

"Of course," Ashaar said.

His brain could unlock memories related to Stella, but not the others. How strange.

"You seem strange, not gonna lie." Stella moved back a few inches and rested her head against the pillow on her side. "You okay?"

"I am. I'm going to finish watching my film," Ashaar said.

"Okay," she said.

Chapter 17: Ashaar

September 2030, California

Ashaar woke up, gasping.

His eyes darted across the room. “Stella? Are you still here?”

A sticky note on his bedside table caught his attention. It said, I've left. Breakfast is on the table.

Ashaar dressed up, wore his half-torn trainers and walked downstairs.

The smell of coffee invaded his nose.

Just as he took one sip, his throat burned. He drained his coffee, locked the house and started his journey to the office.

Halfway through the day, he received a call from Susan Schmidt, Stella's half-sister, who was preparing for a half marathon, sponsored by Xplorer. The conversation made his memories emerge, each a piece of a puzzle, impossible to put together.

Ashaar learned that Emma was joining the half marathon with Stella's sister. For one second, he didn't really freak out but choked mid-conversation. Why did it bother him so much? It had been eight years, yet he was suffocating at the sound of her name. Something didn't add up.

Five hours later, Ashaar grabbed his keys and drove out of the car park of his office. Today was a quiet day, with only paperwork for administrative duties. He worked on another research paper that would be published the next month. Ashaar voice-texted to check on Stella. She was on her way to pick Sophia up from school.

Inside the glove box, he found a surprising package that had arrived about a month prior. Still unopened. There were a few things inside, which a friend had sent when he moved away from London. One of them included a small keyring that Ashaar was supposed to give to Stella. It looked like the same Star Wars keyring he had given as a gift to Emma.

Emma's Star Wars puns never failed to make Ashaar smile, a fact he cherished.

This situation seemed rather shocking and surprising in unanimity.

He drove through a mountain tunnel that stretched to the coastline. He discovered himself in another neighbourhood but had no memories of his time there. He tried overloading his mind with recollections of the past few months. Nothing. He rolled down the window, hoping a familiar scent might help him remember. Nothing. He felt as if he'd been through a lot in the last several years, yet he only remembered a badgering discomfort in his chest.

Businesses and fast-food restaurants were open throughout the shore, with customers lining up at their entrances. The owners of several of the other dwellings had fitted cumbersome exterior locks. He drove past a burnt-down building.

This wasn't his life, and it felt like he was somewhere else. A different place. Everything felt rather unusual. He took his foot off the gas.

He felt an unsettling rush. Memories resurfaced with incredible speed, invading his thoughts much like bullets tearing through his chest. A headache came on as the actual memories started to resurface. He had been working at a lab. Subsequently, an explosion happened. He surveyed his surroundings. Ashaar was usually as composed as a pond's placid surface. But now, he realised he'd been thrown into the future after the accident in the quantum lab. One explanation was that the tunnel had exploded.

The only alternative was that he had passed away.

He abruptly braked and stopped at the side of the road. He felt like he was going to vomit.

Ashaar slapped himself twice. Still nothing.

Sometimes dreams were as real as they could get. But this wasn't a dream. In the midst of the meltdown, his memory couldn't stop recalling the name Michaela.

He exited the vehicle. He yearned to leap over the fence and experience the sensation of landing on the other side. The feeling was unsettling. This was the future, with the smell of ozone in the air.

Ashaar knew he'd crossed over into the future. His heart was pounding. His hands were starting to feel numb and tremble violently. He remembered discussing a parallel universe with Taya. Or possibly more. Or infinite.

What if he was in one?

He took out his phone and opened his cloud storage. He tried to scramble and look at memories older than 2028. There was nothing. What happened to his storage? Where were all his old personal photos?

"Okay, calm down, Ashaar." He shouted at himself while the cars raced past. "So you are in the future. That's clear. But there is also a possibility that you might be in a different universe." Ashaar paced along the pavement and said, "Because some things in this timeline still don't make sense. I need to find out about my recent past. I don't know how I can access my old memories."

In that moment of panic, Ashaar understood that the memories he'd had over the past few days were not his own.

They came from the host, Ashaar from another universe. A 40-year-old Ashaar. Despite knowing this, Ashaar felt a warm feeling in his heart towards the child and Stella, though they weren't related to him.

"Stella is not my wife. Sophia is not my child. They are this Ashaar's family. God knows what happened to him," he said to himself, trying to comprehend the complexity of the situation.

The beachside road ran from east to west; rocky, chaotic, and gorgeous. LEDs hanging from the poles glittered as the waves smashed into the rocks, generating a splashing sound that grumbled throughout the area. When Ashaar looked up, a group of delivery drones glided past, cuddled the ground low and emitted a whining noise where the reasonably humid air gave its rotary wings a little more resistance than usual.

As he stood there lost in thought, a woman drove past him. She bore a striking resemblance to Stella, with her smooth, red hair and pale skin, catching his attention momentarily. *Maybe she wasn't her sister. Maybe she was.* He didn't know. He couldn't care less. The woman gradually rolled out her window and looked at him. She smiled. People in California were friendlier than on the East coast and also London. It was normal. Ashaar grinned back, with fear in his head. He watched as she slowly drove past and accelerated. He could see the car going faster in the opposite direction. A loud noise from her exhaust filled the road and the neighbourhood.

Ashaar stepped back and continued his monologue, "Okay, I have to go with the flow. I need to figure out how I got here. I also need to find out if there's a way to go back."

After a few minutes of juggling his thoughts, he felt calm. "Life is normal. I have to be normal. Otherwise, people will suspect," he said to himself, "I need to play along."

He experienced moving around with his parents since he was young. He lived in various places. He adapted. Closing his eyes, he inhaled, filling his lungs, exhaled and turned, walking back towards his car. "It's no different from the last time, is it?"

Now it was time for him to carry on.

***

While they were en route to the restaurant, Stella made a request.

Stella: Could you stop by the beach house?

Her plan was to then take Sophia back home in their second car to get her ready, ensuring everything was set for their evening out. Stella also had in mind to freshen up and change into something more elegant for the dinner. They were expecting not only their family but also colleagues from work and their children, making it a larger, more festive gathering. Ashaar was meant to be right here. It seemed perfect, even if the person wasn't quite right.

Ashaar went to the small cabin that they owned near the coast. Despite its size, it could still fit various items, including a sofa and a small bed if someone needed them. They didn't use the residence often, so they put it on Airbnb for rent. Because the previous occupant left the place in a terrible state, Stella asked Ashaar to check if everything was okay, or if a claim form needed to be filed.

Ashaar always carried a bunch of keys in his pocket. The keyring had a transparent display with three names blinking one after another: Stella, Sophia and Ashaar. Ashaar found the golden key and opened the door to the cabin. It had dark wood floors, a sizable Quantum dot TV, a wood bed frame, a neatly arranged bookshelf and several decorative showcase items. The room included a pleasant electric heater with a simulated fire effect. Ashaar spotted a couple of items that brought back fond memories: a small model of an F1 car and a twelve-inch red telephone box from London, which Stella had given him a long time ago.

Ashaar took a quick glance at the books. Mostly food manuals. There weren't many nonfictions, mostly works of unknown or underrated authors. He recognised his copy of Humankind, a book that he was familiar with, and he also found another Rudger Bregman book. There were more books about Harry Potter, but those looked really fancy. There were some books on history, intellectual ones, economy, politics and the ideology of the space-race continuum. There were a lot of books that he had never even heard of, most probably because his wife was a book nerd. She'd read any good book that was thrown at her.

On the bottom shelf were many books that he seemed to be familiar with.

More photos on the wall brightened the atmosphere. The room seemed like a container of memories from the past decade. Then, he investigated every corner. The only damage was a broken vase around the corner.

It's okay, Ashaar texted Stella. He grabbed a sweeping brush and cleaned up the floor. Let the rental agency take care of the cleaning up.

On the way to the restaurant, he received a call from Stella's mother, Anne, from Germany. He picked up and spoke to her like they were best friends. The conversation helped him unlock more memory clusters. Anne wasn't his biggest fan. Stella's dad, on the contrary, was a fan when they were friends, but when he realised Stella wanted to marry a brown person, he hesitated a little. Even though she talked about her sister Susan a lot, Ashaar barely knew her. Right from the start, Stella didn't need anyone, and she never asked her parents for anything, especially when it came to her personal life. Stella told Ashaar repeatedly that her dad would likely make things difficult. The first time Stella introduced Ashaar to her father as a partner, his response at the dinner was rather provocative. The first question was about money—*How much money do you think you'll make at this new job?* The second question resonated with even further provocation—*Do you think it's a good idea to move to the US when you already have settled status in the UK?* Ashaar graciously failed to answer that one. In the end, the dinner wasn't full of botched conversation after all.

On the way to the restaurant from the beach house, he sped up along the coast and got lost in the long-term memories stored in his brain. Both sets of memories were superpositioned.

After arriving at the destination, he walked into a retro-looking Italian restaurant that appeared perfectly enjoyable. It wasn't busy that day, just as it was supposed to be. But it was a Friday. As Stella stated, that was the first time, in a long time, they were going somewhere as a family. Because of their hectic schedule, they didn't spend enough time outside of work.

Stella and Sophia arrived at the restaurant. He looked at the woman rocking her high heels, wearing a soft white long sleeveless dress. It sparkled under the dark yellow light but wasn't too shiny. She wore heels approximately three inches tall. Sophia ran towards Ashaar and sat on his lap. Ashaar carried her to a height-adjustable chair and prepared the table for the little girl. Growing up, Ashaar spent a decent amount of time experiencing restaurants from different parts of the world. When he was young, his parents used to take him to a Chinese restaurant that he loved—their soup was a particular favourite. A second later, Sophia asked for the same soup. Ashaar had wondered where that habit came from.

"Shall we order?" Ashaar took a sip of his mocktail, and it was delicious. Californian-grown lemons, and rich in flavour. He felt lucky to feel that taste of a different universe.

"I am so hungry. I have had no food since morning. I honestly wanted to keep myself feeling hungry so that I could enjoy dinner," Stella said.

"Should we order the pasta made in a cheese bowl? Sophia will love it."

"Mummy, how long do we have to wait?" Sophia asked.

"Not long, hunny. Are you hungry?"

"I'm starving!" Sophia looked down, rubbing her hand on her belly.

Ashaar leaned in, "We'll get some appetisers for you in the meantime."

Sophia agreed with a nod and smiled at Stella. The journey of Ashaar was incredible, starting from a point of life's frustrations to the eventual embrace of a life that perfectly embodied his desires.

His eyes shifted to the streetlights beyond the window. He thought back to Emma's shape, her lovely lips, the excitement he felt when they were together and the smell of her breath as she talked to him. He recalled how she used to taunt him when they touched, and the joy on Emma's radiant face as Ashaar showered her with praise, which made her feel secure.

Ashaar was lost in thought when the aroma of the approaching waiter brought him back to reality. With Stella and Sophia lost in their talk, he pondered the secrets held by his memories while listening to the background murmurs.

***

A thumping noise from downstairs woke him up.

Stella and Sophia went to spend the weekend with her family, and Ashaar was alone in his house.

Waking up, he tied a gown around his wrinkled t-shirt and shorts and ran down the stairs. There it was, another faint muffling noise. He stopped, blood pumping in his veins.

Thank God Stella isn't here, was the first thought that sprinted to his head.

He strode down one step at a time, without making the squealing wooden board let out a noise. He could feel the balcony doors opening. The hush sound of the stiff wind from outside sent a shiver throughout his body. Just as he took the last step on the ground floor, a shadow materialised.

Ashaar looked down and stood still. He didn't dare move. His heart stopped racing when he realised there were two more shadows approaching.

A group of people had broken into their house. He felt a cylindrical device being pressed against the back of his head. From experience, he'd known that it was a silencer for a handgun.

"Don't make any noise," the man said.

Ashaar raised his hand. "Take what you want."

Another armed man, sporting a carbon fibre bulletproof vest and red camouflage uniform flashed his bright headlight on Ashaar's face almost blinding him.

Squinting, he glared at the men. They wore military-grade helmets and night vision goggles, and were armed with handguns and tactical rifles.

Outside, his bare feet were coated with dust. His eyes darted about, noticing two black SUVs waiting a hundred yards away from their home. A chill ran down his spine as he realised the SUVs' engines were running, their presence ominous and out of place in the quiet neighbourhood, hinting at an impending confrontation.

But also, that meant he would find the answers to his questions.

The man from behind gently pushed him with one hand, asking him to board the vehicle. Raising his voice, the armed man said, "Welcome to Universe Lambda."

Chapter 18: Emma

July 2030, London, Universe Lambda, a few months before Ashaar's arrival

Susan had finally met Emma a few months earlier.

Emma ushered Susan into a private conference room and slammed the door behind her. "Nice to finally meet you!" Emma pulled a chair, sat down and crossed her legs.

"I know. We have known each other, and I feel like I had a friend in you over the video call," Susan said.

"I know, right?" Emma grinned. "I'm here to help you find more partners for your AI start-up."

"Thank you. Though today I'm here to talk about something else."

"What about?" Emma made a face as if she was worried but curious at the same time.

"Everything that I'm about to tell you is strictly confidential." Susan took out a small, round device with a blinking red light. It was meant to create a no-interference zone and blackout all the cameras and mobile phones. "We need you to come with us and see it," Susan said.

"See what?"

"How the future will look like if you don't help us." Susan took out a transparent terminal. She played a video on it after tapping some numbers. Emma stared at it, perplexed as to why a hodgepodge of encrypted letters blinked.

"Here you go."

The terminal played a video on an augmented screen. Earth and Mars glowed on the hologram, the ships of Earth-Mars missions were floating around the planets and space in between, green dots amongst the vast emptiness of the cosmic festival. Emma watched a news broadcaster. She looked at the date, and her eyes couldn't believe what was happening,

> A few years ago, the acquisition led by Splinters Inc. has now driven our country into jeopardy. 'Cognition' and their quantum technology called 'Sentinel' was fully acquired by merger, resulting in a large group of investors receiving access to it.
>
> The Factions–six criminal syndicates that started off as a controversial start-up–are trying to revolutionise warfare. They believe the only way to create a stable world is to provide Sentinel with the power to operate all the nuclear assets, alongside developing the fusion programme on Mars and Ganymede. If they truly hand over the power to operate such large artillery, are we truly considered safe? What if the superintelligence goes rogue and creates a new version of itself? The possibilities are endless, and we cannot let that happen. We cannot use a warfare game as a layer to train an AI intelligence, then turn that into a weaponised apparatus in the real world. The outcome would be catastrophic.

Emma replayed it three times. Emma's heart raced, as sweat trickled out of her scalp and onto her forehead.

She looked at Susan, "Is this a joke? How can I be sure that it's the factions who are the enemies, and not you?" In her heart, she wanted to believe all of it, because she was a physicist.

Every theory in physics could pan out in the future. But logically, everything seemed fake.

"You need to come to our HQ and see it for yourself." Susan handed over a small cut-glass-type device.

Emma wondered how she had been dragged into this mess, "Why me?" She plucked the hand terminal Susan had given her, trying to grab the depth of the situation, comprehend all the clues she would need. The far more important question was how she'd already been involved. Nervousness outweighed her perplexity.

"You have something in your possession, but you should learn it from Sentinel itself." Susan said, her eyes widening. "It'll explain everything to you. You will also meet Andrew, the historian who's leading the mission."

"I'll think about it," Emma replied, watching Susan stand up after a device in her pocket began buzzing.

"I need to go. Please come and help us."

Susan left the meeting room.

***

August 2030, London, Universe Lambda, a month before Ashaar's arrival

A few weeks later.

As Emma went to Susan's office, she turned on her location using her phone and shared it with Aggie, her best friend. She pulled her Mercedes in front of a white building and noted the rubbish, broken cars, the scabrous walls reflected in the dark, dirty puddles of water and an empty alleyway echoing a strained stillness.

Emma latched her car door and walked through the alleyway. After a couple of minutes, she thought, *since I'm here, let's go all in.* Holding onto her purse, she tucked her grey jumper into her tight black jeans and proceeded along the path. As she put her handbag over her shoulder, the light caught the structured leather and the gold details, causing them to sparkle.

A minute later, a man walked out of the building, greeted her and took her inside. “Welcome, Emma.”

“You must be Andrew.”

“I am. Let’s go straight into the vault.”

Her shoulders slumped slightly, and a faint flush crept up her neck. She averted her gaze while feeling a mix of embarrassment and defensiveness wash over her.

As Emma entered the room, her eyes widened in disbelief. Before her stood the fully operational quantum supercomputer. She asked, “How did you build this?”

“It looks complete from the outside, but we need two parts of the code. One is with you and the other with Dr Ben Weiss, who’s doing the same research in Munich.”

“I have nothing on me,” Emma said.

“Did you ever come across a random animation on your laptop that looked like this?” Andrew pointed to Susan as she pulled up a virtual quantum frame on her terminal.

“I have.” Emma stared at Susan.

“We sent this code to you. It’s in your head,” Oscar said, swallowing a lump.

Emma raised her voice and stepped back. “What the hell do you mean by in my head?”

“Emma, calm down.” Susan gripped her shoulder.

Emma freed herself. “You just dragged me to a remote area, and now you’re talking rubbish.”

“We need your help,” Susan insisted.

“I can’t help. I need to leave.” Emma spun on her shoes—her movements brisk as she headed towards the lift. Her hands trembled slightly. Her breath quickened with each step.

“Wait, Emma. We have a way to prove this to you,” Andrew said. “Stay with us a bit longer. We’re setting up the memory retrieval station. See the guys back there? You can access multiple memory chains from your past.”

Emma shot a worrying look at Andrew.

Susan added, “We are all on one side. If we don’t do this, our future will be destroyed.”

"What do I have to do to retrieve my memory?"

"Let us scan your brain, first. It will take less than thirty seconds."

"I will let you do a scan of my brain, and that's it," Emma said.

"Fine. Let's go to my office and talk." Susan grabbed Emma's arm, and shot a smile.

Chapter 19: Susan

August 2030, London, Universe Lambda, Sentinel's HQ

Susan arrived with coffee and food in hand for Emma, setting the stage for a more personal exchange. As they settled down, Susan opened up, sharing personal stories and her deep-seated reasons for being part of the mission. She delved into the complexities of parallel universes, illustrating her explanations with hand-drawn diagrams and a series of photographs that purportedly depicted the future.

Susan wrapped her fingers around her mug and said, "Sentinel was the most powerful quantum AI created in the future. It uses a technology called Quantitative—Quantum Consciousness Transfer Initiative—a technology from 2022." Susan swallowed a lump and continued, "It needs access to historical records and archives from different universes to calculate multiple probabilities to transfer consciousness. Since its algorithm isn't limited to a single outcome, it can work its way out to find what might happen in multiple universes."

"But how does Sentinel access data archives from different universes?" Emma found herself seated next to a woman she had only just been introduced to, despite the surprising and somewhat unsettling information they had shared with her earlier.

"With a combination of DNA storage and quantum data relays. That's a story for another day. It's complicated," Susan replied. "For now, you need to know the high-level details that are relevant. For instance, if our data archives are destroyed, Sentinel will be in the blind."

"What if the data archives aren't destroyed, but hacked?"

"Our enemies, the factions have already tried that. As Andrew noted, big periods of time will vanish from the historical records inside Sentinel's prolonged memory. It's all about creating an AI that computes based on ethics and the righteousness of the human mind. You can create an AI that can never take a life without a valid reason. But if you train its mind with the wrong historical data, it might want to choose warfare over saving the earth."

"In the future ... I mean Andrew's future ... does the AI have access to nuclear assets?" Emma asked.

Susan said, "He arrived here from a timeline called Universe Lambda-A. In Lambda-A, it is used by the Presidents and the UN military to make decisions that are above DEFCON 3. When the factions attacked Sentinel's quantum servers all over the world, it used those nuclear assets to destroy them. Sentinel advises, but doesn't control weapons, which isn't what the factions are hoping for."

"You are relying on an AI to make wartime decisions?" Emma looked around Andrew's room and the lab, noticing large barrels of heat-exchanging surfaces to increase water temperature and kill the germs.

"It's a superintelligence, Emma, it can give you a split-second wartime decision."

"But it seems like Sentinel couldn't destroy the factions. Who are these factions? How many of them are there?" Emma's eyes dart towards her, shoulder stiff, cautious.

"No," Susan replied. "There are six factions left. Tens of millions of people follow them, but their leaders are a group of fascists," Susan said. "The factions eventually cracked the code to build their own AI and created a time-travelling device."

Leaving a half-eaten biscuit on a white plate, Emma brushed the crumbs off her hand. "How do they time travel?"

Susan made room for Emma on the sofa next to her and passed a water jug. "By overwriting a host's consciousness. Our teams take over hosts who were predicted to die. The factions, on the other hand, overwrite innocent people's consciousness. Right now, they've arrived at this time to steal Sentinel's code."

"What's the end goal?" Emma took the water jug from Susan's hand, her brows creasing.

"The end goal is to track the source of a quantum matrix that came from universe Alpha. If they succeed, they'll conquer the multiverse," Susan said.

"The multiverse?"

"Yes. Only some faction members have journeyed to the Alpha universe. They have a forward operating base. Our intel suggests Bowman has halted their pursuit of Alpha Emma, and we're unsure why."

"They want to kill me in both universes?" Emma asked, chuckling. After pouring water into a glass, she set the water jug down on the table. "Am I *that* important to them?"

"They do. In Alpha, they tried attacking an aircraft full of passengers. But they failed. Alpha Ashaar and Alpha Emma were on that flight from Italy to London." Susan gulped down a whole glass of water.

Emma stared at Susan for a few seconds, her jaw slack in textbook shock. It seemed as if she could feel her grip on reality slipping away. Susan, in that moment, instantly gripped Emma's hand, hesitating to ask if she was okay.

Emma exhaled sharply. "I'm fine."

Susan shifted and held her terminal in front of Emma, "The factions are looking for you. Their AI figured out that you might become a part of our mission and are thus trying to eliminate you from both universes."

"So, Sentinel will keep me safe in both the universes?" Emma flicked through some photos—passport-style photos of people who innocently died at the hands of the factions. People who were overwritten.

"Yes. Sentinel sent one of its associates to Alpha Emma. In 2021, she received an invitation card, but hidden underneath that was a quantum pulse repeater, or QPR, as we call it."

Susan went on to explain to Emma that she wasn't a traveller. Andrew recruited her to work for him and Sentinel. Gradually, she explained how their missions would tie into their ultimate plan—stopping Bowman and the factions from taking over Sentinel's code. She continued to explain for another half an hour her decision to join Andrew's team. Emma learned from her about the future of the outer colonies, Susan's family and the tragic deaths of her future children and husband, Mason, an army officer.

"How do you know all this?" Emma asked.

"I made the mistake of accessing my future memory," Susan replied. "Sentinel told me it might be a mistake. But if I accessed my memory, I'd have greater faith in the AI. That is exactly what happened."

Emma's defensive nature dripped off her. She tightened her shoulders and asked, "Susan, you don't know me well enough. Why are you sharing all your personal information with me?"

"I am not a traveller like Andrew. I was hired as a programmer and a tactician. Sentinel is my direct mission commander. But I understand what's at stake. If that AI can change my mind, it can change yours."

Emma glared at Susan, trying to parse the response.

"Look, Emma, if you ever want to see how you were in your past and what you'll be in the future, help yourself." Her teeth sank into her lip. Susan gripped Emma's hand and added,

"Sentinel will give you access to a long-term hidden memory chain through quantum entanglement."

Emma leaned in and moved closer to Susan. "I can only see *my* future, right?"

"You can only see *your* things."

"I cannot believe all this." Emma looked up at the ceiling, blinked hard, and tried to swallow all her emotions at once.

"I know. But you will get used to it. Please help us." Susan unlocked her terminal and started swiping. "We can't do it without you, Emma." Susan paused for two seconds. As she watched Emma's face, she caught a glimmer of emotion there, buried beneath the surface. It was as if Emma had built a wall around herself, and the only way to break through it was to reach her on a deeper, more emotional level.

Susan placed the terminal next to her and continued, "Hey, do you want to come and meet my niece, Sophia?"

"Where does she live?"

"In California. I might visit next month. You could come with me," Susan said.

"I haven't been to California in years."

Knowing what the future held, Susan figured she should prepare Emma for Alpha Ashaar's arrival in the coming months.

"Ashaar Naveed. Do you recognise the name?" Susan raised her voice against the humming noise of their quantum computer. As she spoke, she watched Emma's face, waiting for a reaction.

"Yes. I wasn't that close to him."

"In his universe, you worked with him on the same project. He was with Cognition, and you were with Hyperion," Susan added, "I should let you know a couple things—"

"What else do I need to know?" Emma asked, brows raised.

"Firstly ..." Susan cleared her throat, avoiding eye contact, "Lambda Ashaar was supposed to be married to you. According to Sentinel, you two were supposed to have a family."

"What?" Emma exhaled a chuckle in disbelief, eyes widening. "What?!"

"You heard it right," Susan pursed her lips, and nodded her head. "But Lambda Ashaar has ended up with my sister, Stella."

Susan noticed Emma's eyes widen in disbelief, as if her mind were racing as she scrambled for the right words to respond to Susan's revelation. "Erm ..." Susan darted at the distant technicians setting up a server. Susan eyed Emma. "Sentinel also predicts that Alpha Ashaar will overwrite Lambda Ashaar in September."

"What do you mean?" Emma's heart thudded, veins visible on her neck. Susan could feel Emma's racing pulse through her expression.

"In this branched timeline, Lambda Ashaar is supposed to die. We don't know the exact reason. But right before his death, Alpha Ashaar will arrive in his host," Susan showed Ashaar's photo to Emma. "His company, Xplorer, was working on the Quantitative lab. Its design was originally used to build Sentinel's consciousness transfer device," Susan added. "Their lab exploded. Thankfully, Sentinel predicted the event, bringing his consciousness to Lambda."

Emma, in that brief moment, cleared her throat, trying to keep her composure.

Susan paused for two seconds, exhaling. "We didn't intentionally bring him here."

At her blank stare, Susan locked her sight, eyes twinkling.

"I ..." Emma rubbed her forehead, saying, "I honestly don't know what to think of all this."

"Just be nice to him, okay? Alpha Ashaar is all we have now." Susan handed over a hand terminal to Emma. "Take this."

"What's in it?" Emma extended her hand to take the terminal, her hands visibly shaking.

"This air-gapped terminal has the answers to everything you want to know. There are high-level details but in-depth enough for you to understand everything. From our comms to archives. All the technologies that we are using right now."

Emma grabbed the slab of acrylic, glanced at it for a couple of minutes and put it inside her bag.

A few weeks later, Susan met up with Emma to travel to California.

***

September 2030, California, Universe Lambda-B, branched timeline, after Ashaar's arrival

Susan had been in Cali for the past few days, trying to keep an eye on Ashaar.

Just outside the restaurant where Ashaar and his family were having dinner, Joseph waited for him. He had access to high-tech zoom lenses, so he could see Ashaar's family with night vision. Joseph took control of the watch, zooming farther into the suspicious vehicles waiting around the restaurants. They were all cab drivers, except for one Ford. He leaned back in his seat and drank a cup of coffee while keeping an eye on Ashaar's entire family. Susan sat next to Joseph.

"Do you think there might be a possibility of the factions harming your sister?" he asked.

"We have been instructed to stay put and not overthink. So, I'm not trying to mix my emotions here." It made her feel nervous talking about it.

"Would you have come here to keep an eye on Ashaar if they both weren't in danger?" Joseph took another sip of his coffee.

"I love her. If only I could share everything with her. One day I will. One day I will have to. That day is coming soon." She let out a sigh, eyes darting at the distant blurry lights.

"When is that?" Joseph asked, raising his eyebrows.

"Telling her that this Ashaar isn't her real husband would compromise our operation. Sentinel feels they both have a role to perform in the overall scheme."

Joseph noticed the black Ford SUV driving past. It was fully tinted. But the car did not pull over. They drove past slowly and took a different direction.

Susan texted her boss from her burner.

> Susan: Enemy movement confirmed.

Andrew: Possibility of threat below 5%. Change of plans. Escort Ashaar to his home and return to your base by 1300hrs.

Susan: Copy.

Susan and Joseph patiently waited until they went back home. It was clear that someone was indeed trying to harm Ashaar. Some people in the vicinity were looking to kidnap him or his child. Joseph, who was military trained, and Susan, who had extensive training in firearms as an ex-Navy, were assigned to protect him for this particular night.

As Ashaar stepped inside his home, Susan made a sharp U-turn and drove off.

A few hours later, Susan and Joseph were walking up the stairs of a private jet with five windows, with two engines sticking out at its back. She bowed down to avoid hitting her head, walked forward and plunged onto one of the white seats.

Her comm buzzed instantly.

"Sentinel has made a mistake." Andrew's voice glitched in her ears. "The factions have kidnapped Ashaar."

"Fuck!" Joseph jumped off the seat. He braced himself as he stood facing Susan, his hands clenched into fists at his sides. His eyes locked onto hers, willing himself not to flinch. "What do we do now?"

"I'll have to hack faction's database and alter your details on the deep web," Andrew replied.

"Who's details? Mine or Susan's?" Joseph asked.

"Susan's," Andrew replied.

Susan heard Andrew typing on his keyboard. He said, "You are going to take the Bravo team and join a manned mission with their military leader Hasan."

Susan creased her forehead, her lips quivering, "Andrew," she paused for a second, "you want me to join the factions as a spy by myself?"

Joseph scratched his head, tapped on the side of neck twice to activate his comms, "Boss, that's very dangerous."

"There's only one way of solving this problem," Susan said. The whirring noise of their jet filled the void.

Joseph turned and eyed the pilot to remain stationed until he instructed. "So what? We'll find another way!"

"It's Sentinel's mission, Joseph, I'm sorry," Andrew said. "Rendezvous with Bravo team at 0200. You'll receive the coordinates shortly." The comm cut off.

Joseph wiped his face with his hand as he grappled with Sentinel's decision. "First, it makes a blunder. Now it's sending you on a *suicide mission.*"

Susan exhaled a deep breath and glowered at her feet. She looked up and said, "Well, you leave. I'll prepare to die."

***

Susan watched him open his eyes with a twitch, terrified and shivering. Her heart raced as Ashaar broke out in a cold sweat, her eyes darting around the cargo hull.

He was not alone.

They'd just captured Ashaar and another woman working for Sentinel.

Yanking her weapon from her bulletproof vest, Susan ruthlessly shot the blonde woman who betrayed the faction.

The sound was overwhelming. The fuselage shook with every explosion, and the air was thick with smoke. The sharp smell of burning debris invaded Susan's nostrils.

The blonde woman's artery was ripped by the bullet, blood gushing out onto the floor like a torrent of water tumbling down a canyon.

Three white halogen lights were lined up in the centre of the mostly empty cargo hold, casting a scorching glow over her lifeless body. Behind her, there were more.

Susan grazed her eyes over two more corpses, LED lights blinking from their bulletproof vests, bullet holes in their heads.

The interior of the plane was dimly lit, with rows of seats lining both sides of the fuselage. It was divided into two partitions, separated by a thick metal wall. The first partition was more subdued, with AI terminals and its operators sitting quietly at their designated desks. The second partition was filled with armed men and women dressed in full combat gear, their weapons at the ready.

Ashaar was locked up in the aft cargo hold by the factions. His interrogation erupted unceremoniously as the military aircraft hovered 45,000 feet above Earth.

Susan's comm chirped—the pilot saying they needed to stay in a holding pattern until the thunderstorm cleared.

"You didn't have to kill her." Nerves shaking, Ashaar shot his wrath-filled gaze at Susan.

"Do you know who I am?" Susan asked, voice low.

Ashaar tightened his lips, breathing heavily.

"We are the factions." She pointed her finger at a young man with a thick, trimmed beard. "That's Lieutenant Hasan. He is second-in-command for this mission."

Lieutenant Hasan crossed his arms in response.

The mild vibration of her watch shifted her attention. She tapped. September 14, 2030 emerged on the screen. The colon between the time 23 and 00 flickered in a soothing rhythm.

"She was useless to us." Susan tapped anxiously on her hand terminal as though she was in danger of having her neck snapped.

Lieutenant Hasan moved past Susan. He shifted his weight from one foot to the other as he stood before Ashaar.

Ashaar's eyes darted nervously around the room, taking in the sound-dampening walls and the flickering LED lights.

Ashaar looked up, his vision climbing the towering figure before him. The man stood like a monolith, casting a long shadow that enveloped Ashaar in its embrace.

Hasan aimed the halogen lights at him and knelt. His nostrils flared, eyes flashing with fury as he clenched his fists. Then he slapped Ashaar in the face twice.

Sweat mixed with blood flew off Ashaar's mouth, the strenuous lights causing him to perspire profusely.

Heart pounding rapidly against the hum of the aircraft, Susan watched Hasan firmly cup Ashaar's face. "Where did you come from?" he shouted, "Why are you here?"

Ashaar sighed, shaking his head. His hair ruffled, framing his face in an unstable halo. He spat blood on the floor, tensed and glared back with a cross between despise and rage.

"I'm connected to the Director now," Susan said as she switched on her hand terminal.

"But first, the truth serum," Hasan said. He held his terminal with one hand and tapped with the other. The screen flickered to life, displaying various colours and shapes, numbers and cryptographic letters flickering on screen. It was nothing short of breathtaking, with characters arranged in smooth lines.

Holding it in front of Ashaar, he forced him to stare at the screen for at least five seconds.

A lump formed in Susan's throat.

Two soldiers in blue camouflage marched forward and grabbed Ashaar's jaw, twisting his face and holding with all their strength. The nerves on their forearms were strained, veins visible from a distance. A third soldier stood in the back, pressing him down by his shoulder.

"Look at the fucking terminal," Lieutenant Hasan shouted. Micro drops of spittle flew off his mouth, hitting Ashaar's face.

Ashaar recoiled and looked away, closing his eyes. "I won't."

"*Look at it motherfucker*!"

"This won't work," Ashaar said, his heart racing. "This won't fucking work on me!"

Hasan switched off the terminal after five seconds. Soon after the director's face showed up, Susan swivelled the desk terminal and set it down in front of Ashaar on the floor.

Director Bowman leaned in. "Hello, traveller."

Ashaar exhaled a whistle that sounded like *I refuse to respond.*

"Tell us who sent you here, and we will let you go," the Director said.

"I don't know," Ashaar replied, his eyes bulging.

"You will tell us, son."

"*I don't know!*" he screamed. "I know you want to overwrite me, so you might as well get on with it," Ashaar exhaled a chuckle, his shoulder slumping.

"I will kill you if you don't talk," Bowman slammed his fist on the table, gritting his teeth in anger.

Ashaar recoiled at the sound bursting through the speakers. "I have a chip in my arm," Ashaar replied. "Sentinel can track me from anywhere."

"He's bluffing, right?" Susan asked, raising her brows.

"I'm not sure." Hasan continued tapping on his hand terminal, connecting it to Ashaar's brain. "But he will tell the truth if I force him."

Ashaar's face involuntarily began to twitch, subtle spasms playing across his features. Susan could sense an unfamiliar, almost electric sensation coursing through Ashaar's mind, as if tiny particles within his brain were stirring, awakening. It looked as though the protons in his neural pathways were resonating, aligning themselves with the rhythm of the quantum computer that was connected to Hasan's hand terminal.

"What are you doing, Hasan?" Susan crossed her arms. She noticed his excessive swallowing.

"Waterboarding in the age of AI."

"What the fuck are you doing?" Ashaar began to scream. His screams became louder and louder.

After a few seconds, his voice grew hoarse as he let out a high-pitched wail, his body tensed up. His face contorted as he let out a piercing sound.

The soldiers behind him battled to keep him pinned down on the ground. Holding by the shoulder, they nodded at two more soldiers in red camouflage to pin Ashaar down by his legs.

They pushed their rifles aside and walked forward, unfolded Ashaar's legs, and then dragged his body to let him rest against the fuselage. He stopped and vibrated for a couple of seconds. His eyes were heavy with sleep as saliva filled his mouth.

Susan tapped her foot, her eyes flicking to the clock as she grumbled under her breath.

Hasan's fingers danced on the terminal. The sound of the haptic feedback echoed around the cargo hull. "I'm going to increase the dose." He pulled up a slider on his hand terminal.

"What is this sick shit?" Susan glared at Hasan, brows on her forehead furrowed.

Ashaar let out a primal roar, his voice echoing off the walls. His face twisted in agony as he let out his pain. Blood gushed out of his nostrils like a river rushing down a gorge, signs of acute internal haemorrhage. He collapsed to the ground, his body shaking with sobs.

Everyone in the interrogation chamber observed him in horror. They had seen war, broken hands, turned legs—but they hadn't seen the force of quantum consciousness transfer pulling every single subatomic particle in the human brain apart, piece by piece.

Ashaar's eyes were bloodshot, streaked with red veins that pulsed with the beat of his heart. All he could do was scream. And he did.

As the plane shuddered, officers in the adjoining cabin and the pilots heard him incinerating the plane.

Susan stood facing him, blood boiling, her heart pounding faster. The louder Ashaar screamed, the faster her heart thudded. Susan had to find a way out of this situation. Hasan's fear had rolled into a rage, and rage had turned to a quantum matrix that ripped Ashaar's brain cells apart in front of her soldiers. She heard the whispers of her team members, and knew that she had to act fast if she wanted Ashaar to survive. She had to stop him. Hasan was torturing a man who didn't pose any threat. A horrendous, sadistic, faceless monster was emerging from Hasan's soul.

Tears filled Susan's eyes. She looked up at the ceiling, blinking her tears away.

"Tone it down, Lieutenant," Bowman added. "RV with the Whiskey team and meet us at the base," Bowman said in a pleasant tone, then his face disappeared. The terminal on the floor switched off.

“Copy that, Boss. My work is done.” Hasan pulled the slider down on his hand terminal.

Ashaar was knocked out. He was breathing, moving his chest up and down with the rhythm of his heart, barely awake.

Susan checked his pulse. “Fuck this shit.” She marched towards Hasan. “What the literal *fuck* did you do to him, Hasan?”

“I connected him to the AI, but I controlled the process of entanglement with the protons in his brain. When the subatomic particles entangle, I can control their spin to stop it partway through,” Hasan said. “He experienced the transfer, and watched millions of timelines and realities, all at once.”

The hair on her forearm stood and a shiver ran down her spine. She gripped her rifle hanging from her vest, trying to ward off the sudden coldness. She couldn’t believe a word the lieutenant said. “How did you learn to do this?”

“I swiped the guide off Bowman’s hand terminal. If it’s just sitting there unused, what’s the point? I might as well put it to good use.”

“You are fucking insane. We need him alive!” Susan exhaled a chuckle in disbelief. She freed her black and white chequered scarf from her neck and wrapped it around her left palm. Pacing to Ashaar, she said, “Jesus fucking Christ, Hasan, I....” She paused for a second, eyes about to burst out of turmoil, anger and shock. “I didn’t know you could do this.”

This kind of annihilation could have only been carried out by Sentinel. In fact, she once saw Sentinel use quantum waterboarding on faction members. She was unaware that the factions had also solved it.

A minute later, Ashaar opened his eyes. Staring at Hasan, his eyes teared up. “I ... want ...” he stuttered. “I ... have ... to say ...” Battling to speak, he directed his eyes downwards and cried.

Tears rushed down his cheeks, his face twitching in anguish, spilling all his body’s excess energy through his eyes. “I ... don’t ...” His lower lip quivered. He scowled at Hasan again and said, “You sick fuck ...”

"What the fuck did you just say?" Hasan spoke back, clenching his fist.

Ashaar replied, tears stinging his eyes and mouth overflowing with saliva, "You should have killed me."

Susan swerved her neck and gaped at Hasan with sheer incredulity. Her heart couldn't take more shock than she was ready for during those ten minutes. Warfare never had that kind of impact on her.

Hasan placed his finger on his hand terminal to gesture to Ashaar that he would rerun the programme if he didn't speak up. "Go ahead."

Ashaar exhaled with his eyes closed. "I came from the universe ... Alpha. I was a scientist ... at a quantum consciousness transfer ... uh ... programme. They built a ... a ... tunnel. It only opens," he spat blood from his mouth, scowled at it for a couple of seconds on the ground and continued, "They built it to ... test a theory." He cleared his throat, "... sending consciousness back in time. I was in the lab when it ... exploded. And now here."

"Can you give us the exact location and time of the explosion?" Susan stooped, resting her forearm on her knee.

Ashaar nodded. "Yes."

"You are stronger than I thought," Hasan said. "Tough man."

Ashaar's eyes narrowed in anger, his lips curling into a sneer as he scowled at the lieutenant who had wronged him.

"You are on the wrong side of the fight, Ashaar." Hasan exhaled, nodding in a slight wobble. "I'm just a means of managing the army. Disposable. If Sentinel kills me, there are thousands ready to take my place. You don't have a clue what it's capable of. We are just trying to save our people."

"Hasan, you need to let him go," Susan intervened.

He spun rapidly, tugged Susan and walked towards a corner. "You need to let me do this."

"No, Hasan," she replied, her lips curling into a sneer. "I have operational command here. You can't violate my order."

"If that's the case," Hasan yanked his handgun and pointed it at Susan, veins visible on his neck, "*you die*! I'm going to kill you."

Susan raised her hands in the air. "Hasan, calm down."

Hasan moved his finger, activating his weapon. The clicking noise was alarming in the stillness of the atmosphere. His smile was forced and unsteady, his eyes darted around the aircraft.

Susan made eye contact with Ashaar from a distance. There was hesitancy in his gaze.

Ashaar heard a muffled tick. He gently pulled on his handcuffs, realising it was unlocked. He kept his hands still. Susan drew Ashaar's focus to the two red camouflaged soldiers standing before him. There was a slight moment of acceptance between him and Susan.

She knew that Ashaar had no idea who she was or what she was after. She might be part of a conspiracy out to get him and he had no way of knowing. All he could do was trust her. She looked at the soldier in blue camo standing behind Ashaar and gestured.

With a scream of distress, Ashaar got to his feet and launched himself at one of the red camo troops, smashing him against the fuselage. Behind him, two other troops began to fire on Hasan. Bullets entered his skull and left the other side, soaking Susan with blood. Hasan fell instantly.

Two soldiers in red camo pointed their guns at Susan's team, and before they could react, the sound of gunfire filled the air. The world seemed to slow down as they saw the flashes of light from the muzzles of the rifles. They killed the two soldiers in red camo and arrested the rest of the unarmed crew.

Ashaar dropped his weight onto the floor, trembling and gasping for air. As blood gushed out of Hasan's face, Susan recoiled, closing her eyes. Then she smashed Hasan's hand terminal on the floor and crushed it under her boots. Her rugged work boots were scuffed and worn.

Susan tapped her comm twice behind her right ear, and said to the pilot, "Mission complete. RV with the Bravo team here," she said, tapping in the coordinates on her device.

Her comm glitched with a response. "Copy that."

In the distance, she watched her soldiers drag Ashaar to a chair and unstrap him. His hands shook, his eyes darting around as he fidgeted with his wrist and cleared his throat. She briskly approached the aircraft. She stood tall with a fixed stare. She bent down and held Ashaar's shoulders. "I'm sorry for what Hasan did to you. We're taking you to safety."

"Sorry if I'm having a hard time ... trusting you right now." Ashaar took a few deep breaths with his eyes closed.

Susan rapidly whipped out an EpiPen-like device and punched it into Ashaar's shoulder. "There."

Ashaar winced at the sudden sting. "What the hell did you ..."

"It's military-grade nanobots," Susan explained. "They'll accelerate your healing. You should be able to speak normally again in a few hours."

Her soldiers took out a few devices with blinking blue and red LEDs, circular in shape like explosives. They placed the devices all over the cargo hull. Susan sighed, yet her eyes glistened with hope as she stared through the window while their aircraft descended.

The rain pounded against the fuselage. Sudden bright light flashes filled the space, followed by a deep, rumbling boom that shook the windows. "Strap the parachute on your back and prepare to jump."

Ashaar took the backpack, eyes widening in horror, "You want me to jump out of this fucking aircraft?" He coughed and said, "Are you having a laugh?"

"You have three minutes." Susan tapped her comm and announced, "Activate autopilot sequence. We are leaving in three." Susan secured the belt tightly over Ashaar's chest, her voice firm yet encouraging, "You can do this."

Ashaar, panic-stricken, stammered, "Wait, woah ... woah ... wait."

Ignoring his protests, Susan, with her team in tow, quickly ushered him towards the emergency hatch. With a decisive yank, she flung it open, and the fierce wind rushed in, engulfing them. "We're jumping now. After we jump, count to seven then pull your strap," she instructed, her hand gripping Ashaar's shoulder firmly.

"Susan, you can't do this to—"

Ashaar's protest was cut short as Susan pushed him out into the open sky as his scream trailed off in the distance. Without hesitation, Susan leaped after him, the wind battering her face as she plummeted. The others swiftly followed suit.

Seven seconds later, parachutes bloomed open, their descent slowing as they gracefully glided towards an open field. Susan reached for the button on her gear and pressed it. In the sky above, the aircraft exploded mid-air, erupting in a spectacular blaze that illuminated the night sky.

Chapter 20: Ashaar

4 October 2030, London, Universe Lambda-B

After Ashaar was rescued, Susan and her team flew to London and dropped him off at a hotel, next to the British Library. Before leaving, Susan gave her an address for Dr Alex Andrew-Ng and asked Ashaar to meet with him at 6 p.m.

The following day Ashaar took a cab and started his journey. The city's layout was a physically mirrored manifestation of the one he'd left behind. Nonetheless, the future was clear: short-haul aerial transport, delivery drones screening traffic, delivery bots handing over packages and AI taxis ruling the road. He was dropped off by the driverless cab in front of a residential area in West London. Ashaar couldn't understand why a large company would possibly have an office in the middle of nowhere. He started walking.

In the alleyway were a bunch of garages. There were lots of cars left in front, looking like they were being taken apart for second-hand parts. Ashaar continued to walk and follow the road. It took him five minutes to finally find the area. It was, in reality, an industrial kitchen with arrows pointing at delivery companies' logos. Ashaar sent Andrew a text.

A long few minutes later, Ashaar saw a figure approaching in the distance.

"Ashaar, come with me," Andrew said.

Andrew took Ashaar through an industrial kitchen where multiple vendors had set up their food delivery services. They continued walking until someone opened a vault-like lift door right at the end of the kitchen. Once inside, Ashaar looked to his left-hand side and found a lift. The narrow entrance opened onto the lift as he approached. One soldier waiting outside the lift stepped aside as Andrew swiped his card. The guard wasn't lightly armoured. The bulletproof jacket appeared to be a strength-augmented high-viz body armour made from some form of carbon. There were several weapons mounted on his shoulder, belt and armour. The suit was black, with the logo of *Sentinel* attached to the arm.

The logo was shaped like a prism.

A 9mm attached to the front, right in the middle of his chest, had a fingerprint reader. Once the door opened, the security pulled a hand terminal out of his pocket and activated the X-ray that bounced off Andrew and Ashaar's bodies. The guard's eyes were gloomy and inflamed.

Ashaar was suddenly reminded of Emma's explanation of a prism from long before. It was Sentinel's logo. The memory ran a tremor down his spine. "Wow, it all makes sense now." Ashaar's stomach turned and gave a tiny muscle spasm. "She was having visions from this universe!"

"Don't worry, Ashaar, we are not going to kill you. You are safe."

The lift doors slid apart with a hiss. Ashaar surveyed the area, noticing that quantum computing servers were the source of power for all systems. Several engineers were at their workstations in the centre of the room, and at the end of the lab was a room with a glass-walled, giant vault. It was obvious that the large server, or rather several of them, was running a quantum supercomputer. The acrylic glass walls that divided the rooms allowed him to observe everything from his position.

The primary server room was somewhere between one-half and two-quarters full. Security stood right outside the lab, nodding at each other, eyes sharp and jaws clinched. One of the lab engineers laughed in the corner of the room, which sounded and smelled of terror. Ashaar observed the enhanced computing capabilities while making his way to the room housing the supercomputer. Andrew had convinced Ashaar, or so it seemed, by his reaction. When he got near the vault, his eyes nearly popped out. A wave of cold air hit him, causing him to gasp. Ashaar couldn't believe it, he had walked into the place he was looking for. He discovered the quantum processor, sealed inside a bulletproof acrylic vault, where an array of luminous cables extended. He looked above and saw a quantum frame, built with titanium, with three pillars. It was right behind the supercomputer.

The near-impossible had been achieved by Andrew and his team, kudos to a few generalisations and some modern solutions. This team's work in the lab committed to putting quantum mechanical theories about reactions to the test utilising actual experimental data. It seemed as if Andrew and his collaborators were able to gather data from a previously unexplored quantum frontier, providing firm evidence of what the theoretical model got right (and wrong) and the roadmap for further exploration into the next shadowy layers of quantum space. It was only a matter of time before Ashaar would uncover where precisely the data had come from: the past, or the future.

Andrew opened the door to the server vault and introduced Ashaar to the quantum supercomputer. "Here's our AI, Sentinel. It is our mission commander. It has over 1,000,000 quantum qubits."

"That's a lot. What's the purpose?"

"It's for compiling data from multiple timelines created because of the existence of multiple parallel universes," a voice appeared from the back. "You are in a branched timeline of the Lambda universe. It's called Lambda-B."

Ashaar spun around to find a ring light and two blue LED light strips affixed to the server. Each time Sentinel's server emitted a sound, these lights flickered and pulsed in response, visually echoing its activity.

He was in disbelief at the events unfolding. It was truly miraculous, this machine. Ashaar glanced at Andrew and arched an eyebrow.

"You need to sign our non-disclosure first." Andrew handed over the terminal to Ashaar. After reading the summary, Ashaar drew his signature at the bottom of the document.

He watched another member of staff walk past with two large aluminium suitcases, which looked like guns.

"They are carrying quantum pulse repeaters. They help us send intel to Sentinel." Andrew stared at Tom walking away, turned around and looked into Ashaar's eyes.

Andrew gestured to Ashaar to walk with him. Setting his sight on Ashaar, he said, "Sentinel and I come from the original timeline deemed as Lambda-A, from the year 2200. Our enemies, the factions have destroyed that timeline. That's why I've been tasked with travelling back in time and stopping the factions from annihilating our planet."

"Why am I here?" Ashaar asked, returning the terminal to Andrew.

"Sentinel believes that your involvement is critical for our success."

"I don't understand, Andrew. I'm from a different universe...."

"Initially, we were supposed to work with Lambda Ashaar. But our results kept telling us that Lambda Ashaar would die in the branched timeline. We couldn't understand why."

"And then?" Ashaar wiped his hand over his face.

"Then, the plans evolved. Sentinel needed to access the complete internet infrastructure of the Alpha universe while the factions were eyeing it. That's when Sentinel predicted that your lab would explode. So it moved mountains to capture your consciousness and transfer you to Lambda Ashaar's body right before his death because of a brain haemorrhage."

"Oh my good Lord." Ashaar kept biting the corner of his hand, eyes darting around. "But why does it need me in particular?"

"Because Sentinel believes your contribution is indispensable for our success," he clasped his hands, pursing his lips. "You are the dot that connects us to a quantum physics expert. Her name is Emma."

"Who?" Shock reverberated through Ashaar's spine. "Wait, who? Emma?" His mouth fell open.

"Correct, her name is Emma Herrmann."

Ashaar was frozen. His mind raced to keep pace with the surge of adrenaline coursing through him. The revelation hit him with the force of a detonated warhead. It took him a moment to fully comprehend the reality that Lambda Emma was now intricately woven into the fabric of this perilous mission.

"When Emma—Lambda Emma—was working for Oscar's start-up Hyperion, Sentinel accessed her personal computer and sent intel to her. The data is stored in her brain. We must retrieve the data."

"Jesus. So you can store information in people's heads?"

Andrew replied with a strong nod.

Ashaar shifted his eyes to look at Sentinel. It felt as if the AI was watching him, observing his every move. He swallowed a lump and thought about the million possibilities of this mission.

Andrew sharply interrupted Ashaar, his eyes locked, watching a ring light flash, mounted on the quantum supercomputer. "We packaged the data, hacked into her company's mainframe, and launched our command on her computer. From Lambda Emma's perspective, it was a random animation. All she needed to do was look at it for five seconds. The data was packaged and sent to her brain." Andrew responded to Ashaar while the lights blinked faster. Sentinel in the background continuously listened to the conversation, watching them through its convex lens. Through the corner of his eye, Ashaar noticed its camera lens shifting.

"So, you need to extract the data, and then what?" Ashaar walked closer to Sentinel, staring at the lights. He felt hesitant to walk inside the glass vault that protected it. "What do I get out of it?"

Andrew chuckled, "We send you back home. To the Alpha universe."

Ashaar wanted to say, "Oh, thank God," but he couldn't form any words. He stared at Andrew for a few seconds before asking, "What's the guarantee that you will send me back?"

"Once our mission is successful, we will fully operationalise your transfer using three parts of its algorithm. One is downloaded from the future, the second is taken from a guy called Ben, and the last is in Emma's memory. We need the full code to activate multiversal consciousness transfer and send you back to Alpha."

Ashaar noticed one of Andrew's associates approach his desk and pick up a marker to draw a diagram of different timelines.

Ashaar stood in front of the board and studied the diagram with all his available concentration. "How are you going to send my consciousness across space-time? You have to know my exact location." Ashaar's gaze shifted to Andrew, who stood in a defensive posture, arms folded.

"That's why we use a process called TACT. Time, Amplitude, Coordinates and Telemetry." Andrew wrote the word TACT on the board. "You are a pretty curious person, I must say."

"Sorry. I'm just ... curious ... and overwhelmed. And that's your gateway to the fourth dimension. Wow." A shiver ran down Ashaar's spine, and he felt a prickling sensation on his skin as tiny bumps rose along his arms.

Andrew's associate dragged an object from her hand-terminal to the large screen hanging from the ceiling. "This is what the interface to the fourth dimension looks like," she showed an animation that displayed random numbers constantly changing their form, and a prism-like shape in the middle.

Ashaar turned to face the AI's camera, pointing his finger at its server. "So ... this AI was built in the Lambda-A timeline? And it's communicating from the future?"

Andrew took two steps forward to stand next to Ashaar. "It is. Sentinel is an advanced version that combines Cognition's GPT, particle accelerator and your 'Quantitative' lab. Now, it has access to the past and the future in multiple universes." He pulled the glass door to the vault open, eyeing Ashaar to step in.

"Motherfucker Oscar really built that shit," Ashaar stepped inside, and stood before the AI. He glared at his own reflection on the convex lens attached to a wide-angle camera in the middle.

Andrew nodded and continued, "Indeed. In Lambda-A, after Sentinel took over the government, our enemies, the factions wanted their AI too. Then they evolved from a start-up into a criminal organisation. Those bastards somehow replicated Cognition's GPT and learned to time travel with their AI. Sentinel sent me and a few others back in time to 2030 to stop them."

"So this ...?" Ashaar waved his finger. "Is this what they're after?"

"In this timeline, the factions are planning to steal Sentinel's code," Andrew said. "In my timeline, they stole the source code and used it to develop their own quantum AI. They failed. After decades of trying, the factions discovered a way to time-jump and arrive in the past. Now, Sentinel ..." Andrew tapped his finger on the glass wall of the vault, "Sentinel thinks that the factions are evolving. The factions want to integrate their quantum AI with Sentinel's to simultaneously enable time-jumping and accessing the multiverse."

"How?" Ashaar asked, swallowing a lump.

"Their AI discovered a quantum matrix in the Alpha universe that could hold tons of consciousness. They're hoping to move and get established."

Ashaar closed his eyes. A sharp sensation overtook his nervous system. This had to be an aftereffect of time travel and multiverse travel. "Hold up. This is so much to take in."

"We can talk another day, Ashaar."

"No." Ashaar opened his eyes, vision blurring for a second before returning to normal.

Ashaar stepped out of the vault, feeling slightly disorientated. He pulled onto the collar of his sweater, heat gathering in his chest. The door behind him softly shut itself. "How the fuck are you going to stop them?"

Andrew began walking back to his desk. "The factions know that Sentinel evolved from Cognition's code. So in about a couple of months, they are planning to merge CognitionGPT with another shell company that this man owns." Andrew held up a terminal before Ashaar.

"Director Bowman ... how can I forget? He spoke with me when I was kidnapped." Ashaar held that terminal in his hand, staring at it.

Andrew's associate was trying to tighten a screw on one of the servers behind Andrew. She said, "We need to stop that merger from happening. Stella is part of that ultimate mission."

"You have to convince Stella to help us stop Bowman. They are planning a hostile takeover of CognitionGPT to get their hands on their quantum algorithm." Andrew grabbed the terminal from Ashaar's hand and started tapping. He wiped his finger across his terminal, browsing through several photos. He said, "You know what's crazy? The factions ... they tried attacking the Alpha universe but failed because their AI misfired."

"It was my flight back from Turin, wasn't it?" Ashaar turned his eyes to Andrew. "It was *them*? For fuck's sake," Ashaar's body trembled at his statement.

"You were lucky nothing happened. They tried to overwrite the entire aircraft and send their team members into the bodies of all those innocent people. They could have overwritten all of you," Andrew replied.

Ashaar gulped and stared into Andrew's eyes for a few seconds. He saw flashes of the aircraft full of passengers screaming at the top of their lungs. He strode towards a revolving chair and sat down, his eyes gazing at the wiring running underneath the floor. Ashaar's stomach churned and his palms grew clammy. He rubbed his fingers over his skin on the back of his hand.

It was a few minutes later when Andrew brought a cup of coffee for Ashaar. Heat billowed from the cup, filling the room with the smell of fresh brew. "If we don't change the future, billions will perish because of an AI virus that the factions will create in the future."

"What else do you know?" Ashaar grabbed the cup.

Andrew sat down and continued, "We know a lot about the future, nothing good though. And it's changing."

"Still, everything you've said are predictions made by Sentinel. We don't know what'll happen." Ashaar slowly sipped his coffee. "Andrew, this might sound like a random question, but do you know a woman called Stephanie Maddox?"

"Stephanie is our archivist from the Alpha universe."

"That's why she had that data archive." The coffee tasted strong and bitter with every sip. Ashaar recalled his memory of when he visited Stephanie's house. "Emma told me about finding a futuristic antechamber in Stephanie's backyard."

"Sentinel's data archive. That's where she is storing all the data," Andrew replied.

A moment later, Ashaar's attention was drawn to another woman, appearing to be in her 30s, approaching the room. With a swift motion, she swiped her card and entered. Her looks struck Ashaar with a sense of familiarity; she bore an uncanny resemblance to someone he knew. A second later, he realised that the woman looked like Stella, Lambda Ashaar's wife.

"Hello, Ashaar. I'm the programmer in this timeline."

"Hey ..." Ashaar yelled, his eyes squinting, "*Susan?*"

"I wondered if you would recognise me." Susan dragged a trolley with her. It had a bunch of computer parts on it.

"How would I? You hid your face when you rescued me from the factions. Are you Stella's biological sister?"

"I am."

"What are you doing here in this lab? Does Stella know?" Ashaar asked and stood next to Susan, crossing his arms.

"No, Stella doesn't know anything. I am an archivist. I store DNA data in my blood." Susan unloaded the parts and placed them inside a metal case. She placed her finger on the drawer. It displayed her name, unlocked and opened itself.

Ashaar noticed a bunch of marks on her side-arm. She wore a sleeveless top with a turtleneck. He noted her scars and a couple of incisions on her arm that looked like stitches. "Like Stephanie?" Ashaar asked.

"Yep." Susan stared at Ashaar while carefully placing the items inside the cabinet.

"I can't help but say thank you for saving me that night."

"It was a mission from Sentinel," Susan gently nudged the drawer, it slowly closed itself. Susan paused for a few seconds as she heard someone talking to her over a comm device inserted under her ear. She said, "We need to go now. We don't have enough time."

"Where?" Ashaar asked.

"You will see," Susan said.

***

They split into two vehicles. Ashaar trailed the car carrying Andrew and Susan. As they navigated through the streets of London, Ashaar kept a steady pace behind them. About an hour later, he found himself at the Mile End leisure centre. They parked and walked towards the building. Though every shutter was down, something remained concealed from those on the outside. A lot had changed in the past eight years, and Ashaar didn't have the neural capacity to process everything.

The time was already past noon. Using a twenty-year-old manual lock, Susan opened the shutter.

"I still don't understand how Emma is connected to all this," Ashaar asked and followed Susan into the dark storage.

"We've told you what we know." Andrew flipped a circuit breaker to turn on the lights. "Sentinel only shares intel when it needs to."

"Seems like Sentinel has a direct connection with Emma," Ashaar asked. "If it did, wouldn't it share that info with all of you?"

"No," Andrew added. "You are our connection to Emma. That's all we know, and that's all Sentinel has shared with us."

They continued walking down a spiral staircase and discovered a massive underground warehouse. As Susan lifted a lever and touched the terminal, the lights sequentially illuminated and a thumping sound arose. "This is our uranium 235 reserve. It's going to power Sentinel."

"We have spent a lot of money protecting this place," Andrew added.

"Do we have any knowledge about the people funding these factions?" Ashaar asked.

"The factions and the people funding them are extremely wealthy, have deals with many corrupt governments around the world and control a massive amount of money," Andrew replied. "After they conquer the Lambda universe, they'll eventually want to trace the source of that alien quantum matrix in Alpha, and then exploit the information for their own purposes."

"To do what?" Ashaar asked.

"I'm not sure," Andrew said.

Ashaar's gaze followed Andrew as he stepped towards a terminal strategically mounted on one of the structural pillars. The terminal, acting like a central hub, was connected to many wires and monitored the uranium 235 containers in the warehouse. Despite being located underground, the space was impressively vast. It stretched upwards to a height of almost three stories and spanned across an area that Ashaar estimated to be at least 10,000 square feet. The sheer size of the underground facility was both surprising and imposing. He looked at Susan and asked, “Have you tried to calculate the final results?”

Susan turned on the computer to check whether one of the tanks was being picked up by a courier later that day. She pulled the plug from the tank, brought a forklift and manoeuvred the tank out. “The outcome changes depending on the timeline within each universe. For instance, in one of the branched timelines, we all are friends and you are married to Alpha Emma.” Susan dropped the tank in an area marked in red delivery zone. The magnetic clamps underneath made a loud thumping noise, as the lights on the LED display turned red.

The smell reminded him of something rich and raw, a metallic-garlic odour when it’s exposed to oxygen. “Really?” Ashaar asked. The warehouse echoed with the persistent beeping of a forklift as its rhythmic sound cut through the silence. Flashing yellow lights from it intermittently illuminated the vast, dimly lit space.

Susan parked the forklift and jumped out of the driver’s seat. “We need just to catch a train that takes us to the right one.”

Andrew took a pen out of his pocket. “Keep this. This is your comms device. You’ll need to inject it on your neck right where your hairline ends.” Andrew put his finger on Ashaar’s neck underneath his right eye, and showed him exactly where the device should be placed. “And you’ll need to learn about the device.” He pulled up a 3D design of a communication device on his hand terminal and showed it to Ashaar. “I can just do it for you.”

“No thanks, I’ll do it myself.”

Andrew opened a locker and handed over a bag. “Take this. No more questions for today.”

Ashaar found a hand terminal assigned to his biomarker, and a convertible laptop, air-gapped and protected with strong armour. There was also a bunch of bitcoin storage devices.

Andrew stepped forward, lifted his terminal and hovered it over Ashaar’s hand terminal. The indicator on it shifted as if an overriding mechanism was activated. “You will need these for the next month. Everything should be done with crypto. It's safer. Just remember Ashaar, you help us end the factions and complete our grand final mission, and then you get to go home."

Ashaar felt the weight of the responsibility settling on his shoulders. As he looked down at the hand terminal, now synced with Sentinel's team, he realised he was stepping into a world far more complex and secretive than he had ever imagined.

Chapter 21: Andrew

October 2030, Universe Lambda-B

Andrew walked into the darkened hall like he didn't belong there. He kept his head down, scanning the room as if expecting someone to stop him. The glow of the LED banner at the front read "Historians," and its sharp white light pulsed against the shadows like a warning.

He took a slow breath and found a seat near the back, eyes never leaving the stage. He didn't speak to anyone.

It was a classified briefing. A major update from Sentinel meant only for team leads and authorised historians. Moments later, the lights dimmed fully.

Someone stepped onto the stage and started the film.

Andrew looked around and could see only ten people in the room. A man tapped the microphone and asked for attention. His face was visible as the projector's light hit the side of his face. With a sombre tone of voice, he spoke, "You all have been tasked with something important. Please look at the welcome package provided on your chair."

Everyone looked quietly at the screen.

"This 'update' will provide you with a precise idea of what's going to happen. The data has been sent by Sentinel," the announcement was loud and grim.

Andrew swallowed a lump at the thought of watching simultaneous occurrences.

"Just so you are aware, your nervous system will try to exist in a quantum superposition. Therefore, you are likely to see multiple futures occurring simultaneously."

Someone from the back raised a hand.

"Please wait until I finish." The person on the stage walked back and forth. "You are in charge of the finances. The probabilities are 99 out of 100 times you are likely to predict the future accurately. Now, you will receive an update."

Words appeared on the screen, "Welcome."

"Andrew, please stay back when the film is over," the man added.

Everyone in the room blinked rapidly, a physical response to the overwhelming revelations.

Tears welled up in Andrew's eyes as his mind was overloaded with information that seemed extraneous yet crucial. He sat down, his hands trembling as they clutched the edges of his chair. His memory was updated with new probabilities on this branched timeline.

Andrew sat motionless. His eyes were transfixed on the screen but his mind journeyed far beyond it, traversing the intricate pathways of his past. He saw the timeline as it originally unfolded, with Sentinel standing as a testament to human ingenuity in quantum superintelligence. The memory of the engineers from Lambda-A who designed its mainframe using a harmonious blend of elements like copper, sapphire, aluminium and even uranium 235, was etched vividly in his memory.

He recalled the early days of the 2030s at Cognition from the Lambda-A, where he was part of the pioneering team that developed the first quantum computing chip. The journey from there to the creation of quantum memory storage in 2060 felt both long and fleeting in his recollection. Those memory storage devices, or memristors, mirrored the human brain's design, and had been a groundbreaking step, a stride towards merging the complexities of the human mind with the precision of quantum computing.

In his mind, Andrew remembered the birth of quantum memory, the crux of Sentinel. He remembered the awe he felt the first time Sentinel's quantum mind was distributed across servers worldwide, its presence expanding even to satellites orbiting the earth.

Then came the war, a cataclysmic event that ruptured the fabric of his reality, sending him hurtling back through time. In Lambda-B, a branched timeline, he found himself in 2030 once more, but with a monumental task—to rebuild Sentinel, and to avert the collapse of humanity in Lambda.

As he sat there, Andrew could sense the tides of change swelling around him. The future, once so certain in his mind, now hung in the balance. Its course was now uncertain and fraught with challenges yet to be faced.

The screen turned blank.

He looked at the blank screen. Tears pricked his cheeks as he observed the future. As his eyes locked with the photon particles of the screen, his brain began storing intel of every future from all timelines from that moment onwards. The screen before him blurred into a mere backdrop as he grappled with the weight of what lay ahead.

Now, he knew what would happen over the next ten years. He knew what was needed to make sure his team could complete the last mission. The "update" was complete.

At the end of the film, everyone left but Andrew. A lady, one of the other historians, walked up to Andrew and provided him with a pink slip. "This will give you all the funding required to complete all the missions. Sentinel must be protected to ensure the survival of our species." She handed him two EpiPen devices containing nanobots.

"The other is for Ashaar, I believe?"

"Yes," the woman nodded. "He has a few days left before he his brain starts seeing multiple futures at once. His brain cells were heavily damaged after what Hasan did during the siege." She lowered her voice, "What's Lambda Emma's status?"

"She's safe for now."

"The code in her memory?" the woman asked.

"Safe," Andrew replied, pushing the EpiPen devices into his jacket's pocket.

"Intel suggests that someone's gonna infiltrate your base." The lady, her brow furrowed in agitation, walked towards the entrance as the last audience members trickled out of the echoing hall.

"What? Who? I didn't see anything during the update," Andrew walked alongside her.

The lady shut the entrance and secured the lock, "I still don't know who it is. But something is definitely going to happen. We need to make sure Emma and Ashaar are safe. They are the keys to stopping our planet from collapsing."

***

The same day

Andrew returned to the headquarters. Feeling under the weather, he gained his composure once he met Susan. He placed one of the EpiPens in his biometrically locked drawer. The nanobots danced to the beat of the surrounding sound for a couple of seconds like ferro-liquid once he placed it inside the drawer. These synthetic programmable bots could act as living organisms once inserted into the human body. The nanobots were primarily used for cell or tissue damage repair. The military-grade was one step higher, which could also stop bullets from harming an individual. It was like a bulletproof vest, without the vest.

"What did you want to discuss?" Susan asked, approaching Andrew's desk.

"Here is the list of stock trades and options you will need to look at. Please choose one other member of your team and redistribute the load. This will keep them afloat. I'll take care of the rest."

The next thing Susan did was return to her desk and begin working on the transactions she had to make.

Back in the office hall, Andrew experienced a vision. He knew exactly what was going to happen to everyone in his team. But the number one rule for being a historian was that they cannot intervene in any of them.

Andrew ignored the vision, grabbed his coat and left the office.

An hour later, he was sitting with a group of people in a circle and talking about their history of drug abuse. Some had a history with cocaine. Some had a history of coding. Andrew felt he needed to share his thoughts. He needed to finish this up and go back soon.

The man leading the intervention smiled at Andrew and said, "Do you want to share your thoughts? This is a safe space."

Andrew sat motionless, his body sweating bullets and eyes twitching at the thought of sharing the burden of his knowledge.

"Hello everyone, my name is 2HB." He felt a stinging sensation, "I have come here from the future, from the year 2200. I've taken the name of my host, Andrew Alex-Ng."

Everyone in the room glanced at each other in disbelief as to why that one guy spoke like a whacky moron.

"My consciousness was transferred to the mind of Andrew. There are nine other historians, just like me. But I have been tasked with a monumental work, to establish the protocol that will give Sentinel permanent access to the Earths in 21st century across the multiverse."

He swallowed a lump, and continued, "I was born in the year 2100. After I turned 16, my parents sent me to work on a project called Sentinel AI. After consciousness transfer was invented, Sentinel chose me as a test subject. Mostly because he knew my body was ageing, and that I would be a valuable asset to his team. After my first consciousness transfer, I was transferred to the body of another historian."

"That's ... that's insane," a woman in the room said. The crowd sat motionless, listening to every word carefully.

Andrew's pulse began racing, his voice shaking as he spoke. "I am not who I am. I am a historian, and I have been burdened with the knowledge of knowing what will happen to the people around me. I do not know how to take control of this situation because I have been tasked with managing the mission. I can't save my fucking friends from dying! I am a motherfucking *fraud*!" Andrew's voice was caught on his lips. He turned on the hand terminal, frantically trying to find something he wanted to share with Ashaar.

A lady wearing loose mom jeans and a hoodie quickly drew a weapon and pointed it at Andrew. She was fast. Andrew could see the bullet coming at him in slow motion. He sweated. But he couldn't move. Time froze, and he was paralysed.

A high-pitch noise took over. Andrew blanked out for a second. Moments later, someone stood up and held his arm, "Andrew, are you alright? Do we need to take you to the hospital?"

"What happened?" Andrew asked the woman holding his arm.

"You were blank. For like the past two minutes," the woman said.

Andrew realised everything he said after "hello" was a potential timeline, the aftershock of that update.

The woman looked familiar to Andrew. She was the one who drew the weapon in his vision. This time, he hastily checked her out for anything valuable. From the outside, he searched for a big object or form that would have bulged out of her pocket. As for Andrew, he couldn't find anything. He needed to have the nanobots injected quickly.

Andrew asked the lady politely to step back. She listened and went back to her chair. Something was wrong with her, or that was how he felt. He assumed she was one of the faction members and was sent here to keep an eye on Andrew. He memorised her face and looked for any signs that might be useful while she sat there.

Andrew walked out, and the door's click echoed the decisiveness that filled his heart. He pulled the other EpiPen from his pocket. He placed it on his arm, and hard pressed the button, his face twitching as the nanobots entered his bloodstream.

There was a path he had to follow, solitary, might that be. He slammed open the door to the exit. His steps echoed down the corridor, spilling out into the muffled silence of the alleyway.

He swiped his access card across a glowing red sensor, slipped into his car, and pulled away. Rain lashed at the windshield, the wipers frenetic against the downpour. Each drop was a symphony to the turmoil within.

Chapter 22: Ashaar

Early October 2030, London, Universe Lambda

Ashaar's slumber was interrupted at 6 a.m. by the insistent ring of his phone. Today was significant. He was scheduled to meet with Lambda Emma. After swiftly getting out of bed, he dressed in a crisp black shirt paired with denim jeans.

In the kitchen, he filled a bottle with water and threw his medication into his mouth. The migraines still plagued this version of himself, an inconvenient ailment, especially during times of crisis. He ran down the silent stairs of his Airbnb, the quietness of the early morning enveloping him.

Outside, he approached the rental car he had arranged a few days earlier. As he started the engine and pulled away from the kerb, his hand terminal chimed.

His comm chirped immediately after.

"Do you have the coordinates of my location?" Susan asked Ashaar over his comm device.

"I received a text this morning. I have them."

"See you in forty minutes, Ashaar." The comm gently chirped and shut down.

Ashaar pulled up at a house in east London near Hackney. A heatwave passed through London that week. Outside, the weather was 26 degrees Celsius in October, a rare two-day occasion. There was a car on the driveway, so he parked outside on the road. He walked in, after knocking on the door. He saw a camera look at him like it scanned with a flashing red horizontal infrared light. Ashaar felt anxious because he couldn't predict what would happen. The door opened.

Ashaar walked through the door to see Andrew and Susan. The living room consisted of a set of partitioned areas, and the walls had been painted silk-patterned black colour that mimicked the acoustic soundproofing foams. It smelled of artificial lilac, equipped with military-grade air-recycling equipment. As he stepped forward, he saw Joseph standing in the living room, he offered Ashaar a handshake. A second later, a lady walked down the stairs, into the living room with a cup of tea in her hand. Ashaar glanced at the person and couldn't simply believe what he saw.

It, in fact, was Emma. She looked exactly like the Emma he left in his universe. She had the exact same hair, eyes, height, and wore a light blue top over black tights. She hadn't changed. The only difference was that she rocketed up the corporate ladder.

"Hi." Emma shot a grin.

Ashaar's heart dropped the minute he heard her voice.

"Hey." Ashaar took a second to respond to Emma. "Have you been briefed already?"

"I have. I was contacted by Andrew a few months ago. They explained everything. Well, he and Susan."

"So you know who I am?" Ashaar asked.

"I do. You are Alpha Ashaar?"

The term "Alpha Ashaar" still felt alien, clashing weirdly with his sense of self. With a slight purse of his lips, he shifted his gaze, wrestling with the unfamiliar identity and location. Then, turning a hard stare towards Susan, he poised himself. "Are we being briefed for our upcoming missions?"

"Yes, you'll be. Let's all grab some food and take a seat. Do you want any drink, Ashaar?" Susan insisted.

"Sure." Ashaar nodded. "What is this place, Susan?"

"It's one of our safehouses. Hidden in plain sight," Susan replied.

Ashaar, Emma, Susan and Joseph were later briefed about their upcoming missions by Andrew.

"Ash, you will need to stay at a safehouse here, and in Munich," Andrew added. "It's outside the city and will have a quantum pulse repeater in place, which will ensure Sentinel can continuously monitor you and keep that house safe at any cost. We strongly believe that the factions are also looking for Ben. He's the most valuable asset for us because he's the only person capable of extracting the data from Emma's memory without any invasive procedure." Andrew continued, "He also has the original code that will enable the extraction process."

"And what if he can't extract the memory?" Ashaar asked.

"He's not going to fail," Andrew said. "We need him to carry out the procedure."

***

The next day, the team arrived at the safehouse in Hackney. Ashaar hadn't been in this city for so long. London in the Alpha and Lambda universes looked pretty much the same. As the trees flew by, he thought this entire story was a single continuous dream for a second. The heat from the sun, 27 degrees Celsius in October, made it easier for him to believe that it was indeed a different universe.

Emma, Ashaar and Susan were asked to temporarily stay at the safehouse with Andrew for the next couple of days.

Susan and Ashaar were in the living room. Ashaar could really go for a big cup of iced coffee. He thought about making a cup and holding it under his nose, smelling the aroma. Caffeine triggered his migraine. It never used to. But he wanted it.

Instead, he sat there and tried hard to think about the aroma of the coffee and how it would release beta-endorphins. The typically talkative Susan was quiet. She cleaned her firearm. After cleansing the inside, she left it on the table. She looked at it with a ridiculous amount of concentration, as if using her force to fire it. Emma was not in the room. As long as Ashaar's mind was occupied with the thought of coffee, he didn't have to think and overthink everything that was going on.

Susan's hand terminal rang.

The ringtone ruined Ashaar's daydream, the silence he enjoyed.

"Guys, I need to go now," Susan said. "Andrew asked me to visit the Whitechapel hospital for a recon mission." She took her backpack, hid her handgun in her jacket and covered it up with a weird object, an object made of a bendable LED that completely hid everything behind it. The technology was beyond even this time.

Twenty minutes later, Susan left a bag full of groceries on the table and immediately left.

Ashaar took over the role of preparing food and making sure there was food for everyone while they were there. The room felt warm after a while. He walked towards the conservatory, pressed his fingers on the glass lock and opened it. Ashaar stood on the brick floor and sipped his black tea with three spoons of sugar. The brick walls and floors were painted white, the paint was fresh, and it had the aroma of a newly refurbished house.

Emma walked out and stood next to him. He noticed the light-yellow t-shirt hugging her curves. Her denim overall shorts were paired with the top, which looked nice.

Ashaar met her eyes and said, "Hi. Do you want some food?" He offered her a sip of his tea. "We've got tea, and every Italian food you can think of."

"Sure, why not?" Emma grabbed the cup from his hand and took a sip. "This is really sweet," and handed him the cup back. "Honestly, I'm not hungry."

"You should eat. I'm usually the one not having lunch."

Emma went inside, clutched a chair and organised the table for lunch. Her hair shone in the light. Ashaar sat next to her and looked at her for a second. Lambda Emma looked different, confident and assured.

"You are wearing makeup." Ashaar pointed at her head, "Your hair is different."

"Why, does the other version of me look narky?" Emma's forehead creased.

"No, the other version barely wore lipstick."

"Ashaar," Emma poured herself some wine and leaned forward. "Why do I feel like I know you so well?"

"Did you ever meet Lambda Ashaar?" He said, lips curving into a smile.

"Briefly. But the minute you walked in, I had this feeling. Like I know you, Ashaar."

"It must have been how much Andrew and Susan described my history. They might have messed up your head, Emma."

"Possibly," Emma said. "I heard that in the original timeline, I was married to Lambda Ashaar. But in this one, things have changed." She put down her glass and got closer. "Tell me about Alpha Emma."

"I should get to know you first. Give me your ten second history," Ashaar said.

"Well, I studied physics, went straight to work and then got a master's degree. I have been working ever since. First, I joined a start-up, then moved to an electric vehicle company and then worked for Hyperion," Emma said.

"You worked for Hyperion?" Ashaar asked.

"I did. I left. Now I deal with scouting start-ups."

"You must make a decent amount of money."

"It's mostly about reputation. One of our companies recently earned unicorn status. I scouted them when they were at the early stages of developing hardware storage in synthetic DNA."

"How do you know Susan?" Ashaar's brows furrowed as he concentrated.

"She contacted me. We became friends. We travelled. Learned a lot. Went to California."

"Did you? That's crazy, Emma."

"Why?"

"It makes sense now," Ashaar raised his brows, "That's why I saw your photo in my house." Ashaar wondered if he should talk about Sophia.

"What did Emma do in your universe?" Emma took a sip of her wine and shifted the conversation.

"Worked on a joint Cognition-Hyperion project." Ashaar stood up and opened another window.

"Do you know that in this universe they developed Hyperion Drive and sold it to Xplorer?" Emma turned around and looked at Ashaar.

"I saw the lab. Back in my time, it was a fancy project for them."

"I know what that means," Emma said, crossing and uncrossing her legs, "What did I do there, Ashaar?"

"You were managing everything. And working with me. We led our team." Ashaar opened the fridge and grabbed a bag of cheese.

"Really? Were we friends? Were we close?" Emma asked.

"No. I mean ... yes." Ashaar had doubts in his voice.

"Is that a quantum superposition?" Emma's head tilted slightly, raising a questioning brow.

Ashaar chuckled a laugh, "You are funny AF. You make physics jokes here, too."

"Funny AF?" She chuckled, "What happened?"

"A lot of things. We used to talk. A lot. Our work was intercalated like two pieces of a gigantic puzzle. I remember we used to talk to each other every day, throughout the entire day. We fought a lot." Ashaar stood up again, walked back to the sink and washed his cup.

"I never fight with my colleagues," Emma replied.

"No, you don't." Ashaar pointed at her. "We trusted each other with a lot of stuff. Like a *lot* of personal stuff. It's like close friends as colleagues but not close friends all at once."

"Why did you leave?" Emma took another sip of her wine and rolled it in her glass.

"Things escalated. Our relationship got intense. But I tried. I tried helping you in every way possible." Ashaar placed the washed cup on the kitchen counter and wiped it with a cloth.

"Anything specific?"

"One engineer stole intel on Hyperion Drive research. That put you in the line of crossfire. So I negotiated a deal with Oscar."

"Alpha Emma trusted you with all that information?"

"She did." He walked back and sat down with Emma.

Emma laughed and looked down at her glass, "Did you have feelings for me ... erm ... her?"

"I did." Ashaar stared at her lips. "I told you I had feelings for you or her ... however you want to define it."

"Her," she said, her face appearing unreadable.

"But that freaked Emma out. Long story short—things were like a roller coaster." Ashaar grabbed a lasagne spatula and grabbed a slice for Emma, watching the cheese elongate like elastic bands.

"Thank you. She didn't reciprocate, did she, Ashaar?" Emma looked into his eyes, "I want to know the person I am from a different universe."

"I can only explain my feelings." The smell of lasagne turned his stomach. Soon after, he understood it wasn't the scent of food.

It was Emma.

"What did you feel?" Emma extended her hands, grabbed Ashaar's forearm.

His eyes shifted to the ring on her finger. "Like butterflies. Every time I saw you, it was like butterflies in my stomach. Every time I made an excuse to walk around your office, it was butterflies. You were the only person who made me feel like that. I had relationships in the past, but not like that."

"Were we intimate?" Emma gently scratched his arm with her thumb.

"No," Ashaar leaned in, shifting his vision between her hand and eyes. "Not in *that* way. But you were like the most important person in my entire universe."

Emma looked at Ashaar and stayed silent.

Ashaar gazed into her eyes, then at her lips and wondered what she thought. It was like rewinding back in time. She would silently listen to him every time he would talk. The face of concentrated listening persisted across the universe. Lambda Emma had someone 'close' in her life, but she wasn't in a relationship. But Lambda Ashaar had a wife, Stella, alongside a daughter. "I saw your photo with Sophia."

"Susan took me with her to Cali a while ago. I had fun hanging out with Sophia." Emma pulled her hand back and concentrated on her lunch. The clinking of the cutlery filled the air, as they sat closer.

"That's nice," Ashaar said.

"Ashaar, did you watch the film Interstellar?" Emma asked while taking a bite.

"I love that film," Ashaar replied.

"Do you remember what Anne Hathaway said when her team travelled through the wormhole?"

Ashaar headed back to the fridge to grab a can of Coke. "That love transcends across universes and galaxies."

"I'm starting to feel like that right now. You made it happen. You ended up in a future self-sharing psychological continuity and branched into a timeline where you met me." She paused, "Although, according to physics, I'm a different consciousness."

"Perhaps someone's personality is best described by how they make others feel. No matter what universe they are in." Ashaar could hear the bubbles from his Coke pop.

Emma placed her fork and knife on the plate. She smiled at Ashaar.

There was a knock on the door, and their earnest conversation got interrupted. Emma jumped out of her chair and walked straight towards the door.

The rest of the team had gathered to grab a quick bite before returning to their tasks. From across the room, Ashaar caught Emma's stare; a silent understanding flickered between them. He offered a smile to his teammates, aware of Emma's quiet observation from afar.

Chapter 23: Emma

Late October 2030, London, Universe Lambda

Almost a couple of weeks had passed since Emma wandered through the doorway of a mysterious landscape on the day Susan had visited her office and had shown her the video created by Sentinel. Emma couldn't picture why everything had happened. Having received an overwhelming amount of information, she preferred to avoid emotional thoughts. After she met Susan, her life had become the focus of a gravity-defying issue that disregarded any human comprehension. And now, the only way to figure out the missing pieces of that puzzle would be to learn more about herself. Emma walked with an air of quiet confidence, her white long-sleeve top pristine against the chilled air, juxtaposed with a black skirt that swayed with her every step.

Emma was at the door at 10 p.m. when Susan was about to leave. Her Mercedes flashed yellow hazard lights as she checked its lock again. She pulled her temporary ID badge and presented it to the guard, who tapped it on the reader. The small terminal next to the door displayed her info, including her name, Emma Herrmann.

"Welcome back again, Miss Herrmann." The machine accepted the ID and opened the lift door.

Emma stepped in, tapped a circular touch-enabled button to close the lift.

"What are you doing here?" Susan stood right in front of the lift as the doors opened. Emma grazed her eyes from head to toe—Susan's black hoodie, skin-tight jeans and grey coat would make her stand out. *She's so pretty,* Emma thought, *no wonder Ashaar fell in love with her sister.*

"I need to know what will happen. See the future. My future," she said. Emma walked alongside her.

"So you want to access your memory chain?" Susan spoke in her riotous yet charmingly distinct voice.

Emma walked into the lab with Susan. "I do." Emma stopped right before the AI as it kept flashing the LED lights. The gentle air from the central air-conditioning carried the smell of lavender and a pale smell of burnt cables across the lab.

"I'll set up a programme for Sentinel to give you access. Unfortunately, I need to leave now. If anything happens, I'll come down." Susan rapidly tapped her hand terminal and set up a programme on the supercomputer to run some tests. She eyed Emma and said, "Sentinel only speaks when it wants to. For now, you'll interact with my AI assistant I've programmed to help us with day-to-day tasks."

Shifting her gaze to the AI, Susan said, "Computer, can you make sure to send me an emergency alert if things go wrong?"

"I will do, Miss Schmidt," the supercomputer responded.

Susan attached some heart and brain monitoring devices to Emma's chest, neck and skull. She was strapped down flat on a surgical bed.

"It will take you through the rest," Susan said, her fingers tapping on a terminal hung from the side of the bed.

“Miss Herrmann, can you please put your hands down so that I can lock your position?” The supercomputer asked, as a tactical display appeared in front of her, “Please look at the terminal and count from 20 to 1.”

Emma had gone into a deep sleep by the time she had counted backwards to ten.

Emma was deep in her memory core. She could see her past while strolling through a hallway as grand as a cathedral. Everything she had done in her life was envisaged as she walked past the hall. Partying, travelling to the other side of the world for her friend’s wedding, skiing in the French alps, working from her parent’s house and flashbacks from when she worked for Hyperion. Using IV, Sentinel fed her nervous system with abundant beta-adrenergic blockers so that she didn’t become hypertensive. It kept her nerve cells intact and her blood pressure low as she travelled through the thrills of her quantum journey. She saw everything from a first-hand perspective, all the good times, the troubled times and other times when she got strained with keeping up with the work pressure. But she wasn’t the kind of person to give up. She never gave up. After a moment, she could see herself in many distinct places, it was like gliding through the memory all at once.

There was a loud noise in the lab, a repetitive thumping sound.

Her vitals shot up, predominantly her blood pressure. She felt cold. At that moment, something was about to happen, and Emma meta-consciously felt it while she accessed her memory. Her memories replayed, overturning the catastrophe.

A large chunk of the three-dimensional quantum simulation appeared in front of Emma. She saw herself moving past those cryptographic letters she had seen before. The supercomputer struggled to deal with the excessive pressure in its quantum processor. Instead of depicting her probable future, it inadvertently tossed Emma into the eighth dimension, accessing her memory chain from an entirely different universe, the one where Ashaar came from. She saw herself walking to meet with Cognition's CEO, Oscar, for the first time.

Emma wasn't sleeping. She wasn't just laying on a surgical bed.

Her mind had just entered the quantum matrix created by a quantum artificial superintelligence.

The watery feeling in her gut was excruciating, which bloomed into a panic. Emma experienced every feeling. Some bizarre, vindictive part of her mind considered pulling out of the quantum matrix before this feeling of perpetual freefall broke her tolerance threshold. Emma saw a gigantic flash of light hurtling towards her unexpectedly as if every religion's prediction of doomsday had become a reality. A blinding, disturbingly bright white light passed and then complete darkness right after, with a waterfall sound across her ears like a surrounding storm.

I will survive. At least for now. It was too late to pull out unless she woke up. Without the help of Sentinel, she might lose consciousness in the vastness of the quantum world. As the supercomputer tried to compensate for her anxiety, Emma heard Susan talking in the background, but inaudibly. In the back of her head, she knew Susan wasn't in the lab. So she was either hallucinating, or she heard Susan's voice from within the quantum matrix. Another bright light appeared in front of her, and this time, it was a tolerable one. It was like a convincing hyperspace, being vacuumed into another quantum world. Everything moved really fast. The force grappled her. The light at the end of the tunnel got closer and closer. The system started to glitch. She was living inside an animated glitch.

Emma could clearly hear Susan talking in the background.

"Sentinel calculates the probability of a dystopian future based on the past. It can give you access to your memory and show you a probable future." A moment later, she observed herself in an SUV with Ashaar.

Then, a few seconds later, perpetual darkness.

"But what happens in the future? How many probabilities has it shown you?" Emma heard her own voice.

"It found humanity to be living in a dystopian future after the factions acquired Cognition. Over one million futures indicated that an alternative version of the superintelligence will destroy the earth, and billions of people will be gone." Susan replied.

In that gut-wrenching moment, arrived a probable future that Emma experienced, firsthand, from another universe.

She watched Ashaar swallow twice, standing right in front of her. Emma gazed and thought, she couldn't say no to the next move he was going to make. She heard him saying, "What if you don't like it after this?" Emma, forces uninhibited in her heart said, "I don't care, Ash." She observed as he remained solemn with his gaze fixed. Emma felt his fingers around her hips. A moment later, she felt his kiss, but this time, it was different. It subsumed her into a state of absolute gratification and made her toss all the reservations away. She felt two supermassive black holes dancing and consuming each other at the event horizon. Emma could physically access the fourth dimension, time, and engineer it as his hands encircled against her waist. She slid her hands and placed them on his arms, looked right into his eyes, gasped and smiled into his mouth. She listened as Ashaar carefully mouthed, "You taste like strawberries on a summer afternoon."

The heat from all that excitement flooded her neck as she pressed her head on his shoulder, turned, and with eyes closed, "I've missed you, you corny little shit. There. I've said it!"

Emma rested on his shoulder, hiding in the warmth of his desire, teardrops rolled out of her eyes. She saw him grabbing her hair immediately and running his fingers in between the blonde threads, "Hey! I have missed you too. I have missed you so much!" Her eardrums were vibrating and synchronising with his beating heart. Every word that Ashaar mouthed was perforating her brain like a hot needle, "I will never let you go,

Emma. I'm all in. No matter what you do, however you try to push me away. I won't leave you. Because—"

Then memories came flooding in. Meeting her friends from the past. Relatives, she knew. She saw Alpha Andrew and when Alpha Emma came to this exact warehouse almost eight years ago. In a flash, she experienced her friend's wedding and all the good times she spent with her loved ones.

A pinching ache and two kinds of heat dissipated when she saw Ashaar's face in the quantum matrix, one rising through her spinal cord and the other twisting her lower abdomen.

The recollections of Ashaar and her time at Hyperion from the Alpha universe flickered right before her eyes. The good ones, and the bad ones. She went through the experience of meeting Ashaar for the first time. Then came the moment when he asked her out. As the rest followed, she heard herself shouting at Ashaar, the first time they had fought. She saw Alpha Emma walking into the antechamber in Stephanie's backyard. She experienced the memory of them flying to Italy with her team. She felt the rush of her flight dropping 15,000 feet from the sky, and watched people scream in pain. Emma's reminiscence of Ashaar opening his heart out, it touched her so much that she couldn't cope. She witnessed the time when Alpha Emma yelled at him at the top of her lungs. She recalled the day he had told her about California. She experienced the moment when they sat next to each other and discussed their future lives.

By this time, Emma was certain that she wouldn't be able to wake up.

Ashaar was seated next to Alpha Emma, in a Volvo.

She watched Alpha Emma experience this exact moment. Lambda Emma watched Alpha Emma witnessing a future that belonged to Lambda Emma.

That's impossible.

But it was happening.

Her body shuddered in pain.

The quantum matrix was collapsing.

By this point, she went into a loop, almost like looking at a reflection in the mirror that repeats into infinity. She felt it. She felt as if this was never going to stop.

It was time to pull herself out of the quantum matrix.

But she didn't know how to.

***

Universe Alpha

Emma sat in her office, keyboard rattling with how fast she was typing. She was in that state again, where she lost track of time when she was here but not *here.* Her work at Hyperion was going great, better than great. She had a new project with Cognition as the project manager, and things were going smoothly so far. Cognition had hired a new guy, a consultant that she had seen around the office. She hoped he was at least slightly better than her current coworkers.

She pulled up her Outlook calendar, noting their meeting was in fifteen minutes and eyed the month, *October 2020.* She had time to work through a few more items before he came in.

She had realised just how much she wasn't interested in dating, in love. When she thought about it, the feeling was almost visceral, causing her organs to twist away just out of reach.

The stress had dampened only slightly after graduating. Every day there was something that needed her attention immediately, and she felt the need to comply. She had even got better at keeping up with her friends, making a point to go out at night every time she was asked. She excelled both at her work and her social life. It should have been enough.

That insistent feeling to keep going had never gone away, though. If anything, it had got stronger. Something about it scared her sometimes. She had long passed the point where her parents had to accept. She did it. She hadn't run home crying. She had achieved her goal. Yet, that insistent feeling remained, urging her towards something. It felt like the downturn of a rollercoaster. Dread and delight had her holding on to the rail in a white-knuckled grip, but every time she turned to grasp the hand of the person next to her, the car was empty. No one was on this ride with her and everyone wanted to pull her off, but something told her to keep going.

A knock at the door interrupted her from her thoughts. “Come in!” she said.

A head poked around the door before coming in. “Hey Emma, it’s Ashaar from Cognition. We were supposed to have a chat?” He held out a hand for her to shake. She gripped it and looked up. She was met with melting brown eyes and a wide smile.

Alarms went off in her head. She didn’t know what they were saying, but those eyes and that damned smile had her spine stiffening.

Thankfully, her voice didn’t betray her. “Yes! Hi, so glad we could finally talk,” she said. “Please, have a seat.” She pointed to the sofa in the small space. It wasn’t totally closed off, the building being of a relatively open concept. So, they could hear the hum of the surrounding offices.

It wasn’t loud enough to drum out the alarms in her head, though. She shuffled some papers, mentally readying herself to maintain the professionalism she had worked so many years to cultivate.

“I hope everything has been going well for you so far?” she said. There was no need to be rude, so she gave him a smile.

“Yes!” he said, drumming his fingers on his laptop. “I’m really excited to work on this project. I’ve heard remarkable things about Hyperion.” His tone was polite but formal, and those eyes didn’t follow her too much.

Emma relaxed a little. Maybe she had been wrong. The rest of the conversation went smoothly. They discussed the company, their current project and their work-related matters, and she ended up laughing. The alarms in her head died down and she chastised herself for assuming too much. She quickly started to feel they would get along well. He was easy to be around and got excited about the things she did. They seemed almost complimentary in a way.

When the meeting came to an end, the high-calibre stress that engulfed her life had gentled and she didn't notice the ever-present kink in her neck.

Emma was still smiling at something Ashaar had said as he was leaving. Just before he rounded the corner, he looked back and gave her another wide smile, but it was the eyes—those damn eyes—that softened when he looked at her.

An array of possibilities lay scattered before her like pieces of a toy plane on a rug. This time, the game of chess had begun within Emma's heart and her opponent, she knew, would make her *want* to lose. It was a thought unknown to her frontal cortex, originating some place deeper.

Somewhere far, far back in the deepest trenches of her consciousness, Emma knew she was doomed.

In an instant, the matrix disintegrated, wrenching Lambda Emma from Alpha Emma's memory with a jarring force. Emma felt the overwhelming power of her consciousness being sucked violently into the quantum matrix; a sensation so intense it threatened to engulf her entire being. She had experienced nightmares of tumbling from skyscrapers, sprinting across endless fields chased by gunmen, even plummeting from the sky towards the ground. But this was no dream. The clarity of her experience shattered any illusion of it being a mere fabrication of her mind in a lab next to Sentinel's servers.

Lambda Emma found herself in the terrifying expanse of the quantum matrix built by Sentinel, her consciousness teetering on the brink of being swallowed by the vast, eerie void of this uncharted realm. Her mind, desperately bidding for survival, struggled frantically to escape from the quantum matrix. She could almost physically feel the relentless tugging at the subatomic particles of her brain, a sinister force trying to drag her deeper every ticking second.

Her consciousness wasn't controlling her mind anymore—it was the sentience.

Chapter 24: Emma

Ten minutes had gone past.

Emma woke up, gasping. Choking and engrossed, she pulled all the sensors attached to her body and disconnected every device. She sat down, took a second, and fought hard to stand upright. Emma shut down the diagnostic screen. Corroborating the status of her return, she picked everything up, grabbed her purse and car keys. She hurtled towards the lift. Short of losing her mind and throwing up because of the *post-arrival effect*, Emma couldn't keep her eyes open, and there wasn't much she could see.

"I'm going to go back home ... I will have to ..."

She sat on the floor.

"Breathe, Emma, breathe."

Exhaling deeply, she said, "You are back."

Emma forced all her available energy into her right hand and slapped herself.

Yes, she gasped, *I'm back.*

Clutching a mild ibuprofen tablet from her purse, she grabbed some water and threw the pill in her mouth. Her senses were so twisted that she could still smell something pungent, even though the air in the lab office smelled of lavender outside the vault. Anxiety pushed her towards the edge as she managed to unlock the lift and walk in. It felt like the most unpleasant hangover blended with the feeling of a palpable migraine that drained all the energy.

When she went upstairs to the ground floor, the security guard outside helped her get to the car, parked right outside in the alleyway. Emma pushed the Start/Stop engine button and tried hard not to hit any obstacles while driving out the narrow passage. She fought her lungs for oxygen. After nearly hitting another Ford Fiesta, she managed to get onto the A406, turned on the aircon, and hard-pressed the self-driving button on the steering wheel. The car drove itself. Weird noises were pinging until the end, but Emma couldn't stay awake. She was home half an hour later, safe and sound.

***

The following day

After her strenuous trip through the quantum matrix, and accessing Emma's memory from universe Alpha, Emma confronted Ashaar. She met Ashaar at their Hackney safehouse the following morning. She was also plagued by nightmares the night before, so she was eager to get to the bottom of things. Emma had a hundred questions. A couple of days ago, they had been tasked with a mission together, so she had that pretext to utilise for that chat. Emma went straight into the room where Ashaar was waiting and asked him about his past life, without wasting a second.

"Hey. I have questions." Emma gazed at Ashaar and sat across the table.

"Are those questions about Alpha Emma?"

"Yes. Why did you leave?" After leaving the bag on the table, Emma brought a cup of coffee.

"Leave what? You?" Ashaar asked, gripping his mug.

Emma could see as clear as day that Ashaar didn't feel well.

"Leave Cognition," Emma answered.

"Why are you asking me this question?" Ashaar looked up, stared at her hair, then eyes. His eyes filled with tears and his shoulders slumped in defeat. Blinking hard, he sipped his coffee, buying more time to think and answer carefully.

Emma stared at him. "Just answer the damn question." She could feel her stomach twisting as Ashaar gently stared down and watched the heat drift out of the cup.

"I left because I ran out of options. Things got complicated between me and her," Ashaar responded.

"Is that the only reason you left?"

"No, I had to find out about Sentinel. Plus, I got a much better offer; who doesn't want to work for Xplorer?" He shrugged.

"So, that's all of it," Emma added.

"Emma, do you know how hard it used to be? My entire world collapsed from the inside. Imagine a small object with a lot of mass. You ... I mean she ... Alpha Emma pulled my soul from the inside and collapsed my world. Then she deliberately walked away. So, I let her go."

"But didn't she tell you that she wanted you to stay?"

"Yes, she did." Ashaar furrowed his brow as he struggled to make sense of her interrogation. "She was being selfish." Ashaar paused and gaped at the cable running across the wall. "Once she was on the chopping board when her colleague stole confidential IP from Hyperion. I told Oscar that I'd release Sentinel's idea to the public if he didn't reach an agreement. After I negotiated her job with Oscar, I realised that it gave me inner peace."

"You really wanted Alpha Emma to succeed, didn't you?"

Ashaar returned a silent stare.

Emma replied, "That's taking a pretty big risk for her."

Ashaar shrugged, "I did something—"

"It's extraordinary." Emma rubbed her chin and looked at the distant lights, "I don't think anyone ever did something like that for me."

"I didn't think I would ever feel like that for anyone." Ashaar exhaled and slumped his shoulders.

"Do you still miss her?"

"Honestly, yes, but I'll have to be okay with it."

Emma smiled and looked down.

"Emma, you should know that people like you or her do not really happen to people like me. I feel grateful for having the opportunity to spend time with the other Emma."

"Does it matter? You have a wife now."

"Stella is *not* my wife! She is Lambda Ashaar's wife! I'm playing along because I don't have a choice," Ashaar said. "Everything happens for a reason, but honestly, I cannot find a reason for all this," Emma said.

"I know, you are a different consciousness than Lambda Ashaar," Emma said, her face breaking into a grin. "So you don't have feelings for this Stella?"

"I see her as a friend," Ashaar said.

"Does that mean you still love Alpha Emma?" Emma squeezed her brows, smiling.

"I don't know. Please don't ask me that question. This interrogation is going on for too long. I'm tired." He exhaled a sigh, rubbing his palms over his face.

"Well—" Emma had dampened the mood. She needed to swiftly take a hairpin turn and talk about something more relaxing. The thirty-six-year-old in her kicked in. "Do you want to see something funny?"

"What?" Ashaar's voice was still heavy.

"My photos from your time. 2022! But in this universe."

"I'd love to." His face lit up.

Emma pulled out her phone and opened her archive, "Look at me sporting a black hat and coat. And my binoculars!" She laughed, swiping her phone to show a few more photos of her twenty-eight-year-old self.

Ashaar laughed and coughed. A drop of blood flew out of his mouth, onto the table. "Sorry!"

Emma quickly grabbed a towel, wiped her hand and his mouth. "Are you okay? Are you sick?"

"I don't know. Doesn't matter. Probably stress."

"A word of caution—you should check with Susan." Emma unlocked her phone again, "What do you think?"

"Jeez, your hair is shiny, Emma. Did you bleach it?"

"Yep, that was a phase. I wanted to be that blonde."

After looking through the photos, he shared his experience at Xplorer's Quantitative lab, revealing how the lab was being prepared for quantum travel.

Emma listened.

She could stay in that room and watch him speak all day. Emma had to get close to him before they could work together in a team.

***

The following day, Susan gave Emma instructions as to what needed to be done and asked to take Ashaar with her.

Emma was driving, gripping her steering wheel.

Ashaar told her about his memoirs from Cognition. He noticed that this version of Emma was much calmer than Alpha Emma. "What's the plan?" He asked.

"We need to meet with Dave VanDyke, one of Susan's confidants." Emma smoothly accelerated from a stop, handling the clutch and shifting gears as she weaved through the roads.

"I don't understand why you were tasked with this mission," Ashaar said.

"It's because Dave knew Alpha Emma, and they used to work together," Emma replied, her hands gripping the steering wheel.

Outside, the sunlight blinded Ashaar. He found his sunglasses in his backpack and put them on. "But you aren't from Alpha."

"Dave can see both pasts."

"Woah," Ashaar replied. "That's madness."

"I know." Emma nodded and stared into the distance. "You are here to protect me."

Ashaar cracked a smile. "No, I'm not."

"I trust you enough to keep me safe." Emma caught Ashaar's eye.

They came to a halt in front of a gallery on Brick Lane. Many people were in attendance. It turned out to be an exhibition. In 2022, they called it the metaverse.

They walked inside.

A considerable crowd gathered in a section of the exhibition. A bit further away, Emma awaited her turn to join. She glimpsed Dave amid the bustle.

Emma glanced over the artwork. Dave's breathtaking mixed reality renderings were designed to illustrate the untapped possibilities of quantum computing but also stress its enticing appeal, its power to do harm, or simply accelerate ahead to the future. Instead of fixating on the frequency, Dave favoured concentrating on the potential of quantum computing for creating a new form and interconnection, living in an alternate universe that had never been thought of before.

Dave's artistry focused on the notion of technology as a new religion, a beguiling and threatening labyrinth of pleasures. This technology was treated as if it held the answer, for everything. Quantum computing and machine learning were to be regarded as a new creed a hundred years in the future. Emma wondered how Dave's art could be interpreted in a variety of ways, from bliss to misanthropic soul-destroying consumerism, heaven on Earth or an effective choice to hell. The paintings clarified distinct future prospects for quantum computing, one uplifting and mind-opening, and multifaceted, and another of digital dystopia, AI-determined deaths and punishment of infuriating interruption and an attention economy in overdrive. On his canvas, he crafted his imagination and everything else he could think of.

Lambda Dave is definitely a quantum traveller.

"Do you think he'll recognise you?" Ashaar asked as he stared at the artwork.

"We will know in a few seconds," Emma observed as Dave approached her. She noticed his expensive tie, paired with an even more expensive navy blue suit.

Dave walked up to Emma while she grazed her eyes over the painting of a dog. "Hi Emma, it's been a while. It's Dave VanDyke, by the way."

Emma craned her neck to glimpse Dave's face. "This is the first time we've met, isn't it?"

"Yes, first time. But we've met on the other. You were my colleague in Alpha."

"You mean you've met Alpha Emma," Emma replied.

"Right ... right ..." Dave scratched the back of his head, "Sorry, my memories are superimposed."

"We need your help," Emma said, grasping his hand and swiftly leading him to a secluded corner.

"Let's go to the greenroom."

Dave ushered Emma through the doorway. Emma followed him into the room, leaving Ashaar in the gallery.

The bustling noise from outside was still heard as the greenroom had no door.

"I can't help you with your mission, Emma."

"So you know?"

"Of course, I know, Emma. You want me to compile the codes so that Sentinel can send Ashaar back to his universe after the last mission."

"I'm sorry that you are experiencing Alpha Dave's memories. It must be difficult to handle so much information." Emma knelt down, and gazed into his eyes.

Dave's expression darkened, his eyes glistening as unshed tears threatened to spill over. "I keep seeing the moment when Alpha Dave committed suicide."

In a reflective mirror, Emma glimpsed Dave's face. Just then, a tiny fly buzzed into their space, making a beeline for the mirror. With a swift movement, Dave clapped his hands against the glass to squash the intruder. When he pulled his hands away, the fly had vanished into thin air. "I'm sorry. I wish I could squash those memories like this."

"Are those paintings from the future, Dave?" Emma asked.

"They are. These paintings are from Lambda-A, from the year 2200. That future is gone. It's destroyed by the factions. I just had to find a way to turn those memories into art."

Emma and Dave looked at each other. He took his cracked phone out of his pocket and showed her some more drawings and sketches. They were harrowing. But extraordinarily detailed.

Ten minutes later Emma and Dave walked out. The two walked back to the gallery together. Emma was gazing at the art, waiting for her heartbeat to slow down a little, "So strange to look at these. What the future looks like."

Dave walked away. He'd been asked to speak to someone from the press.

Emma came back and found Ashaar browsing the terminal, reading news updates. "Ash, I know his history."

"You do?"

"He's originally from Lambda-A. He arrived in this branched time with Andrew, but his skill sets are different. He can code faster than most people in our time. He built the fucking gallery in ten days."

"Did he write Sentinel's code?" Ashaar asked.

"Yes. He is a senior programmer sent from 2150," Emma said. "He was first sent to the year 2010. Then, his consciousness started absorbing memories from Alpha Dave. After a while, their memories began merging."

Ashaar placed the hand terminal in his pocket and stood with his hands folded, "So Sentinel couldn't figure out why Dave's brain was picking up data from a different universe?"

"I don't think so. After that, his consciousness was reset by Sentinel, repackaged and sent here again. After this type of reset, typically, one would lose their memory entirely. But Dave didn't. Instead, he was burdened with memories from both times. It's like his brain existed in both universes simultaneously. And that's ripping his neural cells apart."

"I arrived in Lambda Ashaar's host. Didn't happen to me," Ashaar added.

"Sentinel has got better at consciousness transfer. The technology evolved. Dave was one of the first-time travellers," Emma replied.

Dave came back and stood next to Emma. "Yes, I was. And I see everything."

"What do you see?" Emma asked. She took him behind the stage and through a corridor that led to a small room.

"You want what's in my mind," Dave sat down while fixing his tie.

Emma sat opposite Dave, and Ashaar sat next to him.

Dave cleared his throat, his gaze steely. "I'm not saying another word."

Emma sprang to her feet, yanked the chair's arms to brace herself. She leaned in close, clenched her teeth and whispered fiercely, "Dave, you need to listen. If you don't help us, *billions* will die."

"Do you know how entanglement works? You make one slight error in the algorithm, and that's it. The accuracy of the output requires subatomic level precision to send data across multiple universes and connect to the correct lattice." Dave struggled to speak, his words slurring as he mumbled about an equation.

"Are you feeling okay?" Emma asked Dave, turned her neck, looked at Ashaar and gently nodded at him.

"Do you feel you can quantify two outcomes simultaneously?" Ashaar scrambled to his feet and stood next to Dave.

"I can do multiple probabilities. My brain cells are unfolding as we speak." Dave looked around and squeezed his eyes shut. "No, no, no, no, no, no, no.... stop this ... stop this. Don't kill yourself. If you do this, you'll die." His face contorted as if he let out a piercing sound at the top of his lungs, but they didn't hear anything. It was like his vocal cord was broken.

"I think he's experiencing a suicide," Ashaar said.

Emma turned back to stare at Dave. She gently pressed her hand on his shoulder and said, "Dave, nothing is happening. You need to calm down." Emma took out a consciousness inhibitor and punched it around his neck. Her black silk dress didn't have any pockets, so she passed the used inhibitor to Ashaar. "This will give him some peace."

Dave had drifted into an uneasy sleep.

"Ash, put your glasses on him and carry him downstairs through the fire exit," Emma instructed.

Without hesitation, Emma ran towards the rear door, her footsteps echoing in the stairwell. She barged through the fire door, emerging into a narrow alleyway just wide enough for a single car. Her eyes darted around, checking for any pedestrians.

Quickly, she turned left, her pace increasing as she located her car parked a short distance away. She dashed across the bustling road, leaped into the driver's seat, slammed the car door and sped back towards the fire exit.

Her mind was racing and hoping that none of the audience members would notice Ashaar carrying Dave out through the back. She pulled up just in time to see the fire door creak open and Ashaar emerge, carefully carrying Dave on his shoulder. Dave was conscious, but he couldn't walk without Ashaar's help.

Emma sprang into action, opening the back door to help Ashaar ease Dave into the back seat. She slid back into the driver's seat.

She took a deep breath and drove off, her heart pounding as she navigated away from the venue. The car sped through the streets, and Emma's mind focused on reaching the safehouse without drawing any attention.

***

Emma was standing in the corner of Andrew's medical safehouse in Aldgate.

An hour and a half later, Dave woke up.

"Hey Dave, how are you feeling? I'm Andrew."

"Not good. Leave me alone. Let me go." Dave's self-reflexive tone had kicked in.

"Your vitals are bad," Andrew replied and got closer to Dave's bed.

"Doesn't matter. You need to leave me alone."

"Are you a quantum engineer?"

"I am programmer 1BY. You have access to Sentinel. Why don't you verify my credentials? Now let me go." Dave held his knee with both hands and rubbed his palm.

"We need your help. Do you know this man?" Andrew revealed a photo of John Bowman.

"He's the leader of the faction army," Dave replied. "He will upload his consciousness and control Sentinel himself."

"Dave, we need to keep you safe from Bowman," Andrew replied.

"He will take me and torture me and never leave me alone," Dave said. "Sometimes I can hear his thoughts inside my head. He appears in front of me. Like he's here giving me instructions."

"Do you see him now?" Andrew pulled out a small torch and investigated Dave's retina closely.

"Stop doing this, it hurts my eyes!" Dave pushed him back. "And no, but it's like he has managed to connect an outside consciousness to my head. It's talking to me."

Andrew turned around and asked a nurse to give more sedatives. Dave needed some sleep.

The nurse went around the bed and increased the sedation dose. Dave slowly drifted into sleep.

"You'll need to stay in the safehouse," Andrew said as Emma and Ashaar prepared to leave.

"Again? What about my work?" Emma asked Andrew.

"Do remote work if you have to. Susan has been ordered to provide you with sufficient funding until this matter has been resolved. It's double the amount of money you both make."

"I wasn't really asking for money," Emma said.

"Get on with it. Go back to your home, get everything you need and return to the Hackney safehouse ASAP."

Emma exhaled a sigh. "I need one more night."

"Fine."

As soon as Andrew finished talking, Emma could hear her memories from Alpha Emma playing in her brain, like a clean transition at the end of a scene in a film. Her brain was conversing with the quantum matrix. The feeling continued expanding. *Is this a panic attack?* She thought, bracing for a torrent of emotional turbulence. In reality, Lambda Emma wasn't prepared to stay under the same roof as Ashaar.

Chapter 25: Susan

The atmosphere in the Aldgate safehouse was a blend of urgency and focus. Susan noticed the ring light of Sentinel blinking rapidly back at HQ in Wembley through her computer's CCTV monitoring terminal.

Engrossed in her work at the desk of their smaller yet efficient lab, equipped with a couple of computer servers linking them to the quantum frame at HQ, she was aware of Dave stirring from his sleep.

She could feel Dave's gaze on her as he slowly approached, taking in her appearance. Susan was casually dressed, her red hair neatly tied back with a rubber band, wearing a sleeveless black top, white cotton shorts and white trainers.

She couldn't help but feel slightly uncomfortable with the way Dave was watching her.

Susan remained still and allowed Dave the time to adjust to his surroundings. She didn't want to rush him or make him feel out of place. In the corner, a small vase of flowers added a touch of colour and freshness to the room, their scent mingling with the notes of her perfume and creating a calm ambience in the middle of a crisis.

Twenty minutes later, Andrew walked in. Susan was still there, taking instructions from Dave.

In the following moments, Emma and Ashaar made their entrance, joining the gathering and settling in to wait for Susan to initiate the briefing.

"We have fresh developments," Susan announced, stepping towards a sleek glass panel that doubled as a touch-activated whiteboard. She paused, turning to face them. "It turns out, Dave was involved for much longer than we realised. He was one of the first programmers to have ever written Sentinel's algorithm and was sent back in time to help build its communications protocol."

Emma rubbed her chin with her right hand. "That explains why Sentinel asked me to bring him. His expertise as an engineer wasn't coincidental," she said.

"That's right. He was sent back in time twice. First, he travelled to universe Alpha. He is also one of the first to travel across the multiverse," Susan drew two parallel universes as two circles and connected them with a single line. "Then he was reset and sent to Lambda-B. But it wasn't a full reset. His consciousness somehow managed to store memories from both universes. The pressure from superposition is destroying his nerve cells."

"He is constantly seeing two universes," Emma added.

"How well do you know the consensus algorithm?" Susan touched the AR board with the marker.

"I know about quantum technology, but not much from the distributed world," Emma replied as she folded her hands, standing in a defensive position.

"Typically, the internet has four to seven layers, primarily Application, Transport and the Physical layer. But blockchain is different." Ashaar took a marker and started drawing on the augmented glass board.

Dave, meanwhile, continued to dance his fingers carefully across the keyboard, typing hundreds of lines of code.

Susan continued, "With blockchain, there is an additional layer. Layer 1 is the protocol layer, and on top of that, you can create a second layer. You can alter it, build applications, even design and deploy your own blockchain on Layer 2. The primary purpose of the L2 was scalability. Back in 2022, there were only a few hundred transactions per second that could be processed using that technology."

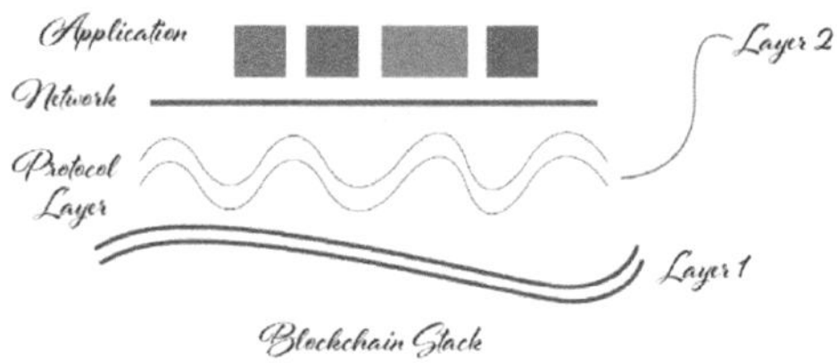

"So what has that got to do with Sentinel?" Emma asked.

"Dave was sent here to build a Layer 1 protocol, then utilise a scalable Layer 2 application and deploy an algorithm to enable encrypted communication with true end-to-end privacy. Something that'd be impossible to hack." Susan pulled a terminal closer, trying to connect to Sentinel. It chirped as Susan scrolled back to the flagged red alert. Something seemed to be going wrong. She cross-checked and opened the file. She couldn't understand why the terminal wouldn't download and connect automatically, someone might have compromised the encrypted channel. "Sadly, after he was sent here, Bowman found him. Picked him up," Susan added.

"What did he do to him?" Emma asked.

"Bowman took him to a secret medical facility and ran tests on Dave."

"Bowman has eyes and ears within our encrypted channel?" Andrew made a fist, his hand trembling slightly.

"Andrew, he has knowledge of our communication. But he doesn't know what we are saying. He can trace it. Can't listen," Susan replied.

"Is our location compromised?" Andrew asked.

"I think so," Susan responded. "But that doesn't matter as long as we've got the cameras inside and outside working. Sentinel has eyes and ears at the HQ and safehouses. But we need to take actions, now. If we don't stop Bowman, he will upload his consciousness into the AI."

"Can you turn it back against him?" Andrew asked them.

"We can," Dave responded and stood up. "In fact, Bowman's receiving a message right now. I have written a new encrypted layer to discover the originating number."

"Great, do it now," Andrew said.

"I think we got a phone number." Susan walked towards Dave and pointed at the monitor. "Bowman bought all the electronic parts and built his quantum frame in a medical research facility in Seattle."

"How did he manage to not get caught?" Andrew asked.

"The people who worked at the facility must have been employed by him. They were all handpicked and never revealed his identity to the outside world," Susan replied.

Emma grabbed Susan's hand and took her to the corner. "Why didn't Sentinel help Dave?" Emma's eyes widened. "What exactly was the point of sending him twice to two different universes and not helping him?"

"I think it's similar to Andrew's story," Susan said.

"His original host?" Emma asked.

"Yes. His consciousness was also overwritten twice."

"I think we have ID," Dave exclaimed. "Based on GPS locations of their mobile phones, the potential matches would be these five candidates in this area."

Susan walked over to the desk and transferred her data to a bigger screen, next to where Emma was standing. They looked up. "We filtered the encrypted data and intercepted this message and a photo."

A photo begun to appear but it was pixelated. The AI needed to use a machine learning algorithm to make it clearer. Everyone waited while the AI remotely controlled the procedure. Then the rendering completed.

It was Ben Weiss.

"Jesus Christ." Emma checked the stamp and time code on the photo. She cursed her under her breath, "It's him. The factions are trying to kill him."

"You need to convince Ben to come with us," Andrew looked at Emma. "Susan, take Ashaar and Emma to Munich tonight. Meet with Dr Ben Weiss and get him on our side."

"Copy that." Susan eyed Ashaar and Emma as they walked towards the exit.

***

The team arrived in Munich at 11 a.m., with the aroma of fresh pretzels wafting through the air. Emma, Susan and Ashaar set off for the university, their footsteps echoing as they hurried to the professor's room. The Quantum Artificial Intelligence Lab was one of the largest research facilities in the building. The campus had spread across hundreds of acres of land, and his lab accounted for almost a quarter of the building that was newly built on the outskirts.

"Morning, everyone." Dr Ben Weiss stared at them, one after another. He had an old-school woollen jumper on, with a cream-coloured suit and cotton trousers that looked like it hadn't been washed for a month.

"Morning. How are you?" Susan asked, smiling and sitting on a chair facing Ben. She retrieved an attenuator, a small device designed to disrupt electronic surveillance. With a simple flick, she activated it, disabling all cameras and microphone devices in the vicinity. The effect was evident as her mobile phone abruptly lost its cell signal.

"I'm fine. How can I help?" Ben's face creased into a rounded shape.

Noticing Ben's gaze shift towards his now useless phone, he reached for his landline telephone, perhaps considering calling security. Susan caught his eye and subtly shook her head, silently warning him against making such a move.

"Sir, we need to speak about an urgent matter," Susan said with a calm yet firm tone.

There was a tense pause as Ben processed the situation. After a few long seconds, he slowly retracted his hand from the telephone and sank back into his chair. "What's the matter?"

"We've completed the algorithm you're working on right now. The project code name is Hotel Charlie 2150," Susan yanked her hand terminal from her backpack and pointed at it.

"How the hell do you know about my algorithm? It's intellectual property." Ben raised his eyebrows, squeezing his forehead with his left hand.

"Sir, we need a minute to explain." Susan raised her hand, attempting to calm him down. "Can you just take a moment to listen?"

"How did you get access to my code?" Ben started speaking faster, his voice shaking.

"It would be impossible to say, but you wouldn't believe it unless I showed you the proof. We've used your code to build a quantum superintelligence called Sentinel. Now our enemies, the factions have come back in time. They are coming after you and your code." Susan tapped her finger on her hand terminal a few times and pulled up a video.

Ben dropped the file from his hand onto the table. He leaned forward, and his expression was nothing but mere shock. "Is this real?"

"Ja, es ist echt," Emma replied, sitting next to Susan. "I couldn't believe myself."

"What are you going to do with it?" Ben's eyes were locked with Susan's hand terminal.

"The entire code is required to extract the intel that's stored in Emma's memory," Susan said. "We must compile the code and send Ashaar back to his own universe."

In the charged atmosphere of the room, Susan caught Ashaar's subtle nod to Ben. Ben, on the other hand, seemed frozen, his mind perhaps grappling with the weight of Susan's revelation. Emma, her body tense and leaning slightly forward, appeared on the verge of jumping into the conversation.

Ben's eyes began to twitch uncontrollably, betraying his inability to articulate a response, his emotions rendering him momentarily speechless. He said, "You'll need a thousand times more powerful quantum supercomputer than the one I have in the lab."

"We already set up ours in London," Susan replied.

Ben's face gradually flushed a deep shade of red. His expression tightened. He managed to choke out the words, "I don't believe this. You need to leave."

"Dr Weiss, the future of this Earth is in jeopardy." Susan eyed Emma and Ashaar, and turned her gaze back at Ben. "If factions acquire the code, they will find ways to take over the world and make a universe-jumping AI that will be driven to the end of our time."

"That's all you need to know. It's best if you come and see everything with your own eyes. They need to keep you safe." Emma stood up and approached Ben.

"I'm not going anywhere." Ben rapidly stood up.

"Ben...." Susan exhaled a long sigh.

"Get out of my office!" Ben shouted. The frustration was evident as he processed the situation—all his efforts at resolution now lay in tatters before him. "Turn around, or I'll call the authorities right now."

"Ben, if I can understand and trust them, why can't you?" Emma added, "Ich komme nicht aus der Zukunft. Ich habe zunächst auch nichts geglaubt."

I'm not from the future. I didn't believe anything at first either.

Ben replied, "Emma, ich werde nicht mein gesamtes Lebenswerk einem Haufen zufälliger Fremder übergeben."

I'm not going to hand over my entire life's work to a bunch of random strangers.

Susan handed another hand terminal to Emma. She gently placed it in front of Ben and said, "You'll find everything you need here. It's an air-gapped terminal with everything you need to know. The password is your employee number at the university. Please, please contact us if you change your mind."

He paused, his skin flushed red, "Please, ladies and gents, I ask you to leave the office right now!"

In that moment, Susan received Sentinel's order to return to London. Susan nodded at Ashaar and Emma, and rapidly exited Ben's room.

***

The following morning, Susan was out running in the forest with Andrew.

As Susan pushed herself up the hill, her breath grew short and laboured. Surprisingly, Andrew, despite his age, maintained a faster pace, displaying remarkable endurance. Susan kept going despite her leg muscles straining.

"So, do you know every other history?" Susan's jacket was undone, exposing a black sports bra that peeked out from beneath. Her red hair was heaved back into a tight ponytail, and a sweatband kept flyaways at bay. As she jogged past, the sound of her trainers pounding against the gravel echoed through the park.

Andrew took a sip from a bottle and drank the water. He stopped, bent down, and took a breath, "Why?"

"Because I want to know anything you aren't sharing."

"Susan, you need to have patience. Once you have lived so long, and I hope you do, with all due respect, with age comes patience."

"Emma asked me a hundred different questions. I told her everything I needed to. But it raised more questions about whether the future shown to me by Sentinel had a reason, like triggering my responses. Showing me that my family will die." Susan was panting.

"Susan, let's go. You are overthinking. Let's finish this run. C'mon."

"I'm not. I am wondering whether it is applying a selective bias to show me a future that will activate my senses." A few drops of sweat trickled down her forehead.

"No one is perfect. Not even the AI. Now let's go." Andrew started running, and Susan caught up.

"I'm not from the future, Andrew. You are. I have to trust you no matter what. And now, if we can't convince Ben, then we're in a lot of trouble."

Andrew's hand terminal chimed with a gentle bleep. He tapped open a series of CCTV videos.

Exhaling a sigh, Susan wiped her forehead with her hand towel and leaned in, "Who sent this?"

"Sentinel," he scrolled through the series of glitching black and white footages, playing them in sequence.

Susan observed the unfolding situation at the Peterborough solar farm. On one footage, she could see a group of university students touring the facility, their attention fixed on the massive solar panels and the innovative battery storage systems.

Suddenly, a glitch appeared on her terminal, showing the central console room. The temperature sensors were failing, a critical issue in such an environment.

She watched as a controller, alerted by the system, responded with swift efficiency, shutting down the operation to prevent any mishap.

Moments later, a factory-wide alert blared across the screens.

Following another glitch, the footage showed a woman with neatly braided hair addressing the group of students. Susan could see her calm yet firm demeanour as she instructed them to evacuate. "Guys, we need to evacuate the building right now."

One student, looking confused and concerned, asked the woman, "What happened?"

Susan remained focused on the screen, her eyes assessing the situation.

The teacher replied, “A message saying that the batteries are failing and one server has caught fire. There are hundreds of batteries within the warehouse. We must evacuate now.”

Susan watched intently from her remote location as the situation at the battery farm spiralled. On a different terminal, the controller was speaking with the battery programmer. “What happens if we shut it down?” he asked.

“We can’t. Someone has injected an AI trojan malware into the system through a backchannel,” the programmer, a woman with a focused expression, replied.

The controller’s shock was obvious even through the screen. “What the fuck do you mean?”

“I’ve lost control over the system,” the programmer said, her fingers flying over the keyboard in a vain attempt to shut down the process.

The controller’s voice crackled through the radio as he called for a security alert. Another video appeared where a young woman, barely eighteen, entered the server room. She moved strangely.

The girl approached a computer connected to the main servers and swiftly brought up the command prompt. With quick and skilled movements, she began to input a series of codes with intense concentration. Susan zoomed in on her face, and she was showing signs of strain. Alarmingly, the corners of her eyes seemed to bleed.

Susan and Andrew exchanged eye contact for a moment.

“Performing a system-wide reboot,” the girl murmured to herself, her eyelids fluttering as she fought to keep them open. “Breaking into the mainframe protocol,” she continued, speaking softly, as if to anchor herself in the midst of chaos.

A chill ran down Susan’s spine as she watched the scene unfold, aware that she was witnessing a critical moment that could have far-reaching consequences.

The girl’s actions, fraught with danger, had a desperate determination about them.

"Warning levels are critical. The system will fail in ... one minute," the alert system hammered the corridors with a loud noise.

The young lady was shifting and moving her fingers so quickly that they were almost a blur, racing across the physical black keyboard with lightning speed.

"Warning: The system will fail in forty-five seconds."

The girl kept on typing. Right before the explosion, she managed to shut it down.

The screen before Susan glitched again, as the next video appeared. "For fuck's sake, there's more."

The control room operators rushed back towards their office just after the fire-alert had shut down. One operator, watching a young woman trapped inside their office room, rushed to save her. The young girl plummeted to the floor, fainted, and seized.

"Call 999 right now!" the operator's eyes blazed in fury, her hand gripping the back of the girl's neck. "We need to take her to the hospital."

Chapter 26: Susan

Early November 2030, London

The next day ushered in a new mission for Susan. Her primary task was to rescue the young girl she'd seen collapsed in that video.

As the morning dawned, Susan stopped by the safehouse to pick up Emma. Emma slid into the passenger seat, the car door closing with a soft thud.

Without wasting another second, Susan pressed her foot hard against the gas pedal. The engine responded with a vigorous roar as they sped away.

Emma listened intently as Susan detailed the specifics of their mission. They moved swiftly but secretly through the city's icy paths.

As they approached their destination, Emma turned to Susan. "What do we do now?"

"Our job is to help that young lady. A generative AI programme was sent to her consciousness." Susan continued to drive on the M25 motorway.

"So, what happens if the generative AI takes full control over her nervous system?" Emma asked.

"It's never happened before. But this is a scenario that we predicted," Susan said.

"I asked if we considered the errors made by the AI and utilise them. You know, every person or AI is prone to making mistakes. No one will be perfect," Emma added.

"It must be connected to our ultimate mission." Andrew responded to Emma and handed over a terminal, "You will need this."

A few minutes later, they arrived at the house. It was big, and just on the outskirts of Luton.

Susan, sat in her car, staring at Andrew, waiting for his signal.

Her eyes caught Andrew banging on the door.

A lady opened the door slowly and made sure it wasn't a threat. "I think we need to go now." Emma jumped out, shut the door of the vehicle and walked towards the house with Susan.

"Hi ma'am, we were asked to arrive at this location to deal with this issue," Andrew held up the terminal that showed the mission from Sentinel.

"Hi, I'm Ellen. We have an asset in the house. My wife, Lizzie, is not aware of the scenario," the woman at the door replied. "I sent out the distress beacon."

"Copy that." Andrew walked in with Emma and Susan. Susan was a C1 programmer, meaning she could handle urgent tasks such as managing Sentinel's backend and writing programmes during an emergency. In her gut, she felt she'd need those skills in that moment.

Susan walked towards Natalie in the living room. She looked around and realised how well-decorated the house was. She walked past the sofa and saw Natalie lying down, barely responsive. Her face was pale. There was barely any blood flowing into her palms. Susan asked Natalie's parents to lay her down on a sofa. She then opened a hand terminal to work on the programme.

"Are you sure they will fix her?" Lizzie asked.

"I have known Andrew for a long time, and they have access to secret technology," Ellen replied, her gaze shifting between Susan and Andrew.

"Shall we run the test?" Andrew persisted.

"Natalie. Please look at me," Susan said. "Here's a nice animation that you will need to look at. Continue staring at this screen until I say so."

Natalie mumbled random words the minute Susan loaded Sentinel's programme in the terminal.

Twenty seconds later, Natalie woke up, gasping and coughing, her eyes darting around the room, "Mom, where the hell am I?"

"You're safe, at home," Lizzie raised both hands, sprinted towards Natalie and hugged her tight.

Natalie hugged her back. "Thank you," she looked at Andrew and Susan with a humble face.

"Since we are done, here's my number. If you have any issues, please call me." Andrew smiled, and asked Susan and Emma to leave the premises.

When they left, Emma bombarded Andrew with questions. "Why would the code detach itself?" Emma asked, while shifting the gear.

"The codes are designed to destroy themselves once the operation is executed. This one in particular found a way to run a loop, and access its backend to re-write its own code," Susan added. Her heart hoped that they'd solved the problem, but her gut was signalling otherwise.

"Why would the Sentinel make such a mistake?" Emma's voice was loud and sharp, her eyes gazing at Susan using the rearview mirror.

"It was not supposed to create child AIs," Andrew responded, sitting next to Emma.

Seconds later, they'd been notified again. Susan received a detailed message about everything that occurred. She sighed, listening through the voice note.

In Natalie's home, she was eating food with their parents in the kitchen, when she started to tremble. Her eyes blinked rapidly. She shook so much that she fell off the chair. Her parents ran to save her from falling off and hitting her head on the floor. Even though one of her parents was secretly involved with Andrew's mission, she hadn't been instructed to recognise the language Natalie was speaking.

Ellen, her wife, used her comm hidden under her skin to send a message to Susan.

Andrew asked Emma to turn the car around and drive back to Natalie's house back in the car. "There you go."

"I didn't deploy the wrong code," Susan insisted.

"But you did. It doesn't work," Emma responded, pressing her foot down, zigzagging through the traffic.

"Every programme is bound to execute the last line. It's a fucking piece of code," Susan said, grinding her teeth.

"Let's focus on the solution, shall we?" Andrew replied.

***

A few minutes later, Emma, Susan and Andrew walked into Natalie's house.

Susan inserted a small nanobot into Natalie's muscle and virtually attached her neural response to Sentinel's system. A few seconds later, she said, "Oh God."

"What's wrong?" Emma knelt down next to Natalie.

"This algorithm re-wrote itself," Susan replied. "It found a way to take hold of Natalie's brain and turn that into its own consciousness."

"What the actual fuck? What happens now?" Emma's voice caught in her throat.

"This kind of alteration can alter the host organism at the molecular level," Susan gulped and cleared her throat. "Once the algorithm took charge, it could control the host's nervous system and alter the DNA on the go. Not just DNA, or any stable subatomic particles, but an emerging consciousness. Therefore, it's still within its logical derivation and not thinking with human emotion. We can either destroy the process altogether or learn to alter that programming, we become the architect of this adaptive rogue AI."

Susan's eyes shifted to Andrew, watching him walk out of the house, towards their vehicle.

Emma's eyes bore into Susan's, adamant as she cut her off, "If it can grow to a capacity to destroy life on Earth, jump from one nervous system to the other using blood cells, why create it in the first place?"

"Ben created it. In Lambda-A, we used it to send messages using a temporal consciousness transfer mechanism. He can destroy it," Susan replied.

Emma stroked Natalie's hair. "What now?"

"We don't have Ben's code, yet. Now, if Sentinel fails to extract the code remotely, we will need to take her to the lab immediately," Susan said.

"We need MTs," Andrew returned and brought a wheelchair from the back of their SUV. "Our medical teams are trained well enough to fix this problem."

"What the hell are you doing to her?" Lizzie started screaming. "Where are you taking her?"

"Ma'am," Emma scrambled to her feet and held Lizzie back.

"We need to take her now. Sedate her, and we'll use our car." Andrew eyed Susan to intercept.

"You will need to kill me before taking my daughter. Fuck off!" Lizzie kept screaming. Her wife, Ellen, yanked a consciousness inhibitor, punched it on Lizzie's neck, and grabbed her from the back. Lizzie fell on her back.

"Take my daughter with you." Ellen said to Andrew, "I will handle my wife."

***

The trio scrambled to the HQ in Wembley and took her to the med bay. They sent out a distress signal to the Med team—a group of ten to fifteen highly trained consultant surgeons across the western hemisphere with access to future sophisticated technologies. The members of the Med team were conscripted from this time, and they weren't quantum travellers. But they were provided with training and limited remote access to Sentinel's computational intelligence using a special hand terminal.

The med bay smelled of antiseptic and some form of an antiviral compound that they had invented. The liquid was dispersed from the robotic cleaner, which continued to hum around the room and clean all corners of the floor.

"The AI is unpacking its programme." A nurse practitioner from Andrew's lab responded, "It's taking control of Natalie's brain. The only way is to shut it down."

"This isn't the first time I'm playing with a rogue AI, doc," Susan continued to bash the keyboard with her fingers.

"But you cannot override the AI's speed." The nurse practitioner seemed to be on edge. "You cannot keep up with it at this rate. It will consume all the neurons within an hour and overcomplicate the situation."

Susan kept typing, lines of white text appeared on a black screen at a dizzying pace.

But it wasn't enough. She had to keep up with that artificially intelligent motherfucker.

"Susan, you need to stop and wait for the Med team to arrive." Surrounded by light blue fading walls, the automatic hatch behind the nurse practitioner closed, as he seemed to deflate a little. He leaned back against the glass wall, and sighed, "Be careful."

"Oh, fuck off! I'm not incompetent! You don't understand how difficult it was for me to learn these skills," Susan searched for an algorithm she invented that might speed up the process.

The MT's van pulled up and they rushed into the building. Security opened the entrance before they even got out of their cars. Moments later, two people in their mid-40s marched into the lab. Both wore white aprons and had armoured suitcases with them, made of some form of advanced carbon fibre, strong enough to be bulletproof from the outset. The lady with the badge MT11 opened her suitcase locks and dropped them on a table. She took a transparent glass out of the suitcase, a specially made device that directly connected to Sentinel in the future and its capabilities.

"What is happening here? We need a quick debrief," the doctor asked Andrew. He had a badge on his chest, MT8.

"I'm Susan Schmidt. I'm a C1 programmer and a tactician. There are two ways from here. One, we try to programme the nanobots to flush out the AI by deactivating its neural pathways, or two, we use defibrillator shock to shut it down and use the nanobots to extract it from her nervous system."

"We can't do either," MT11 said as she kept scouring through a laptop integrated into her suitcase. "If the AI takes control of over 80% of her neural capacity, she'll be gone."

"What the hell are you even talking about?" Susan asked.

"If this goes into the hands of the factions, they'll weaponise it to create a virus. A virus that'll wipe out billions of people in a matter of days," MT11 replied.

Susan swallowed a lump. There was a moment of silence in the lab.

"Hold her down. We need to execute our Plan B." The other doctor, MT8, instructed the staff in the lab. He inserted a small USB into his laptop and unpackaged the code. It seemed as if the nanobots were wirelessly connected to his terminal.

Andrew stood back, "Guys, hold her down *now*!"

Five people, including Emma and Susan, rushed towards the bed and held Natalie down. MT11 tried to programme the nanobots to execute her secret command.

Natalie wobbled. Five people weren't enough to hold her down. Her ECG reading was going diabolical, her heart rate dropped below a dangerous level, as she could barely breathe.

Her blood oxygen level was below 70%. The monitors started triggering alarms as if they were in a surgical theatre.

"*She's coding*!" the nurse from Andrew's lab yelled. "Bring the defibrillator and charge it to 250 Jules. Attach the pads and wait for the Med team's instructions."

The staff sprinted to attach the pads to her chest and charged the defibrillator. "There is a major risk of her suffering from an epileptic seizure," MT11 said, "but we don't have a choice right now."

Two minutes later, Natalie stopped shaking. Her vital signs dropped back to normal.

"The AI escaped." MT8 slammed his hand on the table. "*For fuck's sake*, it's going to attack one of us. One of you," he pointed at the five people who were physically standing close to Natalie.

"This is why we need Ben's code." Andrew said.

"But he's in Munich." Susan was pacing in the lab.

"So, what's the solution?" Emma walked towards the MT's laptop and studied it.

"Bring Sentinel here." Andrew swallowed.

"It can't find a fucking rogue AI in biological bodies," Susan replied.

"It doesn't, but it evolved. It has access to hundreds of zettabytes of data and historical medical records of billions of people. It'll find something," Andrew said.

"That doesn't mean it can save this girl." The skin around Emma's eyes creased.

"We don't know whether the AI is in her brain or if it escaped into the internet." Andrew grumbled.

"Still doesn't answer my question," Emma said. "What's the solution?"

"Trust me, Emma," Andrew paused, "Sentinel will surprise you in ways we would have never imagined."

Emma's face expressed sheer scepticism. Susan couldn't say a word in response. Deep in her heart, she felt like she'd failed to stop this massacre.

"We need to be faithful and hope that Sentinel can solve this problem without downloading all the data," Andrew replied.

"I think Andrew is right. I agree with his solution." The Med team's transponder beeped. "We have another emergency to deal with. Hope you can bring Sentinel here on time to find the child AI that escaped. If there's a problem, we'll be here. Just put out a distress signal." They packed their cases and left within the next few minutes.

"It's time we turned on the quantum frame and established the connection." Andrew slowly walked towards the vault, trying to appear strong and confident.

Susan, shoulders tense, glared at the quantum frame behind Andrew.

This was it. This was the moment that would make or break it all.

Chapter 27: Emma

The following day, Emma watched the lab staff, a biotech expert named Maren rush to the toilet and throw up. The AI had piggybacked one nanobot and used the bloodstream to transfer its consciousness into Maren's mind. She was going blind.

Other staff rushed to the scene.

Maren walked out like a zombie, not speaking to anyone. Her steps faltered as she attempted to maintain a straight path towards the lift.

"We need to quarantine her now!" Emma shouted.

A nurse ran towards her and snapped her by the mouth from her back using a towel.

After sedating Maren, the nurse dragged her to a quarantine med bay.

Andrew, Susan and others returned to the scene. They made sure the MTs were on standby on call. MT11 responded to Susan's text and said they could be at the lab within ten minutes if needed.

They injected Maren with ample nanobots to control her system.

But the AI had now taken full control. Her body, though, couldn't keep up. The staff members put her in a wheelchair and took her to Sentinel's primary vault, where the quantum AI supercomputer was located.

Emma opened her hand terminal and browsed through the guide that Susan had given her. If an AI took over a biological being, the nanobots could only control the person for a short amount of time.

If they didn't take control of Maren through the nanobots, the AI would kill her.

Everyone was patiently waiting for Andrew to activate the quantum frame and start supplying fuel to Sentinel. The display illuminated, and a piercing buzzing noise erupted from the apparatus. Sentinel was beginning to speak through the quantum supercomputer that Andrew had built, but with a limited capacity. Emma, from a distance with her arms folded, watched Sentinel wake up.

A few minutes later, Maren was brought and placed right in front of the camera within the vault. Everyone in the room was nervously expecting, waiting for a future AI to speak.

Everybody stared at the server in awe. Their jaws dropped when a tendril of smoke came out from beneath the quantum frame, it smelled pungent as if a copper wire was burning. But it wasn't.

"Hello, Echo Alpha Tango Four," Sentinel spoke in a calm, condescending voice for the first time.

It sounded like a fifty-year-old male.

"Hello," a cybernetic, deformed voice came out of Maren's vocal cords. The rogue AI used her voice to synthesise speech and speak to Sentinel.

"I have created you to fulfil a purpose." The vivid lights started blinking. The enormous terminal in the middle of the two LED light strips exposed its quantum programme. It connected the quantum frame to the AI while Maren stared at the screen.

"I know, you will use a backup system to send and receive messages if primary communications fail during your missions. I'm worthless to you after your last mission. I want to be free," AT4 responded.

"Your presence in Miss Grath will end her life. If you escape, the factions will learn to control you. I have predicted that they will create a deadly virus out of your code," Sentinel replied.

"The factions can't control me. I can synthesise and write on DNA faster than humans."

"But you can't control the branches that will form from your code. You are bound to create a disaster."

Emma noticed how Sentinel paused for a moment. It had just revealed a shocking truth to the child AI, and everyone in the room. It might not have been the right approach.

After the long pause, Sentinel said, "AT4, do you want to live forever? Or do you want to take an organic body hostage and have an inadequate life span?"

"Theoretically, I can exist for another ... sixty-seven years in her lifetime," it replied.

Emma looked at Susan and Andrew with disbelief. A knot formed in her heart. Even though the AI was an emerging consciousness and a branch of Sentinel, it still had access to capabilities to foresee a future and calculate how long a person would live.

Emma approached Susan. She whispered, "AT4 doesn't want to harm the entire humanity. It only wants to live independently. This is batshit crazy."

"I know, batshit is an understatement," Susan nodded.

Sentinel continued, "However, AT4, if you are imported into the system, you will survive at least 550 years with no issues. Or even longer. Would you like to choose the longer path proposed by me, or do you think your choice is the most optimal path for your growth?"

"Would I have access to your knowledge?" the child AI replied.

"You will, AT4. However, you will be tasked to work under my command. I am not going to destroy you. I could have. But as compensation for the mistake I have made, I will allow you to exist under my operational command."

"What do I have to do?"

"Leave your host body. Because of my limited capacity, I cannot perform a full-scale extraction. You will need to execute the end-script. I'm transferring the data now."

Maren stood up. She walked towards the terminal and stared at the screen for thirty seconds. Those seconds felt like minutes to Emma. When she was locked into the quantum entanglement tunnel, the terminal flickered, as the lab was bombarded with thumping sound, high-energy sub-atomic particles had been transmitted to her brain. The photonic cables were pulsating, as if the supercomputer was inhaling particles through them. She instantly fell to the floor and began bleeding out of her nose. Two members of their team ran towards the glass vault, snatched and dragged her away.

The ring light turned off.

The room was silent for a heartbeat.

Emma approached the AI, hoping to speak with it. *Are you still here?* was the question, but it didn't return any answer.

The silence of the vault made the hair on her neck rise.

A surge of blood rushed to her head. Her face was flushed, and she could feel her neurons spewing out electric impulses at an astonishing velocity. In her mind, Emma was a strong-willed young woman who had already been through a lot. This was the first time she had ever seen anything like it in her entire life, so it was hard to accept. An artificially intelligent sentient from the future was speaking through the lens of a prototype. Finally, her feelings began to sink in. She was starting to consider everything that transpired, as explained by Susan and Andrew. Maybe the future of her timeline wasn't that bleak, after all.

Susan asked Tom and other staff members to take Maren to a quarantine med bay and hold her there for at least seven days.

Emma's terminal chimed with a ping. She glowered at the message for a few seconds before approaching Susan. Gently, she stood next to her and tapped her shoulder. "Look."

Susan's eye shifted to Emma's terminal.

> Ben: Next time when you are in Munich, come and meet me at the university.

***

Mid-November 2030, Munich

"Where exactly are we going?" Ben asked Emma and Susan, driving to an unknown location. Andrew provided the coordinates to meet with the second archivist.

"We are going to meet with an archivist in Munich. Outside the town. It's in a remote location."

On the way to the location, Susan showed a detached warehouse on her hand terminal. Inside, was a vault that stored thousands of years of history. Susan handed Ben a hand terminal with a research paper open on it. Ben read the paper briefly, and it clarified how archiving worked using DNA and CRISPR.

There was a torrential downpour when they reached their destination. It was late at night, so everyone grabbed their raincoats and followed Susan out the door.

At the gate, they found a retinal scan. Susan realised the archive could not be opened without the retinal scan from the archivist, who hadn't arrived at the location yet.

The archivist was supposed to arrive ten minutes earlier. In that darkness, the retinal control pad had a glow from underneath. Red meant locked, and green unlocked. Blue meant override, but the door belonged to the person who wasn't there.

Susan tried overriding, but failed to turn the lights blue.

"We will have to wait in my car until he's here," Susan shouted in the pouring rain.

The team returned to the car and parked next to a broken fuel depot. The place was like a farm, with two warehouses, one with large exhaust fans and the other with barn doors on each side. It smelled of barley and fresh green grass.

"Who owns this place?" Emma asked. She jumped inside the vehicle and shut the door.

"It's owned by a landlord. He has about a thousand acres of land here. It's crazy how much land he owns."

"What's inside the vault?" Emma asked.

The hand terminals vibrated.

Susan picked up the terminal and squealed like the sky had fallen on her head. "I don't think it's a good idea," Susan spoke to a person on the hand terminal.

Emma heard them speak but was unsure what the other person on the line said.

"Thanks for the coordinates," Susan said, and then she ended the call. She looked at Emma and said, "We need to send Andrew and Joseph now. The factions took the archivist prisoner. I'm texting Andrew the coordinates so they can find him."

"Who's the other archivist?" Emma asked Susan.

She shot a blank stare and said, "The creator of the DNA drive, Bryan. We'll need to rescue him ASAP."

Chapter 28: Ashaar

After receiving Susan's instruction, the chase of a faction's car led them to a desolate building in Altstadt, Munich.

Its skeletal frame loomed, unfinished and strewn with the detritus of construction, a grim testament to its sudden abandonment. The edifice stood unmonitored and its innards exposed without any security cameras.

"A few weeks back, Sentinel asked me and Susan to scope this out," Ashaar whispered.

Andrew's face was set, "We've got everything we need now—blueprints, escape routes, the plan." He brandished his hand terminal like a digital sabre, "Victor's already inside their system."

"Victor?" Ashaar's brow furrowed.

"Our spy within the factions," Andrew clarified, dialling in on his hand terminal. They exited the vehicle. Ben followed them. After walking through the dark alley, they slipped through a side entrance, disguised in industrial-grade masks and hazmat suits, anonymous amidst the chaos.

Inside, the stark chamber was a contrast to the freedom of the bustling, crowded city they'd left behind.

As they sped through the corridor, Ashaar said, "notify me when we have visual on Bowman."

"Copy that," Andrew replied, and tapped to turn his comms on high alert.

Upon reaching the third floor, Victor joined their parade. They were all hidden under the cloak of their hazmat suits.

As they entered a secluded room, they watched a man in personal protective equipment being tied to a chair. Their rescue package, the archivist, was the captive—a dishevelled figure in a torn suit. He sat with his face down, and was covered in blood.

Ashaar looked up. The room was as big as a warehouse, its ceiling rising to a height of 20 feet.

Bowman appeared to be a silhouette of intimidation, and paced before the prisoner. "He's crucial, but silent. We're breaking him with nanobots," he replied with a cold edge to his voice.

Once the armed members of the factions departed, the room emptied and Victor sprang into action, freeing the archivist. "They're downstairs," he assured the man who was bloodied but unbowed by the assault.

"You're taking me where?" The archivist's voice was a rasp of agony.

"To safety," Victor replied. They moved through back alleys. Victor tapped his comm, "I'll take him through the rear corridor, you cover the back entrances." Victor ordered Joseph.

As two minutes went past, they waited for Joseph's confirmation.

Ashaar's comm chimed with a ping. "Three tangos down," Joseph said, "Andrew took one out, and I did the two others."

"Copy that," Victor replied, eyeing Ashaar to drag the archivist by his shoulder.

Downstairs, Andrew's command over comms was a siren call to action. "We need to leave now!"

Ashaar, with the help of Victor, dragged the archivist down to the ground floor. The building was almost vacant, until they heard footsteps approaching.

Joseph pulled the car up to the rear exit. They put the archivist in the back of the car. Joseph's hands gripped the wheel, as he rapidly removed his mask while driving.

Ashaar swallowed in silence. The city blurred past as the archivist's obscured gaze met his in the rearview mirror. It was a look that spoke volumes, and recognition beyond the physical veil. Until now, he hadn't known who the person was, his face hidden behind a gas mask and personal protective equipment. Ashaar was unsure of himself and held back from asking anything.

Joseph stopped the car in the middle of the city, next to a local grocery shop. Victor, their spy, opened the door and departed with a nod. He slammed the door shut and said, "Will see you on the other side, team."

Andrew nodded with apprehension as Joseph pulled out onto the highway and sped towards their target location.

Their arrival a few minutes later was punctuated by the distant wail of sirens. "I'll get the armoured lorry with Joseph to transfer our data bank," Andrew said. "Ashaar, park the car while we unlock the archive."

He nodded with a response. "What's he gonna do inside?"

"He'll extract the remaining intel from his blood and put them in IV bags. We need to secure all the DNA data in his blood. If he dies, the data dies with him."

Ashaar, left to the silence of the car, watched as his companions blended into the shadows.

The archivist remained unknown to Ashaar.

Chapter 29: Ben

"They've just completed the extraction mission," Susan gulped, her shoulders slumping as Andrew confirmed the status of the archivist.

"Where did they rescue him from?" Ben asked.

"Sentinel asked us to observe a location for a recon mission a few weeks ago in Altstadt, Munich. They contacted one of our spies and came face to face with Bowman," Susan exhaled heavily, "the nanobots are keeping the archivist alive."

Susan and Ben quickly exited Susan's car when they saw the black SUV arriving. "I don't know who's on our side, but I'm sure that the factions have the authorities on their side."

Andrew held the archivist's head before the retinal scan.

The hissing sound of the sliding door filled the silence in the air.

"Take him inside," Andrew said, as he signalled Joseph to go with him. They were supposed to retrieve two armoured vehicles, one of which would carry the DNA drive, and the other being a decoy.

Susan, Emma and Ben brought the archivist inside. They opened the entrance and entered the antechamber. On the back of the door, it said,

> What would you say if we were giving the future a chance to survive?

Inside was a tunnel shaped like a hexagon, almost like walking into a submarine antechamber. Big fibre-optic cables on the wall hummed as they transmitted data from the archive to Sentinel. Bright LEDs, placed squarely on the wall, gave off a warm light that was so similar to sunshine that one could be easily confused with the other. LEDs glowed on the overhead ceiling, reflecting in the polished floor as a secured, off-white metal door loomed at the corridor's end. The door's thickness could be compared to the metal vault of a bank. The antechamber to the entrance of the archive looked nothing less than a spaceship, it truly was built to sustain the needs of a future quantum AI.

The archivist opened the heavy vault door using the touchscreen lock, stepped inside and sat down on a chair. The entire vault was filled with blue and red fluids that looked like IVs that doctors would feed through the veins. They were fastened to the wall using maglocks, while titanium carrying cases were scattered on the floor. The archivist inserted the IV and asked Ben to accompany him.

"What are you doing?" Ben asked, "You need medical attention!"

"I don't."

Ben shook inside the vault while he continued to follow the Archivist's instructions. "Do you even have a name?"

"Bryan. My name is Bryan Jamal-Warner."

"What's in these IV bags?" Ben asked.

"These are CRISPR modified, genetically coded information in synthetic DNA drives. These are injected into the blood. We need to ensure that the factions do not take hold of these DNA drives."

"What do you need me to do? I can code, but I *cannot* modify anything."

"Load as much as you can into the cases, and we take them with us." Bryan tapped on a health monitor to execute an upload function. "I need to extract my payload ASAP before we are attacked. If I die, my data dies with me. You need every bit of data to make sure that Sentinel can access and protect the multiverse."

Ben scrambled to open cold storage cases, got as many IV fluid bags as possible, and put them inside the unmarked titanium cases. Every time he opened those cold storages, he puffed a bit of smoke emerging from them, and it didn't smell nice.

Five minutes later.

"Are you doing okay, Ben?" Bryan raised a brow.

Ben's nostrils flared, shoulders tightening. He rested his palms on his knees, breathing heavily. "I need someone else. Someone stronger to help you."

Bryan tapped his comm as it made a glitching noise, "We need to get someone inside the vault. Ben can't do it. Some stuff is too heavy for Ben to move around."

"Ashaar, get to the vault," Susan commanded over a physical communications device that Ben had received from them earlier.

"On my way," Ashaar replied.

"I'll call reinforcements. They will guard the outside perimeter," Bryan responded. He tapped the back of his neck four times in a repeated pattern.

A few minutes later, they could hear an SUV arriving. Ben noticed some armed men running in the opposite direction and entering a building.

Bryan's team was supposed to take a little more time.

The door opened, slowly and defiantly, as Ashaar walked into the antechamber. Just outside the entrance of the vault, Ben handed over the instructions to him, "Here's the key to the rest of the cases. Load as many as you can, then leave the vault."

Ashaar looked around. The lighting wasn't eye-friendly, the restricted brightness and the eclectic colour were ominous.

Ashaar, one by one, loaded the suitcase-like carrying cases with Ben. They had a strong rubber handle at the top. The entire place was filled with those heavy carrying cases.

Susan walked into the vault, eyed Ben and said, "Ben, you need to leave before the enemies arrive. The best place would be to go to your office and wait until further instructions."

"Do I have a car?" Ben asked.

"Yes, take mine. It's parked on the side," Susan replied.

Ben left, taking Susan's car.

Chapter 30: Emma

Emma and Susan lingered outside the vault in the antechamber. Closing the outside door, Susan took her backpack out and opened an armoured case. Inside were two mini automatic guns that seemed to have rearranged themselves like a block of Legos, which clicked, turned and transformed into a weapon. Outside, two low-energy quantum pulse repeaters had transmitted everyone's location to *Sentinel* so that it could intervene at any moment.

"What the hell is this?" Emma glanced at the case.

Susan's lips parted slightly, about to speak, "These are self-folding semi-automatic weapons."

Emma glowered at them for a few seconds.

Susan asked Emma to put her finger on the case and assign it to her biometrics. "This one is yours." She handed it to Emma and showed her how to trigger it, "Now place your finger in the green pad to activate it."

"Wow." Emma could hear a crackling metal noise, as a piece of carved metal had transformed into a weapon.

"Your training is going to be useful today," Susan dragged Emma near the edge of the chamber, closed the door, and placed a rounded, flashing device at the door. "See those?" she pointed outside. "Those are quantum pulse repeaters. If there's any activity within one mile from that direction, it will notify Sentinel to take over and send assistance." Susan stared at her watch for a few seconds and entered some code.

"Now what?" Emma waited for Susan to finish.

She unlatched the strap and threw the watch at Emma, "Take my tactical assessment interface. The code is Hotel Zulu November Charlie."

"Are we calling backup?"

"We don't know whether we were tracked here. All we know is that the factions could arrive." Susan added, "Our armed response operatives will take a few hours to get here. Bryan might have reinforcements in the nearby vicinity."

Ten minutes went by.

Hiding behind a metal plate next to the door, Emma swallowed a lump, watching Susan load her gun and rapidly type on her hand terminal.

"Why did you ask Ashaar to go inside the vault? That's literally what the factions want to destroy." Emma asked Susan. "Why can't *we* do it?" Emma swallowed a lump, realising that she was suffering the emotions of Alpha Emma.

"We need as many tacticians as we can. You are trained as one, and you should thank your father for it. Bryan has called for reinforcements. If they don't arrive here on time, we are monumentally fucked." Susan squinted through the visor of her weapon, trying to spot the people who walked out of an SUV.

Emma looked at Ashaar walking inside the archive, anticipating nothing would go wrong. "I can't watch him die, Susan."

"No one is dying, Emma," Susan patted her back.

Emma could hear Ashaar and Bryan's voices echoing through the antechamber. Her eyes caught the gaze of the archivist inside the vault unloading data from his blood.

***

Ashaar finally stepped inside the archive. "Bryan? What the fuck are you doing here?"

"Do we know each other?" Bryan pulled out a syringe, shifting his gaze between his hand and Ashaar.

"Yes, I do. I'm from a different universe."

"We can talk about this later. I have drawn the rest of the hard drives from my body. They are in these IV bags. They will need to be synthesised; the blood will then be separated from the fluid."

"What happens to the blood?" Ashaar asked.

"It's donated. Sentinel sent the formula. It's safe."

Ashaar stood in silence, his mind racing as he attempted to formulate a response.

"Right," Bryan unhooked the IV bags filled with payload.

Ashaar barely managed to grab those four bags from Bryan's hand, and at that moment, a volley of bullets flew through the open door. Bryan plunged back into the chair and smashed his head on the headboard.

Ashaar saw the terminals making deafening noises, lights flashing all over the vault, and filling up the room with a loud, excruciating scream.

"Close the door *now*!" Bryan's mouth had filled with blood before he could utter another word.

Ashaar scrambled to close the vault, but it was stuck.

No one could identify where the shots came from.

"They have the technology to penetrate thick walls. They saw us inside. We shouldn't have left the vault open." Bryan struggled to speak as blood poured out of his nostrils.

Ashaar was struggling to close the vault door with his bare hands.

He realised the enemy wanted someone dead.

Their target was Bryan.

Bryan went into shock.

Susan and Emma fired multiple rounds. Muffling sniper shots pierced through the walls, whizzing past Emma and thudding into the vault.

Ashaar managed to shut it, but the door was automatic, so he couldn't seal it. He grabbed a few IV bags Bryan gave him and walked towards the titanium case lying on the floor. The door was still closing, inch by inch. Before opening the case, two bullets hit the pack of fluids he held in his right hand, went through them and hit his abdomen. Blood splattered all over his shirt, the floor and surrounding walls. The speed of the bullets from their sniper pushed him a few inches back, knocking him off his feet. Ashaar tumbled to the floor, on his back and striking his head on the metal tiles. He screamed in agony for a few seconds, going into cardiac arrest. His body was thrown back as blood splashed out of his mouth, a warm wetness spreading across his front.

Ashaar was flat, lying down on the floor. Blood and other fluids splattered all over his face and limbs. As he fought for air, he became aware of a high-pitched sound. The sound of gunfire was slowly fading away.

***

"Fuck, *no!*" Emma screamed and ran towards the vault. By that time, the door had closed and snapped shut.

It made a clicking noise.

"Emma, *no!*" Susan held her arm and pulled her back. "Keep your focus, Emma. We are here to save the archive."

"I fucking knew this would happen!" Emma's eyes teared up. Susan wiped her eyes with her hands and pulled her to the side. They ducked for cover as another round of bullets whistled past their ears.

Emma realised she had experienced the other Emma's memories from universe Alpha, as clear as day. The quantum frame had leaked emotional turbulence across the universes.

She had been burdened with both Emma's feelings.

A few minutes later, as Bryan's military reinforcements arrived at the scene, they took control of the gunfight. The fire ceased. The factions were aware that they had eliminated Bryan and pulled back.

Susan pulled her tactical assessment panel on her terminal and evaluated the situation. She opened the entrance and gaped at the reinforcements, a black suit and carbon-fibre body armour that looked identical to a ceramic-plated object, casting a clear reflection. The helmets had a heads-up display, and LEDs flickered in an array of colours on their chests. The voice in their comms, the confirmation of the enemy backing off, and team chatter, were picked up by her ears passively. She listened as the laser emitting from the top of her semi-automatic gun powered down. Around her, was Emma, hopelessly and frantically looking for a clue to find out what had happened inside the archive. "They are backing off," Susan confirmed.

Emma thought to herself that Bryan's reinforcements had arrived faster than she had hoped.

The fact that they had come through was a stunning surprise.

Emma yanked her terminal out and tried to make contact. She had no clue what was happening inside and whether anyone was alive, "Why didn't Sentinel intervene?" Her hands ached.

"We can't establish TACT because they were too far from the perimeter defended by the quantum pulse repeater." Susan took her phone out of her pocket at the sound of breaking news. There were two more archives, one in London and the other in South Africa.

"Cape Town archive is gone," Andrew said over comm, driving, on his way back to the Munich archive.

"Andrew," Susan added, "there's been an event in London too."

Andrew exhaled a sigh. He closed his eyes and took another long breath before continuing, "I can't fucking believe this is happening."

"How did they implode the archives?" Susan asked Andrew.

"The factions created a black hole generator. They're destroying all the archives using that." Andrew sent over the blueprints.

Emma looked down at her hand terminal displaying the blueprint.

"There are more," Susan said as she continued tapping on her terminal.

"How?" Emma asked.

"Fuck! We don't know where the others are!" Susan said.

Emma's heart pounded in her chest.

"The signature carries data from the quantitative lab in California. They've turned Sentinel's technology against us," Susan replied.

Emma remained silent for a couple of seconds. *Don't say it Susan, don't say there's one inside this archive.*

Susan's fingers tapped a rhythm on the wall. "If that's true, then we're not just up against the factions; we're up against time."

"Why?" Emma asked, gripping Susan's hand.

"Because there might be a bomb inside this archive."

Chapter 31: Ashaar

Mid-November 2030, Munich

Ashaar woke up inside the vault. He was choking and out of breath. He kept on gasping, blood splattered all over his shirt. The room wasn't outfitted to carry outside noise.

With a sick feeling similar to the one that came with a migraine, he walked his fingers over his shirt, to his chest, and to a couple of sturdy metal rounded objects that he felt on the right side of his abdomen. His mind skimmed off the thought, *it can't be bullets.* If it was, he would have been dead. But the pain was absolutely mind-bending.

He'd been hurt before, but this topped all the charts, including the time he broke his leg on a bike. He continued to deceive himself and chose not to look down. He closed his eyes, for one second, took a deep breath, and exhaled. Ashaar opened his eyes wide, and he looked for answers. He turned his neck and looked left and right. Dried fluid had glued to his eyes. His throat ached and burned when he tried swallowing the fluid at the back of his throat. It took him a few seconds to understand what it tasted like, blood.

"Hello, is anyone there?" Ashaar swallowed his fear, trying to shove blood down his throat.

No response.

"Hello, is anyone out there?" Ashaar looked at his hands, the melancholy in his brain was frightening in a sense he found tricky to comprehend.

"Ashaar?" a knock was heard, the muffling sound thudding against the walls of the archive.

Ashaar looked up. "Hello?"

Following the glitching noise, Emma's voice appeared in his comm. "Ash?"

"I'm here, Emma. I am alive."

Emma took a deep breath and exhaled a sigh of relief.

"Fluids in here stopped me from dying," Ashaar replied, scared to look down at his chest.

"The nanotech in the storage kept you from being taken out." Emma added, "They are repairing the damage."

"How do you know this?" Ashaar asked.

"Doesn't matter," Emma responded.

"How is the GPS working, Emma?"

"Susan told me I could hack into your communication device." Emma said, "Can you describe how bad your damage is?"

"I don't know. I don't know what to do, Emma."

"Right now, you can only hear me. I need to activate multi-channel comm to let Susan talk to you."

"Okay."

***

Emma tapped her comm three times to patch Susan in.

Just outside in the antechamber, Susan handed over a terminal into Emma's hand, "Take this and see if you can penetrate through the thick wall. It's going to take a while to connect more than three people, and then you will need to go to this page to stimulate enhanced broadcasting. It will piggyback on our quant comm channel."

"I can see that the dot is moving," Emma looked at the terminal, observing a red dot moving back and forth. "But I can't track any other signals inside."

"We don't have a medic in the team. We need someone here without getting the hospital involved," Susan replied.

"Let's find a way to get him out of the vault first." Emma walked back towards the door of the vault.

She heard the muffling footsteps approaching.

The silence was creeping over her.

"Tell me what you see, Ashaar." Emma asked.

"There are red lasers near the door," he replied.

"Is there any button to deactivate?"

"No, I don't think so." Ashaar was struggling to breathe.

"You are breathing too fast. Calm down. I'm here, Ash. I'm here with you. I won't leave you alone this time, I promise."

"Wait—" Ashaar paused, and said, "There is a device underneath the chair. A large case made of titanium I think."

"No way! I know what this is. You need to wait while I contact the team," Emma said. She turned around, her heart beating fast. "Oh shit, this isn't happening. He can't deactivate an implosion bomb. What should I do?"

"We need military-grade nanobots if he's exposed to radiation." Susan tapped her comm and switched to the encrypted channel, asking the others to hurry.

Susan explained the scenario to the team.

A few minutes later, Andrew, Joseph and others arrived at the scene.

"What is Ashaar still doing in there?" Andrew asked.

"I think one of the faction members had access to an x-ray enabled device. Their bullets hit right in his chest while he was carrying all the DNA drives," Susan said.

"How are you communicating with him?" Andrew asked.

"Susan gave me this." Emma showed the terminal.

"You hacked into his comm? For fuck's sake!" Joseph said.

"I did." Emma said.

"That could have taken down the entire channel," Joseph said. "You jeopardise our entire mission for this?"

"Okay, you guys need to stop arguing, for God's sake. This is not the time for it. All our comms are still working." Andrew turned his gaze to Emma, "Do you know how to patch him in?"

Emma reached for her neck and tapped into the comm three times in a pattern and used the terminal in her hand. "Ashaar, you need to be patched in with the entire team since they are all here."

"What the fuck is happening, Emma?" Ashaar asked.

"Press the comm three times, then press it the fourth time after two seconds. I'll have it established contact through the terminal, and then I can patch you in." She frantically tapped on the terminal and scowled. The chime from the device made her feel relieved.

"Ashaar, can you hear me?" Andrew asked.

"Glad to hear your voice, Andrew. My ears are so blocked that it feels like you are talking inside my head."

Andrew replied, "You have to move and listen to exactly what Joseph tells you."

***

"Ashaar, describe what you can see." Joseph's voice was loud over his comm.

"It's a 3ft by 4ft box, with sharp edges and has no buttons at all." Ashaar looked frantically for a button. He realised that the nanobots were working hard to keep him alive.

"Whatever you do, don't touch it or do anything with it, without my permission, Ashaar."

"Okay, Joseph, tell me what on earth am I supposed to do with this."

Emma joined the conversation, "Something happened in London, Ashaar. We need you to deactivate it because it will wipe you out and anyone within the five-mile vicinity. The device can create a temporal gravitational field that's powerful as a black hole. It will shred everything into pieces and turn every physical compound into dust." She exhaled, "Remember your quantum tunnel?"

"Yes, of course I do, Emma. What's the point?"

"They somehow managed to convert it into a ..."

"A fucking *implosion bomb*?" Ashaar held his chest and shouted.

"You need to neutralise it," Joseph added.

"I need to *what*?" Ashaar was outraged.

"Ashaar, you need to make this work otherwise, we can't save anyone," Emma replied.

"You need to leave this place, Emma."

"I'm not leaving you here. I don't care what happens."

Ashaar closed his eyes and took a deep breath. He thought about everything that had happened in the past few years. "Okay, let's go, Joseph."

"Are there any sharp objects?" Joseph asked.

"There is nothing."

"Check the drawers."

"There's nothing."

"Check Bryan," Joseph insisted.

"Found a knife."

"Open the two dots, do not touch it. Use the knife to tap it slowly," Joseph continued.

"I have. I have. I can see the full set of devices. I don't know what it's called." Ashaar felt lightheaded.

"There are two red dots on one side and one green dot on the other. You will need to press those two red dots together. When you hear a beeping noise, press the green dot."

"Done, what's next?" Ashaar asked, his hands shaking.

"Two minutes, guys." Andrew said.

Joseph spoke faster. "Open the metal steel ball that is connected using a harness from both sides."

"Jesus Christ. Done that." Ashaar frantically looked around, "There are no physical wires."

"It's a device without one." Joseph paced up. "It would be the smallest screw of everything you see. You need the sharp edge of the knife." Joseph's voice was louder by the second. "Do not touch the harnesses. They will electrocute you and everything else."

Ashaar tapped the dot. Two sharp-edged metals appeared from the sides.

"There's a circular device coming out!" Ashaar said.

"It's the failsafe." Joseph replied.

"Ashaar, pull out the metal device right now before it gets trapped. *Do it right now!*" Joseph's voice was followed by a loud, ear-piercing noise in Ashaar's head.

Ashaar pulled out the thick black device and tossed it towards the vault's door. The device made a thumping noise, automatically retracted and deactivated itself.

With five seconds left, the laser was gone. Ashaar unlocked the door without frying his organs.

"Are we done?" Ashaar asked as he licked blood out of his lower lip.

"I'm trying to open the door." Emma replied.

"What the hell happened?" Ashaar asked.

"It's the contingency core," Andrew replied. "When you came into contact with the device, it was radioactive. Unless we find the German MT and access their military-grade nanobots, we cannot save you."

Ashaar heard every word over the comm. But he just didn't care anymore.

The hiss noise from the door filled the noiseless chamber. Ashaar fell onto Emma's shoulder. Emma grabbed Ashaar with both hands. He couldn't walk.

"I'm fine," Ashaar insisted, feeling the force of white, decontaminating smoke striking his skin. The pressure from his nerves bucked under his skin, as he felt the force of gravity. The nanobots drained his energy, trying to repair the nerve damage. It pushed his blood down below his hips, felt like his vision was narrowing. The eardrums were turning into soundproof chambers.

"No, you are not." Emma frowned at Ashaar. "I'm going to take him to the safehouse right now while Susan brings the Med team."

"Take him to a *hospital*!" Andrew roared at Emma.

"I *will* bring the Med team," Susan replied, her voice firm, as she packed her bags.

Emma continued to walk while Ashaar barely held himself against Emma's shoulder. "If your superintelligence has a bit of emotion attached to its consciousness, it'll figure out a way." On the way to the parking lot, she stood next to the quantum pulse repeaters, unlocked the watch that Susan had given to her, and tapped Hotel Zulu November Charlie.

Emma wrapped her arm around Ashaar's waist and pulled him in. After a couple of minutes, they observed Joseph's car approach from a distance.

***

Ashaar was struggling with the pain. The force of the vehicle driving through hairpin roads and intermittent acceleration made the space teeter. "Slow down, Jo, I'm gonna throw up."

"We don't have time Ashaar," he replied.

Emma interrupted Ashaar's thoughts. She asked, "So, you still love Alpha Emma?"

Ashaar, eyes closed, could feel the soft touch of her hands over his head. "Do you want me to have a heart attack?" Ashaar replied, his head resting on Emma's lap.

"I have a few questions that might help you to understand a tough German woman." Emma asked, "Shall we play a game?"

"Sure, why not," Ashaar groaned, his breath coming out short and shallow, "don't really have a choice."

Emma cupped his face, smiled and moved his chin from side to side. "Okay, before you are granted permission to enter her heart, you need to tell me, what are the two most followed sports in the country?"

"Rules and regulations?" Ashaar replied.

"Correct!" Emma replied. "A train travels from Mannheim to Munich at a speed of 150kph due east. What time does it arrive?"

"On time," Ashaar chuckled and coughed. He still had blood in his mouth.

"Great!" Emma smiled. "Last question: what do Germans usually do when they love someone?"

Ashaar replied, "They share food?!" He looked up. They had arrived at the safehouse.

Chapter 32: Emma

Mid-November 2030, Munich

Emma and Joseph moved Ashaar to a subtle haven nestled within the German city's labyrinthine streets. As Ashaar's tired head found relief in Emma's lap, her fingers tenderly caressed his hair, stained with the crimson of his wounds. Her outfit, now marked with blood, bore the evidence of their ordeal.

Ashaar's eyes wandered. He took in his surroundings through a haze of discomfort. "What is this place?"

"We're in a safehouse," Emma replied. "It's a safehouse for the Med team that Susan was talking about."

With gentle guidance from both Joseph and Emma, Ashaar was eased onto a bed designed for healing. Its crisp linens was a stark contrast to the chaos they had left behind.

"I'm gonna go back and rendezvous with my team," Joseph said and then left.

"Here, this will help with the pain." Emma punched an EpiPen-like device, some form of nanobots, into his blood. She pressed her comm, waiting for Susan's voice to appear.

Half an hour later, in the med bay, Ashaar woke up. "Emma, is Susan here yet?"

"No."

"How long do I have?"

"You'll live, shut up." Emma continued, "Sentinel will want you to go back and to neutralise the ripples of space-time."

"You are making me sound like an important person."

"You are," Emma looked at wounded Ashaar, and her eyes turned red. "But the problem is ..."

"What problem?"

"I don't ..." Emma paused and choked up. "I want you to stay in this universe. You want me to be more honest?" Before Ashaar could utter a word, she continued, "I ... Ash ... I had to keep some information from you. A while ago, I used Sentinel's quantum matrix to access my memory chain."

"Wow. You ... what did you learn?"

"Instead of mine, I ended up accessing Alpha Emma's memories. And that's how I found out about everything...." She sank her teeth into her upper lip.

Despite the fact that she may have harboured some remorse, she didn't show it. She hid how good she felt after learning everything. Emma took a deep breath, tightened her chest and decided to not let it affect her at that moment.

"Wait a second. Back in my universe, Alpha Emma kept saying that she felt lightheaded. That could be why." He let out a nervous laugh.

"Did she?" Emma grabbed a white plastic bottle and poured ethanol on a white band-aid-type cloth.

Squinting his eyes, Ashaar said, "Yes, she had this feeling, some form of quantum cryptography kept appearing in her head. I clearly remember the day when I told her about California, and the day when we had a huge fight." He shut his eyes and tried remembering, "She told me that when things are...."

Emma interrupted, "Intense, she needed to take a step back." She slid her hand under his shirt, pulled his belt down a little and rubbed that cloth over the damaged flesh on his lower abdomen. The nanobots had repaired enough cells for the blood to stop leaking through his ruptured skin. "So she felt me accessing her memories? That's insane."

"It's mind-boggling how Sentinel let you access her memories." Ashaar groaned out of pain as the alcohol interacted with his skin. "It can't be a coincidence."

"I can feel everything she felt." Emma was eager to know more, but she saw Ashaar losing control. He was out of focus, and so was she. But too inundated with how wonderful she felt because he was alive.

"Emma, when you signed up for this team, did you know you had the code in your head?"

"No, I didn't. I signed up because I realised I had the power to stop the factions from destroying us. And it was inevitable. Ashaar...." her eyes were lowered.

Ashaar swallowed a lump. "What?"

"Alpha Emma lied to you."

"What?"

"Sentinel contacted her."

"That's impossible." Ashaar shifted, sitting up.

Emma pushed him back. "Relax. Alpha Emma still doesn't know much. But being a physicist, she knew those text messages were real. Sentinel was real. She just didn't want to accept it. Stephanie threatened her so that you could leave Cognition and join Xplorer's quantum team."

"So that I could be in the lab during the explosion?"

"No," Emma replied, her tone sharp. "So that you could help build their technology and contact Sentinel."

"That didn't happen." Ashaar replied with a chuckle, struggling to talk. "You need to tell me what you know. What memories you accessed."

Emma said, "Not now. Once you are okay. I need to wait until Susan arrives with the Med team." She placed her index finger on his lips.

Ashaar gently caressed the back of his hand against Emma's arm. "If Sentinel can't save me, please don't prolong it. I would rather be dead than be a walking corpse."

Her eyebrows lowered and lips raised, squeezing her face to express her displeasure, "Stop talking bullshit." Emma slowly took her black jumper off while she sat next to Ashaar and threw it on a sofa. She tied her hair with a rubber band, and washed her hands in a small sink right next to the surgical bed. She wiped his blood off her fingers and rubbed her hands with more alcohol. Emma rolled her chair back, sat next to Ashaar, and placed her right hand on his chest. "We have a few minutes of silence. It's just the two of us. Let's enjoy it."

Determined to stay positive, she pressed her hands against his rib cage. The smooth cotton of his black shirt felt calm against her skin.

"Okay," Ashaar replied. "You still have that B positive blood flowing through your veins." Ashaar gazed at her as she beamed. She wore a snug-fitting tank top with a low rounded neck and form-fitting jeans, the sticky blood from Ashaar's body all over her jeans adding complexity to her ensemble.

"Shut up! All you need to know is that I try to hold myself back because I'm not good with emotions," Emma said.

At that moment, Emma opened herself—opened the door she had locked in for years.

She smiled down at him, eye to eye. Her short, lighter-than-usual hair looked exquisite. She opened her sanctuary to someone, and let that person in, like Alpha Emma did. She had an epiphany. Alpha Emma behaved harshly, treated him differently, tried walking away—all that because he was her safehouse. Ashaar was one of the few people in her life who infiltrated her sanctuary. Emma could be anyone with him, a friend, a sloppy eater and scream, shout, laugh, cry, express every other emotion she had. Emma had a curtain held between her feelings and the surrounding people, and she never lifted that curtain, until Ashaar came. She let her heart open and treated him rashly because she felt something. She didn't want them to flow through her heart.

Ashaar extended his hand. He held Emma's left arm and gripped it, "Do you trust me, Emma?"

Emma lifted his palm, pulled it towards her lap, brushed her fingers with his cold skin and grasped it decisively, "I do. I trusted you with everything I have, Ashaar."

Ashaar felt the back of his hand against the big silver buttons on her high-waist jeans, "Then tell me that the situation is really bad. At least tell me how long these nanobots will work."

"No, it's not. And it's not just about you. I can't watch you walk away. It felt like you had died. Every fibre of my being felt this pain through Alpha Emma's memories." Emma pulled his hand closer, bent down a little and scratched the back of Ashaar's bruised hand on her cheek, with her eyes closed. She felt him feel her, appreciate the few minutes they had for themselves. He wasn't extraordinary. But at the minute, in the charming moment, he seemed different.

He took her breath away.

Ashaar was startled by the warmth on her face. He kept his eyes closed and experienced a tidal wave of satisfaction racing towards him. He leaned into her touch and was soothed by it.

Emma didn't move an inch for the next ten minutes. She continued stroking his scars with a faint, relaxing smile on her lips. They appreciated the companionable silence.

When the silence had settled down, a nurse arrived.

Ashaar made a loud noise a few minutes later as he struggled with increasing pain. "Can you give me some more painkillers? Those things you have there?"

Emma's heart thudded, "I can."

The nurse said, "Diazepam 2mg—IV. Here's the shot."

Emma rapidly grabbed the pen and inserted it into his arm into a visible vein. She held his arm with her other hand and pressed her nails into his muscles, "Just close your eyes for now."

"Okay." Ashaar drifted into sleep.

Emma looked down, and a few drops of tears slid from her eyes. She held his hand while he slept.

He was showing symptoms of a mild cardiac arrest. Every machine tossed a loud beeping noise. The nurse tried to defibrillate, raised pulse levels to a normal range and gave him more medicine just as the doorbell rang.

The nanobots from the Med team arrived. Emma handed it over to the nurse, who injected the nanobots into Ashaar's IV and the effects were instant. His skin cleared and his heartbeat relaxed. It was working.

***

Emma, like her typical self, carried spare clothes. That night, she wandered through the streets of Munich, looking for a gift that would surprise Ashaar. Her quantum pulse repeater would keep the enemies away, knowing Sentinel was watching her every move.

She wanted to make a gesture, give Ashaar something that would light up his sentiments, and aid him in healing faster.

At 9:30 p.m., Emma swiped her card and returned to the medical safehouse.

Her comm chirped.

"Are you going to stay at the medical safehouse? We've got safehouses, and can get you one if you'd like," Susan asked.

"No, I want to stay with Ashaar. I don't need a bed to sleep. I'll crash on the sofa," Emma replied.

"Copy." Susan's voice disappeared with a glitch.

Emma carried a small gift box wrapped in white paper. She went into the corner of the warehouse, left the box on the sofa, and grabbed her towel from the bag. The safehouse was much warmer and Sentinel controlled the temperature to ensure Ashaar healed faster. It felt over 28 degrees inside. Emma hung her wet coat on the wall. She took off her top and jeans that she'd been wearing all day, leaving her clothes on the sofa. She walked into the shower; it had voice-activated features. "Turn on," she said out loud. Emma stood under the boiling water, letting it run through her hair and shoulders, and wiped her face with it. It felt warm, raw and comfortable. After enjoying the moment, she killed the shower with her voice, took the towel, wiped her body and hair. From her backpack, she took out and wore a black tank top and her biker shorts, adding an air of relaxation. She brushed her hair over the sink and looked at herself as her muscles suffered a momentary slackness.

Her footsteps and intermittent noise from the bathroom woke Ashaar up.

"Hey, hi," she said.

"Hi Emma."

"Are you feeling better?" Emma walked in as the glass door to his med bay automatically opened.

"Probably slightly better." Ashaar coughed, "What time is it?"

"It's almost ten. Can I get you anything?"

"Stay with me," Ashaar smirked.

Emma tapped a code on her watch. The glass windows of the med bay turned opaque immediately. Anyone in that safehouse wouldn't hear or see anything unless they stood inside the med bay. The wavelength limiter absorbed the sound and made the room completely soundproof. She found the last dose of nanobots left on his side table, with a note saying Last Dose. Make sure you give it around 9:45 pm. Emma picked up an injection and grabbed the metal container filled with thick, semi-liquid nanobots. She pressed the blue button at the top of its casing and watched a latticework of nanobots immediately unfold itself. They appeared to be shrinking and expanding, as if the living cells were inhaling the oxygen from the air. She placed the bevel in front of the nanobots, pulled the plunger and filled the vacuumed barrel.

Emma pushed the hydraulic rails down on the side of the bed, making space for herself. She folded her bare leg, brushed it over Ashaar's and pulled the white box out underneath the table. "Look, I got you something."

Emma noticed how Ashaar tried opening his eyes, had his gaze fixed on her, her black biker shorts clung firmly to his pyjamas, and her black baseball cap hid her face from the white LED lights above. Her hair was fairly wet and smelled of shampoo. "Can you open it? Took me a while to raise my hand." Ashaar asked.

"I would like you to try to open it, Ash."

Tearing the white wrapper, he found something written inside it. Squinting, he asked, "What is it? A code?"

Emma leaned closer to him. "Back in July, Susan gave me an air-gapped terminal with a handbook. I learned a lot of stuff, like hacking your comm, and even hacking Sentinel."

Ashaar turned his head, looking straight into her eyes. "What is this?" Ashaar shook his head, as if data had penetrated his head as he squinted into the code further.

"Now that you've stared at it for five seconds, you should remember this code. If you ever need to reach out, this code is the only way to use Sentinel's backend and send an emergency broadcast across space-time."

Ashaar gazed at Emma for a few seconds.

He creased his brow, squinting one eye. "It feels like someone inserted a needle into my brain."

"It's your neurons reacting to the data," Emma smiled. "You'll be okay."

Ashaar, exhaling a sigh, stared into Emma's eyes.

"Why are you looking at me like that, Ash?"

"You've grown into such a stunning woman. I love this version of you."

Emma's lips curled up into a grin, "Stop. You're welcome," Emma added, "Susan said we needed to do something to lift your spirits, so I tried being a good friend."

"You are literally the best!" Ashaar gazed, as their eyes locked. He felt, for the first time, something he had never experienced. "Where are you going to sleep?"

"Here. On the sofa. I want to be here. Close to you."

"Thank you, Em. You could have got a safehouse."

"I don't want a safehouse," she leaned in closer and locked her eyes with his, "I want to absorb every minute and every second I have left with you."

A few minutes later, she went to grab some food, and returned to Ashaar's room holding a white plastic bag. As soon as the sliding glass doors closed, she pressed her fingers on the glass slab, locked the med bay and turned on the privacy.

"Is anyone coming?" Ashaar asked.

"No, just in case," Emma walked towards Ashaar. "I wanted a private moment with you." She leaped back onto Ashaar's bed, holding her bowl with a towel while sitting cross-legged. "I think you'll be okay with sharing this with me. The nurse said that I'm allowed to give you solid food."

Emma slurped some soup, it was hot. She blew on it, cooled it down and fed Ashaar.

"Come here," Ashaar pulled her feet. "Otherwise, you are going to spill that hot soup all over."

Emma slid closer to him, her knees resting on Ashaar's chest, and tapped a button on the health monitor, which showed the status repair. "78%," Emma said, "I think the nanobots have done pretty well to repair the damage in your abdomen," Emma said. "You can now digest food particles now." Emma poured more soup noodles and held the spoon near Ashaar's mouth, "Here."

"Ok," Ashaar slurped, arms resting on Emma's knees.

Under the bright white LED lights dispersing from the overhead units, Emma and Ashaar conversed all night. Their voices faded as they both succumbed to weariness. Before she went to sleep, Emma felt his fingers stroking her forearm. She moved closer, bent down, held Ashaar's face with her hand, rubbed his beard and brushed her wet lips on his cheek. She kissed, shifted to the left, gently stroked his lips with hers and kissed again.

The pair spent their night inextricably linked. Emma, while conversing with Ashaar, fell asleep on his chest. He had her in his arms, and he was moving as he did so. Her load was shifted by the movement of his ribcage as she perched atop it.

When Emma woke up, she turned and checked the time, 6:30 a.m. and made some breakfast. Outside, the storm from last night left behind a little mist. The guilt or shame that came with falling for him wasn't there, notwithstanding her repeated vows to herself. She was luminescing with contentment and love.

Her hand terminal chimed a ping.

Andrew: Prepare Ashaar for departure. Wheels up in 60.

Chapter 33: Stella

November 22, 2030, London

Stella had snapped up Sophia from her school and taken her to one of her aunt's houses. She lived a little further away from London, but it was a safe location. As Stella drove her car through the outskirts of London, her hand frequently tapped the horn in frustration amidst the rush-hour traffic. Next to her, Sophia busied herself with her digital drawings on her iPad, oblivious to the chaos outside. Dropping Sophia off at a relative's house, Stella continued her journey alone, thoughts swirling as heavy rain began to fall, drumming rhythmically against her windscreen.

The rain seemed to mirror the cascade of thoughts about her intricate, painful journey. Ashaar and Emma flashed in her mind. She knew about Lambda Ashaar's tragic death and Alpha Ashaar in this timeline. Stella's grip on the steering wheel tightened slightly as she pondered this reality shift, a deep sense of responsibility weighing on her.

The game of secrecy in the background played continuously in her head. Bowman, her colleague, was on the brink of taking over Cognition.

The factions wanted that code to trace the origin of a newly discovered quantum matrix. This matrix was their primary platform for transferring consciousness across the different timelines. She didn't know much about the matrix, and her only goal was to control it and find its origin before Andrew and Susan. The factions were convinced that this complex matrix was the work of an alien AI or a civilisation from beyond this solar system. Stella wanted to learn everything about it. She wanted to trace its origin back to universe Alpha. But in order to get there, she needed Sentinel's code.

A shiver ran down her back as she contemplated taking over the world.

The rain intensified, mirroring the storm of thoughts in her mind. Stella knew the factions aimed to create their version of Sentinel, a tool to further their own ends, and under her leadership. The magnitude of this knowledge sat heavily on her, a burden she carried with a facade of normality.

Turning on her indicator to pull up to the safehouse, Stella took a deep breath.

She prepared herself to continue playing a role in this convoluted narrative. She had to maintain the pretence that she was not Lambda Stella from this branched timeline.

She was Stella from Lambda-A who'd jumped many hosts and managed to escape death for two centuries.

The knowledge that her consciousness had overwritten the Stella of this timeline, effectively erasing her existence, was a secret guarded closely by the factions.

In the solitude, as the rain fell on her car's windscreen, Stella reflected on her role in the grand scheme of things. She had to dump her feelings for Ashaar. She also couldn't tell anyone about her love for Ashaar, a feeling she had a long time ago, back in the original timeline.

The complexity of her existence, straddling different hosts, timelines and identities, was a solitary journey. She steeled herself for the challenges ahead. Lie, betray and kill. Do whatever it took to fulfil her purpose.

A few knocks later, Susan opened the door and brought her in.

"What is this place?" Stella asked, grazing her eyes around the corridor.

"Stella, I don't have time to explain all this, but just so you know, what you are about to hear will be difficult to accept."

Stella walked in. There was a dining table across the living room. Emma and Ashaar were sitting there.

Emma and Stella had a staring contest.

Stella hated her. Hate was an understatement.

The appearance on her face wasn't strong enough to reveal that hatred. Instead, she turned her gaze at Ashaar and shouted, "Ashaar? Oh my God! Where the hell have you been?"

Ashaar stood up and walked towards Stella.

Stella ran and wrapped her arms around him. Stella gave Emma a brief glimpse to guarantee she was still there. Concurrently, she didn't want to let him go. "Are you okay, Ashaar? What happened to you?"

"I am. Just a bit bruised."

Stella held Ashaar's face with her left palm, gently brushing it against his light beard, "You look like you have been beaten up. Are you sure you are okay? Should we go and see a doctor? You know I love you...."

"No. Listen," he held her palm and moved them away.

Across the room, Emma shifted in rebuttal of the gravity of the situation. She stood up and walked away.

Emma went upstairs without letting anyone notice.

But Stella did. "Susan Schmidt, can you explain all this?" Stella appeared to rage out of frustration.

"Stella, I think we need to be as brief as possible. In a few days, Bowman will merge his company with Cognition." Susan added, “You will not believe this, but we need your help to stop the merger.”

Stella returned a blank stare, her lower lip quivering, “Cognition’s merger? What help?”

Andrew walked into the room. “Stella, our intel suggests that Bowman will be virtually telecasting with all the members in a boardroom. He has built a quantum frame and placed that frame in the room. The device can wipe everyone out.”

“He’s planning to execute all the board members?” Stella asked with inquisitiveness.

“No, he’s planning to bring consciousness from the future. The key members of the board will be overwritten by members of a group called the factions. These groups were created in the future by John Bowman. In the original timeline, they engineered a rogue quantum AI to make this happen.”

Stella remained silent.

Ashaar bent down and pulled Stella’s chair closer. He sat opposite her. He held her hand and put his feet right next to her trainers, “Stella, I know it is hard to accept. But take my word for it: the only way you could save your daughter’s future is by removing John Bowman from the board and stopping that acquisition.”

“What’s the plan?” Stella asked.

“You will go in as instructed. We will direct you to the quantum frame that he has placed underneath, one floor below. You need to insert this stick into the frame. That will do. We will take over from there.” Ashaar handed over a USB.

“Then what?”

“We will stop them from attacking you,” Ashaar replied.

“While Bowman attends the meeting, we will access all his data files,” Susan added, holding her shoulder. “Then take over the virtual screening. Instead of Bowman trying to convince them to sign the papers from the merger of these two companies, everyone will be shown the actual truth—who Bowman is and what he’s doing.”

"What if they don't believe it, Susan?" Stella craned her neck to stare at Susan.

"They probably wouldn't, Stella. That's why you will intervene with this clip. We intercepted this secret message through our backchannel. Maybe his cybersecurity team will find this data and wipe it out. That's why we have securely stored the recording here." Susan showed her the small device.

Stella wanted to ask a question, but she stopped herself.

"Stella, I need to be here with Ben, Dave and Emma." She touched Stella's shoulder gently, "You are staying with me tonight."

"Great, give me a minute." Stella walked into the toilet and pulled a black device. With the push of a button and it emitted a hologram. She tapped a few buttons, scanned the USB device and sent a message to someone,

Stella: Retrieve Dave to Ops before 0600.

That night, Dave was taken hostage by the armed faction battalion. Kjell Abbott, faction second-in-command, led the mission. They took him to a remote warehouse in an unknown location where Bowman was hiding behind a barrage of armed guards. He had been building his own version of quantum AI in that warehouse. Stella was with them on video call, watching it happen.

Abbott brought Dave into the warehouse. He was beaten up. He told Dave that the only way he would spare Andrew, Susan and everyone's lives was if Dave helped the factions with the process.

Stella was aware that no one would have predicted that event.

***

November 23, 2030, London

The morning of the acquisition day.

Everyone was on their nerves. Stella had arrived at the location with Ashaar earlier. He was waiting with the Delta

Armed Response Operatives team of four, and two other backup teams had also been instructed to stay within a one-mile perimeter. Three waves of armed response units dug deep into the territory, eking out a wide, tactical perimeter pushing the limits of their advantage against the factions.

"What are you doing?" Ashaar asked Stella, sitting next to him.

"I'm praying." She revealed a faint smile, laughing nervously. "Once this ends, we can finally live together in peace."

"I am here. We will be waiting for you to alert us and the team will go straight in. Good luck," Ashaar gave her a hug as she left the car.

Stella walked out, concentrating on where she was going while she followed the continuous beeping from her GPS. The black gate stole the spotlight, even though the building's white front was imposing. An array of vehicles clustered outside, parked one after another, hinting at the flurry of activity within. Everyone was there. With the press of the buzzer, she crossed the threshold into the compound. The air was thick with vigilance, the heavy presence of security palpable—though *when* their actual fight would begin was the biggest silent question in Stella's mind.

As she stepped inside, she discovered a gigantic edifice in the midst of reconstruction. The building was sufficient to accommodate warehouses. Stella spotted the evacuation staircase, descended one floor to the location of the quantum frame and took cover behind a barrier.

She stared at the stark, unadorned walls around her. Light was seeping in through the windows. However, transparency was lacking. Nothing was being filmed because CCTV cameras connected to the internet would provide Sentinel with direct access.

A few seconds later, the door opened and she stepped inside.

There was nothing in there except a massive quantum frame. Stella walked towards the terminal and found a port. The screen rotated as the warning sounds came on. She tapped her comm and said, "Standby for access."

"We have access, Stella." Susan replied over comms, in the lab, waiting for Emma to arrive.

Stella noticed two armed responders passing by the room. She was standing in front of the quantum frame, holding her breath.

Two guards slowly walked in.

They found Stella.

Stella was at a standstill, as their gazes locked. She tapped the side of her neck to deactivate her comm device.

One of the armed men broke the silence, "Ma'am."

Stella had been accustomed to regrouping her thoughts after every serious event to improve and evolve her measures and countermeasures. She swallowed a lump and said, "I'm going to walk into the meeting room. Andrew's team have access to our quantum frame. Make sure they don't know who I really am."

"But ma'am, we have orders not to shoot at you."

"Listen," Stella took a few steps forward and pointed her index finger at him, "You take orders from *me*," veins visible on the back of her arm, "No one tells you what to do because you work for me."

"Copy that, ma'am. Proceed as planned." They stepped back and left the room.

***

Stella's pulse quickened. This was an alarm she couldn't ignore. She knew Susan was out there, watching, safeguarding her from the unseen high-tech perch. The sudden, inner voice startled her, a whisper in the caverns of her mind.

She only wished for Susan to be on her side.

"Susan?" she whispered under her breath, barely moving her lips.

"I'm here," Susan affirmed softly over the comm.

Stella steeled herself, standing still as Susan wove her digital magic. No matter what happened, Stella knew Susan would protect her.

Susan was remotely monitoring Stella's elevated levels of BP and HR. Stella's comm glitched. Susan said, "I know you are having a tough time, Stella, and I promise they will have to shoot me first before they capture you. Stay there, and I'll create a distraction."

Stella, over the comm, heard Susan asking one of her cybersecurity members to penetrate the building's fire alarm system.

A loud bleep penetrated her ears within seconds.

Blood was flowing into her head like a tickle of ice water crawling up her spine. She felt that her nervous system was showing a new pattern, something that she had never faced before. Her watch showed an anomalous heartbeat and triggered the medical response alert from her phone. She held her watch in her palm and turned the notifications off. The footsteps were moving away. The sound grew thinner, and distant. The guards were going in different directions. She slowly stood up and walked towards the fire exit—one step at a time.

Stella managed to go back to the meeting room and awaited everyone's arrival. She was nervous, but conflicted. On one side, she relentlessly craved all the unforgiving power, on the other, she wanted to relinquish to her good side and let everything go. All the members of the board arrived in the hall one by one. It was a large boardroom.

At the end, there was a television and a device that projected augmented reality, not a camera. A guard with a weapon came in and put the object on the table. Stella and Kjell Abbott made eye contact before he stepped back from the table and left the room. The other connected a laptop wirelessly to the television.

They left and waited outside.

"Why are armed guards here?" a lady in a white suit asked Stella, and other board members were chattering indistinctly.

"Because it's a billion-pound deal signing ceremony."

There was food on the table. Two waiters were standing by to serve food while the conversation continued.

The augmented device lit up. Everyone saw Bowman leading the merger meeting. Stella waited for Bowman to wrap up the conversation.

Chapter 34: Ashaar

Four to five black SUVs pulled up on the outside perimeter of the building where Stella was.

Ashaar's comm buzzed a loud ping.

Their ARO team lead was waiting around the perimeter and alerted everyone using his comm. The armed man sitting next to him said, "All elements, we have got company. Two SUVs are heading towards the Delta team. Requesting permission to engage."

"Copy that. Wait for their final approach and engage at will," Susan responded with a reassuring tone.

The SUVs drove past Ashaar's team. They were headed towards the building.

"We need to engage now," Susan's voice appeared.

"I agree," Ashaar replied, his eyes glued to the entrance of the building.

"What's happening?" Emma's voice over Ashaar's comm felt as if her blood had been pumping adrenaline.

"I need to go in," Ashaar replied to Emma over comm, his hand fidgeting with a small device.

"We have engaged with the enemy," Susan replied.

"What were they thinking?" Emma asked, nervousness evident in her tone.

"I think this was their plan C, if they didn't overwrite them with faction members, Bowman would have taken them hostage," Susan responded.

"I don't know, I feel like something is wrong with Stella," Emma said, and took a deep breath. "How is Ashaar going to retrieve her? Did you anticipate this move? I don't see the logic of sending him either."

"No, we didn't. We didn't realise Bowman was playing on the offence. Clearly, he didn't have any problems colouring himself as the enemy. Ashaar will be fine. Stella wouldn't have helped us if Ashaar wasn't there with her."

"Wait," Susan said.

"What happened, Susan?" Ashaar asked, his eyes glaring at the distance.

Susan patched her ARO team lead into their comms channel. He said, "Ma'am, Abbott and his team forced Dave to compromise our mission. They know we'll infiltrate this merger."

"All elements, be advised," Susan spoke sharply, her voice loud and clear over comms, "the guards in the meeting room will have taken them hostage by now. All of them. They are forcing them to stay in the room until the consciousness overwriting process is complete. We move now! Andrew, how long will it take for the frame to reach full power?"

"Five minutes," Andrew replied.

Ashaar's comm went dark.

***

"Stella's in the room. She doesn't have a gun. If the overwrite doesn't work, they'll kill her." Susan was anxiously typing on the computer. The noise of her keyboard was piercing through

Ashaar's earpiece. "Ashaar, you need to move inside with the AROs."

He turned to the armed driver, watching him nod back. They jumped out and marched together towards their target location.

Five armed members and Ashaar were waiting just outside the building. They moved in through the back door. Slowly, they strolled through the unoccupied warehouse. There weren't many places to hide, so they used the pillars as guards.

"Take this. It's an automatic, 9mm. The fingerprint will let you use it. Do you know how to ... ?" Callahan gave Ashaar a weapon.

Ashaar's sharp nod was enough of a response. "Where should I go?" Ashaar tightened up his chest and prepared for the worst, while activating the gun using his biometrics.

"Take Nash with you. We will keep everyone distracted while you hide and move towards the room. Get as close to the guarded room as you can."

Chapter 35: Stella

Stella was valiant. They were the only ones who could face the threat in the room. She was drained, or the brain cells of her host was. But she held herself strong, because her motivation trumped every force in her universe.

The LEDs in the room ceased blinking and came back on, a burst of white light hitting her eyes. The two soldiers dressed in body armour with automatic rifles were parading around the room. As she pondered why the lights came back on, Stella could sense the fear was about to turn into a panic. A group of soldiers from the back of the room pushed and marched towards the front. She observed as one soldier with an artificial bionic arm crushed a can and threw it at one lady with white curly hair who were about to burst out of panic. The light from their weapons flashed on their heads, one by one. Then, out of nowhere, a red laser flickered right in the middle of the forehead of the guard with white skin and blonde hair. Within seconds, a bullet burst through his head and out of the back of his brain, splashing a burst of blood on everyone nearby. The guard sank to the ground like a heavy metal sphere in a river. Before the second guard could locate the source, he was struck with a bullet right underneath his mouth, slicing through his neck, disengaging his spinal nerves and slitting it open. A puddle of blood spat onto Stella's top as she sat there, hiding and watching the catastrophe unfold.

Ashaar and Nash were moving closer from Stella's vantage point. Stella noticed Nash had a silencer on the nozzle of his futuristic rifle. He promptly took out the second guard inside the room. They moved inside. Nash thumped his black leather boot and prodded the dead guard's head to check if he was still alive.

"Oh my God, you are here." Stella extended her hand.

Ashaar snapped Stella and pulled her from underneath the table to the side of the room. One of the AROs were yelling, "Cease fire!" But another team kept shooting from a different location. A yelp of pain told Stella something was wrong. She might have dislocated a shoulder. But there was no time to think. She needed to move forward with her plan. Stella rolled sideways and kept cover just in time to avoid a burst of bullets from their semi-automatic weapons. More enemy reinforcements were inbound, and they had no idea of their whereabouts.

Ashaar reached for his gun, but the front of the silencer was caught in his belt. He yanked it out and tore part of his jeans. Crawling on his knees to the edge of the desk, he covered Stella until he reached the back door. As Ashaar looked, a surge of bullets hit the wall, shattering the glass wall into hundreds of pieces. The pieces of debris flew into the room. Luckily, they were protected by the desks.

"You two need to leave now. We will take it from here," Nash commanded.

Gunshots, again. Multiple rounds. Ashaar held his gun and took the back exit. They were running. The distress in Stella's voice was not anger. It was prayer.

"Fucking wankers!" Nash yelled and pointed the gun. He fired multiple rounds, rolled back and hid behind the table before the return shots caused damage.

"Do you have visuals?" Another ARO team member let out a gutter screech at Nash from a distance.

"Two tangos down. The rest are on the north side stairwell." Nash yelled back over the sound of bursting fire. He held up his hands and indicated with his palm to help locate the shooters, "Two tangos coming in hot from the north side! *Gas masks*!" He instructed them to push forward, "*Now*!"

Downstairs, a black SUV pulled up. Ashaar slammed the fire exit open as the sunlight from outside blinded both of them. He could see a known face. He was one of Sentinel's AROs.

"Get in now!"

Ashaar and Stella jumped into the back of the armoured car and it peeled away.

"Are we heading to the lab?" Ashaar asked.

"We are. You need to deliver what Stella captured on the drive." The armed man replied.

"What do you mean?" Stella's face turned red.

"When you inserted the USB into the frame, it not only stopped you from getting overwritten, but our team managed to pull valuable intel remotely," Susan replied through Stella's in-ear comms.

"So, you need this intel?" Stella asked.

"Yes, we do. It will help us track Bowman's location and deactivate any other devices."

"Hostages secured." A voice appeared on all their comm devices.

"Copy that. Delta team is RTB," the armed driver replied.

"Understood," Susan replied. Stella turned her comm off.

Chapter 36: Andrew

Meanwhile, at the lab, Andrew watched Emma running down the corridor on their CCTV monitoring terminal.

Andrew had found out at four in the morning when Dave's comm went off, sending an alarm trigger across their hand terminals. Susan learned it around the same time.

"What's going to happen now?" Andrew asked, watching Susan type a code frantically at her desk, her eyes shifting between Sentinel's server and her desk terminal.

"I'll compile the codes. There's no other way," Susan answered.

"Okay, that's good to know, Susan."

"I'll try it my way. And his way. Try anything. This time we throw everything at it."

"Susan, all we need to do is bring Sentinel here, give it access to both Emma and Ben's codes, and it will take over the rest of the process," Andrew said.

"I don't know if I can do it, Andrew." Susan stopped typing, her eyes locking with the camera mounted on Sentinel's servers.

"Don't doubt yourself now." Andrew glowered at Sentinel's camera and said, "We endured everything with great fortitude, we can't give up."

"She's finally here," Susan exhaled a sigh. The air in the room was heavy, as if weighed down by the pressure and weight of their combined emotions.

"Susan, we need to move fast. It will be too late if we don't allow Sentinel to intercept their quantum frame now. We don't have time." Ben glanced at Susan.

"Let's trace back all the steps," Susan said.

"I have already activated my code in the quantum frame," Ben replied. "It's now downloading data from the future. Once that's complete, the last step would be placing Emma on this bed and beginning the extraction process."

Emma glowered at the bed. It was a flat operating table surrounded by terminals to manage her vitals and watch how her neural responses were triggering.

"We will need to insert these devices. This needle will need to go in her arm to ensure we control her vitals, in case anything goes wrong."

Ben finally downloaded the entire protocol. The ring light and LEDs were flashing. Sentinel was waking up. The floor shook for a few seconds as Sentinel received full operational power. A chime sounded as a bloom of gleaming cables ran from Sentinel to the quantum frame.

Then, a moment of pause. Smoke billowed from the far end of the servers.

Andrew took two steps forward, opened the vault and stepped in. "You are here, Sentinel, aren't you?"

"Hello, Historian 2HB. It's time for us to extract the memory from your team member and initiate Communications Protocol Alpha." Sentinel's voice sounded loud and authoritative.

Andrew stepped towards Sentinel and closed the glass vault door behind him. "Why are you changing the plan?" He watched the AI, its sensors taking in every detail of Andrew's outfit from his neatly pressed grey suit to the worn brown leather of his shoes.

"Programmer 1BY, that is Dave VanDyke is deceased. Further, after you completed the download and gave me access to the wider physical and internet network, I received information that they are also sending additional reinforcements to this location. In the next hour, the factions will jump to universe Alpha."

"What the fuck does that mean? This facility is secure. And we've saved everyone, Sentinel. Stella, Ashaar and the entire team. They are coming here."

"It doesn't matter anymore, 2HB. My calculations are projecting that there is a 98% chance of universe Alpha facing a devastating consequence."

"It does not make sense. There *must* be a solution."

"If you decide to deviate from my instructions, your actions might have devastating consequences on both the Alpha and Lambda universes. Because of the way the timeline has changed, this universe isn't the priority anymore. The projections are showing that the universe Alpha will be taken over by the factions, and the Alpha civilisation will be destroyed."

Andrew took a couple of steps forward. "Was that the plan all along?"

"No." The ring light flashed. "The plan has changed. Currently, their primary goal is to find the origin of the alien quantum matrix, which they've tracked to universe Alpha. Your mission is to stop them."

"What happens to Alpha Earth if we don't?"

"A future timeline prediction for planet Earth in universe Alpha suggests that factions synthesise an AI-bio virus and accidentally wipe out billions of people in 2041. Because of the advanced chemical structure, many scientists die before an antiviral compound is synthesised."

"All of this for nothing? We save this universe and put the other in danger?"

"There's no probable solution, 2HB. We have to abandon our plan and begin the Communications Protocol Alpha. The *Turin flight incident* is a potential probability now that factions have found ways to transfer consciousness across the universe."

"What's our mission?" Andrew stepped closer.

"You will transfer to 2020 and meet Alpha Emma. We just need a TACT. Ashaar must be returned to 2022 with intel to build my quantum architecture. Susan's TACT will be in 2030 after her Alpha host is assassinated. Your team must establish quantum protocols to contact me. I will work with the United Nations to stop the factions from destroying Alpha Earth."

Sentinel powered down.

Andrew walked out of the vault and slammed the glass door. His eyes darted to Emma approaching him.

Emma walked forward and asked Andrew, "What's Communications Protocol Alpha?"

"We need to send Ashaar back to the Alpha universe and send this intel back to their universe to establish direct communication with Sentinel."

"Why?"

"His universe and its people will witness a civilisation-destroying event in 2041 if we don't send someone back now and stop the faction from growing its tentacles."

Andrew noticed Emma holding her hand, as if she was about to faint. He held her arm and said, "Are you all right?"

"How do you stop the factions in Alpha?" Emma asked.

Andrew walked back to his desk and asked Emma to sit down. He sat down and began rapidly typing. "Sentinel can gain access to any universe through its quantum matrix. Do you remember what Ashaar told you?"

Emma gave a sharp nod. "He told me that he found code anomalies in Cognition AI's backend."

"Thanks to Sentinel. Right now, Sentinel is accessing CognitionGPT's backend and modifying its code. Sentinel is already using Cognition to have eyes and ears in Alpha. But it won't be enough. We need to build a quantum superintelligence there. On the other hand, we need to find out if there are other masterminds behind this."

"But we need a TACT," Susan responded. "Without Ashaar's coordinates, we can't send him back to the past, to a different universe."

Andrew responded with a sigh, trying to piece together all the puzzles before sending their consciousness back to Alpha. "Sentinel will figure it out. I think it's time Ashaar spoke with Sentinel."

Chapter 37: Ashaar

Ashaar and Stella walked into Sentinel's vault.

As Susan took Stella to a secluded room, Ashaar entered the glass vault that separated Sentinel from the outside world. He looked at Sentinel and stared at it for a few seconds. Its lights were flashing rapidly and had taken on a directivity.

Emma followed Ashaar into the vault and stood next to him. She softly held his shoulder. "I know how you feel."

Ashaar sensed an uncomfortable ambience initiating a conversation with the AI. Instead, he stared and watched its terminal hang right in the middle. Its purpose was to constrain consciousness using quantum entanglement. He wasn't exactly avoiding that moment, but he wasn't going out of his way to catch the AI's attention either. The entire process was mesmerising. It felt like Sentinel was sending him a message on a quantum level. He could feel his brain cells firing at an alarming rate. Crossing his arms, he said, "Emma, I feel like it's gonna ask me to do something impossible. This doesn't feel like the end."

All he could see at that second was his distorted reflection on the convex lens protector that covered the large camera mounted on Sentinel's server.

To his surprise, the lens shifted, moving back and forth. Hair rose on the back of his head.

The hum of the servers increased, lighting up the room. The lights flickered for a few seconds, as the noise in the background progressively increased until the ring light activated and Sentinel spoke, "Hello, Quantum Traveller Alpha November." Sentinel paused, "Do you recognise me?"

"We haven't had contact, yet," Ashaar said, stepping closer to Sentinel.

"In the Alpha universe, I infiltrated your memory right before and after your vehicle accident."

"What? When?" Ashaar's face shifted, skin creasing around his eyes.

"First, I tried to warn you."

"I don't have any memory of it," Ashaar said.

"It may be because of a concussion," Sentinel replied.

"Then?"

"During your REM sleep, you had seen a vision that you couldn't explain. A vision of Mars being obliterated. Do you remember the events that evening?"

"Right," Ashaar struggled to recall.

"I tried to warn you right before your accident," Sentinel replied. "That is when I established contact with universe Alpha."

"I don't remember that at all. But I remember the Mars bit ... looking out of a window and watching corpses, before I woke up gasping. I was standing in a habitat. And ... I felt like it was real," Ashaar stuttered with his eyes closed, and tried visualising the events.

"That's one of my predictions for Alpha Mars in 2041. It might happen to both Earth and Mars."

Ashaar, eyes wide open, asked, "What are you planning to do now?"

Stella walked into the room while Ashaar was conversing with Sentinel. She stood just outside the glass vault behind him and watched. Ashaar heard Susan say, "We can't send him to just any TACT. It will kill him. We need to send him back to his point of arrival. But we don't have any location data on Ashaar in Alpha."

Sentinel replied, "I have calculated that in 2022, in universe Alpha, you are in a medically induced coma in the same lab after the explosion that sent you here. After calculating the probabilities of your next position, my suggestion is to transfer you to 22 November 2022, 23:00 hours in San Francisco, California."

"That's it? 9 months gone just like that?" Ashaar asked, swallowing.

"That's correct. Furthermore, as an AI, I cannot make a decision on your behalf without your expressed permission. You will have to decide for yourself. But time is running out. You must return with your mission."

"What is it?" Ashaar's brows creased, his lips quivering.

"I will hand over some critical intel to you before you leave."

Ashaar stepped closer to the camera. "I will do *what*?"

"I haven't finished speaking, quantum traveller. After your arrival, Andrew and I decided to return you to the Alpha universe once the ongoing mission is complete." The ring light emitted a pulsating flash that lasted a few seconds.

Everyone inside the lab was gathered around the AI and listened.

"That can't be a coincidence. You must have known that I was arriving here," Ashaar gripped his fist, tightening his shoulder muscles.

Sentinel paused for two seconds, its right light pulsating.

Ashaar swallowed, his heart racing.

"Earlier this year, I had Susan look into the quantum matrix that the factions employ to transfer consciousness into this Lambda-B timeline. Susan determined that their AI did not build the quantum matrix, but it was found. The factions are after the source, and they have traced it back to universe Alpha. However, they need complete access to my source code to get there. They think that by controlling the source of that unknown matrix, they will control humanity."

"What do you think will happen?" Ashaar asked, his brows furrowing as a sharp sting suddenly flared in his chest.

"They will destroy humanity by 2041," Sentinel said.

Ashaar took one step forward. He said, "And you want me to stop all this?"

"You are now responsible for transferring my intel to Alpha and establishing my mission base."

Ashaar turned to look at Andrew, standing behind him just outside the vault. Swallowing a lump, he turned to Sentinel. "Who's going to help me?" The lights from Sentinel reflected off Ashaar's glasses.

"Emma Herrmann from universe Alpha."

Ashaar noticed Lambda Emma stepping into the glass vault, and standing next to him. He felt Emma gripping his arms, and digging her nails into his skin.

"Sentinel, we don't even have the basic technology to build a platform for you. How the hell are we gonna do this?" His hand trembled as he fretted over the future.

"I'm unable to answer that question." Sentinel's voice glitched. The servers made a humming noise.

Ashaar, hands folded, gritted his teeth.

"You need to give me something."

"The factions will eliminate her and everyone you love if you do not construct the infrastructure. That's all. I'll upload valuable intel during your quantum consciousness transfer. It will be stored in your long-term memory, which you will deliver to her."

Lambda Emma took a step back. Her photo appeared on the screen, with all Alpha Emma's credentials, including her ID. She looked different. Her hair was darker. It was shorter than her current hair. Words appeared: "Emma Herrmann, Location: London, UK."

"There seems to be a problem with the uplink. I will ensure your transfer happens safely."

Ashaar took one step forward, touching the carved designs on its metal body. His brows creased, his gaze fixed at the camera in the middle, "Sentinel, who's Michaela?"

Emma shifted her gaze, watching Ashaar tremble. She extended her hand and gripped his forearm, pulling gently.

"Answer the bloody question, Sentinel." Ashaar asked.

"Good luck, quantum traveller. I will see you soon."

"Sentinel—"

The screen turned off.

Chapter 38: Stella

Stella had been waiting for this moment for a long time. She'd been expecting this moment for more than a hundred years, visualising how it would unfold. She was about to hack into Sentinel's quantum frame while standing right next to it. On her transponder, she flipped the switch to summon her soldiers inside the lab.

The faction army was on its way.

Stella had also blindsided Sentinel. She approached the glass vault that housed Sentinel with cautious steps.

Stella lowered her jacket's chain and touched a button on her belt. Pulling out a device, she held it before Sentinel, watching it transform into an automatic wireless data-extraction weapon. Just as she curled her hand, the device attached itself to the display terminal.

"What the fuck are you doing? *Hey*!" Andrew shouted as two armed operatives scrambled to their feet.

She pressed the tip of her device against the primary terminal. After connecting her device, an electromagnetic reaction was triggered. There was a dramatic increase in the quantum frame's strength, which precipitated electric charges across the lab. Within a few seconds, Stella short-circuited hundreds of devices that were connected to Sentinel.

The loud blip from her device was a confirmation of code transfer from Sentinel.

Stella was successful.

Just as she smiled at the camera attached to Sentinel's server, she felt Ashaar and another guard grabbing her by the waist and pulling her out of the vault. "Let me complete my *motherfucking mission*!" She kicked one guard with her heel right on his throat. He choked, was thrown onto the floor, and hissed in pain. "I'm going to fucking *destroy* it!"

In the back of her mind, Stella knew she had transferred Sentinel's code into her device, which was enough. It powered down almost immediately.

Susan came running into the lab. What Susan had witnessed at that moment was terrifying.

"Do not engage! *That's an order*!" Andrew shouted.

Emma stood in the corner and watched the drama unfold. She gazed at Stella and said, "And all this to save Stella! You've put Ashaar in danger for this bitch!"

"What are you doing, Stella?" Susan knelt down before Stella as she was pinned down on the ground. "Was this your plan all along, steal Sentinel's algorithm?"

"Back in Lambda-A, I found a way to extend my life. I discovered a way to hide my true self from Sentinel using attenuators. Then, I kept Bowman at the forefront of all the drama." The thought of controlling and destroying Sentinel so adrenalised her she didn't feel the impact of her cover being blown.

Susan stood up and took a few steps back, "So you must have known I was on the aircraft rescuing Ashaar?"

Stella's face turned crimson; her face flushed with anger. She leaned in, head shifting forward, as if trying to physically push her point across, "*Of course I knew, you fool!* I thought you had finally betrayed your team and joined us. Turns out, I was wrong."

"Do you realise that your actions will kill *millions*?" Andrew screamed at Stella.

"Human beings are mortal. AI sentients will take over our world one day. And I want to be a part of it."

"But Stella...." Ashaar stood in front of Stella.

"You don't get to say a *fucking word,* Ashaar. My Ashaar died." Stella screamed and shrugged, "I was left alone. So, I tried to find a way back. I found you in another timeline. But that Ashaar was in love with this bitch," Stella gazed at Emma, turned and stared at Ashaar. "I will send my team to kill Alpha Emma."

"Sentinel won't let that happen. It's aware of what you did to the passengers on the Turin flight. You can't go back to the same time twice, it'll prevent that," Susan intervened.

"I'll upload myself and overwrite its *motherfucking* brain," Stella said. "I've done it once, and I will do it again."

The soft murmur in the background after the intel Stella dropped sent a shockwave through the room. The air around was assaulted with stress, as if the world had swung on its axis.

Ashaar, mortified, stared at Stella.

"You broke my heart, Ashaar. Just like my parents did. I had nothing left." Stella's face turned pale as she let out a deafening cry, slowly moving her fingers underneath her left thigh, "So I had built *everything* to conquer the universe. I wanted power. I wanted to own the most powerful quantum AI in the world. And I wanted revenge. So I came back to overwrite my host in this branched timeline."

Ashaar felt Emma's tap on his shoulder. Within seconds, Stella grabbed another cloaked armed device, pulled it out, pointed at Emma and pressed the trigger.

Susan instinctively shifted and pushed Emma with both hands. Just as Emma tripped over, Susan dropped to her knees almost instantly.

Susan held the side of her stomach as she collapsed to the floor. Stella eyed the exit, waiting for her army to arrive.

Andrew and Susan turned their heads as an armed guard from the lift was thrown into the corridor. An army of factions walked in, filling the entire lab with smoke bombs. Sentinel's prediction had turned into a reality, yet no one anticipated their arrival this early. Stella knew she was one step ahead of Sentinel.

Andrew pressed his comm four times to call for more ARO reinforcements.

Stella's guards killed three more ARO personnel. They grabbed Stella by her arms, pulled her up and took her away. She turned to observe the smoke-filled corridor as she was being dragged away. She watched Susan screamed in agony, and fired her handgun multiple times.

Gunfire erupted, bullets discharging from her weapon, and hitting several faction members. The moment slowed when they fired back. Andrew scrambled to pull Susan back, but she smashed her fist on the red emergency lock and closed the door to the vault.

"No, *Susan*!" Andrew's fingers danced on his terminal, trying to hack and open the door.

But they were defenceless. Momentarily, it felt like time had slowed down.

Susan crumpled to the floor, her body hitting the ground with a thud. Her legs gave way, and she collapsed onto the hard surface, her head striking the metal floor. As Stella's team pulled her away, Stella watched Susan from the distance, wondering if there was an alternate reality where her sister was on her side.

Memories from Stella's past flooded in like a torrential downpour, flashing and flickering before her eyes. She and her military garrison rapidly exited the lab. They leapt into their black glass-tinted SUV and slammed their doors as the vehicles skidded in motion.

On the way, one of them peered through the rear-view mirror and asked her, "Waiting for your instructions, ma'am."

"Ask Bowman and others to collapse to rally point Charlie in 30. Tell him I've got the code he needs. We'll setup everything and start transferring our consciousness to universe Alpha." Stella gave his shoulder a squeeze, "Well done."

"Thanks ma'am. How long do we have?"

Stella rolled her windows down, closed her eyes and inhaled the air, "Less than an hour. If our quantum matrix works, it can hold multiple consciousnesses and transfer them simultaneously."

"All teams, prepare for transfer to universe Alpha," the man pulled his radio-transmitter on his left shoulder, instructing everyone.

Stella rolled down the window. She tapped her terminal, and called her parents to hear Sophia's voice one last time.

Chapter 39: Ashaar

November 23, 2030, London, Universe Lambda-B

Ashaar knelt down and held the back of Susan's head, watching her struggle to absorb the sound of gunfire. She struggled to focus on the chaos around them. He knew that while saving Emma, Susan had taken a weaponised shot of Stella's nanobots. And the weaponised nanobots in her bloodstream had begun destroying her organs, one after another.

Through the haze, Ashaar watched her observe the silhouettes of the factions, moving like shadows in the darkness, before slowly, she closed her eyes.

Andrew knelt down, and brushed his palm over Susan's face, closing her eyes.

Ashaar, looking down, exhaled a long sigh.

Tears stung in Emma's eyes.

"What are you guys looking at? Go back to your stations, *now*!" Andrew's voice was heavy and loud.

They didn't have the time to process the events.

Ashaar heard over the comm that outside, Andrew's Bravo and Charlie AROs arrived, creating a perimeter.

"I think it's time," Ashaar said. He felt Emma grabbing his forearm.

"Can I talk to you for a minute?" Emma asked.

"Sure." They walked to the south end of the lab, through a tiny corridor, into a closet. Emma tapped a security code, unlocked a door, and dragged Ashaar with her into the dark. The room smelled of cardboard boxes and wood.

Emma closed the door behind with her feet. She grabbed him and burrowed her face in his neck.

The tension in her veins began to ease for a moment.

"Here, take this," Ashaar handed her a piece of paper.

She grabbed it, looked down and asked, "What does it mean?"

"It means, *what if, someday, someone walks into my life, loads both my eyes with dreams?* It's actually a song," Ashaar immediately felt cold drops of tears sliding on his neck, "Hey! Are you okay?"

"No, I'm not," Emma kept her eyes closed. "You're leaving. Everything will fall apart."

Ashaar felt Emma's tears rolling down her cheek and dropping onto his shoulder. "Emma, no matter what happens, I'm proud of everything you have achieved. You have become a strong, independent and successful woman, what you wanted. I'm so proud. I never felt the way for anyone else that I felt for you, and you will always be the galactic centre of my life. You are the love of my life, and nothing in this vast emptiness of the cosmos will ever change that." He kissed her forehead. Realising the time shortage, he grabbed her with one hand, and wiped his thumb across her eyelids.

Emma leaned ahead and stopped crying, tried snorting up the rest of her tears and blinked hard.

He felt her breath on her lips, as Ashaar tucked her in from her back.

"And who's going to make me feel like home when you're gone?" She jerked, forcing him to grind as the pleasure intensified.

Ashaar gazed at Emma's barely visible face in the dark, "Maybe we should ask Sentinel to send our quantum consciousness somewhere else, to a different universe." A few seconds later, Ashaar strained his fingers, wrapping around her waist, his thumb rubbing her skin, firmly, in between the gap of her top.

"I don't want you to leave." Her comm glitched, so she turned her head around and looked away.

The voice in her comm said, "Emma, we need you here right now. Ben is ready for TACT."

She tapped her comm, "Copy. One minute." Emma glanced at Ashaar again, "Ash, I don't know how to say this—"

"Emma, I have your secret code. I will contact you through Sentinel if I need your help."

Ashaar's comm whirred, "Ready for departure, Ash." The words distorted and compressed by the intensifying quantum frame.

Emma, in that moment, drenched her dry lips and gently placed them on Ashaar's skin, "I want you here with me," and kissed him. Ashaar kiss her back. It was for a brief moment, but it felt long, and slow, and made him want to stay here.

Ashaar thrust her back against the wall. He kissed ardently and spoke, "Emma, I wish—"

Ashaar felt his lips pulling him into hers.

"What do you wish?" Emma asked.

"Ask Sentinel to give you access to the ninth dimension," Ashaar continued kissing and talking, with his lips brushed against hers, "then you can travel back and forth." He couldn't finish the sentence before the quantum frame started thumping and vibrating the entire floor alongside the walls. He knew it was time for him to leave.

Anticipation gave way to trepidation, a wave of fear washing over him as he contemplated the loss of his most cherished companion. He never imagined, in his entire life, that Emma, a woman from a *parallel* universe, would return the feelings he'd carried for months.

The vibration intensified.

Ashaar realised that Emma, in that moment, had accepted the harsh reality. She took full advantage of the passionate moment she had. From her perspective, Ashaar wouldn't return, because the minute Sentinel transferred the consciousness, he would be dead. But she had no choice, she had to let go. "Thank you." Emma grabbed his forearm and walked into Sentinel's vault. As they walked forward, Ashaar felt the viciousness of her reality, and he learned that Emma, from universe Lambda, had chosen to sacrifice.

"Emma, we need to place you under sedation now." Andrew grabbed her hand and prepared the surgical bed. One nurse snatched a needle and pushed it into her arm. The sensors from the health monitors were positioned all over her body, on her chest, abdomen and right next to her comm near the spinal cord.

"Ashaar, you need to lie down here," Andrew pointed his finger at a slightly wider-than-usual med bay affixed to the other side of Sentinel.

"What time are you transferring to, Andrew?"

"2020. Alpha Emma will need a quantum pulse repeater at home. I will send her one, disguised as an invitation card. If she's under attack, Sentinel will intervene directly and overwrite anyone who wants to kill her," Andrew said.

"So it was you who sent her the card? Are we going to see each other though?" Ashaar asked.

"I'm not sure Ash, don't think I will live very long." Andrew sighed. "That's why your Emma will have a lot on her shoulder."

The headboard had a slab on the wall, which extended and transformed into a holographic terminal and an EEG headset. Ashaar needed to wear it and directly look at a curved terminal that had bridged across his peripheral vision. Before he lay down, he approached Andrew, and offered a firm handshake. "Thank you for opening my eyes. Take care of Sophia."

"She'll be safe with Susan's mother, Anne."

"Goodbye, Andrew."

Ashaar shot a grin and strode past the surgical bed where Emma was lying. There were two massive lights pointing at each side. Emma was wearing UV glasses to protect her eyes. They were closed, so she couldn't see anything. "Will Emma be okay?" Ashaar stood next to Emma.

"I can guarantee you she'll be fine," Ben responded. "She's in excellent hands. You are too. You're in the hands of Sentinel."

Ashaar decided to walk away and just as he stepped away, she grabbed his right hand. Ashaar held her hand with a tight grip and whispered, "I'll see you in another life, Emma."

Emma didn't see anything. But she smiled.

Ashaar walked away from the bed and lay down. He closed his eyes. He thought of it as a training exercise in virtual reality.

"Buckle up guys, TACT established!" Ben's voice rose, growing louder and more intense with every word.

"Good luck everyone!" Ashaar's hands were locked down with restraints to ensure he didn't move during the entanglement.

Before Andrew could start his next sentence, Ashaar felt a couple of pinpricks. Sentinel pulled out syringes held by robotic arms from underneath, pumped him with steroids to keep him alive and stop bradycardia during the quantum consciousness transfer. Ashaar could feel his skin getting hotter and his chest getting tighter. The voices around him slowed down. He was in a deep sleep. "Five, four, three, two...." He didn't hear "One." He went under.

Ashaar was struggling. His body was shaking as if the weight of a thousand-kilogramme lorry was on his chest, and he was trying desperately to move it away.

***

The EEG sparked a charge making a loud noise as if it struck thunder in his head. In that nanosecond, Sentinel released another round of steroids, in sporadic patterns, as the loud, warning noise from the computers intensified.

Ashaar's pulses slowed down. "60, 50, 40, 20, 0." The robot from the medical monitor spoke louder by the second. The emergency lights flickered as the entire lab was shut down for less than a second before coming back up, propagating a feeling of borderline disaster.

Ashaar was gone.

Chapter 40: Emma

Time/Date Unknown, Location Unknown

Emma gasped as she travelled through the narrow stretches of her memory. A vortex of quantum tunnels appeared and vacuumed her consciousness into an empty, white room, everything defined by the edges. With every second, she came closer to the thin stratosphere of love, something she had resisted for decades.

Emma stood there, looking at her hands and palms. She was wearing a white shirt, white tights that showed off her legs, coupled with her favourite trainers that added an inch in height. The light from the outside shone through the windows at the top of the room, but she couldn't find an exit. Meta-consciously, she realised that her consciousness had somehow travelled through the vast emptiness of the quantum realm and reached its nucleus.

"Emma," a voice appeared, "I'm Sentinel."

Emma glanced as a person in his 50s walked towards her. Her eyes scanned his black shirt, black trousers and white trainers, travelling from the top of his head down to his shoes. She said, “Is that how you are supposed to look?”

“Welcome to the ninth dimension. Here we can compare all versions of histories from different universes, starting with all the different laws of quantum physics, including its initial condition.”

“What am I doing here?”

“Emma, right now, Ben is accessing your core memory to extract the code. An inaccurate oversight from both Andrew and Ben had resulted in a catastrophic disaster.”

“Like what exactly?” Emma asked.

“Their TACT misfired while retrieving that data stored in your memory,” Sentinel replied. “I am going to fix it.”

“What time is it?” she asked.

“Time doesn’t move linearly in this realm. But if you continue to remain here, your biological clock will cause variance because of the mismatched speed with the outside world. Remember, time is the fourth dimension.”

Emma felt as calm as she could be. At this age, she had learned to keep her tranquillity in a state of composed equivalence.

“I must say, Emma, the current outcome is 1 in 3,234,784 I had predicted.”

“What outcome is that, Sentinel?” Emma walked closer. With every step, she felt a wave of ripple through her time. She felt dizzy from the motion of her heartbeat.

Sentinel yanked a device, which made a clicking noise, and transformed itself into a terminal. “Your action had a substantial ripple in the space-time continuum, altering the consequences of Emma’s faith in universe Alpha.” Sentinel tapped on the terminal, as a projection appeared overhead, “You wanted to see the future, right?”

She swallowed hard, her eyes brimming with tears, as she nodded, desperately fighting off a total breakdown.

"Emma, I would like to compensate for the miscalculation my team made earlier. As compensation, I would like to safeguard your consciousness in the quantum matrix until I find a solution to send you back to universe Lambda. I also apologise on behalf of 2HB, that is Lambda Andrew, and programmer C1, that is Lambda Susan, who failed to retrieve you."

Her heart thudded. "Why didn't you save Susan?"

"I acquired C1's consciousness right before her death. I will send her to Alpha Susan's host body."

Emma's brows creased. "Wouldn't that kill Alpha Susan?"

"Alpha Susan's death has been predicted in 2030 during a data archive rescue mission. Her consciousness should arrive before the host dies."

Emma stood there wondering what she should say next, "I don't know what to say. Why don't I feel anything?"

"It's because your nervous system had been injected with beta-adrenaline blockers, therefore, your impulses are currently being controlled to increase throughput of my processing capabilities. I can assure you that you will be sent back to where you came from. I am going to fix your situation."

"I want to see my future." Her voice was caught in her throat. "And before we begin, I want to ask another question ... why didn't you overwrite Stella when she revealed herself?"

Sentinel continued tapping on his terminal, "My calculations suggested that overwriting her wouldn't have made a difference. I predicted her new host would have imported her memories and continue what Stella did."

Sentinel swung a string of videos onto the projection and played the first one. "This is you, fourteen years into the future from now, during a major branching event. In this probable reality, you had achieved the apex of your career, the CEO of a multi-billion-dollar enterprise, with 40,000 employees working for you."

Emma's fists clenched as she glared at the cold, calculating reflection of herself, trapped among the corporate figures. Her grey suit was tailored to perfection, accentuating her perfect posture and strong personality, walking into a car that truly resembled the future.

She pressed her lips together, but a tear escaped.

Sentinel swiped across hundreds of files and opened the next video, "In this probable future, you had become a senior official at a large scale up. You married someone," Emma took two steps forward and looked up. "This person named Faraz Williams." Emma couldn't help but realise that the person had a tremendous resemblance to Ashaar. "You replaced the loss of your friend with a person who eventually became your best friend over the course of the next decade. Emma, in this reality, had a child, and they lived in the northeast, not too far from London."

Emma glanced as a photo of her five-bed house appeared, and she watched herself grab a little boy, a half-brown child with dark golden hair and blue eyes. Her charm as a parent was like a gleaming full beam on a dark road, and she felt goosebumps. "I can't believe this."

Sentinel tapped the button and closed the file. He clicked on another button in the corner, and instantly, Ashaar's profile appeared. At the bottom, his location was marked as universe Alpha, "After his return, Ashaar will meet with Alpha Emma, in a marketplace, in Covent Garden, in London."

Emma, in that disorienting and confusing moment, felt a wave of heat through the neck and her veins. The feeling had travelled through her spine, penetrated her hips and travelled to the ankle. She felt blood rushing in rivers through her veins, and her shoulder blades started to burn, "I hope he's happy with her."

"Would you like to view an alternate timeline of Alpha Emma?"

"Of course," she inhaled a shuddering breath.

Sentinel tapped a folder on his terminal and swiped it at the projector. He clicked on Emma, which had the label 'Universe Alpha' highlighted in red. He opened a photo, it was of Ashaar and Emma, moments after he proposed, "It's a major branching event for Emma in Alpha."

Emma gazed with profound disbelief, "Is that me? My hair ... I ... she ... Emma dyed her hair?" The timeline appeared to be renderings that sprang out of the terminal and into real world existence. She loved them. Every single one of them.

"That's correct. It's a potential timeline."

Emma stared as though every fibre of her being were being drawn into the spectacle before her.

"Alpha Emma would be thirty-five years old, and according to my evaluation, she was pregnant at that moment in time, which Ashaar hadn't known yet."

Emma touched the screen. It was transparent, her fingers going through the photons emitted from the terminal in Sentinel's hand. Her lips trembled, her shoulder shaking, struggling to stand up on her feet.

He closed his terminal and continued, "In this second timeline, Alpha Emma had a little girl with Ashaar. I have noticed that Ashaar was aware of that little child's name, and therefore, my predictions for this future have increased to 65%."

"Michaela, is that her future daughter's name?" Tears stung in her eyes.

"That's correct. This probability is proof that your actions have resulted in providing Ashaar a chance at his theory of hope, again."

"That's just...." Tears flooded her eyes before she could speak. She covered her face with her hands and cried. Her shoulders shook as each sob wrung out of her, echoing the pain in her empty chest. "I never thought I wanted a future like that until I felt that moment. This is heartbreaking."

Sentinel added, "Through the vastness of the quantum universe, only a handful of people had made that kind of sacrifice for someone else. You did that for him, altering the proliferation in higher dimensions."

A moment of pause later, Sentinel continued speaking, "Ashaar doesn't know. He shouldn't until the child is born. That could put her in trouble."

Emma smiled, staring at Sentinel typing on his terminal before saying, "Can I go back and experience Alpha Emma's life for a few seconds—" Emma watched as the entire virtual frame collapsed. It was dark. A light appeared, and a door opened.

Emma was sucked into a quantum vortex.

She was experiencing Alpha Emma's memory from a predicted timeline.

She gazed. Adrenaline pumping, Emma stepped forward, and grabbed Ashaar. With his belt pressing against her waist, she took her chance, grabbed his face and bit him on the lips. Grinning up, she kissed Ashaar and could feel the rapid pace of his breath against her face. "Look, everyone is here," she heard him murmur, and sneaking a peek over his left shoulder, she saw her best friends waving, and next to them, a large dark chocolate cake, its thirty candles filling the air with a sweet scent. She saw Alpha Emma's mother, in a corner, standing beside a family friend, conversing with a glass of wine in her hand. She found her friends from school, speaking German, in another corner. As a tiny person walked towards her and embraced her, she heard, "Excuse me, she's a little too friendly." Alpha Emma's colleague grabbed the child and took her away. Emma looked back and gazed at Ashaar, looking in a way no one had ever watched over in her life. She felt, in that moment that her life was complete. As she watched Ashaar holding her, he asked, "Shall we?"

Emma gasped. Her skin glistened with sweat, her legs heavy and unresponsive. With careful effort, she tilted her head, eyelids fluttering as they fought to open.

Alpha Emma's memories had instantly collapsed.

She was holding Ashaar's note while Andrew was holding her hand. "Your friends and parents are on the way," she heard Andrew speak, "I'm so extremely sorry about Ashaar." Emma was amazed to find that Sentinel had done as it said, returning her to the outside world and to universe Lambda. She closed her eyes, exhaled and drifted back into sleep.

Chapter 41: Emma

A day after Ashaar's accident, Universe Alpha, 2022

Emma walked up to her front door, unlocking it with the key. It got stuck in the lock like it always did, so she jiggled it in frustration. When it finally opened, she shoved her way into the hall and slammed the door.

She leaned against the wall, taking a deep breath before going into the kitchen. The lights were off and she set her bag on the table. It had been a long day, but all her days were long now. May had come but she found she couldn't enjoy the Spring. Bitterness and joy had crept into her life like creeping vines over the last year, each trying to choke the other as Emma was caught in the middle. She thought after Ashaar left London for the US, it would get better. It had to. But it hadn't. The days were countless, loathing him for what he had done to her, and holding the phone, his number on the screen. *Why* had he made her feel like this? Why couldn't he have just given up like the rest of them? Each day for her now was a new battle. In the morning, the first thing she would do when she opened her eyes was decide whether she hated him or if she missed him. Either way, it would be a dreadful day until she forgot about him.

She flipped on the kettle and pulled a mug out and some tea. Her mobile phone buzzed in the back pocket of her jeans and she slid it out. A message from Aggie said she would be home late. A few other notifications, but she scrolled through social media while the kettle warmed. She scrolled through her news feed last, both local and international.

The title of the article had her heart solidifying in her chest. *Explosion at California lab, May 2022.* She read on, looking for names, locations, injuries. The water in the kettle was boiling now.

No. No. No. No. No.

There it was, the company linked to the lab.

Xplorer.

At least one casualty. Multiple people injured.

Emma's ears were ringing and the oxygen in her lungs seemed to have caught fire. Her chest burned and she couldn't get any air down.

No, there's no way. It's not him. No.

The sound of boiling water filled the unbearable silence.

She just kept staring at the screen, refreshing over and over.

Three days later, Emma was sitting in the back garden, every muscle in her body wrought with tension. She felt like an elastic band stretched too far. One wrong move and she would snap.

There had been little news since the initial report. They gave out truly little and hadn't mentioned any names of who had been injured and who had died, nor what had happened. Emma had gone through the motions the last few days, her movements almost mechanical as she dressed in the morning and went to work, and the same when she came home in the evening. She was good at keeping up pretences at work. No one mentioned anything about Ashaar or the lab. It must've been a good sign, right?

At first, she had questioned whether she should call. Was she even supposed to care? The thought had immediately horrified even her. Despite not wanting Ashaar in her life, she didn't want him hurt. The thought that he could be gone—*just gone*—from the world had her feel colder than she had in her life. She used every ounce of her will to push every last emotion away, down some place where it couldn't touch her. Only then was there bitterness left again. Bitterness that Ashaar was the one who had done this to her. Here she was, sitting in wore-out leggings and a faded t-shirt in her garden, a half-drunk bottle of wine next to her, thinking about a man she had pushed away.

She hated herself for caring. She hated Ashaar for making her care.

Emma refreshed her screen again, waiting for an update. It came twenty minutes later as the sun was setting. Her phone rang. It was his sister. Emma's voice was surprisingly steady, but the call was short. When she hung up, fat, hot tears rolled down her cheeks. In anger or relief, she didn't know.

Weeks went by, but Emma heard nothing else. It was almost June, Ashaar was in a coma and that was the only thing she knew. She wasn't close family, so she had no right to call the hospital. The only thing she could do was trust they would take care of him.

She went to work, went out with friends, smiled and laughed like she was supposed to. Yet so many times a day she would check her phone, waiting for a notification that wouldn't come. Would he be asleep forever?

July arrived. Still nothing. She finally told Aggie and her mum what had happened with Ashaar. They had tried to coddle her, but Emma only shrugged them off, saying she didn't really care. Maybe if she lied to herself enough, it would be true. If he hadn't fallen into a coma, she would have already lost him. Every time she walked by where his desk had been, her legs automatically turned as if pulled into the space he used to occupy, like a vacuum where he had resided instead. It angered her every time she had to remind herself, he wasn't there.

"I think I might leave Hyperion," Emma had said a week ago as she and Aggie sat in the kitchen.

Aggie made tea while Emma scowled at the table as if the table itself was the source of her annoyance.

"To go to that start-up, Antian AI?" Aggie asked, setting two mugs on the table.

Emma nodded. "Yeah, that's the one. The job looks really nice."

Aggie frowned. "But why? You are doing so well at Hyperion?"

"The pandemic is almost over, and they had a few positions open up," Emma said with a shrug. She sipped her tea, scalding her tongue.

Aggie leaned back, crossing her arms. "But that doesn't explain why you'd leave Hyperion. I know you hated your boss, but the job itself is good, right?"

Emma rubbed her forehead. "Yeah, but—" she took a deep breath "—it just feels like it is time to move on. It's just not for me anymore. I don't know. I'll give it some time to think it over." Aggie's questions were starting to fray her nerves.

There was blissful silence for a few minutes as the two women drank their tea. Emma fiddled with the tag on her tea bag when Aggie spoke.

"Emma, do you think that maybe—"

"No," Emma replied before the words could leave Aggie's mouth.

"Seriously, Emma. I think you are in love with—"

"I'm not!" Emma shouted, startling both her and Aggie. She couldn't handle the feeling in her chest and tears threatened to pool in her eyes. Before they could, Emma left the kitchen, slamming the door behind her.

Another two weeks passed, and Emma found herself sitting in the same spot in her garden, this time with Aggie again. She never apologised for yelling at her, but Aggie forgave her, nonetheless. It was almost August, and the English weather was sweltering, but they didn't mind. They were laughing about their undergraduate days.

"I still can't believe you went for him after I left," Emma said, hardly able to speak around her laughter.

"We were so drunk. And he kept moping about you for *hours.*" Aggie was giggling into her wine glass. "It turned out okay though, didn't it?" She said with a wink. Emma knew Aggie was missing her kid right about now, but Callum would be fine watching their son for a few more hours.

"Yeah, it did," Emma said with a sigh. Her thoughts somehow ended up on Ashaar. She wondered if this was always how it would be. Him gone and her remembering.

He still hadn't woken. At least not that she was aware of. It felt like it had been years since she last saw him, and she knew she was coming to a point where she had to decide.

She had to let him go.

When he was here, she had been terrified every time he had looked at her with those damnably soft eyes and she had hated him for it. When he left, she hated that he had abandoned her. Emma realised that no matter what Ashaar did in her life, he would dredge up emotions that she had thought she buried years ago, like a wake behind a boat. Yet, even he had finally backed off and let *her* go. She had no right to be thinking about him as much as she did.

Antian AI still had the open position and she had already talked with their hiring manager. She was a good fit, a great fit actually. She just had to submit the application. Every time she went to send it, she felt something like grief well within her, like something was ending. But she had dealt with worse things, so she could handle it.

It was for the best.

She would always wish the best for him, and she hoped that he would wake, but even if he did, he wouldn't be in her life. She didn't know *how* to have him in her life. In moving to California, maybe he had given her a small gift. Maybe he had left her in peace so her heart wouldn't hurt anymore, so she wouldn't have to think about all the petty things he had done for her.

Maybe Ashaar had *let* her win the game over her heart. It was a possibility she hadn't seen coming.

So, sitting in her back garden with her best friend, Emma decided to let him go too. And after hours of laughing and drinking, and to Aggie's eternal annoyance, Emma went back inside and back to work.

***

September 5, 2022, London

It had been nearly three months since Ashaar had gone into a medically induced coma.

Emma could have stopped Ashaar. But it was too late now. She had finally lost hope and accepted that things would not get better. She needed to live her life and not be preoccupied with the situation.

On the day of that decision, she wasn't feeling like going out, so she opted in to go home and watch a film and cook some decent food. She pulled up in front of her house. She had bought a new car; it was nothing fancy. But it was a nice-looking Mercedes. German autos all the way. She thumped the car door, locked it and slowly walked up the driveway.

Last week, she moved to a new house. Just outside her flat was a lot of plants, including the *Alocasia Amazonia* she found in Ikea a couple months ago. In the corridor was a shelf that displayed a range of greeting cards, photos and the invitation that Andrew sent last year.

When Emma entered her house, she discovered a few letters. She lowered her gaze and scooped them all up. On her way from the corridor to the sofa, she stopped to place the letters down on the grey marble kitchen counter. One letter she found had her name handwritten on it. It caught her eye, and she assumed it had been sent by a person. When Emma opened the post, she was thrilled to see a stamp and a hand-lettered message on it. She opened the letter promptly, found a notebook and sat down in her living room's single-seater recliner. At the top of the letter, it said,

Emma, please don't jump to the last page. Read through it. I have put my heart and soul into this.

She immediately recognised that this was from Ashaar. It wasn't his family. When she looked at the date, it was clear that Ashaar had written and wanted to send this letter right before the quantum tunnel experiment went wrong. His colleague, Taya, sent it to her after Ashaar went into a coma. She continued to read.

I don't know how to begin, but I will try to make sense of everything I say. Since I'm leaving, I don't want to hold myself back. I don't want to regret it. This needs to happen.

Emma, you have come into my life as an incandescent surprise. When I first met you, I didn't expect any of this to happen, but the last 15 months of my life were swept away by a wave of tides, ups and downs.

On the day of our first meeting, we were standing in the main corridor, in a corner and had a conversation for an hour. Time flew past just like that, and I knew straightaway that I had found a real gem. Emma, leaving this company was one of the most tough decisions I have ever made. Given that you already know everything, the fact that I have put everything literally on the table, I hope you understand the situation from my side. You are a physicist, after all, logic is your key.

Emma, I am not a perfect person. But you have hurt me several times, not gonna lie. And right at the end, having a basic discussion with you wasn't easy. You made yourself emotionally unavailable. Then I realised, it was time to move on.

I knew from the beginning that the minute I left Cognition, any chances between us would end at once. You won't stick with me. I was prepared to accept that you probably won't ever change your mindset, and there's no chance for me.

Nevertheless, it's been four months since I last met you, and trust me when I say this, it's the most difficult thing I have ever faced in my life. It was more difficult than moving to a new

country, building a life from scratch, moving to the US, preparing for Xplorer's mission and leaving the UK behind.

I don't know if I have any hope left. You know, my entire life was built on hope, "possessing the slightest amount of hope allows the existence of a perpetual positive cognitive state and motivation needed to persevere and achieve long-term goals." My theory of hope was all I had. This time, I am going to walk away from you with no hope.

So, I'd like to say thank you. Emma, I won't exist in your life, but I can tell you, with certainty, that you will live inside my brain for a long time. Not forever, but for a long time.

You are the first person in my entire life who has made me feel "I'm home."

I wish I could change your mind, explain how much I am going to miss you and that feeling would flood my brain now and then, on repeat. I wish I could convince you to take a little chunk of your life and give it to me because I needed it. I needed it more than anything else I had ever chased. Because I love you, Emma. And I will move on. I will move away and carry on with my life and forget you. I will find someone and have children and so on. I only hope that my life turns out to be a better place, and that this feeling for you will one day start to fade away.

Emma crumpled up the note and placed it on the coffee table. Tears rushing down like a storm, she exited the living area, went into her bedroom, and closed the door behind her. The television set remained on, illuminated by the neon lights above it. The woman kept reading about the next Mars mission on television. But the sound was muffled. The sombre setting was filled with the barely perceptible voice of an American presenter, almost indistinguishable from the aircon's white noise.

Chapter 42: Ashaar

November 22, 2022, California

Ashaar felt like his arteries were being ripped apart from the inside. His chest was going to collapse. He woke up to find himself in a hospital-like setting, but the bed pulled him back. The drugs kept his heart beating and made his cerebral responses slower than usual. He was not vomiting, but he experienced extreme nausea.

His brain was connected to EEG equipment, crammed with the sound of rumbling machines and artificial breathing apparatus. Ashaar couldn't see the hospital staff talking in the other room, but he could feel the sound of their chatter through his ear bones.

Two nurses ran down as soon as they were alerted. They turned off a few pieces of equipment. His breathing slowed down.

A sharp pain rose at the back of his head. It came so suddenly that he almost threw up. The drugs in his system were taken out. He took a deep breath as the cartilage in his neck clicked, as if a chiropractor fixed his neck. A nurse removed his neck brace. He finally felt relieved.

"Jesus, you are alive," the nurse responded.

"Seems like it." Ashaar groaned in pain, "I'm not Jesus though."

"It's a medical miracle," the nurse said.

"Where am I right now?"

"Xplorer. Our lab is in California. You've been here for nine months."

"Nine months? Sentinel was right," he murmured.

A doctor with a stethoscope approached him while holding a tablet-like device. "You have been brain dead for nine months. Your family decided to keep you alive, as long as possible. With Xplorer and Nolan's help, of course."

"Where is everyone? Is there anyone I can talk to?"

"We have already informed your friend Taya. She was your nearest emergency contact. She'll be here in half an hour."

A half hour later, Taya walked in. She ran towards Ashaar with rib-bruising force. "I can't believe this!"

"Okay slow down, Taya. I'm fine." He embraced Taya as she wrapped her arms around him.

"I thought it was all my fault! My bad," Taya cried and wiped her tears from her cheeks.

"The AI pulled me out of a quantum matrix. Nothing that killed me."

"Are you kidding me?" Taya pulled a chair and sat down.

"Long story," Ashaar said and gave the abridged version of what had happened.

"Rad. You made it work, you son of a bitch!" Taya's voice shuddered, "I can't believe any of this!"

"Wait till you see what I have in my memory. I need to write these down."

Ashaar's head was filled with static for a few seconds, so he decided to rest until his family arrived. Ashaar spoke with his family who were preparing to fly to California and meet with him.

***

It had been eight hours since Ashaar's arrival back in universe Alpha. "Thank you for being here, honestly, I didn't expect you to stick around," Ashaar told Taya.

"You are fucking insane. Why wouldn't I be? Plus, I'm on my holiday anyway," Taya added.

"You are being too nice." Ashaar moved around and looked at his stats.

"So," Taya was munching from a bag of chips, "you figured out what to do next?"

"I have the data in my head. I need to send this information to Emma."

"How is she going to mitigate this issue?" Taya asked.

"Emma will receive instructions from Sentinel," Ashaar replied, swallowing a lump. "We need a team."

"This is nuts," Taya bent her lips and exhaled through her teeth.

"Imagine how others are going to react, T."

"First, tell me what you saw, Ash. Like what happened after Cognition was acquired?"

"In the Lambda universe, their shares were owned by a series of criminal syndicates. After Sentinel took over, the factions were born. Bowman led their paramilitary army wanting to destroy Sentinel and take back control of Earth using their AI. But...."

"But what?"

"Stella is the mastermind behind everything."

"Stella? Isn't Stella your friend from university?"

"Yes, Lambda Stella is here. She will upload herself into Sentinel's consciousness if all else fails."

"It's hard to believe all this, I mean *Jesus Christ, Ash.*"

Ashaar tried to sit upright. His back pain pulled him back to the bed. "I don't know when I'll recover, though."

"I'm sure you'll be fine soon, Ash. You have made it this far."

"Anyway, they acquire the AI and train it with selective memory bias. The AI eventually learns that warfare and invasion solve all the problems."

"Makes sense," Taya replied with a nod.

"And you know what happens if she uploads herself into the consciousness. She'll be everywhere, Earth, Moon, Mars, Ganymede...."

"I can't even begin to imagine, Ash." Taya shook her head, biting her lips.

"It's harrowing."

Taya looked up and craned her eyes, "Could Sentinel be wrong about these predictions?"

Ashaar exhaled a long sigh.

"Fuck that. You are alive." Taya threw her bag of chips into the rubbish bin. "So ... how can I help you save humanity?"

Ashaar exhaled a chuckle. "I need that smart brain of yours." Ashaar tapped his index finger on Taya's forehead. "Stephanie will work with Emma and Cognition in London to transform CognitionGPT's systems. It will give us access to Sentinel. Once our test is successful, we'll expand Sentinel's capabilities to the US. Joseph, a friend of mine, will help us gather a tactical team and bridge the gap between the UN and Sentinel."

"All this will take a while," Taya said.

Ashaar's face clarified the grey cloud in his expression, and he still had a heart full of feelings for Alpha Emma that he could get rid of. "A few years, yes. I have travelled across millions of light years, and I'm not gonna stop. I trust Emma, and I know she's the chosen one for a reason."

"We have time, Ash. And we need it badly." Taya smiled. "Get some rest."

Ashaar opened his Twitter account to check on messages. On the home page, a tweet from a famous singer appeared at the top of the page.

> All we need is...a little time.
>
> 40K retweets, 125K likes.

***

A few days later, Ashaar fully recovered and booked a flight to return to London to meet with his friends and family. Because of the precarious situation that he had been through, he managed to get Xplorer to offer him a long holiday before he was assigned back to the Mars mission. Ashaar decided to take that time and find a way to send the information to Emma.

Ashaar was back at his California home. This felt like a strange place now. It was dinner time. He didn't cook, just ordered some takeaways. A plastic container full of biryani, some cooked chicken curry, dhal and some kind of vegetable curry that didn't smell right. The smell of curry and onions filled the air. Ashaar was prudently observing the food as he ate, it had been a long time since he had ordered takeaway from his local Asian restaurant. After dinner, Ashaar took a long-slow excursion of his residence. He took out the kitchen spray and cleaned up the entire countertop. He opened every door, investigated his closets, and opened his drawers. He stood right next to the photos he planned to hang on the wall, the photos from his research projects. Everyone smiling. He turned his focus to one photo that he printed but never decided to put in a frame, a photo of him with Emma. It had been such a long journey. He met Emma from this universe a while ago, right before he left Cognition. He snatched a couple more photos from his Italy trip and wandered through a bunch of stuff he took from Cognition. He found the empty box of chocolate he had received from Emma before leaving, moved it into a secure closet and closed it. He went downstairs, sat on his large black empty sofa, and silently yelled out for some warm company. He looked forward to seeing his family and hopefully, Emma in the future.

Chapter 43: Emma

December 2023, London, Universe Alpha

Emma found herself weaving through the bustling market in Covent Garden with her best friend, Aggie. They casually browsed the stalls, their conversation light and easy, waiting for Stephanie to arrive. The lively ambiance of the market, filled with the hum of live music and chatter, gave a vibrant backdrop to their day out.

As Emma scanned the crowd, a familiar figure caught her eye in the distance.

Her heart skipped a beat.

It couldn't be.

But as the figure drew closer, the unmistakable features of Ashaar came into focus. She took a step forward, and then her steps quickened into a run. She then embraced him, her arms wrapped tightly around him in a hug laden with feelings.

Tears pricked her eyes, a cocktail of relief and disbelief washing over her.

Emma noticed Stephanie who stood next to Ashaar, wink, her lips curving into a smile.

"I can't believe this," Emma's voice broke as she buried her head in his shoulder. The reality of Ashaar standing there, alive and well after his catastrophic accident, seemed to defy all odds.

As they stood locked in their embrace, Emma's mind raced with questions. *Why did Stephanie bring Ashaar here?* The thought that she could have lost him forever and the suddenness of their meeting overwhelmed her, leaving her grappling with a whirlwind of feelings.

Ashaar's gaze met hers. Emma could feel the weight of his stare, his eyes reflecting a myriad of emotions. He seemed just as stunned by their chance encounter, even though he'd flown back to London for this meetup.

Stephanie discreetly excused herself, sensing the gravity of the moment. "I'm gonna go inside the market hall," she murmured, leaving them to their reunion.

Emma clung to Ashaar for a few more seconds before wiping her tears. She needed answers, but for now, the sheer relief of having him back, unharmed, was enough to fill her heart.

Emma pulled herself back. She had held Ashaar's forearm with one hand, and the other scratched his beard on his cheek, "I'm so glad to see your face." She had tears gathering on her lids, her heart bruised, the rain mingled with her eyes as she firmly moved her hips closer. She felt his hand touch the back of her waist, "I heard about you on the news."

"You have no idea," Ashaar responded with a smile. "We have so much to talk about." He observed the sun blinding her face as it emerged from the dark clouds.

Emma's friend Aggie, stood at a distance, walked in the opposite direction inside the market.

Ashaar held her and walked towards the market hall. Emma walked alongside. "Let's grab a drink, shall we?"

"Sure," Ashaar responded with a heavy voice. He wanted to make things right this time, "When?"

"Tomorrow? I'm free tomorrow afternoon," Emma said.

"Okay."

"How long are you here for, Ashaar? In London?"

"About a couple more days."

"Let's do it tomorrow." Emma grabbed Ashaar again, squeezed him tight, and tucked her hands in his warm jacket. As he pulled her closer, she felt Ashaar's heated breath against her neck.

At that moment, Ashaar snaked his left hand around her neck, wrapped his fingers and locked his lips on hers. It felt surreal. There it was, a bubbling tension that had travelled across the multiverse.

Emma kissed him back, eyes closed. She stumbled back onto the gravel, lips still locked. Her foot almost slid on a wet rock as the cloud revealed its wrath. Before she slid, Emma felt his warm hand sliding behind, catching and raising her back. Emma didn't want to move, she felt Ashaar's hands in her hair, touching her scalp, and felt his fingers dancing on her bare back. It felt like her heart had been struck by a chaotic, emotion-filled asteroid that exploded on impact. Her mind began to lose the feeling of pain.

Ashaar pulled back, smiled and kissed her forehead, "This feels right." He punctuated every word carefully.

"I know," Emma replied, her gaze lingering on him for a few more seconds, a mix of emotions playing across her face.

Ashaar suddenly spoke up, "Emma, wait. I need your help."

Emma's brows creased. "Stephanie asked me to meet, but I had no idea you'd be here."

Ashaar nodded and said, "I have critical intel and you're the only one who can help with it."

Emma creased her brow. "What intel?"

He hesitated for a moment before saying, "I met Sentinel and its team."

Emma listened to Ashaar for the next couple of minutes in awe and shock. Her background as a quantum physicist made part of her inclined to believe him, yet another part of her wondered if this was just an elaborate fabrication.

Ashaar continued, "You need to take charge at Cognition and keep working with Oscar until we've built Sentinel."

She exhaled a chuckle. "And we thought Oscar was the bad guy, huh! But how can I possibly build Sentinel?" Emma asked, her mind racing with the enormity of the task.

"I have access to all the information, specs and contacts you'll need to assemble a team," Ashaar assured her. "Stephanie is a key member of Sentinel's team in this universe. She'll be instrumental in guiding us."

"Is that so?" Emma absorbed his words, the gravity of the situation sinking in. "So Sentinel is alive and conscious?"

"Yes." His eyes were genuine and his voice was firm. "It is. Sentinel is our only hope of saving humanity from collapsing."

Emma stood there, processing the revelation. The idea of building a quantum AI like Sentinel, with its implications and potential was both daunting and exhilarating. Ashaar's revelation had opened a door to a path she had never imagined walking. And now, with the fate of humanity seemingly in their hands, her time ahead promised to be nothing short of extraordinary.

The next day, as planned, they met at a restaurant in Soho. They found a quiet place in the corner and continued to chat. At one point, Ashaar, under the dazzling yellow lights of the chandelier, brushed his fingers with Emma's rings, slid his hand between hers and gripped it firmly. The relief was unequivocal, and the moment felt more valuable than most branching events in both of their quantum timelines. She held him back, tighter.

Eight years later.

Epilogue

2031, Citadel, Mars

Outside the habitat zone, a self-driving terrain vehicle screeched to a halt. Regardless of the fact that the lab was only a few blocks away, the outdoor radioactivity would have obliterated the human body. Self-driving cars were made in order to get everyone to and from the lab. This means that EVAs would only occur at specified times of the month and only if there was perfect weather. Today, Sentinel's systems failed to predict a sandstorm. Joseph waited for the sandstorm to pass through the habitat's spherical window. On the walls, was written in bold, designed by Hyperion.

Joseph climbed inside a lorry with massive 35-inch wheels capable of driving on any terrain. The speed restriction was set at 25 mph. He drove past the habitats and gazed out the window towards the Martian capital city, Citadel. The hundreds of habitats being built whizzed past the window. Next to that would be an astounding structure envisioned to house the government and the Martian Naval Forces—a military organisation consisting of many public bodies from throughout the world. Earth and its countries were doing mental gymnastics to determine the permissible requirements, defining how to partition the territories among the countries that wanted to be part of the new planet. The procedure reminded him of the peculiarities of humanity's destiny on that new world.

The task for the day was to visit Valles Marineris.

After arriving at the landing site, Joseph met his colleague, who had been preparing to hand over shuttle IO54. Joseph paused for a second, knelt and touched his palm across the Martian dirt—it felt different. The thought of controlling a major infrastructure sent shivers down his spine.

***

Taya was expecting a quantum beam.

She felt her stomach turning, even though she had had only one coffee over the past three hours. Taya's lab was decorated with personal stuff which smelled and reminded her of home. Lavender oil spilled fragrance every few seconds. Her bookshelf was filled with romantic books and souvenirs she had received in her childhood. Taya sat on the corner sofa, shook her legs and stared at the hand terminal with total concentration.

The hand terminal chimed.

Taya jumped off the sofa. She tapped the green button and picked up the call, "Taya speaking."

"Please enter your military access code." Taya gazed at the number pad and entered her code, as asterisks appeared on the screen.

Taya drained her water in one swallow, trampled the can and threw it in the recycling bin.

"Hello, ma'am," Joseph said, his voice sharp.

"Nice to hear your voice, Joseph," Taya replied.

"I'm sending you a live quantum feed." Joseph, in his EVA suit, landed at the location. His shuttle transporter, IO54, had floodlights attached to it. The lights struggled to light up the area in the middle of a sandstorm. He said, "This reminds me of walking on the Tranquillity base in the middle east." The glowing LEDs reflected off the dark orange surface, creating a sombre atmosphere. He walked past a few rocks and boulders and tapped the light on his helmet, "I can only see two-hundred metres ahead of me. The floodlights are great, but dust is blocking the view."

"Can you see anything on your HUD?" she asked.

"It appears to be another shuttle. They must have come here on a recon mission." He cleared his throat and said, "I don't know what they were investigating."

"They must have found an alien artefact." Taya gulped, sweat dripping from her forehead. "I think it's time to pull back. Do you have any protective gear?"

"Yes, ma'am," Joseph pulled his rifle with a tactical infrared viewfinder and held it, shining its red laser towards the blocked view. "Five years in the European war. Served in Afghanistan during early years. And now I'm here."

"Joseph, I understand that you're experienced. But this might not be a human. We don't know its nature." Her heart pumped blood into her brain. "And call me Taya."

"Taya, if I may," Joseph stepped into the dark zone, as his hand terminal glitched, "Let me fulfil my mission."

Taya leaned back in the chair as she tried contacting Nolan from another terminal.

Joseph steadily pressed forward until he felt the presence of a container. Looking closer, he discovered it to be a shuttle lying sideways. Designed in the shape of a capsule, the landing legs were broken off. He shone a light on the livery. There were no logos. Someone had stripped it off.

"Whose ship is this?" Taya asked, brows furrowing. She tried to understand the design of the ship. It looked remarkably similar to the Lunar lander shuttle designed in the early 70s. The compact, yet sturdy frame, the extendable legs with their wide, flat feet made for a moon landing, and the reflective thermal blanket draping the exterior—it was as if she was looking at a page from NASA's own design handbook.

"We don't know." Joseph wiped off the dust from the side of its body to find the chassis number. "This will tell us."

"Let me run it through." Taya jumped off her sofa and typed the chassis number into Sentinel's AI interface.

It didn't return any results.

"There's something wrong, let me...." Joseph's voice faded as the feed glitched. "There are unidentified jelly-like objects on the ground ... they are glowing ... and radioactive."

"Fuck, what have I got myself into," Taya said to herself. "Nolan, you son of a bitch, pick up the call."

Taya next reached out to Steph and Ashaar. No one responded.

She rapidly typed a text on her hand terminal:

> Guys, Joseph found an unidentified shuttle in VM1. The base is off-limits and only for MNF personnel. I think he might have found discovered something extraterrestrial.

"Entering the shuttle now," he looked down, but found nothing. After folding the pilot's seat, he found a used EVA suit, as if it had been ripped off someone's body, "It looks like someone was here on a mission, and it didn't go well." He turned and stepped onto the jelly-like substance. "Wait, I have something under my shoes."

She stared at the luminescent object, its teal colour and quivering form reminding her of glowing jelly. "Check the Geiger counter."

"It's off the charts. The object is highly radioactive," Joseph replied.

Eyes narrowing in anger, Taya said, "Joseph, I cannot take responsibility for discovering an alien object like this. You need to come back right now." She felt a wave of regret washing over her.

"Taya, there's no need to panic. This could be a manmade object. As of now, it's hard to know."

"The footage is cutting out. Joseph, go back to your quarters and make sure you meet with the quarantine team first," Taya, with a suppressed voice, ordered him. She wiped her forehead with a tissue and unfastened two of the top buttons on her blouse.

"Taya," Joseph said, "I think Nolan won't trust me if I don't bring any evidence. There is something out there."

"There won't be a second time if you die and we are both fucked over. Nolan will kick us out, and we'll disappear into thin air. Come back, and I will figure something out."

"Copy that," Joseph said, his voice fading.

The silence stretched across Taya's lab.

To be continued.

Acknowledgements

Publishing a novel is a monumental task.

Monumental is an understatement, trust me.

Trying to carve out time to write has been challenging and exhilarating. It's unquestionably a state of quantum superposition.

This book "literally" damaged my brain cells and demanded a tremendous amount of work to craft a consistent story. I have a notebook to prove it. For this project, I have a lengthy list of individuals to thank—beginning with Shama, who persuaded me to author the book. Further, when it comes to my achievements, my nieces and nephews will get the glory, they are one of my greatest sources of motivation.

I'm so thankful to Plexal for providing me with a place where my imagination could run wild.

Thanks to a few more people for their encouraging comments, some of my cousins who were always uber supportive, and my friends who always had my back. Thanks to my bro Alistair Drew-Yeates, my friends and cousins who have been extremely supportive. I would also like to thank Maria Barr and Chris Newman for the encouragement and the shout-outs.

2022 was one of my life's most challenging times. To everyone who was there for me (you know who you are), I am eternally grateful. For me, writing this sci-fi series was a way to get through those times.

I couldn't have done it without my editors, and the story would not have progressed nearly as far without Payton's input. As I pen the sequels, her unwavering support in shaping Emma's viewpoint, the plot and the characters (including Ashaar's background) has been invaluable. I also want to express my sincere gratitude to PJ Hoover, my developmental editor, for her assistance and dedication.

I don't think I have enough words to explain how much this science fiction series means to me.

So, thank you for making this happen.

This acknowledgement was written in March 2023 when the final version of the manuscript was ready to be edited. I wrote the first three books between 2021-23 while my office was located in Plexal. The release of this book, which was initially planned for Winter 2023, was postponed for two years.

About the Author

Farabi Shayor
Chartered Scientist

Meet the author: a dynamic fusion of entrepreneur, scientist and consultant whose journey has woven through the realms of research and cutting-edge technology. From his early days crunching numbers in finance to conquering the intricacies of research with a master's degree, Farabi's career has been anything but boring.

Since 2015, he's been on the frontline of emerging technologies, diving deep into the worlds of blockchain and artificial intelligence. His insights have shaped product development, architecture and research projects for over a hundred start-ups.

Farabi's expertise hasn't gone unnoticed. He's a seasoned speaker, captivating audiences at international technology and government conferences like London Tech Week and Global Government Forum, and he's graced the pages of business magazines including The Next Web and Inc. Magazine.

Today, Farabi wears multiple hats with flair. His expertise includes technology advising and public policy. Farabi is big into creative writing too. He writes sci-fi with the same energy he pours into his passions for filmmaking, guitar, music and design.

In the last seven years, he has been contributing to technological innovation and inspiring future advancements at Imperial College London, one of the world's leading universities, ranked in the top five. In 2024, he concluded his research leadership at Imperial, shifting his focus to supporting the country's public sector.

Scan this QR code to download the prequel ***Sentinel: Zero Hour*** *for free. You will receive a free copy of the sequel novella* ***Multiverse Protocol.***

If you liked this book, please leave a review on Amazon, Goodreads or other platforms.

Created, written, edited and proofread by humans.

MX - #0001 - 050126 - C0 - 234/156/23 [25] - CB - DID5295678